POTPOURRI FROM
A BLACK PEN

Other writings by the author

Cleopatra, and Other Poems, 1955 - Exposition Press

From a Tin-Mouth God to His Brass-Eared Subjects, 1966 - Greenwich Pub.

Good Evenin', Midnight Blues, This Mornin', 1989 - Carlton

Dusty Shells from the Peanut Galley, 1992 - Rivercross Publishing., Inc.

Co-Author: (Living Biographies) *Call Them Heroes,* 1965 - Silver, Burdett

Chapbooks:

Love Poems for a Black-Indian Grandma, 1976 - Holt Press

Poems of Love to a Lady, 1992 - Green Meadow Press

Polemics for Pocahontas, 1993 - Green Meadow Press

Poems from a Stolen Diary, 1993 - Green Meadow Press

Poems for Poca from a Jamaica Hospital Ward, - 1994 - Green Meadow Press

Short Fiction Appeared in:

Short Story Scene, 1973, Globe Book Company, Inc.

Reaching for Tomorrow, 1976, Globe Book Company, Inc.

POTPOURRI
FROM
A BLACK PEN

Many Musings That Have Passed

Through the Years

James C. Morris

RIVERCROSS PUBLISHING, INC.
New York • Orlando

ISBN: 0-944957-53-6

Library of Congress Catalog Card Number: 95-16113

First Printing

Library of Congress Cataloging-in-Publication Data

Morris, James Cliftonne.
    Potpourri from a black pen : many musings that have passed through the years / James C. Morris.
        p.   cm.
    ISBN 0-944957-53-6
    1. Afro-Americans—Literary collections. I. Title.
PS3525.07455P68 1995
818'.5409—dc20   95-16113
                                                                                         CIP

Dedicated to Those *Spicers* of Life
Only!
(and, Of Course, to "Poca!")

What Is Inside These Pages!

PART I

"That's What *I* Think!"
(ESSAYS)

Whatever Happened to the 'Uppity Nigger'?

Having always been a lover, an avid lover, of words, their meanings, derivations, their births, their deaths, and changes, I had wondered in recent years what had happened to the Southern bigot's pet phrase for me and my rebellious black type—the phrase: "uppity nigger." Anyone who grew up in the South, and, I suppose, in other quarters of America some thirty or forty years ago, is quite familiar with this term, and all of the unnamed implications which accompany the cognomen. It, of course, meant the militant Negro who refused to be "put in his place," or to act sufficiently subservient.

So often, because of my proud black stubborn streak, I acquired this appellation from the local whites and at a rather tender age. I recall refusing to bow or doff a cap or shuffle or automatically grin whenever I was in the presence of whites. My poor grandmother knew of this streak and she feared for my safety. My uncle, a well-meaning, hard-working foundryman, knew this, and he, too, feared for my health status.

I worked with my uncle at this brutally tough iron pipe-making shop, and I remember an occasion when I was about eleven or twelve which brought my attitude into such sharp focus. My two cousins also worked in this viciously heated foundry with me. Our job was to shovel, wet down, stir, and spread the warm sand that was used to protect the iron pipes and fittings, which were turned out by the white molders. Naturally, such semi-skilled jobs were done by the whites! These molders were perhaps the most anti-black members of the human race! I really mean that. Their greatest joy, it seemed, was to revel in telling what they called "nigger jokes," expecting to receive the most appreciative and loudest guffaws from the black listeners. And because the jobs as "sandcutters" were scarce, and the tenure as such, a laborer depended upon the whims and the vicissitudes of the molders. Quite often the ribaldry and joyous laughter, even at their own expense, did not go unrestrained on the parts of the poor Negro workers in that shop.

Well, one of the "Mister Charlies" had the undivided attention of the black workers one day as he unfolded one of the most distasteful and degrading "nigger jokes" I had ever heard, and at the age of twelve. The "haw-haws," the "hee-hees," and "ooh-wees" exploded at once throughout the huge foundry. Black men and boys fell back, their shovels slipping uncontrollably from their grasps, their shoulders shaking. They beat their hands, using their caps or hats to slap them against their sides. They roared. It was one of the best jokes this "Mister Charlie" had ever told! That was definitely certain! Uh-huh! Yes, all of the grateful Negro listeners agreed and screamed once more with their laughter—all that is except for one little skinny black twelve year-old, who continued "cutting" and spreading the very warm sand over the molding floor.

Suddenly, the laughter that had so freely bounced from the dusty beams, had danced from the dirty light fixtures hanging down from the vast ceiling, and had skipped along the floor, died away. Only the sharp *chip-twang* of my shovel broke the spreading silence. Slowly, I felt an electric sharpness sparkle through the heavy air. I stopped, leaned on my tool, and looked around. All eyes, I mean *all* eyes, were riveted on me. I began to breathe heavily. Mr. Charlie-the-Teller-of-Nigger-jokes turned to my uncle. He spoke slowly and nasally, "Hey, Ernest, whut's with this youngun heah, this nephew o yourn? He didn like th joke, huh?" He snickered in a high-pitched tone. I bristled, pinpricks tingling the back of my neck. I stood tall, stiff as a pine board. I could almost taste the volatile situation that was rising at once. So did kind Uncle Ernest. He remembered my "uppity nigger" make-up, so he interposed quickly, his breath coming hard and fast, cutting off any explanation on my part that he was sure would spring out of me.

He said slowly, "Ah, nawsuh! nawsuh! Indeed not! It ain nuthin like that, suh. Ma nephew heah jus don do too much laughin at nothin, you might say. Yall could say he's sorta serious-like, if yall know whut Ah mean." The pain came through him although there was that proverbial smile on his black and sweating face. I saw his hands twitch slightly. I started to speak. I was cut off. Being black, and several shades below the blushing level, I only flashed my eyes, turned back to work, squeezing all the hate and hurt into the new grip I put on my shovel. I heard this rank storyteller answer, "Oh, awright, Ernest. Jus thought he might be one of them young 'uppity niggers.' You know bout them kin. They think they moren whut they is."

"Yessuh! Yessuh! ah know whut yall mean, but Jim heah ain nothin like that—nawsuh!" My uncle knew better, my two cousins, who had stood there all the time, knew better. And I suspect the white story-teller thought otherwise, but could not prove it—or cared to. And so the delicate matter was dropped.

Of course, Uncle Ernest told his mother, my grandmother, with whom I lived, the whole story. Grandma gave me wise lecturing on learning to suppress the urge to retaliate, to serenely bear the nomenclature of "uppity nigger" silently, until I was old enough to escape these mean circumstances or to know how to intelligently combat the opprobrium with greater experiential wisdom, if not with grace.

Yet throughout my young teen years in Alabama, the "uppity nigger" title was levelled against me and those of my friends who also resented the term vehemently.

But then college and the war came in between, bringing radical changes in my life. Into the Army, overseas for twenty-two months, foxhole living involved, back to New York, no longer in the South (for Grandma had died during my stay in England and France). Great moves and movements rapidly took place, bringing changes more "swift than eagle's wings." And then the giant Civil Rights Breakthrough. And thus, the term "uppity nigger" was no longer in vogue, nor did it seem pertinent in the closing sixties and early seventies. America and her centuries-old sticky "race relations" problems had come to terms!

I was so glad and relieved in many ways for its passing. But yet, having been a "fool" for words, linguistics, isoglosses, and semantics, I rather mourned the demise of "uppity nigger." *What? Were there no more residual white bigoted memory flashback makers for the "good old days," when* (to pardon this terrible upcoming pun): *whites did more than call a "spade a spade"?* But I knew, reader, I just *knew* that words, like the concepts of reincarnation, have ways, ways strange or otherwise, of returning to verbal existence in new and/or protracted forms and uses. Yet, I almost grieved, I repeat, over the loss of my childhood knighted title. *Oh, I. A. Richards, Sturtevant, Hayakawa, what happened to my phrase?* No reverberatory decibels of sound replies hit my mental walls of awareness! When had all whites grown so gentle and humane in regards to name-calling? Gone! Gone! Gone like the Model-T, gone like the drugstore ceiling fans, gone like the hand-turned vanilla-made-at-home-ice cream! And I felt this touching loss of that which was almost akin to apple pie and the flag and motherhood, and, you know, things indigenous like that. The Age of Modern American Enlightenment had arrived, and I was too reluctant to accept it! Does the fifty-age bracket make one a masochist, or was I the only oddball on the block?

Then, patient reader, the other day I found the phrase! I found the phrase! And of all places, I found it in a beautiful pharmacy shop in midtown Manhattan! True, reincarnation had "re-semanticized" it somewhat, but it was there! It may be strange how "uppity nigger" was discovered, but it *was* discovered! As it is my normal wont each Saturday morning, I stepped into this drugstore to purchase my usual face-scraping steel blades, the social security deodorant, and other such useless youth-extending nonsense. You should know what I mean, especially if you have hit fifty and are hopeful and vain and love mirrors.

Well, it being the baseball summer season and it being New York City, and it being the home of the famed Yankee baseball club and it being the great imbroglio season concerning a current "feud" surrounding a certain baseball attraction in the form of a personality on the Yankee roster by the name of Reggie Jackson, the discovery of my lost verbal friend should not have been too surprising. But it was, and here is the situation that presented itself: As I walked in to await my turn, there just ahead of me, her back toward me, talking in a rather loud and somewhat animated voice to Pharmacist Sol, was this little modishly dressed white lady. Evidently, the Yankees had played a game the night before this late June in 1979. I caught the tail-end of the conversation, I suppose. I heard Miss Animated One say to Sol, "And so that Reggie Jackson struck out three or four times, huh? And I am so glad! You know, I just can't stand that fellow, that Reggie. He's so, so (Here Sol recognized my presence, nodded, and kept listening. Miss "A. O." didn't notice my being there. She kept up the speech.) . . . so, so *arrogant*. That's the word, so *arrogant*! (She really got into her emphasis thing! She started to repeat herself). Yes, he's so strong. . . ." (Here, the final word trailed from her lips like the movements of a dying quail a lucky wildgame hunter has just winged. She turned and *beheld* my dark Saturday morning visage there on The Avenue of the Americas. Her skin, being fair, unlike mine in that long ago circumstance, flushed a deep red, a kind of Chinese red. She lowered her eyes, turned away abruptly, paid her bill, took the packages, and left me laughing and rejoicing insanely! Sol smiled broadly. Little Lady, Little Caucasian Lady, wherever you are, I was laughing and rejoicing insanely not at your obvious embarrassment, although it was stamped so, so ludicrously all over your face. I was laughing because you had done for me, this ex-Alabamian, what that egyptologist had done for the world in 1924—you had unearthed, intact, my long-time dead verbal friend! And I want to thank you wholeheartedly. That was all. Honest!

Yes, I have found that there still is an occasion for more learning, for more teaching—and in mid-town Manhattan—and in 1979! Say, you linguistic fellows whom I had clamorously called for earlier, don't bother to answer. I don't have to annoy you after all. I have been saved. Although *arrogant* or *arrogance* is not quite the same, structurally-speaking or pro-nunciatively-employed, it can serve as beautifully a replacement as I could ever hope to find for a grand phoenix-raising of the buried and feared lost "uppity nigger."

Perhaps, and I say a very strong *perhaps*, it was fitting, although it added another dimension, or slant, to this essay, that I came across the following news item in the *New York Times*, dated July 4, 1979, a scant five days after the *arrogant* incident:

14

"On the eve of the 40th anniversary of Lou Gehrig's fare-well speech at Yankee Stadium, Reggie Jackson was honored before last night's game at the Stadium by the National ALF foundation, the organization that seeks to find a cause and cure for amyotrophic lateral sclerosis, the disease of which Gehrig died two years after his speech of July 4, 1939.

Jackson, who wears No. 44 for the Yankees as a link to Gehrig's No. 4, has been working as honorary chairman of the foundation for more than a year and a half in an effort to increase public awareness of the terminal neuromuscular disease and raise money for research. In addition to acting as host at a fund-raising auction last year, Jackson recently completed a series of ALS public-service announcements for radio and tele-vision."

(O Death, where is thy sting? O fate, where is thy cave?)

On Blacks and Cadillacs

My ever unfailing point of view on this topic may create for me more black and motor manufacturer alienation than I would or could ask for. But since I have always played a kind of "lone wolf" role, and have always been enamoured of such songs as: "It's a Lonely Old Town", "All By Myself Alone," and "Me and My Shadow," I do not feel that I would undergo any great traumatic change, or any other change, for that matter. And so, I shall step off into the murky and unknown waters of controversy and drown or float or breaststroke to an island of safety.

I am rather miffed, or, to be honest about the whole thing, I am *more* than miffed, when I see so many of the "black brothers" (a term, incidentally, in many cases could go better unnoticed, for all the sincerity that is pressed upon the phrase) cruising around the city or motoring cross-country in their Eldorados and Broughams, feeling, I judge, most appropriate and well at ease in their secure glory.

Now I am not against the higher-priced vehicle—not a bit. But what is my personal apple cart is the symbol of affluence that the black man is seeking so often to display. This, I am afraid, is entirely contrary to the point of view relative to his sense of affluence and social status regarded by the white man.

I am reminded of a statement uttered by a poorly-lettered black mother to some young white friends some twenty or so years ago. Her son and his wife had just moved into the block into a new home, and the five of them had just finished bringing in the last of the household. They had sat down for a breather, I guess. They were talking casually among themselves, when I heard the mother say in a voice filled with honesty of belief. She said, "Yeah, young people, that's right, all Negroes love Cadillacs. Yessir, they all love Cadillacs."

As I said before, this was said some twenty years ago, but somehow the weight of her observation remains heavy with me today. And I suppose it will stay with me as I see and come in contact with the fast-rising numbers of blacks who "own" and/or "pay down" on these magnificent four-wheeled vehicles.

Peculiarly, however, my disturbed condition over black-operated Caddies does not rise from a distaste for the car. It stems from a socio-psychological aberration, one that was placed well-deep in my psyche years and years ago. I shall tell you the correlation to this attitude in a moment or two if you will care to stay around and read or listen. Maybe then you will understand and extend a degree of commiseration my way, and set me up as a lasting memorial you might pray *for* in your daily evening prayers. Maybe.

Now, one of the most upsetting factors in my life has been a sense that one can readily predict my personality traits, my predilections, and my predicted reactions and responses. In other words, and perhaps, this stems from an inborn, inbred, sense of individual pride for me and my desire to always be *me*, and none other. I do not feel it essential or necessary to follow the flow and will of the group or the whims of a particular sect. I've had a long-time aversion for this concept. It especially rings forth whenever the idea that the white man can identify, catalogue, and determine my wishes as a black man. I suppose that could be the reason why I grew up with an almost denunciatory reaction to such foods as "chitterlings," pork fatback, collared greens, and, yes, with a later disregard for the black-associated *watermelon*. Then, too, perhaps my disdain for these so-called Negro or "soul-food" snacks, may have grown out of the realization as to *why* such eatings were preferred by blacks. It seems certain to me that much of the greater dependence upon such "nutrition-givers" evolved from the fact that such food staples were often the *only* food staples the poor blacks and earlier slaves were able to secure. The more wholesome, more delectable, and more choice menus were prepared and bountifully placed before the whites or the more affluent members of society. Rightly or wrongly, this sense of the historical inequity has persisted, haunting me through my "growing up" and now my "aging" years.

Let me tell you a little story, a true one, of course, to press my point, in reference to my preference for the watermelon. (And I have been called to task, chided, for this attitude more than once.) Then maybe you may *really* empathize—not seek to further besmirch my already blurred character.

In 1943, I had the misfortune of training in the Army in Illinois in the late fall and early winter. Now, if you know anything about the wide open plains of Illinois, you know that the weather, and particularly the winter kind, is no respecter of human flesh. November is fickle and angry enough, but when you're in Illinois, that month offers Mother Nature the "heebie-jeebies!." And in the United States Army Engineer Corps!

Another misfortune was being with a "gung-ho" captain commander who actually rejoiced in a tough training regimen. Therefore, it is small wonder that my outfit found itself involved in that month, in that place, under that Army officer's command, on a 125-mile "forced march" hike! The distance was horrible enough. Of course it snowed on us. Of course it rained on us. And of course the field kitchen crew that was travelling with us by truck lacked the proper know-how to maintain a gas flame to prepare the distasteful as well as tasteless viands! This gang also must have *guided* those freezing rain and snowdrops *toward* each boiling pot and frying pan! All that was not under-cooked, had turned to a kind of "fast-food" mish-mosh in a kaleidoscopic manner. Even the most corrugated of soldier gullets had to reject the mess and turn away in deep famished disgust.

So, it was in this weakened and wet condition that on the third day we spotted an empty, well-gleaned cornfield—cleaned, that is, except for a few little forgotten or disregarded fall watermelons! Hunger or near-destitution can make stalwarts and "derring-do-ers" of us all! So, as soon as we espied those lonely melons beckoning for us, what were we, black, cold, damp, and starving G.I.'s to do but obey the invitational waltz, so to speak, aimed our way by the watermelons? We rushed the wet field with a whoop, and not a single melon was left to die a wallflower! We were so gallant! We also were growing full!

Now, to get back into the story "slant" of this piece before you grow tired and escape. Passing us, going in the opposite direction, was a band of white troops. (Of course in those days, Dan, the Army was segregated! What do you think, huh?) They saw us greedily and happily munching the melonic gold. They did not witness the non-functioning cooking equipment nor the non-functioning cooks. How could these fellow-warriors suspect that hunger, blind, wretched hunger, was behind it all? So it was natural for several to yell out and deride our choice of dining victuals.

One, brighter than all the rest of the passers-by, and perhaps more observant, *and* better *home*-instructed, yelled out most piercingly, destroying our "quiet hour of charm." He erupted, "Hey, man, looka there. Them boys done found themselves some good ol watermelons—they sure have! They'll do it evertime, huh? They'll do it evertime! Hee-haw!" The voice echoed and re-echoed across the cold fields.

Those bitter words sliced through me, sharper than any bayonet thrust could ever be made to do. *They'll do it evertime! They'll do it evertime!* The voice kept ringing. Suddenly the pangs of hunger were no longer there, all joy of that saving fruit discovery turned flat and soured in my mind. It might not have been true—this idea of "doing it every time." That's not the point. The white voice had tauntingly said it and I *was*, along with the other dark faces, eating *watermelon*! Couldn't deny it. I slammed the half-eaten piece of melon to the gray-brown soil, the black-speckled seeds scattering all over from the impact. That was it! The Majority Man's younger representative had stated a premise that he knew was a black or Negro or colored or "nigger" truth. He *knew* me, my habits, my limited "great expectations," and I had not let him down!

18

From 1943 until now is quite a tough stretch of time, no matter how you measure it—the hands of a clock, the leaves of the calendar, the passing generation, passing in full bloom itself—it is a long interval. I have not savored or wanted to savor a piece of watermelon in all that time-span—not since that certain distant November in an Illinois cornfield.

As you can see, I, like anyone else, do not wish to be boxed in, stamped with or without my approval, America. This neatly sort of ascertaining my interests, my levels of aspiration, makes me all the more combative. Some years ago, there ran the words of a popular song: "No, you don't know me." Those words are my prohibitive bulwark against being taken for granted. No one is to assume my actions or my reactions. Even if my tastes *did* run toward the likes of the Cadillac automobile, my vainglorious nature, if you must name this "mental block," would force me to refrain from such a vehicular automotive association.

Oh, I've heard the arguments time and time again many of my friends and acquaintances have proferred for their inclination toward the "caddy:"

1. *Well, you know I never had much of anything as a black youngster, so I've decided to taste a little bit of life's goodies.*
2. *I just want to prove to "Mr. Charlie" that my tastes run as high as his, by George!*
3. *Heck, you only live once, you know, and you sure can't take it with you!*
4. *If you're gonna go, you might as well go in style.*
5. *Well, it's my money, you know.*
6. *So, I have big bills. I'll always have big bills until the day I die. I'm a black man, remember!*

And so on and on, ad infinitum, and so on and so on and so on. And you know one thing? All of the cited arguments carry their *own* weight. So my anti-Cadillac thesis runs against a tough field of reasoning. And maybe *my* own reasoning may be labored and even specious. Who am I really to project an argumentative old point of view? I can only say that my thinking was first formed in childhood, but it was irreparably concretized and made more so, whenever my aging mind would wander to an emptied farmer's field in a cold and wet November in central Illinois where the sophistical voice of a white soldier-trooper repeated itself once more and once more.

And, good people, I don't want to "do it every time!"

For Sale: Manhattan Island—Fistful of Trinkets and Twenty-four Dollars

I suppose, if for no other reason, because I have a scant drop of the North American Indian blood in my otherwise Afric-oriented veins and arteries, I have had more than a cursory interest and concern over the treatment and status of the "original Americans." It is common knowledge that the Indians, being chiefly agrarian and trapper-minded, cultivated no great need to reshape and re-arrange the natural use of the most common resources the immediate environs had to offer. This, of course, was in sharp contrast to the motives, needs, and presentiments of the latecomers to these shores: the Caucasians.

I understand readily the ease with which my redskin brothers met and greeted Columbus and his "real" India-seeking entourage. It is only natural by the precepts of God, Jehovah, or Manitou to be so friendly, exuding warmth to the wayfaring, and in this case of Columbus, the seafaring wanderers. I can accept in later decades, or years, the instructional classes in gardening, homecraft, and chef-preparing succulent dishes which the Indians offered these hungry, freezing, and lost *Mayflower* junketeers. Yes, I can accept that. It is still a part of or an appendage to the be-kind-to-the-stranger-within-the-gates philosophy.

But what has rankled my mind over the long and arduous years of my life has been the greatest real estate "rip-off" ever perpetuated against any landowner, whether the landowner was selling a ten by sixty foot strip of soil or three hundred thousand acres of the stuff. I am specifically referring to the famous, or better perhaps, the infamous, sale of this island of Manhattan for a fistful of Woolworth-like trinkets and a quarter hundred shekels! Charles, can you imagine! Even a piece of muskrat-inhabited swampland one billionth the size of Manhattan, this water surrounded land would have brought so much more in the honest marketplace, and on a different Wall Street speculator's integrity. But trinkets and twenty-four dollars!

As I said earlier, this treatment bothered my sense of fairplay and justice and sensitivity and all that, for a long, long time. How could anyone, anywhere, be so child-like or stupid or careless? I presented this problem to my early fourth grade American geography and history teacher.

She merely frowned at my juvenescent wandering mind. She had no answer. I then pursued this socio-eco and historical blunder through junior high school, high school, and even through my undergraduate days. Either I was awarded silent and severe stares or a whole string of unintelligible rigamarole of explanation, which never quelled my inquisitive passion. Nor did this offer me any sympathetic obliquity at all.

After passing out of my undergraduate exposure, and entering postgraduate involvement, I knew at last that any answer to my age-old inquiry could not be found within the ivy-colored halls of academe—certainly not where the lecture-body was predominantly of the Caucasian persuasion, and who I felt would feel either annoyed or embarrassed discussing that well-known territory sale. I just knew the professors or historians of American development would be only too happy to refrain from this topic. Therefore, I saw no avenue where I might travel in valiant search of the answer that would explain in any justifiable stance the shortsightedness of my Indian dwellers of New Amsterdam.

Then it hit me! Where I should I go, that is, to find perhaps a momentous explanation. And so often, it seems, our minds run in the pattern as exemplified in Edgar Poe's wonderful short fiction piece: "The Purloined Letter—" One overlooks the obvious, the covert, the near at hand source, seeking divination of a problem. I had not even thought over all these years of mental anguish to go to the primary source.

So, being a new "native" New Yorker, I felt I could find a member of the Algonquin or Seneca or Iroquois living here on this "tight little island," who could possibly explain the reasoning behind that treacherous land-grab job. Luckily, I did find one member of the old Seneca group who was securely and intellectually gifted in the ways of history and the art of artifacts among his ancestors. And I approached the gentleman upon an occasion and he listened carefully to my query. Then he clucked most wisely and noisily, saying, "Why, Jim Morris, you should have asked your great-grandmother. She knew." I explained that I never knew my part-Indian great-grandmother Harriet.

"Besides," I added, "she was only part-Indian, so perhaps she was not privy at all to such historical relevance. But, more than that, friend, she had lived in Alabama, quite a long ways and quite a few moon changes from New York."

"That wouldn't have mattered," my Seneca pal went on, "she would have known anyway. And, then, too, your grandmother Anora should have told you the answer to that land-grab thrust, as well as many of the other indignities handed out by the white man all through these centuries." He gave me a sharp glance. I was lost, confused.

I came back with, "But what do you mean, they knew the answer, they knew the answer? *What* answer?"

21

'Oh my, Jim, Jim, Jim Morris, poor brother of Marching Bear, of Pocohontas, Chief Sitting Bull, and all the rest. You are indeed a poor possessor of insight, despite what should have proved a perspicacious amalgam. But evidently the strain didn't filter down to your genes." Brother Seneca did seem worried about me.

And now I was fully ready to blow a gasket, growing more and more agitated at my obvious stupidity, and at the self-assured, regal-bearing Indian fellow. I did feel like a moron. My friend smiled comfortingly, however, at my discomfort, patted my shoulder. "Let's take a little longer walk down Fifth Avenue here in mid-town, huh? I want you to see the answer for yourself." I was more than glad to do so, to do anything to relieve me of a sense of ignorance. I was in awe of this apocryphal being walking beside me in all of that human movement. The Indian friend said, "Say, Jim, what would you say that most of these travelers have in their mouths or in their hands right now as we pass them?" I tried to, and did stall, staring around blankly. Nothing came to jog my mental wheels into motion. I stared again at the faces and hands of each one who jostled by. Suddenly I recognized what *thing* so many of these people were carrying! They were smoking, carrying *cigarettes!* I told my instructor of my slow observation.

"Right," Mr. Seneca laughed in a highly-pitched tone. "and," he continued, "didn't we introduce Chris Columbus and Sir Walter What's-His-Name to the wonders of tobacco?" I nodded a firm of-course. "And," he picked up from my assent remark, "what today seems to be the number one dreaded disease in America?"

"Cancer," I said.

"Right again, Morris," he laughed quickly once more. "And, my friend, what cancer seems to be the most virulent cancer?"

"Lung cancer, of course," I shot back. I knew my diseases!

"Again, what, dear dense, a-little-part-Indian-but-mostly-black good brother, has been claimed as probable causative for this deadly type?"

"Cigarettes, smokes," I replied.

So then I turned to add something finally erudite and revelatory to this illuminating conversation, but I looked and the wise man was now nowhere in sight. He had somehow melted or merged with the throng on Fifth Avenue. I heard that familiar laugh, rising above the street sounds, cutting through the streams of blue smoke and burning tobacco odors of the crowd.

The sale of this Manhattan island suddenly appeared so many times more costly to the American white man than the inconsequential fistful of Woolworth-like trinkets and twenty-four green ones.

Yes. So many times more costly.

The Poetry Contest:
Catalyst for Creativity
(Sub-Topic: "The Spectator's Point of
View") Prepared upon Request for
National Council of Teachers of
English - 11/79

Since a dynamic speaker is supposed to show great erudition through an innovative and arresting approach to a topic, and since I have *always* been dynamic *and* arresting *and* innovative, let me not become crass and mundane and stray from my *norm* today. But please bear in mind: I was assigned the sub-topic—*assigned*—so any problems that might pop up, ascribe them to the powers beyond this wretched victim's tiny sphere of influence!

Now let us go. The story goes, once in a dry, dry country, the subjects of a king pleaded for new sunken wells to relieve them of the awful drouth conditions that swept the land. The king, a good king, as far as good kings go, (which may not be far in your eyesight) did oblige, and he dug enough wells to ease the suffering populace. The people were pleased and quite soaked, and they reacted so. But there was one fellow, however, who went to the king because he complained that he was still "athirst." He cried that the leader had not provided him with a pitcher or some other container with which to take some of the good "aqua" stuff home. Thereupon, the good king said stoutly, "Ah, my good man, I dug the wells, I provided you with the water. In order for you to appreciate the bounty, you must bring something *to* the wells." The subject, though *drily*, finally understood the regency's point of view. He left and, according to history, was last seen scrounging around for a pail, any kind of pail, with which to take some of the cooling juice homeward.

I hope my opening gambit on the topic is fairly and clearly established: The biggest problem, I have found, with the listener or reader of any poetic attempt, is the degree of receptivity to which the spectator offers to what has been placed before him or her. It may not seem too important to the casual observer, but to one who is keenly aware of the

23

poet's painful attempt, the attempt to reach you, to touch your "vibrancy," so to speak, it is dreadfully important that a real communicative system be set in motion at the outset. One must bring an open awareness in order to truly receive honestly, with no preconceived attitudes of "hang-ups" toward the poet and the poem. Whitman, that *good gray poet* of Long Island, said that in order to have a great voice, there must be a great, or even greater ear. The ear he meant was the audience, the dynamically sympathetic audience. In other words, like any of the other arts, poetry demands a clear response to let the creator know if he or she has caught the "ear" of the listener. An artist is only as good as the public will let that artist be! And so much greater is this need of good listening when the writer of verse is the young student—a neophyte at best!

Now what is this "vibrancy" that this glib Jim Morris here refers to? Maybe we would do well to review how some of the masters of the "quivering metaphor" and the "shimmering simile" defined poetry—this almost elusive muse. Carl Sandburg saw poetry as being the "combination of hyacinths and biscuits." Carl also said that it was a "sliver of the moon in the belly of a frog." Billy Wordsworth termed poetry as the "recollection of things remembered in tranquillity." How about old crusty Bob Frost growling something about poetry starting out vaguely, then ending in "wisdom." Yet perhaps the most profound statement was offered by that recluse of a gal from Amherst: Em Dickinson. Emily said in words to the effect: "Whenever I read or hear a line of poetry whose power seems to explode in my head, then I know that I am into a real poetic experience!" (Maybe I did paraphrase her poorly, but do not interrupt me now—I am just beginning to roll!) And as a concluding consideration which might assist the honest spectator, how about the statement that speaks of poetry as "saying that which could not be said, and saying it beautifully." Often I like to feel that it could be a kind of *deja vu* experience—a feeling of having felt the emotional "truth" before, but had lacked the insight, the ability, or the intellectual strength to say it as magnificently as that writer of the particular poem had just phrased it, or had "poeticized" it.

Now this moves us into a more concrete and definitive area where the honest appraiser, the spectator, has to tread, and tread firmly. That is: *How do I evaluate what I have heard as a member of the audience with which to give the "performer" my best and most constructive criticism?* There are two possible attitudes which are commonly adopted, and *both* are most disadvantageous to the student as well as to the spectator-evaluator. The first I have named the "over-zealous" approach. We have seen this type of observer, I am certain. To him or her almost any effort free of grammatical faults is excellent, a typical masterpiece! Then there is the other observer, no less guilty. This one is the very antithesis: *Nothing* on the part of the young writer is noteworthy. "After all," this critic intones, "this is merely a child; there is nothing outstanding here. It couldn't be!"

Both of these stances are only slightly less than horrendous. The "over-zealous," or the "sweetness-and-light," evaluator harms himself or herself as well as the student by failing to give a sensible and constructive appraisal of the work. This makes the job of discovering real merit almost impossible. The cloud-nine-riding student is presented with a false sense of his or her talent, latent or otherwise. On the other hand, the "praise-parsimonious" spectator goes very far toward destroying what desire the student may possess. It could also easily help kill any further attempts on the poet's part to better the creative efforts. At the same time, the critical observer closes both eyes to the possible evidence of genius that may be lurking on the premises of the minds. Now please do not get the idea that I am implying that there will be several or even *one* poet prodigy in every listening situation. Maybe there will be none. It really does not *have* to be, you know. That is not the point! But it is obvious that each listener will discover some students who are better able to express themselves than others.

Another question arises: How, then, can the observer *properly* praise or respond to the work of all students without harming the more proficient ones and those who are not so capable of presenting meaningful expression? A Mr. Paul Marks, professor, in an earlier work, entitled, *The Craft of Writing*, experienced similar problems which confronted him in the classroom. He had a student who was so *abnormally* crippled that the usual procedures of earning a livelihood, or living a fruitful life, were impossible—only writing seemed possible. The author pointed out that criticism of the severest nature was so important in this case. In fact, it was needed more so here than for the other students. Such an instance may be rare, but indeed a problem of this nature does arise. I can vividly remember such a classmate in my undergraduate days at Columbia in a poetry-writing class with the late Leonora Speyer. So pedantic, so didactic, and so "Long-fellow-ish" were this young lady's arduous examples, it was very painful to witness how her work had to be so sharply "broken apart!" Even *I* shuddered, and who was I to shudder in those olden days at anything metaphorically inept—no matter how stultifying it might have been! (In fact, some of you may ask who am I *today*, for that matter!) A meaningful spectator, therefore, should at all cost offer criticism, regardless of how it may appear at the time to the poet or to the colleagues around him or her.

As long as I could remember, I was in some class of creative writing, and especially poetry, throughout my high school, college, and post-college days. Therefore, I can accurately speak from experience of the hazards

25

of criticism too glibly done as well as criticism over-intellectually embroidered. I recall one classic example that befell me in one of my high school writing classes. My dear friends, at the time I felt that I would challenge Bill Wordworth in his *best* days with his grand and renowned "Lucy" poems! Oh, but I had *done* one! Eagerly I handed it in to the instructor. The remark which I received emboldened across the grubby sheet probably set me back creatively about sixteen decades, give or take two. The teacher had written in large letters for *all* to see these words, only these and nothing more: *Too cacophonous!*" First of all, because of my lexicographical aridity, I had to rush to the open arms of the Webster to see just what the word meant; and again, I was lost as to just *what* was too cacophonous—the *entire* language, or certain *words* and *phrases* that I had used, or *both*? (Later, you snickering ones, through my own discovery, I found out that it was *both*!) But this helps, I hope, to demonstrate how detrimental this kind of critical evaluation can be. In another instance, I was the victim of a very kindly disposed teacher. She, too, proved most inadequate. This beautiful soul treated everything I wrote as if it was the essence of perfection. To her I had already scaled the dizzy heights of Mount Parnassus, and at an age that would have rivalled Tennyson! That was ancient history. It was only some fifty years or so later that I was successful, minimally so, in receiving letters from benevolent editors stating that a particular work of mine was acceptable. And it was *not* because I did not flood their offices with *glowing* attempts!

I hope this further points out more graphically my stand on the worth of the evaluating spectator. You see, we, the honest appraisers, must in many instances re-evaluate or re-direct the values we often infiltrate our criticisms with. We cannot ask what is the happy medium between the two poles of reasoning. Frankly, if you august minds here today inquire of me, I have to declare that there is *no* medium, no middle ground. It is essential that we face this evaluation monster upon an entirely new plane. The spectator has to be an excellent psychologist, both in sensing value as well as maintaining an interest, a high interest, in each effort. I repeat the word *each*. Remember, at this stage of the poem we are dealing with the *finished product*. The idea-embryonic, the idea-formed, the idea-constructed, are all now passed. The young writer is seeking approval or understanding of this end-resultant reaction, so to speak. And we must let the writer's own desire serve as the best measurement for continued stimulations, since the infusion has been made. Praise cannot make the young poet more or less proficient at the craft, to be sure, but it does offer the creator a greater faith to accept condemnation with the same spirit in which he or she accepts the accolade.

Another vital element in evaluating any creative work is the necessity of viewing the effort in terms of the student's *own* realm of experience, or something I should like to call the *personal individualized frame of reference*. Too often the observer has failed to consider the importance of the pupil's grasp of the world about him or her, the real value of local color. I am not saying that a New York City youngster who has lived within earshot (and maybe *I* should pun here and say within "shot ear," but you wouldn't understand such brilliance!), within earshot of the subway's roar, cannot vividly give a charming story of life on a Minnesota farm, or paint a convincing word-scene of Pike's Peak. But how much more truthfully, how much more critically, and how much more accurately, can the writer depict Manhattan and urban life! Here familiarity does *not* breed contempt! Of course, the reverse holds true for the rural youngster as well when he or she tries to report genuinely on the city scene.

The discerning spectator will do well to remember such an open truth when he or she is appraising any expressions of the emotions. And the faithful ascription of this principle can go a tremendously long way in aiding the young writer—and especially the poet. It can also aid the evaluator by affording a more *pleasant* experience in approaching this poetic art.

As a final parting shot, I guess, in this probably disjointed missive, let me say that if we as genuine critical spectators of the poetic self-expression ever expect to succeed as the "encouragement-dispensers," we have to consider every possible situation and see every student as a *single objective*, and see every poem as a poem unto itself *alone*. True, these are rigid requirements. But we *must* seek to individualize the collective whole, if you get what I mean, and knowing *your* very brilliant minds again, I know that you do. But doing so, maybe—I say *maybe*—we can outlast the cruel adage that you know so well: "Those who can, do; those who cannot, teach, or evaluate."

Little patient ones, here I could wax on and on even more logically and even more eloquently, but I must resist temptation! I have to let your greater voices be heard in this lovely conference room. Then, too, I have to remember that the great voice demands a greater ear. Now where on earth did I hear *that* remark before?

Oh, I know. *Now* I remember—so there now. And thank you for your kind indulgence.

Name-Changing and Name-Calling

Let me say at the outset that perhaps had it occurred at some other time and in some other place, it might not have evoked questions I never did gain answers to. But it did occur when it did, and in New York City, and that's that.

Maybe the happening would not have meant so much to me, but it had happened during my first months of teaching in the New York City public school system. And I must point out that junior high school music teacher Alan Pitskovsky was an excellent teacher. He was warm, creative, and quite an artist on the keyboard. Alan and I hit it off at once, as they say in clichéland, "famously." He won the pupils' hearts and respect with his music and his obvious concern for them as young adults. He won my heart, as I said before, and we became quite friendly and very close. Since it was far back in the days of 1952 and not too many years after we both had come through those foxhole days of World War II, and since Israel was the neophyte, struggling state, and since we both felt a new urgency to conquer new worlds, we'd spend many happy and reflected moments together.

Alan and I sensed a new day "a-borning" in this post-war world. We sensed that we had some role to play to make it better, and that role would manifest itself best in the classroom of the public school in the junior high school area especially.

Yet through all of his *joie de vivre*, I would often note a bit of apprehension, of sadness, in some of his conversations. Upon prodding Alan about this shaded area of his optimism, he would say, "Yeah, but you know my heart is in music, jazz and pop, and I play in spots in and around the city, upstate, in Jersey, and Connecticut."

"So?" I asked, "What has that got to do with this undergrowth of morbidity I detect?"

"Well, you know, Jim, the war's not ten years past, the holocaust, the suffering, the remembrance of all the promises of a better social order for all Americans. And yet . . (Here his voice grew a bit more sad), and yet, in order for me to get more playing dates, especially out of the city, I've often had to change my name, or to hide my identity."

"Change your name, Alan? Why? Isn't 'Alan Pitskovsky' good enough as, say 'Howard Jones' or 'William Albert'?" I sensed what Alan was getting

28

at, but I really didn't want him to arrive at that point. "Say," I cranked on, trying to display my classical Shakespearean upbringing; (I remembered *Julius Caesar*) "remember old Cassius' remarks to Brutus when he was trying to poison his mind against Julie Boy: 'The name *Caesar*, the name *Brutus*—they both spin off the tongue just as easily.' Now those weren't exactly the grandiloquent verbiage, but you get my meaning, Al."

"No, Jim," he said, "it's not the same—not yet in America. The killing of six million Jews hasn't impressed the United States that much after all. Too often, there are too many doors closed in my field if the owner or the powers that be know I'm Jewish, or even if they feel it sounds 'Jewish,' whatever that means."

"Look, Alan," I soothed, "no one knows better than I, black, and undubitably black, what it means, and one bred and reared in Alabama, the hotseat for religious and racial bigotry. But for all that, I would not re-paint or bleach or uncurl my hair if I could." I felt that this very serious and talented Jewish boy from Brownsville would see what I was reaching for.

I paused, saw him nodding in comprehension. Then I went on, picking up a humorous though bitter-strained, way, how a conversation piece was kicked around when we soldiers were overseas, and the Allied Forces were closing in on the little goose-stepping dictator. The talk that was so often brought up was how to best punish Adolph in the most humiliating and excruciating manner. Some of the G. I.'s said, "Let him be imprisoned in one of the chambers where he had ordered so many of his victims gassed." Other suggestions were bandied about, some gruesome, still others almost satiric. But the final suggestion which seemed to have gained the creator of this idea the "Can-You-Top-This-Award" was this one. He said, "Aw, naw, men. All that is too easy. Here's the topper of all toppers. Listen: Paint him black, put a yarmulka on his head, and drop him off in south Georgia!" The roar of us all told the speaker that he had made the best one: *Paint him black, make him Jewish, and put his butt in south Georgia!*

"So, you see, Alan Pitskovsky, it could be worse. You also can see that I understand the nauseating problem. But we can't run from it." We both laughed at that bit of malevolent humor. We both also knew that each one knew what it meant to be (a) Jewish, (b) black, (c) and in America. *Shades of Gentleman's Agreement!*

Because I was at the time only a substitute teacher, and I was ousted by a regular-appointed teacher, I soon left that junior high and moved to another. It was through this abrupt change that I gradually lost contact with my newly-made friend and musician. Oh, we'd talk by phone now and then; but soon I began teaching in Queens.

29

Alan Pitskovsky did call me around late December to announce that his name was now officially "Alan Pitts—" no longer Alan Pitskovsky. "How do you feel about the *Change*, Al?" I queried. He said he felt great, that an onerous load had been removed. He wouldn't have to undergo the questioning, the interrogation, now that his name was more acceptably "American." The stigma had been removed. He really did seem relieved, almost jubilant.

That was the last time I had any written or verbal contact with Alan Pitts, neé Pitskovsky. I am certain that he found good and satisfactory jobs and club dates after that move of name-changing.

Of course, Alan's decision should not have been such a disturbing factor on my part in regards to his, as the old Latiners would say, his *modus vivendi*. For, after that, the most salient and forceful objective in this world is one's *method* of working or *getting on*, especially if you're of a minority group in America. Still, my perturbation over my music teacher friend did linger and linger.

Nor was his name-changing the only occasion I came across in those days some twenty-five years ago. I remember I had in one of my English classes a youngster whose name was Anthony Bell. He came to me one afternoon upon some occasion. Anthony was a nice chap, respectful, quiet, and bright. He said almost abruptly, "Mr. Morris, guess what: I'm Italian." I looked up at Anthoy rather quizzically, wondering if his was a case of adopting his new father's name, his surname, that is. "Oh, no, Mr. Morris, you see, it's not too hard to figure it out. You see, my real last name was 'Bellini,' but my father said what with so many people's attitudes not so nice toward the Italian people, he changed it to sound more *American*. See?"

I saw. As Anthony stood there before me, my mind raced back to Alan Pitts. I wondered had he "made it," had he "overcome" the stigma his genealogical impuissance had willed him. I wondered also would Anthony Bell, nee *Bellini*, find the "good life" in these United States by the simple stroke of a re-spelling of a surname. Then, as an extension of my confusion, my clouded avenue of lucubration, I posed this cute question for myself: "Knowing the many unpleasantries, the many hardships, which are circumvented if you were of the 'white, Anglo-Saxon, protestants' persuasion, wouldn't *you*, Jim Morris, make the change?"

I did not answer because I knew that my so-labelled "rate of high visibility" made it impossible for me to make the change-over. Oh, I remembered many "blacks" from the early Southern days who, being of extremely fair skin, and of a particular hirsute texture comparable to White America, had unobtrusively slipped into the "other-land" of advantaged America, relinquishing forever the octoroon or even less Negroid red and white corpuscular make-up. I wondered about them. Had they achieved, to a major degree, happiness? Greater security, maybe? Peace of mind? Who knows?

Still, getting back to Alan and Anthony once more, did they really do as Shakespeare's lamentable character expostulated: "Deny thy father?" And of course another question sprang up before me, one which shifted the guilt-feeling of "escape" from the Pitskovskys and Bellinis, the "passed-over-into-the-majority-camp-existence blacks." I placed it for the moment at least before the muddy and muddied feet of the creator of this situation: Mr. Average White American. This was the query: "Why have you demanded such a terrible price of exclusivity that these (to me) reprehensible acts of escapism would *have* to take place? What parliament of narrowed minds forced you to set up such purlieus of the soul that Americans, good, loyal, Americans, would even want to "deny their fathers"? To paraphrase an earlier American excoriating voice, "Is 'making it' so sweet; is success so enviable, that one as willing to submerge his original identity? Forbid not, Almighty God!"

I have heard and read of such instances when members of the Jewish faith, or religion, would hide their Star of David emblem, "unkosherize" their meals, to avoid distasteful situations which were sure to arise. And isn't it revealed so often that many of the Italian stars, singers, and actors, once they have achieved a permanent and lasting notch in the entertainment world, tell us their real, "Old Country" surname spellings and enunciatory and pronunciatory treatment of these names? Now I know some names are pretty difficult to translate or say in Americanized English. Or these names may be too long for advertising purposes. I don't mean these instances. This I can readily understand and accept. It's the sense of fleeing one's "roots," one's ethnicity of derivations, that tends to disturb me greatly.

Does America set up a duality of expectancy for one group under certain given circumstances, and change or restructure it upon another occasion? I am thinking: Alan Pitskovsky and Papa Bellini didn't have to "Americanize" their surnames at the local draft boards during World War II. Private or Corporal or Sergeant Pitskovsky or Major or Private First Class Bellini sounded pretty good "over there." There had been no need for family tree identifications then. Why now: and back home?

Now I must terminate this possible insoluble line of reasoning here. One must not maunder lost in the loquacity of his or her own biases too long. But, reader, some things do bother me and name-changing for material and social gains tends to force me to rage and do a bit of perhaps useless name-calling.

I do hope you will accept this rambunctious rage. Deep down I'm really not all that irascible—honest!

Suburbanites: What's the Color of Your Village Green?

Now I don't mean to constantly drape wet blankets upon the beauty of the world around me. I do have more jocund moments than despairing ones, despite the appearance to the contrary from time to time. Yet, this essay will lean into the dark side again. And, to be honest, maybe this seemingly dark side investigation of human action will prove eventually to be the brighter side after all. Anyway, that which calls our attention to an inequity can often serve as a tremendous purgative for cleansing the beclouded minds of us all.

I have always smiled inwardly and outwardly over the neighborhood integration or segregation status so long and so durable a clause in our country; especially has this been puissant and lasting in the greater urban areas of America. To bus or not to bus has hinged, or its concepts have impinged upon neighborhood make-ups, the 1954 school separate-but-unequal-issue coming to a constitutional permanency for the land not-withstanding. My smiling has emanated from the situation that local school boards have or have allowed themselves to become the whipping boy, and they have been pilloried beyond recognition in so many in-stances! And perhaps it is easy to see why the local school boards have taken much of the rap of segregated neighborhood sentiments for several reasons. And we know deep down the housing patterns are largely the insidious monsters behind much of the de facto segregation. Because the school board generally is loosely held together, and its autonomy is so weak or so amorphous, it can offer no worthwhile supportive relationship for so democratic and moral an issue as opened and open community living or societal intercourse.

And on the other side of the coin, the status quo or restricted cove-nants on housing and neighborhood sharing have great and invincible allies in the form of watchful lobbyists. Note the term "watchful lobbyists" sets up the basic note germane to this essay. And I am here attempting the poetic licensing of figurative language to embellish upon that phrase, I am going to hazard a guess that you will allow me to treat "watchful lobbyism" as a metaphorical entity here, to let it, more or less, symbolize more than the actual physical efforts, the often furtive movements of men and women, organizations, dictum, and operating to defend its posture. Rather, I propose to plead your indulgence and ask you to understand my approach when I label such actions as a watchful lobbyism of the mind. Hold on before you seek to become royally donative and shower me with expletives at this my brash coinage attempt. I shall make every effort to oblige you with a clear (as clearly as I am humanly able to) definition by example and by imagined reasons for such a definitive and demonstrative point of personal view.

I feel that this lobbyism of the mind stems, like so many biases, from a one-time, a one-instance, circumstance times ago, to what it has come to today that is almost a built-in Pavlovan reaction. Of course all of this "explaining" of the rationale is based upon, largely, the concept, as the song said, "You've got to be carefully taught to hate." Nevertheless, carefully or casually, the existence of this "restricted neighborhood belief" on the part, largely of the white constituents of the American society, the final results almost develop into a sort of inborn oppugnance to change? Thus, the two American societies exist, and shall exist until radical reorientation of attitudes reverse themselves.

It is almost funny where the attitudes of the average white about the maintenance and/or creation of the white enclave or enclosure stand. Many feel that it is a kind of God-bestowed right to set up such restrictive thinking. And the unusual thing is that upon so many occasions this restricting technique is so quietly or unobtrusively done! Perhaps that is the most enervating aspect of the whole idea or charade construction.

I am reminded how this all-white neighborhood feeling can run so deeply and so counter to the thinking of many otherwise "liberal" whites. A few years or so back, I was talking with a Jewish colleague teacher at a lunch-time break. The topic for that day stemmed from a news item concerning certain gangsters who had been apprehended. They were members of the white mafia-like group. We were talking about the utter reprehensibilities as displayed by one of the men in custody. This led me to reply what gall the fellow showed, what insensitivity he displayed for the crimes that he had committed. Eric Dromburg agreed. Then he said, "But you know, out on the 'Island,' in Nassau County, where I live, why, one of the biggest 'biggies' in the business lives just down the block from me in Farrowsville."

"Oh, yes, Eric?" I asked, "and how does the community feel about him, his presence, his family, and all? Or is the neighborhood aware of his certain predisposed livelihood predilection?"

"Oh," Eric Bromburg answered calmly, in an almost matter-of-fact manner, "he's a very responsible member of the neighborhood, quiet, polite. Keeps to himself and his family mostly. He doesn't bother us and we don't bother him. Acting like that, how can we mind, Jim, buddy?"

"Yeah," I said slowly. Then my mental rottenness slipped right out. "Right, Eric, right." I paused, then I went ahead: "By the way, didn't you say some time ago that no blacks or Spanish live in your particular little neighborhood?"

"That's right," Eric Dromburg replied quickly, "but we really have no type of apartheid-like policy, not at all. No siree! But, come to think of it, I really hadn't thought about it."

The lunch break was over, as the pragmatic time buzzer didn't break down, but sounded off in its usual plaintive tone. We had to get back to teaching the "young" (thought not necessarily "gifted", not all black).

Since that brief encounter with Eric Dromburg, I've often thought about his genuine response and the whole whites-for-whites-though-may-not-be intentional-community attitudes. What leads to such narrow, such shallow reflections on one of the major cancerous growths on our national body politic? Then I ran across a rather illuminating text recently by the behaviorist-philosopher, Harry A. Overstreet. In his book, *The Mature Mind*, he goes at length in describing one of our greatest shortcomings as human beings. Overstreet attributes much of our areas of despair and confusion in our adult world to the danger of the immaturity of the adult mind in the physiologically mature body of the human being. He goes on to say, "The forms that adult childishness can take are almost infinite in number. They exist not merely in those unfortunates who have to be confined to institutions, but in countless thousands of men and women who look adult, are taken to be adult, and are granted the full prerogatives of adulthood." In the same contextual relationship, the writer goes on to add: "The immaturities, moreover, are disguised from society at large, since that society has as yet developed no constant habit of appraising adult behaviors as immature or mature."

Here I inject my metaphorical implication, for this adult immaturity way of life, by saying this lack of mental growing up chronologically can be laid to the hardly recognizable nurtured stereotyped belief pattern, even manifesting itself among another maligned minority!

And so often this "watchful lobbyism" becomes so natural, the dispenser of such prejudice is not aware of this prejudicial slant! But it is there all right! And what makes the total problem so arduous lies in the very nature of the white American belief of the self-righteous responsibility to maintain and superimpose this attitude of separate living and housing quarters for the white and black races in this country. Until we can no longer fail *not* to sense this kind of immoral living in our land, there will always be, always persist, the existence of misunderstanding, mistrust, and the false sense of superiority and inferiority that sweeps the local and the national scenes.

Perhaps I could do well to end this "dark side" (What a nasty self-induced pun, considering the great abundance of melanin in my epidermal outer covering!) on another set of viable statements by Mr. Overstreet, and again from his *The Mature Mind*: "Not all adults are adults. Many who look grown up on the outside may be childish on the inside. Psychological age, moreover, as distinct from chronological age, is not merely an academic curiosity. Whether a person is average advanced, or retarded in his mental, emotional, and social growth may be the concealed reason—and the chief reason—why his adult relationships with his world are as they are."

". . . with his world are as they are. ." Huh. Well, there is the ancient adage that the Devil may quote the *Scriptures* for his own favors with great avidity and assiduity. Maybe you see me as Mr. Mephistopheles. I do beg you do no such thing. As I said at the outset here, many times, the better reminding or pointing out of our faults can act as a genuine catharsis. I do hope so for the Eric Dromburgs and others in our society.

Who needs any "watchful lobbyism of the mind" as we move toward life in the twenty-first century?

Neither I nor you, nor our children. And especially, *not our children!*

What Political Role Should Organized Teachers Play in America Today?

As members of the society at large. They have allowed themselves to be shunted as a whole, disregarding their responsibilities as citizens of society. We cannot make such an-all embracing statement without due reservations, but, in the main, educators have refrained from taking a vital role in our politics. There are several reasons, possibly, why such an attitude has remained so long. One has been the queer notion on the part of some teachers that they had to abstain from politics because it was thought to be below their professional dignity to put a finger in politics. Just why this odd reasoning persisted, no one can state accurately, but I daresay that this is a carry-over from the old order when education was a kind of blood-bought thing, only acquired by the select few. We can hear a few wags remark that the taint and the smearings which have been discovered in so many instances where politics is concerned, a few more upstanding citizens would refrain from such legislative involvement! But back to the main thrust here: Their philosophy (these old order educators) was that anyone could enter politics, but not everyone could receive an education, an education comparable to their professional demands. This concept might have had some basis, however flimsy, but since the aura of exclusiveness in educational opportunities has been lifted, it is only the foolhardy who will entertain such a thought today.

Another reason for many teachers to steer clear of politics lies in the local autonomy often vested in many of our schools' administrators and superintendents. These overlords of education look upon the teacher's activities other than the schoolroom and school organization with an air of utter disdain. Patterns of behavior not synonymous with the particular board's approval are forbidden. And many teachers who would gladly take an active part in politics find themselves weighing the decision between participation and loss of their jobs. Perhaps these are isolated instances, but I suspect that they are not as isolated as one would suppose.

Now I do not propose to say that teachers should not be closely examined upon their personal activities as well as their understanding of the subject matter they are to handle. But let this be an honest examination presented by qualified examiners who will weigh all of the values

36

inherent and otherwise. By all means the teacher must take an active part in political action, whatever the creed, so long as it is within the framework of our Constitution and societal obligations. How can any teacher preach full participation in our democratic system to students unless he or she makes his or her contribution a living, dynamic one? There are no more cloistered halls, no more hallowed schoolrooms, set apart from the local and national communities. Economic interdependence, sociological interchange, and political developments which have taken place during the last two or three decades make any division between education and life impossible. This does not mean that it cannot individualize its members. Just as any other profession does not set certain patterns or policies for its associates to adhere to, so must the teacher be free from channelization. The instructor must be allied to any other group in the society which suits his or her interests. The main thought I wish to state here is that the teacher must not ostracize himself or herself from society; nor must the teacher be forced to disassociate himself or herself. If this should develop, the entire educational system will break down, and the young minds of the classrooms will be unable to grasp any meaningful way of thinking or to show individual growth.

This last point leads us into the question of *subversives* in the teaching profession. First of all, let me define in my own thinking what a subversive is. According to my concept such an individual is regarded as one whose intent is to overthrow our form of government by force or by violence. Certainly, no individual whose intent is to overthrow the existing government, or who preaches such doctrinaire should be permitted to the teaching field. That much is definite! But a possible point of conflict may lie in the authorities' minds who determine the definition of a subversive. There has been great stress placed upon this issue, with no resolutions in some parts of our country yet. But much of the examining and qualifying has been placed with emphasis upon the leftist point of view, thereby leaving many demagogical theories of the right untouched. It is true, however, that there is often a great difficulty in pinning down the native fascistic philosophies. But in order that we have a "more perfect union," *all* elements, whether obliquely expressed, or blatantly shouted, must be eradicated. There can be no other way.

This eradication referred to above cannot be successfully achieved through any such things as loyalty oaths alone. It is too simple a task to swear to a principle for the sake of convenience or expediancy of a given moment. The job is tough, a job which must be taken without hysteria or subterfuge on the part of the examining officials. These officials should be well-trained, public-minded men and women who can approach their work fairly. Otherwise, we might create a state of affairs wherein clannish appraisal will be the judgment, and suspicions can become magnified.

By studying, weighing, and weighing other ideologies does not mean that our own way of life will be put in jeopardy. Rather, by so searching into the various political and social attitudes, we can better appreciate our own concepts, observing our defects as well as our attributes. The school, therefore, must serve as the awakening medium for students to look into the hearts of all issues. The student must not be taught what to think, as the Hitler Youth Movement in Germany tried to promote. The school's job is to encourage the student to think, and think for himself or herself. Anything less than this is tantamount to a condemnation.

Of course this attitude will undermine many of the old practices of the traditional subject matter in the curriculum. Old principles were relegated to self-containing cubicles, unrelated many times to the entire education program. Today with the emphasis moving away toward a "modified core or "experience" program, learning should be an all-embracing experience. Acute authoritarianism is being lessened. The whole child and his relations to the society, redeeming or otherwise, will have to be accounted for, die-hards notwithstanding. Future teachers and educational workers must be trained to take this new approach to education as they are prepared to face the classroom. We must remember that the problems of society do not stop at the door of the school. They are truly a part of the environment which is, in turn, an important constituent of *society* itself, and this *society* in its largest and most powerful sense!

"Daisy, Daisy . . ."

Well, I know it had to arrive. It had to come. It had to reach fruition, to gain its maturation point. But I just did not want to see it come to pass. Honest. But with the E.R.A. proposition certain of eventual passage—and something, by the way, which is so long overdue—the wheel of progress had to revolve or to resolve itself unto this zenith.

Oh, I'll get to my sadness in just a moment. Right now I'm just too full of the bitter wine of remorse to appear in anywise sane or salubrious. Yet the reason for this deep depression lies in a simple observation I have recently made. And what did I view that swept me into a state of nausea of nostalgia, you ask? Well, please do not laugh when I tell you, you hear? It is this: Lately, I've seen many, many young ladies riding the two-wheelers, bicycles built with the *crossbar*—bicycles built for the *male* consumption. Or so I was led to believe in the old days of my lost and time-destroyed youth.

In those golden days it was absolutely unthinkable for a nice young lady to be astride a velocipede constructed for men and boys! It was so unthinkable! Again, I suppose, in the old days of my lost and time-destroyed youth it was unthinkable for a young lady to be seen doing many things thought to be within the province of the masculine-gendered world!

I am certain this line of really errant reasoning on my part will help to tag me as the proverbial last of the red hot male chauvinist pigs, owner of that narrow, dust clouded brain, a severe proponent of the "place-for-the-woman-is-in-the-home" philosophy. But, please do not ascribe such a title to me. I am not that type, really! Such an attitude today could certainly get my whole corporal being into a heavy dark kettle of boiling aqua. Can't you just hear the well-meaning ERA-ers screaming for my bald and/or balding pate. "Say, throw the bum out, back to the lions and the brass knuckle users! He deserves no better fate than that. Some men are such sick losers!"

Well, ladies, I assure all of you lovely creatures on the surface it does seem that I do not care a whit for human equality. I am truly pro-feminine in all ways except for the way that seeks to maintain the difference in the use of the feminine gender when it comes to sharing the masculine velocipedic vehicle.

I can take the uni-sex hair styles, similar levi slacks-wearing, similar camper's boot-wearing. I can even accept and promote an open and free market in all employment and social position situations. My dear ladies, I will go so far as to fight for your admittance to all former male drinking bar establishments. But for bike equality—save this ancient reprobate this singular debasement, this obvious defilement!

Let there ever be: The male bicycle for the male cyclist and the female bicycle for the female cyclist. *Please!*

Looking at the Classroom Teacher Dress Code

It is true—an undeniable truth—that the American Civil Liberties Union acted in good faith and forthrightness in defending the teachers' rights to dress in a manner "less rigidly patterned," if I may create a term, in the classroom. Here I am referring to the state and local laws which forced the administrators of some public institutions to cease and desist from demanding, for instance, the wearing of ties and less flamboyant attire on the part of the male instructors, and the non-wearing of, say, slacks and/or other pants-like dress, and more disciplined dress codes on the part of the female instructors.

One's civil rights, remember, must be, and are protected by a special amendment, labored over and spelled out by the sagacious law-givers when this property was in its historical infancy. I do grant that it was correct and proper that particular teacher unions readily and staunchly bounded to the rescue of the "beleagured" teacher who sought to dress in a more relaxed manner. Anyway, who is the ferrous-fisted hierarchy that can tell one how to clothe one's self? Remember, this had verily become the age of relaxation, of realism, to bring one's approach in the classroom in nearer accord with the pupils. After all, students must not have to regard the role and the personality of the smart new instructor as the type so commonly pictured in the old school "marm" and school "master" attitudes of stern and icy civility! Ah, no! So why not dress in a way more casual, and thereby gain a closer, warmer relationship with the youth before the teacher? Didn't the birch rod and dunce cap techniques, teacher-oriented and centered instruction, go the way of the "home-on-the-range" buffalo herds.? And why in heaven's sake should we expect students to wear ties (on the part of the male constituency), for example, to leave off wearing slacks and shorts (on the part of the female constituency)? And, naturally, the best way to solve the problem was for the teacher to show by *example*! John Dewey, *the* John Dewey would approve—and that would be approbation sufficient for the teacher.

Thus, the de-emphasis on the classroom dress code was engendered and enkindled. Now what is my biased and provincial "beef," as the saying goes? Well, let me project this at once: My objection to, say the optional

41

wearing of ties for gentleman instructors, for example, restricts itself solely to the elementary and middle school levels. I state this primarily because I feel that these early pubescent years are the most impressionable years of a child's entire life, and further feel that in countless cases, what with a sudden plethora of media-crowded concepts, some bad, others terrible, and some too soon presented to the immature and malleable mind, the classroom, the early classroom situation, is the only haven the pupil may run to for many of the basic elements so necessary in "growing up." The outlawing of "birching" the child, the misguided concepts concerning the child, (and here we refer specifically to student permissiveness), have left the student with little of elemental value guides, with few concrete objectives, images, that he or she can build on, or cling to.

No don't gain from my "rantings" here that you are captured by a vacuous, embittered old man, a recalcitrant "ancient mariner" of an English teacher who resents a kind of denigration of image, a kind of regret over the loss of "special respect" treatment. Nor should you receive the notion that I am still crying for the waltz and foxtrot in an age here where the "disco" and "salsa" beats have come to maturity. Nothing could be so far removed from veracity! I may not display the best "hustle" steps on the dance floor, but I do know what moves I am *supposed* to make! You must be made really cognizant of that certainty! I am not of the sour or fermented genus *vitis* (*grape*, to the uniformed, botanically speaking) type.

Rather, I envision the whole aspect of this easing up of the dress code reaching further and deeper into the other areas, areas of graver and more resolute intent. I am thinking of the need so often for the young formative mind to see the mother and father image within the personality scope of the grade teacher—not to picture the abecedarian as "big brother" or "big sister" to whom the child may or may not or need not respond, depending upon the specific situation and the time element. As one of the old gray-beards whose job has been over the years to offer seminars and some guidance instruction to the younger and often neophyte teacher, I have witnessed more times than not the resultants that are the remains of a misguided young teacher's attempt to play the thespian art of "big brother" or "big sister." I have also seen the disillusion, the painful realization of the error of such an approach. And it is never a pleasing painting of the human soul.

As the immediate supervisor of a language arts program in a local junior high school in the city, I had the occasion to receive a most earnest, seriously dedicated young man, ready to "give it his all" for those tender early teenagers, John Murer was such a gracious and determined teacher—personable, if you can consider the hyperbolic meaning of the term: *to a fault.* He came into the school term that September brimming with ideas and ideals. John had been apparently a kind of collector of

42

artifacts relative to the Arthurian and Robin Hood histories; that is, he had gathered countless and some illustrious and illustrative materials on knights, knighthood, and mythology. Many of these items and articles, some obviously rare and expensive, he gladly brought to share and use with the students in his planned and structured layouts. But John Murer had one unredeemable enemy: John Murer. He saw the *chargers* under his tutelage as his kid brothers and sisters. They soon grew to sense this unguided or misguided almost freedom from classroom law that pervaded this very "nice" atmosphere. To them he was truly a "with it" teacher. Often they would sit at his desk, call out with a "hey, teacher," showing no sense of discriminatory regard for the classroom situation here.

Of course, when "Monster Morris" would walk in amid such confusion and freedom of movement escapades, the tones would quickly change on the part of the pupil populace, unoccupied seats suddenly realizing they were to be filled with bodies after all!

Upon more than one instance, I directed to John: "John, you're a bright, ambitious, and dedicated teacher already, it shows. It all pours through like a fresh beacon of joy. But there is one element, my boy, which may topple you and destroy your refreshing outlook on teaching. It may also mean you'll be forced to seek an early egress, believe me. John Murer, exert more discipline, set that imaginary line of demarcation, that threshold over which these lovable children may not step. They'll understand and they will accept *and* respect you even more so, come next June. Otherwise, you might be willing to 'toss in the washcloth' before Christmas!"

John Murer understood, I am of the opinion, but I think John Murer felt the situation would become less severe, and thereby even enhance the learning atmosphere. How could anyone think of dealing so harshly with such bright eyes and voluble voices!

Needless to say, Mr. John Murer was asked "out" by the administration shortly after Thanksgiving that November.

I shall not belabor the point here with the insipid "I-told-you-so's." "I-told-you-so's" are not in order at any time like this. Rather, the "I-wish-we-could-have-saved-the-situations" are definitely needed, for this was one genuinely concerned bright language arts teacher that I lost, or rather, that those *bright eyes* and *voluble voices* lost. And seeing the scarcity in so many instances of good, bright, and dedicated male language arts teachers, especially in the middle or junior high school division, it was indeed a tragic loss. I never heard whatever became of John—I only hope he was able to be the learner in this sense, that he found his techniques of approach to be somewhat too flocculent or susceptible, and that he gained a more disciplined order to his methods. He certainly had the creativeness, he had the gregariousness, and he surely possessed the charm.

I do hope my kind of "Dear John" story did not lead you too far afield, for I hope, too, that my analogies and anecdotal additives are part and parcel of this total picture: *the gaining and maintaining respect for the teachers, and the incalculable role learning must play in each school child's life.*

Oh, sure there has grown more militancy on the part of the too-often harried and underpaid classroom instructor since the dismal days when my mother and two aunts struggled in the one-room, all-grades, shacks in Alabama and North Carolina. There *had* to be this new urgency to focus proper attention upon the importance of the teacher. This I gladly accept and realize. And perhaps, although obliquely so, when my emphasis is pressed for greater care and special consideration for a teacher code of dress, I am really "opting" for a kind of superexaltation to be directed to the position and status of the teacher. By demonstrating that we are a bit special, that we do exert a tremendous influence and impact upon the present and future development of the child, we can cause an even greater effort on the part of these youngsters. If our dress behavior is of the same taste and style *and* manner of the ones we have before us in the classroom, I wonder what great impressions in *other* areas of learning disciplines are affected by the obvious and primary contact—the eye—children have before them.

Having been a kind of "sick stickler" for more representable attire and care on the part of my pupils over the some forty odd years in the classroom, and especially in the wearing of ties by the boys on special occasions, I am regularly confronted with the ex-junior high student, now in college or in the wider and more demanding occupational areas in the marketplace today. And countless ones greet me with an appreciated (or so these young men now declare!) reference to the "law" I hammered out about the wearing of "those ties." One particular fellow, now a work-supervisor for United Parcel Service met me recently in the "City," and said, even before a warm greeting was made: "Mr. Morris, do you still have those awful ties you used to make us boys wear? I hope so!"

"Why, Kirk?" I compelled to ask at once.

"Because, Mr. Morris, that was one of the greatest discipline builders I ever had to undergo. The Army, the banking job I had for a little while, and all, that forcing the tie upon me was great. It was rough then. I didn't understand what it was all about, but it became so much clearer after I left you years later."

I laughed most happily as I saw Kirk Powell point and tighten his tastefully selected cravat under his shirt collar. If I had had doubts about easing my classroom dress code ethics and considerations, the statement Kirk made to me the other Sunday morning dispelled such thoughts as they so often say, with "deliberate speed and accurate intent!"

What Price Prejudice?

Ambrose Bierce, the late extraordinary writer, said, "A prejudice is a vagrant opinion with no visible means of support." William Hazlitt, in his *Sketches and Essays,* declared: "Prejudice is the child of ignorance."

Both of these observations are most valid and admirably said by these two eminent men of letters. They are both worthy of our fullest cogitation. Prejudice *is* predicated on such flimsy and on such baseless foundations. It is born of know-nothing parentage. We all know this, and yet this toxic present turpitude lingers and lingers in so many walks of our American life. Of course behind the ignorance, or I should like to say, underneath any element of prejudice is its foundation of fear, ironclad fear, signal of that of which we know nothing. And one of the most painful aspects of the evil is the method by which it is carried down through the ages from father to son, from father to son, and so on.

I would not be so chagrined except for the fact that in this progeny-passing of the baton, as in the relay racing situations on the cinder track, so seldom is the stick dropped to break the chain of bigotry-transporting. And I am further chagrined when I hear an otherwise "sensible" voice exclaim, "Well, you know, we *all* are a *little* prejudiced!" It galls me for two reasons. (1) The speaker seeks to intimate that prejudice is a kind of God-given, hereditary human trademark, a burden or cross, something created beyond the individual's power to control, regulate, or even destroy. (2) The speaker uses this position to assume that I, too, am not devoid of the curse of bigotry. And these two positions simply rankle me beyond all sense of self-contained order. The contention that *everyone* has some prejudiced taint upon his escutcheon, willed upon his behavior, is like using the philosophy of the non-self-determining proponents. This preachment swears that mankind is either bestowed with this social shortcoming or he is too weak to sidestep this damning problem if and when it presents itself. In any event, it is a sad commentary.

On the other hand, the belief that I am unable to escape the reaches of prejudice and prejudiced attitudes is saying that we are in a debilitated state of existence, therefore, we are not expected to grow beyond this level of human existence. Racial and religious prejudices can possibly be compared again to one's attitude toward the reptile, commonly gentle or

45

unusually deadly. A youngster never led to exist under the fear of the snake's reputed enmity, has no innate dread of the stated danger. (And, really, how many children have ever been bitten or attacked by the creature to be able to display first hand experiential reason for avoiding the snake?)

I am more than amused and amazed at the vituperative spoutings which are so often ranted about Italians here in the United States, for illustrative purposes. It appears to these sick minds that every criminal act of crime-laden report is linked to someone of Italian descent. And these same "poison-pourers" go on to belittle the place of the Italian and of the impressive contributions these people have made to our society. I dare not offer here any individual listings of the Fermis, Carusos, Michaelangelos, Puccinis! That would prove too obviously easy and too far a step to go to prove a point. Rather, let me address these verbal atrocity-makers with a primary fact that should reduce their blather to less than zero on the scale of verbiage-poisoning: *The same language that these bigots employ to degrade the Italian people—the English language—over 52% of its origin can be traced back to the Latin or Roman tongue!* (That should cool their *hot-garbage-can* mouths at least until sundown!)

One of the most commonly deceptive lines of reasoning for many whites' attitudes toward the blacks rests in the *how* of their measuring rod techniques. To far too many white people, blacks are measured by the worst, the most unfortunate, elements of the black society or community. The lowest element, therefore, becomes the norm for Caucasian measurements of success or of abnormalities for the black race. Any outstanding figures in the community become a kind of exception to the rule. Now, on the *other* side of the coin, blacks are expected to see the social deviates, the social misfits, in the white world as the *exception*—not the rule, or norm for measurement. Perhaps this immoderate attitudinal position is the very bedrock upon which our poor black-white relations rest in America today. But to conclude this thrust on a more sober and sobering note: I am afraid that until this feeling of consideration is altered completely and *honestly*, the perpetuation of the problems of prejudice in this country will not minimize themselves. They will proliferate. Again, "to thine ownself be true" is still in good order, although the voice in *Hamlet* had neither America nor race relations in mind—unless it was the human race at large.

Now, we are all conscious of the importance of bringing to the surface an awareness of an evil. Anyone can do that. And I think that I have just performed this task, if not wisely nor well, but with at least a gesture of good intent. But the really decent "gadfly artist" goes a step further, the step that produces at worst a line of suggestion for the rectification of a sickness—a kind of "here's-how-to-change process."

So, with or without your permission, let me pose two possible ways to overcome this individual personality of bias. My suggestion will cost nothing, add nothing to your physical posture or situations. Nor will it expose you to open ridicule from the most august members of your peer-age group or cult. Here's how, I believe, you race and religious hatemongers can overcome this affliction; Each morning when you *first* tumble out of bed, slip sleepy-eyed into the little private room that you use for your daily ablutions. Now gently close the aperture to the other members of the domicile. (So often your nearest relatives cannot comprehend some private executions!) Place your visage just as is when you've just left the all-night bunk piece of furniture before a well-cleaned mirror. Stare closely at the face staring back. Now if you can accept that reflection without an honest grimace, "You're a better man than I am, Gunga Din!" Chances are, however, all former concepts of egomania that granted you the belief that you were so much better than those you had held in a kind of despicable tolerance, will fade on the waves of the incandescent light that made you this startling revelation in the first place! Ah, yes, the nullity will come out!

I can't prescribe and predict guaranteed initial results. But I am more than eager to lay my sceptered title on the line that after several of these aurora hour visual rituals, you will willingly accept the fact that personally you're not such an over-heated potato after all. I might be totally incorrect, but I'll lay you my most jam-packed port-manteau that there will be a softening in your sense of vaunted self-esteem. I am most eager to learn of the results, s' *il vous plait!*

Well, the other suggestion may sound a bit more odd (but what is more odd than acts or attitudes of prejudice?), and it may appear quite quixotic, but it is worth the attempt, I feel. Let me state unequivocally, haters, if you must give vent to your mental spleenage outpourings, why not turn your prejudicial bent toward the following members of the human race: Hate only the human beings whose epidermis coloring is a decidedly cerulean blue, whose vitreous humor containers number only one, with that orb resting securely, Polyphemus-like, in the back of the head. And, further, despise those who possess fingernails-less digits which can be observed on only two of the four hands that they have.

"But," I think I hear you ejaculating quickly, "there is no such human being in existence—so far as science has indicated at this moment in the world!"

"Yes," see me smiling most indulgently, "no, God never did get around to manufacturing such a member of the human species. So I suggest that in some chimerical fashion, you create one and use it as a straw object—a punching bag sort of entity—to hate. In that way, you can "have your hate and beat it, too."

Unmaking the Drug Scene

Anyone alive and conscious and "kicking" today cannot help wondering and growing quite apprehensive at the sudden proliferation by the young in the use of drugs and alcohol. The fast rise in the consumption of beer itself can lend a sense of trepidation (or I should think) in regard to this situation. I don't think that I have ever seen so many brownbag-enclosed beer cans and bottles in the hands of our teen agers as I have seen over the last year or so. I shall not beat upon the point of the abuse of social ethics or of environmental pollution damage this is all causing. Neither will I dwell upon the personal moral issues involved here. I can say without contradiction that more experienced scholars on the effects of alcohol consumption can say more and with greater authority than I could ever point out.

I opened with the observation on the heavy use of beer at the outset in this dissertative espousal because, I suppose, it is the least damaging of the mind-altering or mind-disturbing substances of all. If one is to believe statistics and all of their implications, the use of such drugs as marijuana, hashish, "high-inducing" capsules, and cocaine, that monster drug, is staggering! (And no pun was ever intended here!) And although the use of the harder drugs is prohibited, the almost complete abandonment with which, for example, young people on the streets of the city "light up a joint," as the saying goes, with no indication of fear that they will be apprehended by the police, is truly astounding.

I am further reminded of the eye-opening revelation by two very recent news reports I saw on the "tube" a few evenings ago, a revelation which in itself led me to many avenues of thinking. The first item showed the wide use of marijuana by the young workers and other youthful executives down in the Wall Street area of New York City, and, as the reporter pointed out, fearless of an arrest or "bust." The pushers, their attire certainly not exactly in camouflage, along the streets of the stock exchange vicinity, seemed only concerned themselves with transacting the deals, and the buyers seemed only concerned with completing the trade and in the fact that the twistings or pills were the "real McCoy"—nothing more, nothing less!

The other news scene on the same theme of drugs among the young, centered upon its widespread use of beer and wine and liquor by those who frequent Jones Beach, some forty or fifty miles away from the packed-in atmosphere of the concrete. Many older citizens, it appears, had complained because of the tremendous litter of cans and bottles scattered around this magnificent shore playground, tossed there mainly by the youthful contingent. Again, the reporter focussed his attention upon the young people seen at this time as bright articulate boys and girls, many of whom came from the upper middle class and more affluent segments of our society. The question was: "Aren't you young people afraid that the police will arrest you?"

The answer that came back was, "Naw, man, we don't fear the cops. Oh, now and then they 'bust' some of us, but we'll take our chances, man. We'll take our chances."

"Tell me," the interviewer went on, approaching another side of the issue, "what is there that is so great in this heavy use of these stimulants, these often deadly-proven drugs?"

"Well, you see," chimed in another voice, this time a little blue-eyed girl who was not more than fifteen, if that much, "things get pretty boring, and these drugs and stuff keep you in a constant 'high,' a constant 'high.' You just feel good all the time!"

And it was that young girl's last remark that set my course for this perhaps testy and hastily contrived essay here: *You just feel good all the time!* Feel good all the time. I shall make my point of conjecture plain. The fault, I'm afraid, lies not in the cruel fact that these youngsters are destroying their lives so foolishly. What then, you may rightfully ask, if the fault does not lie with these pampered, middle class, neglected, and often ignored affluent Americans, who must bear this culpability?

The fault, I fear, may rest upon the shoulders of the older generation, the parents and guardians of these young lives. The fault may rest in a larger sense in America's rapid striving for the *materials* of life today. Have we over-emphasized the "good life" ethic without stressing the laborious journey one must make to get there? And what about the "good life"—is it for real, and is it all-essential for happiness and security? What is the escape route to "feeling good" all of the time? Have home, religious, and social values in general become so, so debased, so watered, so refined, that things of spiritual, of academic-intellectual worth—the mere *joie de vivre*, of learning for the sake of learning, gone out of the American encyclopedia of living? Truly, I do not know.

What happened to the kids who used to get "high" over Bill Shakespeare's soliloquies, Picasso's abstracts, Harriet Tubman's magnificent ingenuity and bravery, Dos Passos' realistic fiction, John Brown's human fanaticism, Marty King's blind dedication to a cause that transcended all levels of fear, of personal safety, and self-preservation? What really happens?

49

Have we the adults been too self-conscious about "making it" ourselves to have had the time long enough to see the inutility, the futility of this generation's silent cries for help through its self-destructing manner of searching for "M.O.: Found in a Bottle—" to paraphrase from Edgar A. Poe, and call it, "Modus Operandi Found in a Bottle"—as a way out of a wilderness of personal loneliness?

I don't know, people. Me, being the devil's most dedicated advocate, I only pose the question. I do not, nor can I, supply the solution. And this concern does not make me "feel good" at any time!

Don't Let the Thought of Death Kill You

To enliven things, perhaps this peregrinatory exploration will speak about death, that veiled abstraction that has always upset, intrigued, baffled, teased, and lured the ablest minds of the ages to investigate. Maybe it is truly the most magnificent of topics because it is the one, the sole, the solitary thesis, that renders all thinking and expostulations most equal. It is that subject that has evoked, I daresay, the greatest number of euphemistic derivations in the English language. More metaphors and similes about death have kept poets mentally fat, verbally speaking, over the years, with their simply describing the relative qualities of death and dying!

Yet we who follow closely or only rather desultorily the concepts of our particular holy writs failed to accept the *Scriptures'* repeated statements that death is as natural as life, that living is the prelude to dying, that it is at the other end of the spectrum. Perhaps it is so because we fear the unknown. Perhaps it is like the traveler who, having traversed a million or so miles along a well-companioned highway, suddenly finds his footsteps leading toward a dense, dark, and heavily-matted underbrush. And there is the penetrating silence, the greatest of all boons to a world of loneliness. Yes, I do believe that is the major factor in our dread of death—the apprehensive approach to a universe of loneliness! Wasn't it loneliness that made old Robinson Crusoe shout for joy unmanageable upon discovering those huge human footprints along that sandy and pebbled island beach? And doesn't the old black spiritual moan out on dying: "I don't mind dying, but I have to go by myself"? And don't we find over and over again the recurring theme that man is terrified of the unknown quality or qualities inherent in death only because of the dread of loneliness, of being forever alone?

Of course, this pulls this thesis into another street of wandering discourse for a moment. We do know that human beings originally came together as a unit, as a community-oriented existence, out of the need for self-protection, but more than that, man grouped his physical and mental resources to avoid boredom and the pitfalls of loneliness. Ah, yes, we do need each other for more survival strength!

51

Now that we are certain that this is an undeniable truth, what bothers me is: *Since we want and need communal living, why do we treat each other so badly?* We really are pretty empty-craniumed, to state the least. If we know that food, water, sleep, and rest are so basic as ingredients for the sustenance of our well-being, we will scrap, fight, beg, borrow, and purloin for these essentials. Yet although we know that we are truly inter and intra-dependent each upon the other, dreading the emptiness of the grave, and fear of the world to come, we erect gigantic barriers to obstruct this mingling, the intercourse of everyday communicational necessities!

These obstructions take on so many forms, too. We know that there is, at least in this particular sector of the Western Hemisphere, the great obstruction known as race hatred and skin coloration denigration. Now just who set up such arbitrary nonsense is not for me to hammer over. Sufficient it is for me to happily state that I do not have to bear that responsibility, thank goodness! Nor will I have a hand in promoting the perpetuity of this doctrine.

Then again, how about the centuries-old bugaboo that keeps the disturbance pot boiling: religious intolerance? And I am willing to wager my last sou I have hoarded down in Local First National on Main Street that all of the creators of these excellent concepts of life and living did not intend that the later practitioners resort to such narrow-minded application of precepts. I thought the objective of Islam, Judaism, Christianity, and all the other established religious fixtures in this world was based, above all else, on love or reverence for fellow human beings. I do not believe that any group was taught what I like to call human harmony genocide. Rather, there is the basic objective of seeking the good life, discovering the peace and tranquil experience awaiting just beyond the "shade." Maybe I am totally wrong and inept in my logic-philosophy (generally I am!), but I dare to feel much to the contrary in these my exhortations.

Then naturally up pops the third and maybe the most ludicrous of all bugaboos that pits one human segment of the American people against the other. We all recognize it as national origins fear. We somehow feel (that is, Majority American) that your beginning in another country and reaching here later than, say, the "old-time-*Mayflower*-like" arrivals—this tends to lower you on the scale of American preferential treatment and exposure to the bounties of this land. Now if that isn't the most blameworthy of all posturings! On this issue, I shall paraphrase Carl Sandburg in his great book-length poem, *The People, Yes*, of 1936 vintage. The situation: An Indian IWW soapbox speaker was addressing a crowd in Denver, when an Irish cop on duty yelled to the Indian, "Aw, why dontcha go back where you came from!"

And if that subtlety is not enough, let us look at the remark attributed to the political wit and life-in-general pundit, Will Rogers, part-Cherokee and part-white: It seems that a member of the once supra-patriotic and super-narrow in its outlook, DAR, told Will: "I'll have you know that my ancestors came over here on the *Mayflower*, humph!"

Will Rogers is said to have drawled, "Wall, Ma'm, can't quite match that. My folks didn't come over on the *Mayflower*, but a whole lot of 'em was there to meet the boat!" (And can you imagine this DAR xenophobe's complete contretemps had she addressed, say, Chief Pontiac or Pocahontas!)

Now all of this rambling might have tossed you and me off the original "death" track, in a manner of facetiously speaking, but I hope not. Because we all know the dread of our future passing on into that Beyond, from which no one has successfully returned to date, and because that greatest fear is the fear of loneliness, and because the grave spells loneliness, it, therefore, appears so essential for me to wake us up and remind us how we have let ourselves fall heir to a fear of our own silly and unnecessary creation.

Dear neighbors and colleagues, let us live a lot together before the moment comes when we'll have to die alone!

The Teacher-Poet and the Student-Poet in the Classroom (Presented to the N. Y. C. Assn. of the Teachers of English a few seasons ago)

It has been a common contention among many educators that the working artist seldom acts as the proper instructor in the field where he practices. Some feel the great need for the artist himself or herself to seek full achievement within big or her own realm blocks the real effort to give aid to the young creative student. Others contend that the poet, who has been trained in this peculiar specialty, cannot tolerate the mixed metaphor, the misplaced synecdoche, the broken limb, or the smashed dactyl produced by the student-poet. Still, there is another camp of non-believers who thinks a poet cannot make a good teacher of verse because he is too close to his or her art to distinguish or clarify the efforts of the others and to translate these emotions to students.

They all may be right, but I wonder though when I consider such poets who were teachers at one time: Sandburg, Frost, Van Doren, Ciardi, Cullen, to name a few. You might say, "Well, ask their students in order to gain a true evaluation of their effectiveness as teachers." But I still would doubt that their pupils suffered by being under the influence of these masters. And I do not buy the old crutch! "Those who can, do—those who cannot, teach." A poet is a human being first and he is an artist second, in that order. In fact, the two basic ingredients are inseparable.

I further contend that the teacher-poet knows first-hand what goes through the mind of a poet struggling to find expression. As Sandburg said, it must be a combination of the common and the exquisite. And as Robert Frost once wrote, as recorded by Miss Elaine Barry, in *Robert Frost on Writing*, "The artist's object is to tell people what they haven't as yet realized they were about to say themselves." Once the student can feel the need to see *all* of life's expressions as being capable of poetic derivation, then the road to poetic happiness will be realized a little more clearly. It is the job of the teacher-poet to help the student-poet come to realize the prime objective of the poet and the poem.

Again, and not to brutalize a point in showing the advantage of having the poet in the teaching situation, can be observed from a personal point of view. As we may all recall, most poems and poets, when we were children, seemed so distant and unreal, something and someone to be feared, or at best gently tolerated. But when the teacher-poet is there, living, sharing these emotional involvements, then this image takes on a more realistic consideration. I know, for my humble jacket pockets are constantly filled with student examples of poetic efforts which have been done and shoved into my hands as I pass along the halls. This, indeed, helps to erase much of the aura of mystery.

Many of the older concepts of the poet and the poem were of another vintage, from another place. Most of the themes were teacher-imposed, and many of the themes were not fully explored before the teacher addressed the pupils with: "Now, tonight go home and write a poem about the first leaf in spring." Believe me, readers, I have nothing against leaves, (In fact, some of my best (*friends* are *leaves* — especially tender green ones!) *If* leaves were the topic that the pupil really felt emotionally attuned to; or if the teacher had made the topic of that leaf in spring so *dynamic*, so completely *fascinating* in advance, that Johnny Fullback was impelled to respond with a "perm," or "pome," or even with a "poem!"

Please do not gain the impression that I am all-omnipotent on the poet in the classroom, for I am not (I'm possibly not even a good poet *out* of the classroom!) but I do know after twenty-five years with secondary and college students, and with elementary pupils as well, that poetry appreciation in American schools must be sold and re-sold every term I face a new sea of swirling faces and button-bright eyes. The themes must be vital to the student and to the student's mentor! They may dwell on a crack in the street, a broken leg, a burning house, or even upon a family spot. But the student must *feel* what he or she is examining at the moment is *worth* feeling and feeling *fully* about.

Let me further create for you a "world I never made" of utter discontent. It is so true that no teacher can create the talent, but the instructor can help *recognize* talent; he or she can help clarify thinking, and awaken pupil sensibilities to the merits of honest self-expression. I am most grateful to the late Pulitzer Prize poet, Leonora Speyer, under whom I had the honor of studying the craft of poetry-writing for four years at Columbia several "eons" ago. This gentle and fine writer would constantly admonish us with: "Now, I cannot make you poets; I can only make you aware of your poetic potential." Another problem that plagues the student is the age-old American concept that poetry is for "sissies." But I counter with, "That may be, young people, but if only you could put in a very long distance call, charges reversed, of course, to Goliath! He could easily

55

contradict such flimsy thinking. And David penned some of the finest lyric poetry ever recorded!"

The student must be made conscious of several things in trying to grasp an initial idea of what is being said in a poem. One basic question is, "Who is doing the talking: Is it the writer of the poem, or is he speaking through someone else! In other words, through whose eyes is the statement given, or is the situation being observed?"

A second basic question becomes: "Who is the audience, or the listener, toward whom the sentiment is directed? What kind of personality is being affected, or is seeking to be affected?" Often, once the pupil and the teacher have established this fact, the understanding of the poem or the poem-idea becomes easier to realize. A reader would certainly be more receptive, for example, in the remarkable sonnet, "Yet Do I Marvel," by Mr. Countee Cullen, famous black poet, if the reader could know that here the poet is addressing everyone in general, and yet is addressing no one in particular. Hence, universality and individuality. Especially do we get this painful beauty in the truth when he closes his query on why God, though omni-aware of all things, would decide to "make a poet black and bid him sing!"

And there are countless examples, especially in the lyric poem, where the more personalized approach must be examined closely to see who the *addressed* is.

Another impact or important factor in evaluating the poem for the student-poet is perhaps the simplest question of all: "What is the circumstance that surrounds the speaker, be the poet as poet, or be the poet as mouthpiece? In another now almost cliché-beaten question: "What is the relevancy here—can the pupil relate, find empathy, or even sympathy, with the problem that the poem makes as a poem?"

A possible final consideration that must be resolved is: "What is the reaction to the poem and its situation by the reader?" Does the student smile, laugh, grow defiant, reflective, resigned to the effects of the poem itself? Does Browning's "Boots, boots, tramping up and down again" help to determine the pupil's reaction? Is it the insistent rhythmic patterned structure, or do the quietly disturbing lines by little-known poet Robert Davis, that say in his poem, "Dust Bowl,": "The dust sifts down—blows in . . . our mouths are filled," create a different response?

So poetry, modern poetry especially, has a difficult task indeed in trying to pinpoint our values and to make them clearly acceptable to the student-interpreter and the student-creator. As I. A. Richards says in his most provocative book, *Practical Criticism*, all of the emotional tendencies: *love, hate, fear, tenderness, concern*, must find their way into the poem—and be found there *without* sentimentality. And of course we are duty bound to ferret out these qualities and make them more palatable for this questioning and creative student. All of these considerations must be accounted for in part, if not in total, if the *full* impact of any poetic experience of real worth is to be realized.

If all things are equal, the student-poet should find support for his imagination through sympathetic understanding. One thing the teacher and poet, or teacher-poet, can and should do is to write with the pupils. Show examples of *style, form,* and *idea.* He or she should write the *cinquain,* the *haiku,* the *rondeau,* the *sonnet,* the *limerick, villanelle,* and so on, to show the variety that may be achieved as a writer for experimentation. The teacher can also demonstrate to the young poet what a poet must go through to finally gain a certain end-result. Poetry contests, much like the Japanese emphasis upon the haiku, may be tried. Outside local poets could be invited to assist or offer demonstrations on the art of *freeing* the word images. Three groups that would be most willing to give in-classroom readings I am most certain are: The American Academy of Poets, Association for Poetry Therapy, and Poets and Writers, Incorporated.

One approach for poetry-writing which has been tried in my junior or middle school is what we like to call "picture-poeming art." Here the poet may work alone or with a neighbor to illustrate his or her poetic ideas. Poetry certificates are awarded, including news publicity locally. By involving the student-poet in a *vivid* way, much of the trepidation can be removed.

It may be only a coincidence in itself, but recently I was delighted twice within a three-month period to receive two slim copies of *first* (sic) editions of poems published by two of my former middle school students. They are now in higher schools of learning and still writing, I hope! I would like to feel that they profited from some of these devices of encouragement. But, on the *other* hand, perhaps they have succeeded famously *despite* my methods and my imposed presence in their midst, (I hear you mumble but quite audibly!) Heaven forbid such a *rotten* thought! That is most unbecoming of you, you know!

-Spring, 1970
Hotel Americana, N.Y.C.

How Do You Measure a Man?
How Do You Measure a Dream?
(Thoughts Mulled Over on Dr. Martin King's Birthday)

How do you measure a man? How do you measure a dream? From where do you begin, and how do the measurements really start? Someone far wiser than I once said that a man is as tall as the shadow he casts at noontime. Another said that you measure a man by the height and breadth of his dream, his range, his scope of feeling, his power of empathy and sympathy for the people around him. These all, perhaps, are true, all fitting for a man or woman who moves obtrusively into our midst and rearranges the patterns of our culture, our thinking, our sympathies. That man or that woman is a rarity indeed. For he or she who rises among us, above us, and reshapes our destinies — that person is truly a creator of very, very tangible human visions!

Only a handful have walked this world, only a fistful have stood on the edge of time and brought a new evaluation of mankind's existence, his true worth. Only a handful have commanded the established old order, the mores of entrenched concepts since our beginning almost, to be deleted, to be wiped away, making way for a grander, more profound evaluation and response to humanity's needs. Only a handful have been so touched by Providence to make us honestly examine ourselves minutely, to see what we *really* are, to make us see what we should become, and to make us witness how we can more nearly approach that ideal plan the Maker had ordained for us in the very beginning.

On January 15, 1929, the day dawned, possibly cold, blustery, for the United States of America, in a quiet minister's home in Atlanta, Georgia. Maybe the year of the baby's birth, 1929, was portentous of the child the man was to become. Let us remember that 1929 was the season of the great Fall, the market event or advent of the beginning of the deep Depression Years. Nineteen hundred and twenty-nine was perhaps our most momentous year, our domestic hour of despair. Certainly the times that followed, the events that were spawned in that era, gave grim testimony to the need for a new faith in ourselves, in our world at large.

Martin Luther King, Jr., born on that day, in that year, was, as some philosopher once remarked of such special souls: "Some men strive at the very outset to attain greatness; some men reject the search for greatness, and some men have greatness thrust upon them." They seem to be born unto the mantle they must wear, and wear doggedly, wear it proudly. Dr. King was surely a man who destiny demanded that he perform America's great social miracle, to really create a firm foundation for hope for all the world some thirty years later.

Many have declared that Dr. King provided the black people of America, and the world for that matter, a greater and purer estimation of their own human worth. This is true, no doubt. But friends, I would rather feel that this brilliant, selfless minister of God give to *all* of America—yes, to all of the world—a greater estimation of this country's human worth, human wealth, its potential for true greatness.

Yet when time seeks to measure this giant of a being, when time seaks to measure his dream, linear, spatial, and countable dimensions fade, get lost in an infinite sphere of human wonder. For who can really measure this black man's worth, this man who forsook the comforts of a quiet Southern parish to push and fight for the dignity of the human soul! For who can measure the spiritual strength of this man, who, when viciously stabbed near the heart by a deranged woman, while he was lying near the threshold of death, *still* had the unheard of compassion to suddenly whisper, "Don't hurt her, look after her; she needs help!" For who can measure the fullness of such a man's soul whose hope was rocked time and time again with the hate sticks of dynamite, and yet who calmly said, "Let us pray for the perpetrators, replace anger power with love power!" For who can really measure or fashion the size of a dreamer who, upon receiving the fifty-three-thousand-dollar Nobel Peace Prize stipend, handed every penny of it over for the cause of peace and for the ultimate dignity of man! How can you measure a man, who, when definitely facing snarling dogs, policemen, billy clubs, and firehoses, still stoutly told his followers, "We shall *not* be moved, and we do honestly believe that we shall overcome someday!"

Now who can forget this man whose voice roared to millions on that heat-baked August day in 1963, from our nation's capitol, who insisted that he had a dream, a dream tightly wrapped in the American Dream, that he envisioned black boys and black girls playing and learning with white boys and white girls, even in the red hills of his home state of Georgia, living and learning in a new era of love and understanding! He was the man who, on that unforgettable day, facing 300,000 glistening faces in Washington, roared to this multitude that he had a dream that one day Jews and Gentiles, Catholics and Protestants, believers and non-believers, would stand together, hands linked, to tell a watching world that America was truly a "land of the free, and the home of the brave." We can never forget, too, that this was the Dream Maker who said that he had been to the *mountain,* had glimpsed over into the Promised Land, and that he was not afraid to die!

Yes, Martin King was cut down in his thirty-ninth year by the warped and poisonous elements of our society. He was suddenly removed from our community by a sniper's bullet on a Memphis balcony some thirty-odd years ago, still trying to do, as he phrased it, "God's work." Yes, that magnificent, resonant voice, the *natural* voice, was stilled. Yes, his *physical, mortal* pleading, cajoling, crying for social, economic, moral, and religious justice was ended. But, people, the wellsprings of his hope, which are the wellsprings of all God's children, the power of his visions, which are the visions of all God's children, the granite-rock of his dignity, which is the bed-rock of the dignity of all God's children, have never once diminished. Nor can these inviolate principles be dwarfed or eroded. These are the true beacons of piercing light that we, though often reluctantly at times, reach for, long for, and pray for, will forever burn into the deepest recesses of our souls.

And, kind audience, on this day, as we attempt to pay feeble tribute to this incomparable figure of a person, let us in our own private and public fashion dedicate or re-dedicate ourselves here and now to work still on the foundations of love that his heart, his hands, his soul fought for so diligently, and struggled to establish. Certainly, the job is huge, the edifice of truth hardly begun. But with each of us vowing that the monument to faith *can* be constructed, we *can* push that dream nearer to reality.

How *do* you measure a man? How *do* you measure a dream? We cannot; we do not try. We only thank our God for a soul like Martin Luther King, Jr. whose blueprint for love has laid the groundwork upon which we can build. Let us now proceed!

The Cat in the Well

Ding, dong, bell,
Pussy's in the well.
Who put her in?
Little Johnny Green.
Who pulled her out?
Little Johnny Stout."

—*Mother Goose Rhyme*

Now in the name of all things sanitary and clean and fitting for human ingestion, or whatever, I wonder and I am appalled that the above-named nursery rhyme got to first base with the Society for Decent Literature for Children!

First, who in the name of all things holy and pure and right and so on, would relate an incident about a cat falling into a well of drinking water? Can you imagine what that means to a child's tastebuds or quenchbuds to read about a cat tumbling head first or head last into a well? I am cognizant of the fact that cats are known to be the cleanest and most meticulous of all lower—and some higher—animals, I might add—with their constant licking, preening, preening their fur, and their checking their skins and whiskers to spot foreign visitors who might wish to come calling on their body politic unannounced and uncalled for. But even so, what can a child think or feel when he or she lifts a glass of what aqua purists love to candidly call the "sanguine-effects of well water?"

Nowhere in that shocking rhyme is there any mention of the water, because of more than possibly being polluted, being boiled after that, to destroy what germ impurities that the cat's unceremonious dousing was certain to produce.

Second, dearest reader, I must hand you another angle which I suspect you have overlooked and its deleterious effects upon the unexposed and tender juvenile mind. The issue is this: *Why didn't the rhyme go on to castigate, or at least suggest that Johnny Green be soundly* (or *is it roundly*) *buffeted about for doing such a dastardly deed toward Miss Pussy?* And such an act, you must admit, is wholly anti-social and anti-humane totally! We have since time immemorial preached and clamored for fair

61

treatment for God's animal "critters." The mere fact that we have such noble and well-meaning outfits, as the A.S.P.C.A. to protect animals, domesticated and otherwise, serves as proof positive that we are not totally immune to this needed respect and regard for animals. And what about these great animal preserves in certain parts of the world—positive attitudes again prevailing? Yet, not one—I repeat, not one voice in fiery protest was uttered or sputtered against that despicable John or "Johnny" Green! And we say that we respect the tenets of fair play and lend impeccable regard to jurisprudence considerations! World, don't make me upchuck, if you'll pardon the expression just here.

It is true that the poem about poor Miss or Ms. Pussy did go on to weakly subject John Green to a reprimand, but it seemed to me that that reprimand was merely a "going-through-the-motions" sort of thing, if you grasp what I sincerely mean. Nor was there any magnificent adulation or medal dispensation granted to "hero" Johnny Stout, who was, no doubt a contemporary, and a fine example of human concern, of that stupid and unfeeling rotten Johnson Green. Where is the accolade, the reward, the bronze statue erected in Cat's Lover's Garden to honor Master Stout, truly a hero—if not respectfully and humbly regarded by humans—to the members of the feline world, from Atlanta to Angora, from Nagasaki to Nantucket, from Vero Beach to Vera Cruz? Where? Oh, where?

And we lament the quality of Tommy's and Mary-Ann's reading abilities and their literary interests at large! Even at the outset—and Mother Goose Rhymes were meant to afford the earliest, *refreshing* exposure for the interests of junior and juniorette!

It should be small wonder, therefore, that I, as a junior high or middle school language arts instructor, have such an arduous time in seeking to bring my early teen-yeared charges to appreciate and enjoy the beauty rewards of the literature of our language, or of any language, for that matter!

"Ding, dong, bell, Pussy's in the well!"

Really, it's enough to make one turn to pre-boiled and honestly sterilized soda pop! And I do not feel surprised at the rising sales of old-fashioned "soda water," and at the pitifully low consumption of well water among the precocious young of our modern society!

The Essence of Trust
(An Essay for Young Children)

A man told me that he owned hundreds of dollars, much property, and boxes and boxes of jewels. But he said that he was an unhappy man. Unhappy and owning all of that named wealth? I couldn't believe it! Here I would have been so glad, so proud, had I possessed even one twenty-fifth of a part of that! And he was unhappy! This I could not accept! No way! "You see," said the man with a deep crease across his face, "I have all of this money and all of these goods, but I cannot sleep at night; I cannot eat during the day. I am always in a state of confusion and fear. Always."

"Fear?" I asked this man who, incidentally, did look extremely perturbed. "Why on this wide earth would you be afraid?" I asked him. "You have all of the secure things in this world."

Ah, no, my friend," he went on, cutting me off, "you said the word. It was *secure*. You see, that's just the trouble. I am *not* secure. I cannot find anyone or any place that I feel safe enough to keep these for me without thieves entering and taking it or the person holding it for me without his taking it, also. You see, it is not easy to be a multi-millionaire."

"But, sir," I went on, "surely there must be someone or some place where you may deposit your assets and feel that they are safe. If you feel that way, you can never find real peace or contentment anywhere in this world. There must be someone that you can trust. There *must* be!"

"Ah, but you see, the worried man with the creased face said wistfully, his voice trailing into the musty and misty evening, "There really is no one that is trustworthy. No, no one to trust anywhere." He walked away, looking to his right and to his left. I felt the very air around us grow heavy with despair and utter weariness—with dejection.

Children, that was a long, long time ago. I have not seen the gentleman since then, but his face, his voice, his uneasiness have lingered with me all these years, students. Isn't it a sad existence when you discover the tragic fact that you can trust no one? Isn't it? Now, if you, as a class, have ever been left alone in an *un*supervised situation, chances are it meant that that teacher or principal or other grownup has put *implicit faith* in you and in your personal sense of worth.

To be accorded trust by another is not an easy task to handle. Two problems can evolve or arise: One, it can put the trusting person in a most disappointing situation if that trust is broken. And two, it can put you, the one *believed in,* in a most awkward and embarrassing spot if you *break* that trust.

No one has ever stated that it easy growing up. It has never been easy. Temptations, false excitements, friends who seek to *get you in trouble,* your own possible weakness for trouble—all these make for worry, to say the least. It makes growing up and growing into your teen years even more difficult. No one has ever promised you that it would be smooth sailing. *This I must repeat. No one.* And the weak, the mentally incompetent, the ones who just don't care about *personal* pride, and those like that, simply fall by the wayside. They become your famous *drop-outs;* they become the *dummy-ones* who discover too late what life and *self-pride* are all about.

I don't know about you, but whenever I feel a little careless about my self-image, I think about someone like Harriet Tubman, an uneducated tiny black kid, and then a woman, who had enough *self-motivation,* enough *self-pride* to refuse slavery and its sickening conditions. She led over 350 runaway slaves to freedom. Why? Well, chiefly, class, she was able to because those hundreds of slaves, those Quakers who befriended her, those other people of goodwill—they had *faith* in her! They entrusted their very lives to her, this little five feet two-or-three inches of female superiority!!

And when I think of this little woman who lived from 1820 to 1913, whose statue still stands upstate in Auburn, New York, as a symbol of strength and *trust,* I don't get careless anymore. And, students, I think that you had better do likewise, and start from this moment on. The world is *waiting.* The world is *watching!*

PART II

"Told in Short"
(BRIEF FICTION)

A Little Boy's Anger

You know, folks, I once was angry all of the time. I really don't know exactly why, but I was. It seems to me that I was always being fussed at by my mother, who is a widow, or yelled at by all of my teachers. I don't know, it just seemed I couldn't get myself together. If you know what I mean. You ever been in that kind of a set-up? Huh? No matter how I would attempt to explain something I had done or had not done, nobody seemed to be listening or cared.

I remember once, a long time ago, when I was eight or nine. It was when I lived on Sattern Boulevard in North Brooklyn. That section of Brooklyn was very old; the houses and all of the buildings were just leaning upon one another for support—or else they might all just tumble down in a big dusty, loud heap of junk, dirt, and scrap. And men were always seen loitering and hanging around the street, up the alleys, down the block—doing nothing—just hanging around all of the time—just hanging and hanging around.

I guess it was then, one hot, stifling summer evening when it all started. You see, we were playing three-sewer stickball two blocks down from our house. I had no brothers or sisters, so I was very close pals with Doug, Henry, and Moe. Then there was Gus, good old Gus Lawson. As I was saying, we were playing punchball—no, I don't meant *punch*ball—I mean *stick*ball. I had just whammed a double down the street, past the flying feet of Gus and Moe. It was a beauty of a hit! I dropped the broomstick and I ran! Now, I'm not the greatest two-base stickball artist in the world. And whenever I managed to belt a good shot like that, and especially past the speedy Moe, I knew I had done something. And those two guys were fast! Boy, could they fly! I went zipping down the basepath, my face tingling in the hot summer air.

Then it all happened—I mean, I guess it was the thing that had made me so angry so many of the years and times that followed. Oh, I forgot to tell you at the time my "pops" was alive then, and he was home. He had come home early from his job down at the paper factory or some place. He had been pretty tired because of the heat and the pain that was in his right knee. You see, Pops had been a soldier in Korea. He had been a tank gunner, or something like that. He had got his leg hit and the

Army doctors were forced to take off the lower half of his shattered leg. Well, as I was saying, Pops was home resting when it took place. I was pretty close to my dad. He had been a super ball player, a basketball player before the war. He had even had a try-out as a backcourt man for the Boston Celtics. Honest. Pops was just that good.

But that's another story. Well, as I was saying, I had just hit that fabulous hit, this two-bagger, and I was flying around the bases like a gray cat with a hotfoot on all four feet, when it all happened. Some voice down the long block behind me boomed, "Fire! Fire! Let's go look at it!" It was then I stopped and looked back. Doug and Moe and my other buddies had stopped and were pointing and running the opposite way. I looked back once more and saw dark streams of smoke shooting out of a building that looked as if it was in my part of Sattern Boulevard. My heart stopped still! My legs wobbled a little bit.

I raced back faster than anything to my house. Sure enough, it was a huge fire. Smoke was pouring out of the building even faster, even darker. Flames licked through open windows. My heart hammered as I leaped up the steps, only to be stopped, held back by strong dark hands. "Don't go in there, Paul, don't go in there. It's safer outside!" The voice was firm and the hands held me in a vise-like grip.

"But—But," I stammered, "where's my Pops Where's my Pops?" I tried to tear myself away again, but I could not. Pops, I remembered, had taken off his artificial limb and said that he would take a short nap after a beer and a cigarette. Moms had gone to a church meeting about a prayer-meeting or something, so I just knew Pops was alone.

Soon the sound of the sirens screamed through the moist heat. Crowds seemed to have congregated out of nowhere. "Let 'em through, let 'em through!" someone shouted to the people. The crowd did not move back. Someone yelled, "Throw something at the damned truck." These apartments ain't fit to be saved. Block 'em, baby, just block 'em!" In the meanwhile, the fire was crackling now, leaping in giant red finger waves through the upper floor windows. I struggled, gouging my fingers into those giant arms that had me pinned tightly. I couldn't move. A lady I'll never know started crying great gushes of tears. "My God! My God! They can't get through to save that building. My God! Please stop it! Let the firemen get in. Please!" A half-filled beer can hurtled through the blazing air. It narrowly missed one of the firemen with a hose. All of us who had been huddled on the nearby stoop were rushed and pulled away to a safer distance. Shouts and crying sounds, curses, and screaming spattered the night in this part of Sattern Boulevard.

Finally, the big rocks and half-bricks stopped flying, and the firemen rushed through, their aerial ladders swinging into action. Some of the others with gas masks pulled tightly into place dashed up the stairs, banging on doors and cutting away at the doors. After what seemed like a thousand years, two firemen, smudged with smoke, brought down a body that was very, very still. It was *Pops*! I could tell because one of the person's legs was missing. "Pops! Pops!" I screamed. He looked like a damp dishrag.

I strained to rush forward to him, but still I couldn't. I stared around me, and looked at Moe who was crouched there with me. His eyes were big and red from the reflection of the fire, the smoke, and the lights. Somebody asked, "How is he? Will he make it?" to an ambulance driver, or one of the fellows who assist with stretchers. They anxiously looked at Pops' covered form. The ambulance man paused, swallowed, and waited a lifetime before he answered in the slowest voice I believe that I had ever heard. "I'm afraid he's dead. He's just stopped breathing—just then. He took a lot of smoke, you know."

"Oh, no, my God!" that same women screamed, "if only they could have got through, he'd be alive now!"

I buried my burning face in that lady's aproned lap. It was such a comfort. That stickball two-base hit faded. I faced that big, blank-faced crowd. I spit and beat my fist on the ground!

A Time for Remembering
(A Flight of Desperation—Post World War II)

"I wouldn't go back to see Mr. Mills for a job, honey." Her voice sounded thin to her, too thin. It wouldn't do any good to talk to Lawrence though. She knew that he had made his mind up. "You know how you and Mrs. Mills can't get along." Lawrence said nothing as he moved his chair away from the black stove and ran his fingers through his hair. She started to go on but decided to say no more, and took the little aluminum percolator from the center of the stove to quiet its spasmodic bubbling. The burnished water had to stop burbling up and down, up and down like a liquid jack-in-the-box. It made her nervous, jumpy. Outside the gray rain kept stabbing the water-soaked earth. These November days were pure hell. It was even better when she had been alone, waiting for him to come back from Germany, from the war. Then, at least, she was able to hope that he was happy, or perhaps, well and safe. But now back in Blakesburg, discharged and disconsolate, she knew and shared his distress.

The wind had risen and it was rattling that loose paling on the side of the house. *Phla! Phlat! Phalt!* Lawrence had promised to fix that plank last week, but he hadn't done so. He had promised to do a lot of things when he got back. Yet somehow he couldn't seem to get started. He was going to college, he was going to leave Alabama. But now he was going back to that confounded store to save some money so they could leave. Often he would say to her, "Baby, we're going so far from this hole until it will take ten dollars' worth of postage to send a postcard." She smiled at the thought. They were going North—to Chicago. He had told her about State Street, Calumet, South Side, Chicago University. She didn't want him to stay here in Blakesburg with its two main steets, its flat-faced people, its monotonous existence.

Nettie moved over to him and stroked his hair. What could she do? Mrs. Mills didn't like Lawrence one bit and she would make it hard for him if he went back to the store. She had called him a "sassy, half-educated black boy." But Mr. Mills had always liked him, liked the way he worked, and so Lawrence had stayed, working after school and during vacations until he left for the Army.

Suddenly Lawrence reached up and held Nettie's hand, squeezing it. "See, sugar, this won't be for long—just long enough to save some money to get th' hell out of this town."

She smiled broadly and looked down into his soft brown eyes. "I know, Lawrence," she whispered, "but you don't have to take that twenty-two a week job. I don't want you to have it. Get your unemployment money and you can be brushing up on some of your studies at the same time. You know dentistry calls for a lot of work."

"Yeah, I know."

"What difference would two dollars make anyway? I can work at the laundry. We'll get by, honey." She knew that she shouldn't have mentioned about working at the laundry. That's what made him angry. But the laundry paid fifteen dollars a week and that was almost twice a much as a colored girl could get anywhere in Blakesburg.

Lawrence flared up. "Now listen, honey, listen once and for all. You'e *not* going to work at that damned laundry. That's no place for you. That damned laundry is nothing but a legitimate slave pen for colored girls. The work's too hard, salary's too low, and so are the minds of those white bastards who run it. Almost every night I pass there I can hear the muffled giggles of some Negro wench and the snarled pleas of one of those Cracker-sons-of-bitches as they are having a lay. Net, it makes me sick! When I hear them I get as mad as hell at both of them."

His words wounded her. How could he even have a thing like that on his mind! Why, during the three years that he had been away from her she had not permitted any man, white or black, to put a hand on her. "Why, you don't think I'd tolerate a thing like that, do you, Lawrence?" Her own voice grew sharp, as sharp as the shrieks of the wind swirling the rain around the house. She went on. "You know me better that that. It wouldn't be for long. Besides, it pays more than anything else I could get to help you."

He answered hurriedly. "Now, you know I didn't have you in mind, darling. But I'm just telling you the kind of place it is. You know that, too. We'll make it even if it does take a litle more time. Furthermore, I want to lay off the "Fifty-two Twenty Club" till things get a little tougher. Or until we get to Chicago and can't find anything to do right away." His voice was quiet and almost passionless, yet she saw a bright gleam shine from his eyes. He continued, turning to her, banging a fist into an open hand, "No, the thing that burns me up is the fact that if some colored boy even so much as lifted an eyebrow at one of their women, be she bitch or mayor's unspoiled virgin, why, the trees on the hills out there would hardly be tall enough for the poor boy's butt. Not that I give a clogged-up river's dam about their colorless women, but it just goes to show you."

71

How violent he had become since the war! Net breathed slowly before she spoke this time. "Well, it's the girl's own fault. That does not mean . . ." He cut her off.

He seemed to ignore her. He had become flushed and words began to jump out, one after another. "And if any man lets his wife work there, then he doesn't care much what happens to her reputation."

"I can take care of myself," Nettie remonstrated. "No man will go farther than a girl will let him. I'll say again, it pays more than any other job in Blakesburg."

"It should, Net. Look what those bastards get on the side in addition to the long hours. That laundry produces more illegitimate children of different shades in a month of dry Saturdays than all the whore alleys of Birmingham do in three years."

His words cut her again. "Now you're being plain low, Lawrence, and you know it." Nettie moved swiftly toward the window and stared out at the rain. What a nasty day. There had never been any summer; no bright sunshine had ever slanted through the matted leaves of that chinaberry tree in the yard. It had always been a raw, wet November. And, right now, it seemed, it would never be any different. There had always been hoarse-voiced sparrows huddling under the rosebush by the steps—no robins and field larks had ever skimmed across the brown Bermuda grass on the lawn. It had always been a raw, wet November, her mind repeated. There would always be such a sloppy day. Nettie tried to remember the bright, glittering days of summer but they seemed so far away. Tears gathered in her eyes but she refused to cry. Lawrence didn't like weepy girls. Said strong women gritted their teeth and plunged ahead. Said weepy girls made him nervous, fidgety. But it was so hard not to cry, so hard not to cry, not to cry.

"Want some coffee?" she asked as she turned back to him, shaking the tears from her eyes. He mustn't see her crying.

"Unh-hunh, please."

"Cream?"

"Unh-hunh." Then he brightened, "I'm going to have some music with my java." And so saying, he went into the living room to select some records to play on the turntable. She knew he was going to play records. He always did. Presently from the kitchen where she was getting the cups and things, she heard the old strains of a popular song. It was the one to which they had danced so often before he went away. That was their favorite song.

Please don't let our one dream leave you

Why did Lawrence have to pick out *Remember Our Love*? They were together again. There would be no more separating again, ever, ever. But it *was* a beautiful song. She fumbled around in the cupboard for the sugar.

Old Mother Hubbard went to the cupboard to get her man the sugar bowl. She finally found it.

Please don't let false friends deceive you

Where is the cream? The cream? The CREAM? It's over there, Nettie, next to the chicken by the ice. See? Oops! careful, that sugar bowl almost dropped to the floor. Lawrence only played that record when he was low in spirits. Can't much blame him either. He's been through so much, so much—seen people killed, dying, starving. Gosh, we girls didn't quite know what it was like. JesusGod! some of the cream spilled on the stove. Steady yourself, Nettie, you sentimental ass! Now he's back and things are worse than before, worse than before. I'm nervous because Lawrence won't let me cry. I want to cry. I've got to cry. All women have to cry. Those who don't are queers, or so they say. But Lawrence says I mustn't cry.

Don't let separation grieve you

At last she had everything—cream, sugar, cups, saucers, and spoons. Where was the tray? Had to serve Lawrence on the tray. It would make him feel good. Here, Nettie, here up on top of the third shelf, see! Lord, what a sweet song, what a wonderfully sweet song! The fellow singing was none other than her tall, coffee-colored Lawrence whirling her over the dance floor in the gym at the high school prom! He was singing the words softly in her ear. She was—what—what did the science teacher call that element that was lighter than air—was it helium? Yes, helium. She was helium, floating with Lawrence without restraint. *What if my bra should pop now and me on this dance floor, boy, would I be embarrassed!* "Oh, Lawrence," she murmured aloud as she went back into the room still dazed. His sudden "hunh" startled her and she smiled sheepishly. "Oh, nothing, nothing at all. I—I was just thinking about something," she said quickly.

The record spun on.

Remember our love.

Remember our love. She had to, she would. That was almost all a colored girl could hang on to, especially in Blakesburg, in Alabama, in the South, in America, for that matter. *Remember. Remember.* Sure, she would remember, only there was so much to remember. Wasn't there ever anything to look forward to, anything? She had stood at the window, remembering in a dull, half-awake sense, the bright yesterdays, bright sunshine, bright summer, bright everything. Only the music had sharpened it all, darkened everything, making a focal point of her remembering.

Her hand trembled as she poured the liquid. Tears welled once more in her eyes as the hot vapor rose and filtered past her face. Lawrence saw. He turned quickly to her side and took the pot from her hand. "You're crying, Net. Let me do it."

73

He smiled faintly, his white, even teeth showing. He looked at her and filled the two cups silently. "Unh-unh," the sounds came forth as heavy and as flat a possible. "It was the steam that dampened my face," she lied.

Lawrence smiled again and said nothing. They sat down in silence sipping the hot stimulant, listening to the clarinet crying out again *Remember Our Love*, crying out above the rain and the *phla-phlat* of that loose paling. Evening slipped in as they danced.

The weeks moved by intrepidly.

Nettie felt it would happen; she knew it would, but she just didn't know when. And now that it had happened, nothing seemed to make sense anymore. Now the young colored woman of twenty-one had a large space for tears, only there were no tears to fall. In their place had arisen a hard lump, an ache that hung in her throat like a piece of meat not well chewed. It stayed there and water would not wash it down or vomiting force it up. It seemed there to stay.

She arose vacantly from the chair by the window where she had been sitting all day. She tried to take a bite to eat. Although Lawrence had been buried for more than three days she had not eaten any food. Everything spoke of him: socks, his shoes in the closet, his neatly stacked books, his GI trousers, still baggy at the knees where he had bent down so many times during the last weeks at the store. They were still shouting of him to her!

She mouthed a spoonful of cold beans which one of the neighbors had cooked for her and then she turned back to the chair. Gosh, food just didn't taste right when you ate alone. Yes, the philosophers were right: man had to live in a herd, had to have a companion for support. A woman had to have a man, husband or otherwise. Nettie went into the living room and clicked on the radio. Somewhere out of the ether came . . . *separa-tion grie-ve you remember our love. Oh, no, who had authorized who to play that song? That man didn't know that that was their song! It was theirs, theirs, theirs!*

"It's ours! It's ours! Ours! Who told you that you could play that thing? Who told you?" she sobbed loudly. At last the storm had broken. Tears came from everywhere and it seemed as if she would cry her insides out. She would cry herself limp like wash-clothes. How long Nettie had lain their slumped over the radio she did not know. Neither did she fully realize why her hands were so swollen and bruised. She looked vacantly at the long nail scratches on the veneer top of the radio and then she understood why. She had gone temporarily insane. Nettie did not recall beating her fists against the thing, yet she must have for there were the signs to testify. And her hands were bloody and sore. She had gone off on a mad tangent and her sense of recollection failed her. When she finally recovered and straightened up she felt her stockings cold against her legs. She had urinated on herself in her frenzy, Oh, JesusGod, this was foolish, stupid! All the fear and hurt she had stored within her breast had been expelled. And she could not help herself. She was weak.

The exhausted woman moved almost unconsciously back to the room where the stove was smouldering ruddily, throwing out heat against the December chill. Huddled alone she re-lived the horrible days which had just gone before. In a few days it would be Christmas. Lawrence had said there would be few extra expenses for the holidays so they could leave for Chicago right after New Year's Day. Now, now he was dead and New Year's Day was still quite a ways off. She recalled how it had all happened. Mrs. Mills' niece had come to the hardware store one evening to look at a new bathroom sink to be installed. She had gone in the back with Lawrence to see it. Then she screamed that Lawrence had suddenly grabbed her. But Nettie knew that it had been a framed lie! There were no other people in the store at the time except Mrs. Mills and her niece. Mr. Mills was away and the whole thing had been framed. Nettie just knew it. Then it all happened so rapidly till she could hardly remember anything. Lawrence came running home terrified and angry. He gasped out the story to her and then he quickly slipped away, grabbing a heavy coat and some money.

She had never seen such terror, such hate, twist his face before. "It was all a dirty lie, Net, sugar, a damned dirty lie! I never touched that woman, never touched her! You were right. That Mrs. Mills and that niece planned that trick!" As he scrambled out, he shouted, "I'm going to Chicago. Come to Tommie's house. Don't stay down here. I'll be there. You know the address!" He slammed a blue-white kiss against her mouth and vanished into the pine thicket that bordered the swamps.

The young woman put a hand to her lips and the kiss still felt hot and scorching that he had put there. She was like a hot coal all over, like the stove that glowed before her feet. *Lord, help me! I knew that it would be like that. Women are too cunning for a man.* Then they tracked him down in the swamps, shot him, shot him before he could defend himself. Now all she could do was remember. There was no future, no shiny tomorrow alone. *Now may th Lawd rest his soul deep river my home is over Jordan cause a swinging golden chariot is coming for to carry me home Lord child ain thata pretty casket all purple and velvety inside it shore is a pity these younguns nowadays is so headstrong and he was a smart good boy bet that casket musta cost a pretty nigh on to a thousand dollars honey. That's right, talk about being headstrong. Of course Lawrence's casket didn't cost a thousand dollars but it was all I could afford. You folks gazed down into the face of a hero, my husband, my own coffee-colored Lawrence with* the softest dark eyes. *I'm not angry with you, honey, not for listening to me. That's the way you wanted it and that's the way it had to be. Only, Lawrence, today I cried. Not too much, I don't think, but I cried. But, honest to God, I tried not to! I know you don't like weepy girls, but you have gone a long way from me now, farther than the months before when you were over there in Europe someplace. And you will never be back. And those wenches, (excuse me, dear, I didn't mean to use that word—doesn't become a girl, I know, but what would you have called them?) those two wenches are still alive, still moving about in their "protected" world. And you, you are gone. The one promise I had to cherish has gone, too, gone like that summer sun I couldn't remember, Jesus God, help me, what must I do?* The room reeled crazily before her.

Nettie slowly came out of her stupor of self-pity. Her head ached. Now she began thinking, thinking very hard, trying to remember if she had ever known any happiness, if she had ever known any peace. It seemed that the gods of evil had always pounded hard at her heels. She had started college and then her mother died; she was forced to stop. She married, then there was the war. Lawrence had come back safe and unhurt, only to . . . to . . . her thoughts broke off. A black wave surged over her. Everything had turned against her. She was a marked woman. Was there ever a time when she would know happiness? What was the necessity of hope when frustration forever reared its head? "But," she pondered, "I could have had happiness if Mrs. Mills hadn't hated Lawrence." Her other denials were caused by things bigger than herself—death and war. But this last vestige of joy was shattered by a thing her size, someone of her sex, her dimensions. And she would know revenge.

The gun was cold against her bosom and it was heavy. She had never fired a gun before and the thought made her nervous. But Nettie shoved her fists farther down in the pockets of her brown coat and headed on toward town. The frozen ground was hard beneath her feet. The steady *crump-crump* her feet made over the cold surface jarred her, making her teeth rattle. She mustn't turn back now, she mustn't, for it was now or never. The icy wind which dipped down from the straggling Blue Ridge Mountain tops bit through her like evil needles. She was cold, shaking, but she had to go on. The street led only one way. Thus would be her last tribute to her husband. Inside she felt like a taut steel spring, ready to jump forward, release her pain. *Lord, I've never even been close to a gunshot except once when Lawrence showed me how a gun operates. And then I had to press my thumbs against my eardrums to deaden the sound. But the POWMM still frightened me. I still can remember the little tree the bullet hit—how the top hopped off as if in surprise. I can still see how the skinny trunk stood straight and keen like a broken-off pencil, quivering. But I must go on. I must go on. How could everything have gone so wrong!*

76

The colored girl was no longer nervous as she turned on High Street. It was evening and the bright lights hurt her eyes. It was the Christmas season, but it held no joy for her, nothing but a dull, metallic ticking which represented her heartbeat. What would Christmas be like without Lawrence, with nothing but the hideous hours alone to hound her? As she passed the endless stream of the red, green, silver, and white lights and decorations she saw the colors as one long blaze of fire, its heat driving out the chill. Now and then as she moved along she caught the long hungry looks of some of those flat two-dimensional faces. One white man bared his teeth and winked. Nettie walked on. An unshaven black man slouched past her and whistled softly. She glanced neither to the right nor to the left, her feet keeping up the mechanical pat-pat along the pavement. She felt like an automaton, her knees stiff. She would accomplish her mission. *Baby, we're going so far from this damned hole that it will take ten dollars' worth of postage to send a postcard.* This time she did not smile—she only grunted painfully. Lawrence had gone farther than that. All the money from every mint in the world could not afford enough postage. Across the endless space, from out of some far off place, she heard *remember, remember.* This evening she had not forgotten. She would not forget.

She stared up suddenly at the cheap neon sign which blinked on and off at her sardonically: MILLS' HARDWARE STORE—LET US SHARE IN YOUR HOMEBUILDING. The young woman stood there and took a deep breath. *Let us share in your homebuilding!* The store had shared all right; it had done the whole job, completely. Only it had destroyed her home, her heart, her everything. Now it was her turn to do some sharing, to let it take part in her misery. She looked up and down the bleak street before she went in. Everyone had practically gone to supper. Only here and there moved a few bundled figures at the far end of the street. That was good. Neither the store's truck nor Mr. Mills' car was parked at the curb. It was as if everything had been planned for her. Mrs. Mills would probably be alone.

She walked in after pulling the gun out of her bosom and shoving it inside her coat. She hurriedly glanced around. No one else. There sat Mrs. Mills, her wide, pink forehead pale against the lamp's reflection on the cluttered desk. "Yes, what can I do for you?" she asked monotonously before looking up. Nothing had perturbed her. When the woman peered up through her rimless glasses and suddenly stared, she seemed to sense the hate that leaped from Nettie's eyes as they bore steadily into her own. Anger flashed from them and all she was able to utter, half rising, was, "Why, Nettie." Only until now had she appeared moved by that lie she had told, that collaboration with her niece.

77

Nettie had never felt so composed in her whole life. And now it unfolded before her. Those long hours of pain, longing, frustration, all gathered to a bursting point. This time she wasn't weepy. She remembered how Lawrence wouldn't approve. A hard smile formed on her face and she gritted her teeth. "This is what you can do for me, Mrs. Mills," she heard herself saying, "you can catch up with your conscience. It rotted years ago and now you may join it."

The half-scream died on the white woman's lips and was drowned, in the roar of the gun. Blood spurted. Shooting a gun was easy, mere child's play. The quick squeezing of a trigger and all the hate and suffering that was built up over the years was wiped out in a split second. Nettie stared fearfully at the body as it lay sprawled grotesquely over the desk. The right hand still clutched the pen. Then she moved back out of the store swiftly. The neon sign was still blinking, but no longer sardonically. She glanced the full length of High Street. It was still almost deserted. Now she would run, run anywhere. Run to Chicago like Lawrence had told her, like he had tried to do. She was a murderer and she would be hunted. She shuddered.

Apparently the people had assumed that the gunshot was the bark of fireworks which the children were shooting. As she hurried down the street, she looked back and saw the long maroon car of Mr. Mills pull up in front of the store. She turned and slipped into a side steet and began running toward home. She dropped the gun in a sewer. *No, I mustn't run; someone would suspect something surely.* She changed her mind and decided to head for the swamps.

Night had settled in definitely and the darkness made Nettie's steps more confusing, more uncertain. *Christ! They'll never catch me! Not like they did Lawrence. Lawrence, darling, baby, did you see me, did you see me; I didn't cry, did I, I paid her back, Lawrence, paid her back for you, for me, for us. You should have seen the crazy look of terror on her wrinkled face. Must've been just like the look that German soldier you killed had. I didn't forget and turn weepy, did I, honey? You can't do much hiding in the woods in winter. Nothing to conceal you. But I must keep going; I've got to keep on, get out of Alabama. Nothing left here now. Nothing. There's nothing left anywhere.*

The dry leaves crackled under her feet as she left the clearing. She stopped, caught her breath, listened—no noise from town yet. A dog howled mournfully back in the hills. Sounded like it was lonesome. It made her cringe. If she could only make it a bit farther into the thicket. Somewhere there was a cave, a narrow hole where she used to go when she was a child. It lay hidden down in a narrow ravine and honeysuckle vines crawled over it. She could hide there for a while if she could find it. Back behind her, or was it in *front* of her lay Big River. She had not been in these woods for a long, long time. Perhaps she had forgotten where it was. There used to be a big sweet gum tree just above the cave, but where was the tree? She looked feverishly at the trees. They were all the same, all big sweet gum trees!

A police siren suddenly rose shrill and eerie through the evening air. They had found out and the police were on the prowl now! Nettie imagined how stirred up the town must be, how the angry whites were turning frenetic like madmen. *Lord, where is that tree, where is that tree!* A car droned down Highway 63. She moved to another spot. She was growing panicky and she began running again, this time wildly, the dead sticks stabbing at her legs. She had to stop, compose herself, get her bearings. The siren grew louder. Her nostrils spread and her lungs felt as tight as a drum. She peered through the darkening woods and listened as another car whined down Highway 63. She moved to another hill exhausted. Everything was quiet again as she scrambled, crawled, scuffled her way down the sharp declivity. The briers of the mountain brambles tore into her legs, they ripped through her gloves into her hands. The blood was warm to her numbing fingers. Why did she have to run, why, why? It was all so unreal. Just the other day, or the other year, Lawrence had struggled hopelessly out in these wilds somewhere. Would her fate be the same?

She rested awhile and looked up slowly, and there before her eyes was that sweet gum tree! Big and black and beautiful! *That's it! That's it!* Panting she crawled down the hill and felt her way up the opposite side until she found the opening of the cave. It seemed so much smaller now. How often she had explored this place when she was a child, peering into the dark gaping hole fearfully. This evening there was no sign of terror for the narrow hole. This was shelter from the wind and from the mob which she knew was somewhere back there hunting her. She would be safe here if there were no dogs, if there were no dogs. "If there were no dogs," she chattered again and again. And in the morning between four and five she would go to the highway and try to thumb a ride on one of the first trucks heading North.

As she pushed her body feet first into the narrow cave opening the gritty surface of the rock forced her clothes up to her panties and the frosty ledge stung her thighs. She pulled the vines over the covering and lay there panting, whimpering, and aching. A slow pain gnawed at her stomach and the food which she had rejected in the past days loomed large before her eyes. She whimpered again quietly and the old familiar tears crowded her eyes, smarting, blinding, but she refused to let go. She couldn't let go, not now. Nettie stared down at the phosphorescent numerals on her Bulova which glowed up like little fireflies. 8:12. Good Lord, she would have a long time to wait if they didn't find her. Off in the distance she heard the faint *pop-pop* of firecrackers, or were they firecrackers? But she had had her celebration, had lighted *her* firecracker. Only her way of expressing the Yuletide was different. It had meant death. But she was glad, so glad because all the remorse which she had known was swept away on the tail of that one bullet. She looked down at her hand but could see nothing. Everything around her was black, velvet black. Her fingers trembled slightly beneath the torn glove and the frost continued to bite. She could no longer hear the wail of the siren.

Nettie slept. She did not know just how long because she did not peer at her watch. Her ears caught the *tramp-tramp* sound and rustle of dead leaves above her. Voices were muttering something as lights played lurid shadows on the underbrush. The lights picked out the bare trees. They had come looking for her! Had found her! She felt as exposed as the blackjacks that stood on the hill. Her heart thumped. Now she knew what her husband must have experienced when he was caught. It was terrible, a terrible sensation to be caught like a rat, wedged between two rocks. And she had been so sure here was safety! She was afraid to move. One single beam knifed down the ravine and rested upon the vines. Nettie shoved her body farther into the cave. A voice rasped out above her. "It ain no needa going down thet goddamn gully. I tol Clance the bitch probly hidin with some a them nigger famlies."

"How the police shore hit was her?"

"Well, who else could it been? Thet jackleg nigger preacher who lives neah her said he seen her pass his house this evening bout dusk dark. Wouldn't she be sore after we got her man?"

"She ain heah. No black bitch got sense er nerve nough to bring her ass out in these swamps. Not col as hit is."

So Reverend Jackson got scared and told. I thought no one saw me leave. What chance do I have now, what chance?

"But, wait a minute, ain these heah fresh tracks?"

The frightened woman held her breath, clenched her fists until they ached. She heard excitement rise and then she heard another voice. "Hell, naw, some kids was out heah the other day. I tell ya, fellers, she ain out heah. Besides, if she is, she cain git out. Both ends gonna be watched. Yall know thet damn river is behind the thicket."

"Th Sheriff issued orders to check all incomin an outgoin traffic on the highway an warn th drivers to be on th lookout."

Oh, Lord, that is my only chance! But I won't give in! I won't give in! She closed her eyes.

"C'mon, we gonna search ever nigger shack in Nigger Town. Thas where she is. That bitch'll never git away. If she ain in one of them houses we'll git th dogs next time."

"This is the goddamnes crap I ever run into. First, thet nigger, an now his woman. Pore Miz Mills was such a fine woman. Such a fine woman."

The men must have been smoking, for the faint odor of burning tobacco reached her nose. Her legs, arms, shoulders, had begun to cramp, the pain running through her entire body. The words began to lose meaning. Loosened pebbles rattled down the hillside, sounding like large hailstones to her. *This is how Lawrence must have felt before they got him. Lord, I never knew fear could be so fierce, so dreadful. Why don't they go, why don't they come and get me. If I stay here long enough, this cold is going to kill me. JesusGod! I'm so hungry!* She lifted her body up to ease the cramping some. *Must hold myself together for Lawrence as well as for myself, but this waiting is killing me. I can't stand much more, Lawrence, honest to God, I can't!*

"Buddyboy heah says he knows her. Says he's knowed her for a long time. Kinda uppity like her man was. Says she's a mighty fine-lookin bitch, too. Don't let me see her first, boys. I ain had no nigger stuff since I was a youngun. No tellin what I might not do. Don't let me see her first." Nettie heard him chuckle, and she shivered.

The figures began to filter away and Nettie breathed easier. Sweat chilled her body. She peeped down at her watch and it showed 12:30. The footsteps now died away and only the wind still raked through the dry leaves and the white pines above. She would attempt to signal a truck nevertheless. Perhaps a colored driver would run the risk to pick her up. Perhaps he would feel sorry for her. There was nothing to lose. To stay here cramped in this hole she was certain to die; if she ventured to the highway maybe she would have a chance—maybe. *What if it would be a white man*—she trembled at the thought. *But it is my only way of escape. God knows I've got to get away, someplace, somewhere.*

She lay a while longer listening to the passing traffic. She had to go because they would come back with those bloodhounds. Nettie made up her mind: she would go to the highway and wait. When she dragged herself out of the hole, her legs felt dead and they crumpled beneath her. She began to cry softly, crawling back up the hill. The sharp stones cut wickedly into her knees but she went on up until she made it. *Maybe it is a journey into eternity, perhaps I am going into the final phase of my life. Lawrence did. I must go on. I must go on.* That highway was a good quarter mile away but it seemed a journey, indeed, into eternity. She fought her way through the bushes and entangled vines.

One she tripped and fell, her hands cracking through the thin ice sheet of a mud hole. Nettie made no sound as she arose. A tear stung her face and she brushed it away. *I'm not crying, Lawrence, really. Just some water sort of splashed up on my face.* She smiled forcefully at herself. Nettie remembered the sympathetic smile that he had given her before

81

when she had cried. *Honest I know how you feel about a thing like that.* She wondered if he had smiled from some distant place this time. She knew that he had. The wintry stars stared down into her eyes and she struggled on to the road.

As she reached Highway 63 twin lights of an oncoming car came into view. Her heart leaped! Should she signal for it to stop or should she lie there crouched under the bank of the road. *Perhaps this is my chance, perhaps this is my chance. O, Lord, I'm so cold, so cold. Don't think I can resist any longer. Don't think I can.* The lights grew brighter as the car approached. Nettie stood up and prepared to wave when suddenly she recognized the spotlight beam of the car, reaching across the road from side to side. *Lord, they almost got me! They're patrolling the road!* She lay there and listened as the sound of the car faded. Then she heard the distant yells which seemed to be coming from town. As she raised and peeped over the road she saw a reddish glow beginning to spread over the sky, the resuscent tinge growing larger and clearer. It was coming from the direction of Colored Town. Had the mob carried out its threat to search every "nigger shack"? Was it their house the mob had set fire to? They must have done it. This was civilization, thousands of miles from the jungles, yet it was as barbaric, as savage—more so—than the rites of some jungle tribe!

While the terrified woman had fixed her gaze upon the light in the distance, another vehicle approached almost suddenly upon her. And she could not dash back to safety, so she turned and signalled to the driver. It was a truck headed North—one of those fruit trucks—she rushed out as the driver slowed down. It was a colored driver. She thought she could almost feel the tremors in his dark features. Maybe he would feel sorry for her and give her a lift. *But he doesn't have to feel sorry for me. He must realize what I did, why I did it.* She made quite a spectacle standing there, scratched, bleeding, half-frozen. Her voice failed her temporarily as she whispered, "C-Could you give me a ride, take me away from here?" Nettie could go no further, she choked up completely as she gazed up into the driver's face.

His eyes widened and his own voice shook. "I-I wish I could, girl, I wish I could, but you mus be th woman them policemen warned me about. Baby, they would kill me and you both if I picked you up. They sho would. But I ain seen ya if if they asts me, I ain seen ya." Then he cranked up and the spluttering of the truck smothered Nettie's pleas as she watched hopelessly and saw the red tail light finally fade. The red light still bobbed up and down long after the truck was out of sight. Would they all do that—the bright headlights of hope, then the red tail lights of despair?

She stumbled back crazily, weak over the embankment, feeling old and lonesome. Her mind shoved the story of Reynard the fox before her, being chased by the incessant, relentless dogs. *But Reynard got away. He got away, Lawrence, and you didn't, darling, you didn't. And I wonder if I will.* She hunched there and saw the hands on her watch crawl around, then she saw them running around, racing for day, for her doom. 3:30 and still in these swamps. The glow from the fires had faded and everything was still save for that cruel wind. *If I could swim Big River, maybe they wouldn't suspect it. Might as well die drowning as in any other manner. It would be less horrible.*

So she got up again, this time to go back through the thicket to the river. That seemed to be her only chance. But Nettie knew that she could not swim. But she also knew that now Big River was her only possible way of escape. She had become desperate.

As she turned to go, Nettie heard the roar of another truck up the road. She stopped, crouched, waited. This might be the last one, her last chance. A shudder ran through her. Disregarding all caution, she stood up tall and waved frantically as the truck ground to a full halt. She ran to it, gripped the door handle as the driver poked his head out. He had an army wool-knit cap pulled over his ears. *Oh, I didn't mean to stop him—he's white!* "Yeah, whatcha want?" the driver asked as he looked down at her. Then as if he suddenly remembered the warning in town, he exclaimed, "Hey, you, you must be that gal who has caused all that hell back there in town. Ain't you the one the cops told me about? You really have raised a ton o hell, gal, a ton o hell." Nettie said nothing and unblinkingly stood her ground. He looked at her intently. He went on, "You sure have got a lotta nerve stopping *me*." He paused before continuing. "I'm white, ya know." The shivering colored girl said nothing. The man surveyed her face, her body, its torn and abject appearance. A smile slipped across his face. He spoke slowly, looking around furtively, "Say, I'll make a deal with you. You know, I'm supposed to turn you in. But I'll make a deal with you."

Nettie sensed what was to follow and a smouldering anger coursed her whole being, made her tingle. She flushed and drew the ragged coat collar tighter around her throat. She was naked before the searching eyes of this white man. Never before had the colored woman experienced such humiliation. Her hand released its vise-like grip on the door handle and she stepped back. Her whole body was quivering. The driver knew the answer. "All right, suit yourself, goddamnit," he snapped. "It's your own hearse." He settled back as if to go on. The motor started up. From somewhere in the hills Nettie thought she heard the baying of dogs.

"Wait, wait," she said hoarsely, "don't leave me here! I-I haven't said that I wouldn't listen to your proposition." *Oh, Lawrence, what must I do!*

This is as low as I can stoop. Should I trust him? His face is white. He has to think in terms of white folks, too. Oh, those dogs, those must be those dogs I hear. She faltered, "What sort of deal are you talking about? Her words frightened her. The wind cut through her hair, blowing it across her face. She winced.

The man smiled broadly and replied, "Don't hand me that bull crap, baby. You know what I mean. I've got some blankets folded up back there we can use." He jerked a thumb toward his truck bed. He went on, "You can hide back there. You don't have a damned thing to lose anyway."

He was right; she didn't have a "damned thing" to lose. Then she recalled what Lawrence had said about the laundry. She had reached the end of her rope. There was nothing more to lose. Everything had been irretrievably destroyed. "All right," she whispered feebly, and went around and scrambled up into the cab. He ran an ungloved hand over her knee, her thigh, and she shook like a leaf. His breath came upon her face hot and moist. Was escape worth this?

"Naw," he mumbled, "wait until you warm up some. And until we get farther away from here. Go through this flap here and you will find some blankets in this corner." He indicated with his head and raised a tarpaulin covering. Nettie hesitated for a minute before she crawled through. Was this merely a trap, a trick. But there was no time to hesitate now. A slight gray pall was stretching across the skyline ever so faintly. But morning was on its way. She found the blankets and spread them alongside the fruit crates and stretched out, staring into the blackness. The bounding truck rolled her back and forth against the boxes. The heavy odor of oranges and cucumbers was sharp to her nostrils. She did not know what new dangers lay ahead. She was too tired to care.

The truck roared on and then it came to a halt. Nettie raised up and heard the driver get out. In a flash she got up. She heard him talking to some men outside. Their voices soon came in clear to her. Her heart stopped, froze! Quickly Nettie folded the blankets as neatly as possible and crawled along the floor of the truck. She squeezed her aching body between the stacked crates and waited. She was concealed, yet she felt exposed, afraid to move. Why had they stopped, what was wrong? Then the voices became distinct, nearer. The young truck driver was talking, talking very rapidly. "But I tell you, I haven't seen nothing of a woman—black or white, young or old—nobody since I left town. Can't you take my word?" His voice rose shrilly, sputtering.

"Jus th same, mind if we take a look inside? This heah is a big thing. You know, ya kin never tell bout you young fellers today. That War seemed t hev changed some of ya."

That sounded like one of the men who had stood out on the hill last night. *Oh, no! Oh, no! Don't let them come in here!* Nettie felt a warm trickle of perspiration as it wormed its way from her armpit down her side, across her stomach. The heavy footsteps pounded upon the runningboard and then a light flashed in among the crates of fruit and vegetables. *They can see my foot, they can see my head, my left shoulder! They can see all of me!* The beam flicked off and the man grunted, "Hmmmm, I see ya got plenny of cover back there. Goin fer?"

The driver spurted out excitedly, his voice was strained, "Yeah, yeah, going back to East St. Louis. The blankets left back there by my buddy. Left him in Montgomery."

"Wall, you fellers really got the neat habit. They all folded up like the work of a woman. Wall, no needa us holdin ya up any longer if ya got thet fer t go. If y happins t see thet bitch, be sure to turn her in. Cain afford to let er git away with this. Won't nobody be safe in thet goddamn town. Good luck, feller." They left and Nettie heard the driver step up into the truck, turn the motor over and head off again. She almost retched. The girl almost fell into a dead faint.

After about thirty minutes' driving he slowed down, turned off to what sounded like a dirt road. The woman peeped out. She heard him raise the flap and whisper, "Psst-psst!" Nettie was still too weak to move. "Hey," he called softly once more. Then he cut off his headlights and came back to the rear of the truck. She heard him breathing heavily. She crawled from her hiding place, still shaking. "Well, I'll be goddamn!" he grunted. "How in th hell did you do it—I mean this hiding and all?" He helped her to her feet and she felt his hands trembling. He was scared, too.

He spoke again. "How did you do it, the hiding and the blankets, I mean?"

She could not say anything for a moment. Words clung to her mouth, and tears bubbled forth. "I-I don't know. I just don't know. But, But, But you won't let them get me, will you? Will you?" Her fingers dug into his field jacket. He must have been a soldier, too. Then she went on, "I heard you lying for me back there. Oh, my God, thanks, Mister!"

"I was lying mostly for myself. I got myself into something a helluva lot bigger than I dreamed of. Umm-umm, a whole lot bigger," he breathed.

"Thanks just the same," Nettie countered. "I heard you say you were going to East St. Louis. Could I go that far with you, please. Please, Mister? I'll stay hidden out of sight. You must have been a soldier, too."

"Yeah, I was a GI. Most everybody was I guess. Why?"

"So was my husband. Then you can understand what it is like to come back discouraged, disgusted, beaten before you can get started. And, Mister, my husband did not touch that woman. Believe me! He was a gentle human being. And he was going to become a dentist, too, if . . . if . . ." Her voice trailed off. She was breathing easier now. She

85

wanted more than ever to live. Lawrence would wish it, too. "You won't turn me in, will you?" She softly begged again.

"I was when I first picked ya up, but now I've changed my mind. I'll risk it. I understand a lot of things now. My wife died when I was overseas." He sounded wistful. Then he said to her, "Let me spread the blankets out again. You promised me, remember?"

"Unh-hunh, I remember," the tired woman answered as she waited and then lay down on the warm blankets. Sure, she remembered, but not what *he* remembered. She did not feel cold fingers, numb hands, fumbling with her skirt, her underthings, her taut, tired body.

Nettie only remembered the crying record and a tall man whirling her over a shining dance floor. *Lawrence, Lawrence, we're taking this trip together still, darling!*

As the shafts of the cold morning light nosed its way through the cracks of the rumbling truck, the woman slept.

And in her sleep she remembered.

Blinded Glory
(Short Story) 1949
(A Black Man Finds Himself)

Ellsworth Jackson Farnsdale was a Negro. He lived, worked, and died in Georgia—in a small town—Cox Bridge, Georgia. This is the story of a terrified man. Ellsworth was a doctor, and what's more, he was a good doctor, a good, country doctor, but he was a terrified doctor. Years of struggle and study had not driven this fear out of his system. Except for a brief span of years when he studied medicine in Tennessee at Meharry in Nashville, his life was woven and twisted into the red clay of southern Georgia.

Negro citizens of the town looked upon this tall, robust man as a living example of success—kindly, sincere, and patient. When he attended the high school mothers would point to this serious youngster with pride and tell their errant and less-industrious offspring to watch the road that Ellsworth was taking. He had no time for such triflings as football, basketball, or any athletics. In fact, the only extra-curricular activity in which this boy was engaged was the high school choir. He studied. None but Ellsworth Jackson Farnsdale knew why he refused to take part in anything else, no one. He was afraid to get hurt, to injure somebody. This was probably why he pursued a course in medicine—he hated pain and was filled with compassion for the sick and wounded.

After graduating from State College, he received a scholarship to attend Meharry Medical School. Nobody could understand the almost inexpressible joy which he derived from that scholarship. With trembling hands he left his smiling mother and sister at the station and went off to school. His life there was uneventful save for a companionship he struck up with a fellow medical student from Chicago, William Speers, a dynamic, almost reckless fellow. He was able to see through the cloak of fear which Farnsdale kept pulled tightly about him. "You're just frightened at your own foolish sense of insecurity," Speers told him one day, "your own fear. Why don't you come to Chicago to practice after you finish here? You need to get up North or to a big city to feel the stiff competition of the fast moving world."

"No, Bill," Ellsworth answered slowly, "I am going back to Georgia. That's where I will work. Let the more ambitious boys like yourself aim for the bigger and more glorious things. If I can help to show the colored people in Cox Bridge the necessity of good health and have a few patients, I will indeed be gratified." Farnsdale knew that he spoke only a half-truth. He did want to return to Cox Bridge and administer to the poor people there, but he wouldn't be totally satisfied. He was too afraid to make his way in a strange place. He only dreamed of a simple practice, marriage, if possible, and that would be all.

Farnsdale returned to Cox Bridge and hung his shingle in small letters, ELLSWORTH J. FARNSDALE, M.D., outside his home. Almost before the paint on the sign had dried people were rushing to his little office with this ailment and that complaint. Some paid, some did not, most of them couldn't, but Ellsworth did not mind. At least he had found the seclusion which would help to shadow his everlasting fear. "He's a mighty good medicine doctor," the citizens were saying, "a good boy with a level head." This was uttered by the Negro population. And the whites of the town spoke in tones not too much differently from the ones used by the colored people. "Thet nigger doc is a damned good boy, a respectful citizen. He's going to do a powerful lot to keep the other black bucks in check." And Doctor Farnsdale, (and we can rightfully use this title now), Doctor Ellsworth Jackson Farnsdale went about his duties with the respect of a man proud of his profession, but not vainly so.

Then Ellsworth married. Mary Finch was from Atlanta. She had come to teach at the high school and met Ellsworth at a luncheon given in his honor. And the friendship developed into the ultimate. Perhaps this was what the doctor needed, for Mary was an energetic person, friendly, courteous, and yet straightforward. "Ellsworth," she would often say, "it's a pity that you won't leave this town and go where you could reap some of the benefits from your long years of study. It's all right here, but this is not enough for you. I believe that you are afraid."

Mary had hit a sore spot and she did not know it. "Afraid?" the doctor would retort, "Afraid of *what*? Why should I go and leave the Negroes here without a doctor?" But he knew that his wife had told the truth. He *was* afraid, but not even she was to know it.

"Well, you needn't snap my head off, Doctor Ellsworth Jackson Farnsdale!" she would always reply. "After all, you could at least get paid for most of your work, you know. And that's not such a crazy idea."

After that they would be silent, Ellsworth turning to his prescriptions, and Mary to the secretarial duties in the office. But this fear was gnawing at the doctor like the teeth of a mouse, gnawing and gnawing away slowly. Often Ellsworth would awake in the night and stare into the blackness as if to reach out and grasp it. He looked upon it as a living thing which became his companion as he drove out to the rural sections at night. It was there and he could not name it.

The years moved along. Now Doctor Farnsdale was a fixture in the community, the local boy who had returned to his place of struggle. And the people were proud of him. But a change had begun to take place in the town, in Georgia, for that matter. Suddenly the tenseness developed into a taut circumstance. The Negro people began to clamor for the right to vote in the primaries and the white businessmen did not like it one bit. Many of the white townspeople would come to Ellsworth and ask him about this new uprising. The quiet doctor would say that he knew of no such thing. This was true, because Doctor Ellsworth Jackson Farnsdale withdrew deeper and deeper within himself and studied with more fervor.

He had only heard, but he did not clearly know anything about it. He was a man of medicine and it was not his job to mix medicine and politics. The mixture could not prove favorable. Politics were politics and medicine was medicine he would repeat over and over again. "But you should help the people out, Ellsworth. That is your job as an influential man here in town. The people would believe in you; they know that you would not lie," his wife protested once after they had entered into such an argument. "Both things are good—politics and medicine. One helps to bring out self-expression and the other removes physical illness. They're inter-related."

But the doctor would have nothing to do with the organizing of the people, to help them understand the political maneuvers of the town and county. Yet, out of a daring urge one day he approached one of the town commissioners and said, "Mr. Haines, my people have been asking me to see the possibility of their voting in this spring's primary. What must I tell them?"

"What must you tell them, Doc? Now, Doc, you know they don't know what they're talking about. This is a white man's business. Who would they vote for anyway and *why*?" the commissioner chuckled.

"Yes sir," answered the trembling man, "you're just about right." He echoed the chuckle, the laugh of a man who knew that he was betraying his people. Yet he had to laugh for he had to get along in this town. No one really expected *him* to get involved in anything like this. He hurried on back to his office and told Mary about the incident.

"Why, you coward, Ellsworth!" she blurted, "you perfect coward! How could you have said a thing like that?"

Her words cut him deeply and he said nothing. There was really nothing to say. His wife had not understood him after all of these years. No one had understood him—he had not understood himself. He merely bit his lip and turned to his work. "But," his wife continued, "I suppose that you are well content in the idea that you can tell the people that you tried, you tried, and there was nothing that you could do about it. After all, you're only a doctor. And don't tell me about that politics and medicine don't mix again. I'm tired of hearing that. This is not politics. A Negro doctor must be more than a doctor. He has to be a guiding light to his people."

The silent man finally found speech and he scathingly answered, "You should have married a damned congressman if you're that wrapped up in the government functions!"

"Now don't you turn ridiculous, Ellworth!" But Mary was more subdued in her retort, for Ellsworth seldom used profane terms unless he was angry, and she knew that he was pretty sore.

Mary did not tell anyone about the incident which had occurred between Doctor Farnsdale and the commissioner, so Ellsworth still moved and worked as usual. But the spring primary was at hand, and, strangely enough, the Negroes turned out in tremendous groups and stormed the polls, demanding to vote. No one could hardly understand it. But secretly the colored population had engaged a political lawyer from Atlanta and it was agreed that his identity would not be revealed. The movement had caught white Cox Bridge off-guard. The whole town was buzzing. "This sounds like the work of that goddamned nigger doctor," the white businessmen rasped. "He lied to Haines." And so the news spread like wildfire. The colored people who did not know who was instrumental in the strange turn of events all agreed that this was the work of this tall, silent black Emancipator. This *had* to be the work of the "medicine doctor." and Ellsworth staggered about in a foolish daze. He was caught between two forces—between the whites' angered belief and the unwise Negroes' joyous concept of his actions. He was trapped.

One night after the incident had subsided he was driving along a dark country road still deep in this perplexing problem. Suddenly as the doctor slowed the car to avoid a deep rut in the road, white men surrounded his car and forced him to halt. He was grabbed and jerked from beneath the steering wheel before he could realize what had taken place. He was pitched to the rough road. "You were very, very slick, ya son-of-a-bitch! Ya thought ya'd get away with lying about that voting, didn't ya?" And before the frightened Ellsworth could get his bearings, sticks and fists rained down in his face. His head ached. He tried to cry out that he knew nothing about the mess, that he was honestly innocent, but the words stuck in his mouth. He fought back as best he could but there were too many. Then suddenly he visualized his wife's face, how proud she looked when the news trickled to her that he had been the one behind the voting after all. He remembered the voice of Bill Speers: *You're just frightened at your own foolish sense of insecurity.* Then Mary whispered: *I believe you are afraid. Why, why, you coward, Ellsworth! You perfect coward!*

He smiled grimly as the cutting voices shouted, "Take 'im to thet tall hick'ry tree. Thet goddamned tree won't break!" Then flames were built about his bound feet. Ellsworth Jackson Farnsdale suddenly realized that this fear had an answer; he had been afraid only of Ellsworth Jackson Farnsdale all these years. His entire life span was unwound before him, his youth, his studies, his practice, his complete life.

As the fire began to burn his bleeding body he raised his voice and hoarsely yelled, "Build your fires! Yeah, yeah, I was behind it all. Build your goddamned fires, higher, higher, hotter! I fooled all you silly bastards!'

And just before the pain from the searing flames burned away his consciousness, he raised his eyes toward the shadowy outlines of the sleeping town and his dying laughter reverberated throughout the countryside.

State Line

He spat and then spat again. Blood and salt. Salt and blood. God! but he was tired—dog tired. He stopped and listened—dogs again, those goddamned hounds, howling and howling their heads off and bursting their lungs, still following. Nearer and nearer they sounded, still following. They sounded like something from Edgar Allan Poe's horror stories.

"Ow-ooo! Ow-ooo!" Those damned dogs.

God, if he could only tell how far he was from the State Line, then he possibly would have a chance, but it was as dark as hell and even darker. It was darker than the nights when he was on patrol duty in Italy—yeah, a thousand times darker, because then once in a while a flare from enemy territory would break the blackness. But out here in this damned section there was nothing. He couldn't even strike a match and how he wanted to smoke! It was like a mad itch and he couldn't scratch, yet he had to—it was like the time near La Spezia on patrol duty behind the enemy lines when Paul Black had to sneeze and the sergeant told him to hold his breath if he and all of them wanted to live. But Paul just had to sneeze, just had to. He swallowed hard, held his breath until tears and sweat streamed down his face. And then—he sneezed, and then—the Germans heard, and then—they opened fire, and then—Paul was hit—and dead. Just like that.

Lord, but why in the hell did he think of that at this particular time of all times? He couldn't say, but everything crowds the mind when a fellow is in a tight spot. He was at home in America, but still he was in a tight spot. Swamps, water, eerie sounds, men trailing him, men and those goddamned bow-legged bloodhounds! And he could still hear them a long way off but coming nearer and nearer. He was burning up all over like he was full of pepper or ants or something like that, yet it was a chilly night in Arkansas and he had no coat on, just that olive-drab GI shirt. S'funny to be chilly and yet hot as fire at the same time—it didn't add up, didn't make sense. But what in the hell *had* made sense during the last forty-eight hours?

A shirt—ha, that was why he was out in these God-forsaken wilds—all because of a shirt. Jeezus, he was back home and running just like he had to do if an ME-109 was overhead spraying bullets at him, or just like

92

he had heard a damned "88" screaming near—just alike, only it was a little different feeling. Over there although it was as terrifying as hell he still had the strange comfort that he wasn't running and scared by himself; there were his buddies, he could hear their fast-plodding boots racing for shelter, too, and so a guy didn't feel so damned lonesome and scared. But out here, there was no one, not even his "officer-boot-licking" sergeant; for although he disliked him so much there still was the feeling that he was the sergeant's equal in a situation like that. It is bad enough to be lonesome, but try to mix loneliness, fear, and a big dash of anger together, and the concoction would terrify the bravest heart.

He still rested for he was tired as hell and cold and hot at the same time, and he felt so hungry and smoke-thirsty. No, he had better not smoke for somebody might see the flame. And how near was he to the State Line? He couldn't be too far, but it was past midnight and day would soon be breaking. If he could only make it to Oklahoma—to the Oklahoma border, then maybe he would have a chance to get away at least for a while. He suddenly knew how the children of Israel felt coming out of the land of the Pharaohs in Egypt. He knew how they felt when they knew they were nearing Canaan. He knew that Oklahoma was no Promised Land, but for the moment it could serve as such. But how much farther did he have to walk or run or hop or crawl or—roll—how much farther? He listened and the howls of the bloodhounds didn't seem so near—they seemed to be fading. Were they, or was it his imagination? There were so many things unreal which seemed to take on an entirely different aspect when a person is in a tight spot. Some fellow had said that even noonday brightness takes on a midnight hue sometimes if a guy is scared enough. But, no, he stopped breathing so his listening faculties wouldn't have the slightest impediment to prevent them from functioning perfectly; but, hell, his heart was pounding like a ten-ton sledge hammer and he couldn't stop that. He listened, straining for the sheerest noise, but, sure enough, the howls were fading! They were fading! Maybe they got off on the wrong track after he had crossed that little creek or maybe those mad pursuers had turned back. Lord, if they had! Now he could breathe easier, louder. Before he had been too scared to risk breaking wind for fear someone would hear and that would have meant lights out. He had been too scared to break wind—suppose some folks heard him say that; they would laugh, laugh like hell for that sounded silly and exaggerated. But honest, he was that scared. Now he did and his stomach ceased to cramp some. *Better keep moving, better keep moving,* his mind was saying, better keep moving. And as he began to walk on through the underbrush the words began to sound off in definite rhythm and his feet took up the beat—*better keep moving, better keep moving,* BETTER KEEP MOVING.

He knew that he wasn't too far from the line now and if he kept going west he was certain to reach it by morning—only if he could keep moving till morning and throw that fiendish pack off his trail. Gosh, but he was making more progress than he had realized. That little saying in his mind about "better keep moving" had given him new and determined drive to keep going. And that big North Star was still there to his right and so he knew he was heading west. The more he thought about the distance the faster he walked. Everything had grown deathly quiet save the crackling of his sore feet on the underbrush. And his feet were sore, too, wet and aching. Still he had to get across to Oklahoma, because possibly he could make it on to Muskogee where Janice, his girl, was. She could help him get away. The more he thought of the State Line the more he thought of Muskogee, Janice, and freedom. Janice was there teaching school and what would she think of him? What *could* she think of him? He couldn't help doing what he did—couldn't help it. White people asked too much of colored folks, too much. And since the war things had appeared different to him; he saw with a clearer vision the bloody curse of American democracy—especially American democracy *Southern* style.

But this wasn't the time to think of democracy any style; this was the time to keep moving, make it to a safer part of the country. Nevertheless, everything rushed through his distorted mind—a panorama of ideas and wild, confused thoughts. In fact, everything crowded his mental focus—the beginning of the whole thing, the altercation, the bruise spot on his jaw, the swollen section of his leg from the kicks, the nasty snarl, the scream, and the dastardly lie that white girl had told. Everything danced before his eyes and he began to walk faster to outrun his thoughts and side-step those last bitter memories of the last forty-eight hours. Then faster, faster, he ran, and even faster, his breath burning his lungs; he would outrun his thoughts. But he forgot, or was too confused to remember that thoughts always go ahead of you, thoughts of past events encircle you, follow you, become a vital part of you. Remember Tennyson said that he was a part of all that he had met. But it didn't make sense. Then there was that mad stillness and blackness which made him recall those black nights on guard duty when he was stationed in England when the moor fogs would rise up like a huge cloak and hug him, choke him, and make him clench his teeth and grip his rifle in fearful anticipation of something from another world lurking in the shadows. But he was one helluva ways from the English moors and English fogs. He remembered that he was in America and in Arkansas hunted instead of hunting and guarding something. And the realization of his predicament snapped him back.

Why the hell did that girl have to lie—why did she have to tell that dirty lie? All he had asked was: "Could I look at some of your shirts you have on sale here?" And she proceeded to ask the size, color, and so on. She brought him one and haughtily dropped it in his hands.

"If it is possible, I would like to see more than one because I am just out of service and I have none except this army issue which I have on."

"You'd better be satisfied to get this one. You fellows come back and try to demand too much."

Try to demand too much! Too much! All he wanted was two shirts—just two shirts: there wasn't anything too demanding about that. It was a dire necessity.

"I'm not trying to ask for too much, lady; all I wanted and would like to have is two shirts to change."

Then—

"Who are you to tell me I'm lyin': I'm not one of your nigger wenches who you can talk to just any old way. That discharge emblem you niggers wearin' have just about gone to your heads. The sooner you remember who you are, the sooner you can get along better down here."

"I-I-I beg your pardon, Miss, I didn't er . . ."

She went on, "Stayin' in Europe and everywhere else sorta makes you think you're a white person's equal."

Jeezus, listen to all that noise and speech that lady made!

"Well, lady, I only come in here to try to make a purchase—not to start an argument. I'm sorry to have bothered you."

Then that hideous scream that followed and the crowd which all seemed too quickly have gathered. Southern white womanhood had been molested and things had begun to boil over! He recalled how he was surrounded while that whore, or whatever he could think of as far away from a lady, blurted indignantly that she had been insulted by that nigger! Someone in the crowd wanted to know what he had said.

"He asked me to have an affair with him. Said that he had been over in Europe and he knew about white women and wanted to have an affair with me." The words fairly hissed out.

An affair with her! That bad looking woman! Why, even a guy with the clap or pox would shy away from her, and this fellow of all persons! Then, too, he had more respect for all women than to pull a thing like that. Didn't he have a sister, and how about Janice? She didn't mean what she had said, surely not; she must have been joking. Then they started beating him, kicking him before he could even attempt to explain or defend himself. And the names they called him—God! He tried his level best to be calm and cool, but somebody struck him on the head from behind almost knocking his teeth out and he felt blood coming out of his mouth. White faces everywhere, scrawny, lined, red, and vicious. He could not resist striking back, defending himself. Suddenly he remembered some of his old judo tricks and as a big beef-faced cop moved in to stike him again, he ducked under the stick and caught his swinging arm and flipped him headlong into the infuriated crowd—and he ran, raced down the narrow alley, across the railroad tracks, and over the bridge into Colored Town and home. He remembered how he half gasped his episode to his terrified sister and crying niece. Then he headed for the swamps to make a get-away. The whites had risen up as one to track down this demented attacker.

And now he still heard the frightful crying of his sister, "Muskogee, Sonny, Muskogee." That was over two hundred miles back. He looked westward and pictured his Janice over the State Line and crazy patterns and jumbled pictures kept dancing before his eyes in kaleidescopic fashion. And it was still black save the beacon of that North Star blinking at him, whispering, "Keep plugging, keep plugging. I'm still here keeping silent vigil." And on he plunged.

Ooooooh, hell! Crash! and down his left leg went into a hole. Excruciating pain, blood, and then he slowly pulled his foot out of the unseen hole. His foot had sunk in an old stump hole and the remaining roots had served as vicious daggers. He sat down cursing under his breath letting the warm blood run down in his shoe, between his toes, making them sticky and gummy. This was the last straw; this was it; he had to give up. But, no, he couldn't stop for somewhere to the west lay Oklahoma and freedom possibly. *He had to make it.* He couldn't be too far now, for some colored fellow he had met the night before had told him that he was only about fifty miles from the state line, and he had really been travelling some since then. But he couldn't make it; that goddamned nasty cut was killing him. He tried to rise and then weakly sat back down and cried big, futile tears.

He couldn't tell just how long he had remained in this painful position, but two things aroused him from this nightmarish slumber: the sound of early morning sparrows in the slight gray haze in the eastern skies behind him, and the warm trickle of urine down between his legs. It was morning and the North Star was gone! Soon he would be there across the State Line and freedom. The mob would only probably chase him out of the state. As he stiffly rose, pains shot all through his body like a billion needles—his body screamed for rest, but he couldn't rest. *Gotta go, gotta go,* his mind kept saying and repeating over and over again. And there was that BETTER KEEP MOVING still sounding back of all this, so he kept on. He had been going due west and he was right. He looked ahead and there appeared some sort of sign not more than fifteen yards in front of him. *What did it say, and was that really a sign?* It appeared almost phantasmagoric in the gray shadows of the early morning. *But this*

96

was it! He had made it, he had almost made it! This reminded him of how relieved and joyous he had felt when his outfit landed on Sardinia. He had made it!

With mad anticipation he raced to the sign-post and it read: YOU ARE NOW ENTERING THE STATE OF OKLAHOMA. There was some more to read, but he wasn't interested; he had read all that he needed. *Oklahoma*. All of the wild escapades the night before and the night before that seemed like a frightful dream that was finally over. There really had been no fight, no white girl, no running, no bruises, no hunger, no terror. He felt like a new man, like Adam must have felt when God breathed life into his human frame. He lifted his puffed and swollen eyes and aching arms to God and prayed and hugged that sign-post.

A single shot. He turned half way around, his body stiffened in stark surprise and fell headlong head and arms across the State Line, fingers clutching the brown grass, the other part of his body *still* in Arkansas.

"*He almost made it*," one voice drawled, "*thet bastard almost made it*."

97

PART III

"Morris' 'Bitter-cisms'"
(MENTAL RUMINATIONS)

94 Mental Shavings

PART I. AND MOSTLY LOVE?

1.

Funny how this world changes
Just to resist change itself,
And is only *made* to change
When any change takes place.

2.

Nothing is new under the sun,
But we all pretend there are countless things.
And many of us begin to believe that there are.

3.

Nothing is positively more predictable
Than a politician on election day
And all the elected days that follow.
We know all this, yet we waste our vote anyway.

4.

I'd offer a "penny for your thoughts,"
But I don't have change.

5.

"All the world loves a lover,"
But the lover still has to pay his own way,
As do most of those who love to profess they love
As part of the world the lover loves.

6.

The next time you say, "Don't quote me,"
I'm going to *not* quote you,
And see how well off you'll be *then*!

7.

Amazing how many of us swear to be
Great Christians and Upright Jews
And will flatly refuse to show true love
And share the same living quarters in the U.S.,

Thereby forfeiting a true chance to be
Great Christians and Upright Jews.

8.

Don't "come and get it"
If only you have interest in the dessert.

9.

Anybody can "pass the buck,"
And most do if the buck proves
To be only worthless.

10.

He readily boasts of aquatic prowess
When he knows the pool has just been drained
And the ocean is much too cold.

11.

"The cat's got his tongue."
Only trouble is: The cat won't keep it.

12.

A man, dreamless and lonely for years,
As he trudged life's uneven highway,
Suddenly found one day a most beautiful silk-
Ribbon-tied box, paper, gilt-prettied up.
The glittering bow and breath-taking object stopped him.
His heart skipped the proverbial beat
As he stared at the wonder-box clearly marked:
"Unused Dreams Inside."
His hands trembled, his eyes misted up,
As his shaking hands untied the beauty.
He knew some unfortunate soul would toss
And turn somewhere in anxiety.
"Here," the man thought, "is why someone somewhere
Must weep red tears of regret this night.
I must search inside for identifying sign.
I'll see the dreams and find the owner."
"At least," the man continued, "there are those
Left who still can dream."
Slowly he unwrapped the box, his heart still
Beating wildly, fingers twitching excitedly.
He peeped within. There was nothing. Not even
The shadow of a dream. The dust of emptiness
Made him sneeze, and tears welled within his eyes.
The man dropped the box by the side of the road,
Glad and relieved that he was not alone in this
Big and dream-forsaken world.

13.

In a world of mixed-up verbiage and the big lie, baby,
We do go, so well together, so very well together:
Me an *enigma* and *you* a *paradox.*
But somehow we come across with a common language
Known only by losers at the game of love.

14.

I've always known where THITHER is,
But I've never run across YON, not on
Any map in any book or road map.
Perhaps, on second thought, once having
Been to THITHER, YON doesn't amount to much anyway.

15.

Nothing is prettier than being cursed out
In a language you cannot understand.
Yet the mildest expletive in the mother tongue
Sets your anger aflame as nothing else can!

16.

"Oh," he boastfully admitted, "I've known
Quite a few ladies in my life, but I've only loved my wife!"
To which his listening wife *nodded* in strict *disbelief.*

17.

The biggest problem with being in love, son,
Is that you never know when she will fall out of love.
So as to never lose in this piddling game,
Always be mindful to beat her to the punch.
And don't worry: she'll soon follow suit
And forget you faster than you can remember her face.

18.

The funny thing about jealousy is that
There is nothing funny about jealousy.

19.

Since the whole world is based on love,
I can readily see why there are rotting underpinnings.
What can one expect of an edifice
Built on such flimsy foundations!

20.

She tried to break my heart
So I beat her to it.
Now she will never catch up
(Unless I want her to.)

21.

Trouble with selective love and loving
Is that too often we select and love
The wrong things for the right reasons
And the right things for the wrong reasons,
Which leads me to conclude that marriage
Is the last resort for a happy relationship
(And it's so risky, too!)

22.

Marriage is an institution, a fine institution,
For one who wishes to be institutionalized
with guided restrictions, uncompromising guards,
And being only as happy as she says you are to be.
And, anyway, who needs happiness to love?

23.

"Love 'ain't' what it's all cracked up to be!"
No? Well, what is nowadays, unless it's Humpty Dumpty,
And he needed all the help he could muster
To be able just to *re*-survive!

24.

Love does make all of the little problems go away.
They go away to return compounded into one giant iron-bound one.
Most loves do not forget to remember:
They just forget to remember not to forget,
Which is a double-said way of saying: "So long, honey,
It's been really something else knowing you."

25.

When you're waving that final goodbye to her,
Better hire a siamese-twin octopus to do the job
For added, realistic, and lasting emphasis.

26.

It's funny how enterprising beach lifeguards are:
How they search for more female near-drowning victims
To be sure they haven't lost the mouth-to-mouth
Resuscitation know-how.
Now about little old ladies and fellows,
Well, now wouldn't that be another story!

27.

Love is the root of all money,
And so he went out to own a forest of
Very fresh saplings. (And flourishing ones, too.)

104

She had to relinquish the title of "call-girl"
Simply because nobody would call her.
And when *she* did, nobody would answer!

29.
I say let love grab you, twist you, shake you,
Chill you, hammer you, shove you, pinch you,
And turn you every way—but *loose!*
And stand you, stand there, look love dead in the eye,
(The way you'd look at a major sun eclipse
Without eyeball protection!)
The results will be the same!

30.
Now when the honest-to-stomp-down-goodness
Kind of love rolls your way,
Whether in the dark, mildew of a midnight
Or in the eyeball-open-burning glare of noon sun,
Or in the quieting hush-ness of a fall evening
Somewhere in Upper Vermont
Or 'way 'cross in Pine-Cone, Montana,
Or in noise-filled, auto-jammed, skyscraper-knocking
East Chicago, Illinois, or Metropolised New York,—
When this kind of love lopes in, kid, just duck!
If you can, or if you cannot,
Put up a daggone good resistance fight.
But whatever, let love know you're no meek milquetoast,
Hang-dog type of a fellow. Hang tougher than tough.
And (who knows) just as love came barging in
With no rights of yours respected and all,
Then maybe love will limp and slink out the backdoor
Of your life once one more time.
And you can live again, not forgetting, however,
To look over your left or right shoulder from time to time
Just to be chary, and just to be safe, you know.

31.
Well, we've known all along my heart was tissue-paper thin,
And that the least pull would rip-rip that heart apart.
We both knew this—even at the very on-set and out-set.
Yet you tore it into the tiniest of pieces for the wind to
Play havoc or pick-up and scatter game, which it did,
Sending each piece into so many unreachable and strange
Universes of abject wonder. And now I'm in pretty bad shape.
We both knew this would happen. We both knew it.

32.

You "brought me a 'new kind' of love."
True, but I haven't got used to the old love yet,
And you know how slow I am to change.

33.

Goodnight, Sweetheart, whenever you are, wherever you are,
And. . . . .*who*ever you are.

34.

Dear, to "make me what I am today,"
Must have taken an awful lot out of you.
Really, you shouldn't have bothered.
I was so beautiful the way I was.
(I really was.)

PART II CRIME AND THE CRIMINAL MIND

1.

They say you cannot cheat an honest man. Perhaps that's why I'm always being "had."

2.

Inner cities boast endless petty crimes that make big city headlines. Outer cities point to fewer but bigger broken laws.

3.

"Wine, women, and song" have made many a man go wrong who was headed that way anyway. (Only with these he went faster.)

4.

Oh, but had I known "the gun was loaded," I more quickly would have pulled the trigger.

5.

The judge gave him twenty-five years for his law-breaking activities, then added five more in case he'd try to have some cut for good behavior.

6.

The Judge asked, "Did you abscond with the company money?" "Abscond?" came the query, "No, Judge, I had a good time with women and drinks and the horses."

7.

It was an Inner City crime with Outer City implications.

8.

When the Next Big Global War comes along, I intend to be the very first one to volunteer—for peace.

9.

Odd, but a war of nerves is more devastating than the war that wrecks the physical aspects of the body.

10.

Yes, I raised a patriotic son. He even volunteered when the armistice was just signed.

11.

I'm the total consummate thief, I even steal from myself just to keep in practice and in trim.

12.

I took the high road to crime because it had the brightest lights, the clearest signposts, and the smoothest walking surface!

13.

After the man who robbed me was hanged, vociferously did I fight to end the viciousness of capital punishment.

14.

If I had to live my life over, I don't think it would be behind bars or within the bonds of matrimony.

15.

Some headlines are so glaring they encourage and attract the criminal mind.

16.

Often the quieter the judge, the stiffer the penalty. And often the louder the judge, the stiffer the penalty.

17.

Would-be murderer, why not choose to kill some *time* instead?

18.

He's a reformed convict: He's now re-formed his strategy for new assaults on society.

19.

Although he was in for life, he made big plans for "tomorrow and tomorrow and tomorrow."

20.

Many times when a judge rests a case, it's because he's tired of the palaver and rhetoric on both sides of the case.

21.

Why complain, my pet? We all can't be a modern Marie Antoinette.

22.

The inmates at the state prison voted the warden the "one most likely to . . ." (And he did.)

23.

In criminal accounting, the first to go
Is always the "small-time Joe."
Both you and I know

Just why this proves to be so.

24.

Is it a crime to "take the bull by the horns?" Ah, no, the real crime is ever deciding to let go!

25.

Nothing is more heinous than the white collar criminal who is so unctuous, honey double-sweetens itself in his mouth.

26.

I wonder why more public cooks aren't jailed?

27.

Most criminals who turn state's evidence and *sing* to the authorities, usually wind up off-key and behind the turnkey.

28.

Oh, boy! I have what it takes! Yeah, and the police are on the lookout for you to take it back, too.

29.

I encouraged my husband Joe to be a criminal because I wanted somewhere different to go to visit weekends. I think Joe understood, too.

30.

Give him the bullets—he doesn't need the gun.

31.

"Judge," said the man in the docket, "I'm so confused, I don't know if I'm going or coming!"

"Man," said the Judge, "relax. You're *going!*"

32.

Funny how the biggest liar is the first to swear it's the truth, unadorned, and solid!

33.

Just before the smooth-talking New York real estate salesman had just completed the sale of the Brooklyn Bridge, a giant cable snapped.

34.

"A doctor started me out on a life of crime!" he wailed. "A doctor? How?" was the question.

Answer was: "He was my pediatrician."

35.

Most police join the force to avoid a life of crime. Others join to lead such a life.

36.

That gossipmonger dug up so much dirt she buried herself in the debris, thank God!

37.

You think the economy is bad in England *now;* just suppose Robin Hood had stolen from the rich to give to the rich!

38.

He was very short on the truth but very long on lies.

39.

Do you think "Ma" Sutton could have made a cool million if she had penned a book, *My Son the Thief*?

40.

We—you and I—know every group has its own "Mafia"—yet we are so brutally prone to attribute this title solely to the Sicilian mind at once whenever the term is mentioned—another one of our dumb failings!

41.

He was such an inveterate thief he went around and picked up cases of measles and ringworm.

42.

What! Wouldn't it be horrendous if the police-trained canine should defect?

43.

Funny indeed how we applaud one who steals a whole Brink's car with millions, and madly castigate the purse-snatcher who swipes a handful of pennies.

44.

"When did you first exhibit proclivities for the role of thief?" asked the psychologist.

He answered, "When I first stole my baby cousin Effie's diaper pins while she slept beside me in the same crib."

45.

The story was so fantastic! Did you make it up?
No, the story made *me* up.

46.

Are you head of the law enforcement in this town?
No, just the law.

47.

After my brother the lawyer finished handling my case,
The jury promptly put my brother in jail in my place.

48.

"Here I am lying in this jail
With my face turned to the wall!"
(At least, friend, you do have a wall.
Just suppose you had no wall at *all*!)

49.

"Our father who art in Heaven,
Hallowed be Thy Name."
Lord, set me free from these cold gray bars
And I promise I'll pray just as hard all the same.

109

And, Lord, if you really want me to,
I'll even pray more sincere for you!

50.

Now, Judge, if you up and send me to jail, I'll never, never forgive myself!

51.

When the judge throws the *book* at you, at least try to pick out a funny page to read.

52.

Why is it all butchers grow the *biggest thumbs*!

53.

They suggested that I straightforth be remanded to the prison for the criminally insane, but I wasn't too crazy about the idea.

54.

Crime in the streets is not nearly as commonplace nor as vicious as most crime behind closed doors.

55.

I'd rather be a little fish in a big pond than a big fish in a small pond, knowing how water can evaporate so easily.

56.

A judge may forget, but the convicted one always remembers.

57.

"How's prison life?" he was asked after serving fifty-five years.

"Oh, I've seen better days," he answered, "but I can't quite remember when."

58.

I'm not trying to form a corollary here, but have you noticed the overwhelming number of Blacks and Spanish-speaking young men who make up the prison population, and the overwhelming number of Blacks and Spanish-speaking young men, women, and children who make up our great ghettoes—huh? Now, mind you, I'm not here to form any kind of corollary.

59.

The convicted man had so much class he wore his silk tuxedo when he went to prison and tipped the guards for escorting him to the prison gates.

60.

"Ooh," said she, "I never saw a man I didn't like, good or bad!"

"A double ooh," rejoined her love-starved friend, "I've never seen a *man*!"

61.

He was arrested for eating garlic in the small elevator, did you say?
No, he was arrested for not having enough garlic to go around.

62.

Say, here's a quick test for your stereotyping inclination: A Black man and a White man are walking together down a jewelry-shopful street. Someone shouts out, running toward the pair, "Stop that man! Stop that thief!" How many of you instinctively would grab for Mr. Black, huh?

63.

Strange, but we as beings profess to abhor crime and the criminal, but look how popular the criminal bent in drama, for example, has caught our fancies from Shakespeare on down to Ellery Queen (and beyond!)

64.

Odd how the greater our nation's affluency, the greater the crime rate and evidences of moral decay. Sort of reminds one of old Sodom and Gomorrah, eh?

65.

The only being to steal for "peanuts" should be Jumbo, and with his advoirdupois, he really doesn't have to steal for *any*thing!

66.

"Officer, why's crime so out of hand in this small town?"

"There's an easy explanation, sir: faster cars and fewer traffic jams around here."

67.

What's worse than being a police officer's wife who lives in fear for her husband's welfare is the wife of the big-time crook who knows the intent of her husband is to create disastrous and so often fatal situations (and without remorse).

68.

Hey, Warden, who's that banging on the bars to get out, Joe Judd?

Naw, that's Bill Willis rattling to get back *in*!

69.

"At least," moaned the inmate inside for homicide, "the man I killed didn't have to suffer as long as I have—and *will*!"

70.

In prison it's not daylight that is so long; it's the dark-time that seems interminable. And can you imagine the life of an inmate in the Land of the Midnight Sun when the sun reverses itself!

71.

Perhaps there was a gap in clear communications here, or something, but when the old jail resident asked the newcomer, "Say, what're you in for, murder or theft or libel?"

The newcomer replied promptly, "Naw, for twenty-five years."

72.

"Well," opined the inmate with Gertrude Stein-ish metaphorical tendencies, "if I were between a 'rock and a hard place,' I'd take the hard

111

place because a hard place might afford some give here and there, but a *rock is a rock is a rock is a rock.*"

73.

He chose to go to prison because he loved the color and cut of the prison garb. That's why the fashion-design-minded should not take all things so seriously!

74.

All's fair in love and war—if you're on the winning side.

75.

Gladly, anytime I'd go to prison for years if the warden will give me my own passkey.

76.

I agree: To the victor belongs the spoils—if they are rotten and foul-smelling.

77.

He was jailed for lack of evidence.

78.

You've convinced me. Now convince the judge—and yourself.

79.

At last, at long, long last, I found twelve honest jurymen, but no one to prosecute. Now what'll I do? (Why not investigate these twelve honest jurymen? I would.)

80.

That Judge Joe Jacobs was slow to anger, but quick to prosecute.

81.

Now just *how* venerable are the members of the Supreme Court? (Why not ask them? These venerable members of the Supreme Court will readily tell you without hesitation. (Whether you'll believe them or not.)

82.

Ah, bring back the "good old, crime-free days!"
You mean before Adam and Eve?
Of course, honey.

83.

He was such an honest and model prisoner he drove himself to the prison and served a spotless four months of a seven-year term.

84.

The saddest thing perhaps about his act of thievery is that he purloined a penny whistle that wouldn't whistle (and it cost him a ten thousand dollar fine!)

85.

As a close friend I elect you to faithfully defend my right to be wrong (if ever I chance to be!)

86.

Sir, as a traffic officer, I'm arresting you and I'm impounding your car. Why, sir?
For having a car so old and moving so slowly in a thirty-five mile an hour zone, you're being charged with parking.

87.

I went fishing for evidence but I got hooked on truth on the scales of justice.

88.

By the time *he* finally got out of law school, Blackstone had turned to white sandy gravel!

89.

It's not the drug users I abhor so much as I do the purveyors and profit-making leeches who help to initiate and perpetuate the need for the drug users in the first place!

90.

Letting the "punishment fit the crime" would do you a most grave injustice, for a single smile from you could gain you seven-to-ten on a felony charge for doing bodily harm.

91.

Name me the cure and I'll find the ailment, or kill some soul in the process!

92.

It doesn't matter who was the greatest gangster: Jesse James or John Dillinger or Pretty Boy Floyd—they all fell dead each with his head full of lead.

93.

When I said, "Go West, young man," I didn't mean for you to stop in California. I meant "West" in its metaphorical and metaphysical larger sense!

94.

Possibly the best way to prevent all future wars is to cut down on the child-population, thereby reducing the war loss count. If this should keep up long enough, the world will have to re-introduce a new Adam and Eve—right where we came in in the first place!

PART IV

"Verse in the Long Run" (THE LONGER POEM FORM)

A Statement for "Satchmo"

oh, little black man
of the immeasurable soul,
with that silver-bright liquid music

that honey-flowed from
your trembling horn-of-jazz-a-plenty,
now that you have put aside that tool of joy,
have passed that handkerchief
for the final moment of exhaustion
across a steaming brow,
please tiptoe in cushioned shoes
across the crystal floor of God's heaven,
over those streets of jaspered beauty,
close your eyes,
rest from your cares.

Tonight, all of the Storyvilles you immortalized
with your *scat* growl and bubbled zest,
rise up as one in polished memory of your name,
sing your name,
letting words soar to spheres unknown,
reverberating from all Mt. Everests of the world.

the Storyvilles can never forget what new-born pleasures
you gave them.
Paris, Rome, London, Accra, Dakar, Moscow—
these were home to you,
and you to them.
Wherever you went souls, revitalized with the saints,
went *marching in!*

Oh, great black man
with the frog-throated voice,
who's going to bind the forces,
hold them in place,
now that you are stilled?
Dolly and that *St. Louis Woman*—

will they find their rainbowed ends, answers?
Their dreams of contentment—
will they be realized now,
now that you have left the "scene"
after pleading their "righteous" cases
for all these years on riverboats,
dancehalls, dust-covered floors,
in grand ballrooms,
one-night stands,
in peanut shacks?

What *is* going to happen now,
O Mr. Jazzman's jazzman,
O Mr. Ambassador, "Daddy," "Pops,"
of the hot licks and happy runs?
Is *Mack the Knife* leaving town for good
with his *Back 'o Town Blueberry Hill*—
What *is* going to happen on *Blueberry Hill*—
no more thrills, no more willowed windsongs there?
Will the *Harvest Moon* still spill over the spot
in mantled darkness?
And *Froggy Bottom*—
who's going to help the souls down there believe
that a light-beamed tomorrow's coming,
especially for them, especially for them,
and *Beale Street* and *Basin Street*
and Lenox Avenue?

It's a long, long haul from selling coal
to painting happiness stars.
Few can make it—few ever do.
But you did, *Louis*, you did!
you made the trek over the broken glass
of disappointment,
through barbed-wire barricades of despair,
of that ever-present monster *Fear*.
made it without the schoolroomed books,
without ivied halls and tasseled caps.

and kings, emperors, queens, potentates—

all begged to "sit in" on your *sessions*,
because they knew greatness.
nor did you have to claim a *cause*—
your voice, your horn, your strength
to weld man to man,
voice to voice, dream to dream,
were cause, and cause enough.
though the world may not say so at this hour,
we know we were made ten thousand years younger,
made a billion-billion richer
by that spirit you've left upon this land.

o mourners, recipients of jazz' happiest sounds,
toll the malevolent bell slowly, so slowly,
pull down the shades of *l'allegro* for a spell.
robe yourselves in somber silks, your softest hues.
the man with the horn has ceased to speak,
the man with the horn has bowed his head.

now, houselights, fade two by two,
drop one by one, like teardrop pellets
on a kettledrum, upon this silent stage,
as death rides in on a minor scale,
as death shifts in on a minor scale,
as death slides in on a minor wail,
as death freezes in on a cold, blue note.

7/27/71

News Inventory

So what else is new?
Oh, I have uncovered many things,
many things that would raise your brow,
make you sit up and take notice.

I have found out that the end of the rainbow is at its beginning;
the Man Without a Country has a brick bungalow in the suburbs;
Gunnar Myrdal has identified an old European Dilemma;
that Frankenstein is going steady with Little Bo-Peep;
and Red Riding Hood is green with envy!
So what else is new?
Oh, I've uncovered many things,
many things that would raise your brow,
make you sit up and take notice.

I have found out that Eldorado was *not* a Spanish dream,
embellished upon by Edgar Poe—
Eldorado is located on a map, drawn to scale, one and six-tenths miles
from Johnsville, U.S. Route 1007—
only Rand-McNally has the exact topographic description in a secret vault,
and plans to commercialize it just after World War III;
that music charms the savage breast,
but drives the civilized insane;
The Trail of the Lonesome Pine is not as lonesome as it used to be;
I have learned that Miss Greta Garbo did not really "vant to be alone;"
that "Beauty is *not* in the eye of the beholder"—
(that which is homely is homely in *any* man's visual neck of the woods!)

So what else is new?
Oh, I've uncovered many things,
many things that would raise your brow,
make you sit up and take notice.

I have learned that books banned in Boston are read there *first*,
and City Fathers operate an Underground Lending Library;
that breast-fed babies hate their mothers, but love cows;
that the affluent are not *less* promiscuous,
but can afford to be *more* discreet;
I have it from unimpeachable source that the South is really going to fall
    with "the fire next time,"
but Jeff Davis is coming back to live in a five-flight walkup on Seventh
    Avenue in Harlem;
that Schubert's *Unfinished* will be completed by a computer for electric
    guitar and bassoon.
I have discovered that, after all the heat and hate in this world,
a little cross-eyed, broken-toothed girl, giving away rose petals, is going to
    set us straight;
that America will send over an Indian sailor and discover Europe and
teach the natives how to make true Pilsner beer;
I have learned that Little Jack Horner lived in a *circular* house and never
    celebrated Christmas;
that Christ's modesty is too self-incriminating for this crotchety world.

So what else is new?
Oh, I've uncovered many things,
Many things that would raise your brow,
make you sit up and take notice.

I have been informed that all of the "Arizona Bad Men" were killed with
pea-shooters by a band of Tom Thumbs before they got one-half mile
    west of Philadelphia;
that Mr. America is in reality *Miss* America who took up weightlifting;

I have learned that children have dug up the secret of love
but won't give the formula to anyone over fifteen—
I mean they really know about *love!*

So what else is new?
Oh, I've uncovered many things,
many things that would raise your brow,
make you sit up and take notice.

I have discovered that the British have lost their English accent,
and speak with a distinct Mississippi drawl;
that Mr. William "Count" Basie really taught Mr. Erroll Garner, who, in
    turn, showed Mr. Van Cliburn;
that the deadly espousers of hate and separatism are great lovers of the
    human race and unity when they are alone;
I have found out that there are no "blues" in all of St. Louis;
that there *was* joy in Mudville because Casey hit a "four-bagger,"
but was the victim of bad press coverage;
that girls have finally admitted they chase more than they are chased.

I have learned that children have dug up the secret of love

So, what else is new?
Oh, I've uncovered many things,
many things that would raise your brow,
make you sit up and take notice.

I have learned that a moment of truth
is equal to a lifetime of despair and doubt;
that tall trees do not grow on low ground—
they just *seem* taller;
that over-hygienic practices have killed off more romances
than dirt has ever mutilated;
I have seen more hobgoblins, Ralph Waldo Emerson, than you could
    shake a stick at,
especially in the hallowed and cloistered halls of learning;

121

that Utopia is just around the next corner shooting craps with Prosperity,
but this highway has no curve for the next 20,000 miles;
but I have also found out that *Hope* has "Come-on" signs all along the
 pike;
and I have discovered the words *children* and *truth* are spelled the same—
only the *adults* pronounce them differently;
that "Faith of Our Fathers" was not always the strongest faith;
that the jug is more precious than the liquor it holds;
I have learned to dream in reality and thereby lull myself to sleep;
that the color of a man's skin, like the size of his heart,
identifies himself only with himself and none other.

Yes, I've uncovered many new ideas
and reviewed ancient ideals,
have learned to live with countless things,
but mostly I've learned to live with myself.

I have learned that children have dug up the secret of love

so nothing else need be new!

1968

"We Consider Them Heroes Around Here"

(Statement purportedly made to a news reporter by two young teenagers
when asked how they felt toward the two whites who firebombed a black
home in Rosedale, L. I., in an effort to keep the black family out of the
almost all-white neighborhood, early in January, 1975)

oh, poor dumb, and twice-more dumb children,
with eyes of shatterable stone,
whose bones are narrowed to mere spikes of clay,
mere stiffened blades of winter-burned grass,
of seedless wheat, earless corn,
whose tongues are split by the magical evil
of a modern-day sorcerer's apprentice,
these utterances that i give you
are poured out, brimful of compassion;
these snowflaked tears of salined sadness are poured for you.
(and yet they really are not for you,)
for how much of this hallowed existence
you yet have known, encompassed,
have tasted beyond the dry-rot attitudes
that have already made shambles of your lives—

lives that could have flowered into wholesome minds,
now made emotional wrecks of what could have been wall-to-wall, world-
wide hearts?

look how you so early in pubescent growth
have shattered your vision,
muddied your once clear pools of inner peace!
see how vast rivers and rivers of future tranquility
have been dammed, clogged, cut off before the waters
could sluice away all pseudo-ethnic fears!

why should your earth in its infancy run to rust
before you could quarry under stone to know its gold?
why should your rose lean budless, drop leaves,
and sprout knife-thorns for you,
while your tender hands bleed,
and you did not even plant the cause!

you are not the gatekeepers of hate —
only the children of the gatekeepers;
you are not the perpetrators of sin —
only the offspring of the sinners;
you are not the originators of the evil —
only the mouthpieces of the evil-doers,
programmed into splintered ways of treachery!

"we consider them heroes around here."

(the firebombers you so labelled in your childish praise) —

and well you could, children, you whose tomorrow
has already stretched back into
the shades of a long miasmal yesterday,
since we have re-defined our *heroes*
and their roles in our national scene today.

(didn't a *watergate*-accused one consider himself a martyr?
didn't a leader of great and moral trust reject a request for forgiveness?
didn't many suspects in high places receive plaudits for war-time mas-
sacres,
and *expediency* became the watchword that retched before the altars of
our gods?)

the shame, the terror, boys of rosedale,
lie not in what thing you have pronounced,
rather, the shame, the terror, rise like banquo's and caesar's ghosts
from those who have taught you to say what you have said,
from the putrescent lips of those who begot you,
the institutions who knew all along the direction
such wayward words would lead:
the temple, the church, the school,
the little league this and local chapter that—
these all were the immaculate conceptual designs of hate—
you merely the unwitting vessels through which
the flow of life must pour,
must pour its lava of hate or its *milk of human kindness.*
and the abject silence to counter your young voices
offers bitter testament,
lends but a shadowy aura of suspicion
to my total wonder of it all.
the adult world must know, but will not let *you* know,
that yours (words) are timebombs
that split belfast into civil pain,
that yours (words) are timebombs
that lay the groundwork for the middle east futility,
allende's chile,
castro's cuba,
viet nam, lower and upper,
boston and her busing and her schools,
warsaw and watts,
that yours (words) are timebombs
for all the larger and lesser evils that beset us!

oh, trees, so young, so unfit already
for greener, larger growth,
no suns of power can ever grant you
deep-seated security,
no multi-aria-ed birds can ever blend songs
through your leaves,
nor can children of another dawn
scatter their prisms of happiness
under your shade. . . .
unless—unless—
unless a force far greater than that
which has used you today as tools
can wipe clean the slate of your false notion

of every man's worth—

unless unless
unless and until
such an awakening blooms into your bloodstreams,
fires your total beings,
your present concept of *heroes*
will continue to rain down
streams of pity for you
and for those who cursed you thus—
streams of pity for you
will escape my burning eyes.

1/75

"Requiem for Pablo Neruda
(Died Sept., 1973)
No me faltase en vida,
sino en meurte—
Neruda to Cesar Vallejo

today this arching moment
this sickening second
of new-discovered sorrow
i have beaten down cacophonies
of new-discovered sorrow
from the decibels of my voice
this voice that once so stridently
rasped your name
i have cooled the fires
have doused tall-flowered flame
that once burned away
silvered memories of you *pablo*

the raucous black crows that swarm your fields
fields alive with growing spring
crowned greater with the density of hope
where lovelier birds would sing
these crows that devoured each fluting dream
are all now forever slaughtered by me
with these hands red-ripe with predators' blood
predators that lie stretched before my feet
as did those sailors aboard that craft
lives cut short by doubting mariner

125

blue with invective on pallid lips
within gelid eyes
given way to riotous death

such an act my seem spurious
overburdened with tedious laughter
but see the way the globe of my desires
has turned its axis swift
but see the way i have returned to comets
that once spelled out wisdom of your speech
the comforting blanket of your charm
which vanity made me spurn
but see the way hurricane winds that ripped to earth
each guidon of joy
your strong arm raised to *eros* to *truth* in my name
but see the way such storms have whispered
down to a zephyred beauty
breathing a perfumed wafture
upon your petalled mouth

lately how often have i screamed in a canyoned silence
seeking to flee the leaning sword of damocles
in times like these
lately how often have i witnessed other shadows
other forms substances yielding
thinking those deep-pooled eyes
still more plumbless than your own
thinking their uttered words
far more prophetic than the syllables
you scribbled upon the sands
words you laughed into the arms
of rolling trade winds that swept over chile
and worlds and worlds beyond
thinking their pungent claret
more red more heady with *truth*
than your own cup of musky wine

now this lamentable downpour
that weeps to slush these arid lanes of my desire
has come too late for new-spring sowing
for future harvest bins
for the drouth of my sorrow to know release
to rest assured mind assuaged

(and how i have aged)—
has come too late to resist a roaring fall
(and more's the pity of it all)

turgid drumbeats of mockery reach my ear
this timeful *now* this wintered *here*
and each drumbeat but a venated leaf
of tortured grief
hammering a frost-eaten ground
filling an emptied cornucopia of whirlwind
reaped from a desert of sifting sand

but such are the ways
these arrowed ways
pablo neruda
that point my tomb of uncreative despair
where now your sharp prophecies evoke shimmerings
from a million evening stars
but only over my decaying universe
whose ears are stopped with clay
whose eyelids are sewn shut with wastrel threads of darkness

too late i and my universe seek to raise this monument
to the purity of your song
to the clarity of your warning
too late we have sheared our everests of vaunted glory
too late too late too late too late
so *pablo pablo neruda*
outwardly we weep
for the *inward* dreams you offered
that i and my world were far too blind
to keep!

10/73

In Memoriam for Bill Blaes, Teacher-Friend
(Killed in mysterious plane crash)
-1962-

the broken candle leans still,
a sputtering flower of light,
though acrid wind disturbs
this solemn ring that guards the dead.

127

and death, or the state of death,
unlike its counterpart life,
awaits no longeer with pale fears crossed
clawing the impending silence—inevitability's stoic doom.

a silver-tan moth
(order of lepidoptera,
of nocturnal or crepuscular habits)
born of a spring's ripening into summer,
in bold and great committed circlings
you move from tinted candle flame
to rest upon the hand-closed eyes
of this one i loved so freshly dead!

o moth, silver-tan, that is,
(order of lepidoptera,
of nocturnal or crepuscular habits),
of all the countless objects,
things, materials, identities, labels,
            objets d'arts, etc.,
you could have found upon which to rest
            inquiring feet,
your fatigue-burdened wings,
why did you choose these shuttered eyes,
now darkened beneath twin-ashening lids
of this my time-deep-stilled friend?
are you, normally timorous one,
ephemeral sojourner of light,
nightly flutterer—
are you immune to such a profound passing?
or is it because you know,
unlike we human ones,
once breath-gasps conclude the mortal frame,
this higher order of beings,
that we so highly praise,
once it turns to outer darkness,
it is no more than sodden stump,
than alga-ed stone,
than crisp, venationed leaf,
than bird egg
once the bird has flown?

o moth!
o crooked candle flame,
say it cannot be so
not to me who's left here alone,
nor to my friend who somehow had to go.

"Looking for the Moment"
(A Declaration of Interdependence)

I'm looking for the moment
when "all god's children"
will really be *all* god's children—
and not a man-appointed select few.

I'm looking for the moment
when the term: "brothers under the skin"
has given way to "brothers *outside* the epidermis,"
and there can be no question of genuine brotherly love
and all that piety-sounding goodness;

I'm looking for the moment
when "a little learning will (*not*) be a dangerous thing,"
but will be a germ fatale,
and the cure will not be a thing
to be avoided or denigrated;
I'm looking for the moment
when all the mirrors of the world
will have cracked into a zillion pieces
so we can stop looking at ourselves in admiration,
and come to see each other in a true wholesome light;

I'm looking for the moment
when all the tenets espoused by all the ordered religions
of the world will dump all philosophies but one,
and that is: *respect for each other boils down to*
respect for ourselves,
that heaven's highway is not as rocky as non-believers
would have us believe;

I'm looking for the moment
when problems of "race relations" will only refer to:
stock car or horse or foot,

and not to the disgusting over and undertones
they now generally suggest;

I'm looking for the moment
when no one will need "an ounce of prevention to
pit against a pound of cure,"
and "socialized medicine" not the pariah big business
and the AMA declare it to be;
I'm looking for the moment
when we show genuine shock at the foul-mouth
and not at those other souls who remember and respect
the sensibilities of those within earshot,
and the very young;

I'm looking for the moment
when marriage vows don't get confused with divorce ceremonies,
and live-in arrangements will die a fast and most
inglorious death so children can realize that there
is sanctity in marriage after all;

I'm looking for the moment
when whites don't shift their seats
and their eyes when they sit next to me, to black me,
in a public situation, even to this day,
then feign a total sense of innocence if suspected;

I'm looking for the moment
when integrated *working* conditions
spill over naturally into integrated *living* conditions,
and we don't grow into a nation of races divided
on a part-time living basis,
when five o'clock no longer casts such an ominous shadow
at clock "punch-out" time;

I'm looking for the moment
when priests, ministers, and all members of the cloth
are no longer put under the microscope of social and moral
scrutiny due to the few miscreants who abound to taint
the name and tone of the altar;

I'm looking for the moment
when we realize that "all the world's *not* a stage,"
or does not have to be regarded as such to bolster

our pathetic ego-trip desires and inclinations,
our self-created image about our pristine imageries;

I'm looking for the moment
when the bibles of all religions gather *less* dust
than the "porno," soap opera, and murder video contraptions
this wide country over;

I'm looking for the moment
when blacks realize that often we, too, worship at hate's citadel,
and raise obnoxious flags of pseudo-piety at the originators of such hate,
and that any form of retaliation, whatever the reason,
has no place in true soul-searching processes for honest
development of peace of mind;

I'm looking for the moment
when those profess to "make-the-world-safe-for-democracy"
will stop and destroy every indian reservation in this country
set aside for the "original settlers" in this land;

I'm looking for the moment
when "majority" man and wife who so open-heartedly adopt
the lost, the destitute child from foreign shores,
yet find it convenience-policy to overlook brown and
black babies down the block or around the corner;

I'm looking for the moment
when the *real* traffickers in drugs and degradation are exposed
for the *big* business cartels they really represent,
and can no longer hide in anonymity or in the inviolate
legal verbal manipulators so they may yet "reign supreme,"
while short, *small*-time hoods of the minority elements absorb their rot;

I'm looking for the moment
when big publicity seeking leeches, no matter their creed,
color, or "persuasion"
will be exposed for the gutter scum and maggot-growers they truly are
and their blind followers who relentlessly accept their pathway
through the slime and mental torpidity on their way to
private and personal hells come that dead reckoning tomorrow;

I'm looking for the moment
when we can become as contrite in daylight

as our consciences make us appear when we're alone
before going to sleep at night;

I'm looking for the moment
when "responsible" adults excoriate the "art" of graffiti for
what it really is: despicable desecration of our visual and moral sensibilities
and not some "personal venue" of "expression"—self-expression,
thereby, promoting such desecration to a point of no possible return;

I'm looking for the moment
when youth will admit there *is* joy in honest labor,
and that age *does* know a little something about this world after all,
and that same age can advise and consent upon more than one occasion;

I'm looking for the moment
when mothers and daughters put aside their antipathies
and see themselves as they really should be,
when fathers really become the honest "heads" of the house in
a most viable way, giving less attention to homerun hitters,
blocked punts, and placing a "pair" in the fifth at Hialeah;

I'm looking for the moment
when executive privileges are *rightfully* earned and *not* gained
through clear cases of deceit and/or favoritism;

I'm looking for the moment
when our big corporate entities stop whining poor mouth about
such giant "losses" when their single leaders still reap millions
year after year, gained upon the backs of the little men and women
in their employ;

I'm looking for the moment
when we refuse to deify the mundane, the cheap, and the crass,
and turn to admire the simple beauties in genuine human exchanges
of honest ideas and heart-felt emotions,
when the video and television monsters will no longer be the signal
bell in the village square of our existence in america;

I'm looking for the moment
when america will be more concerned with a sense of inner security
than with the gaining of the two-car garage, the fur-lined mink,
the cloud-touching antiseptic condominium
to emulate the selfish monied few of the world,

when there'll be scant need for the annual pleas of the Salvation
Army and the child welfare committees, not to mention the homeless
that wander a wilderness of despair in a community running over with
    plenty;

I'm looking for the moment
when we won't have to worry about "giving millions for defense,
and not a cent for tribute,"
as the "bigshots" of the world will realize that wars are not fought
for pride, apple pie, baseball, and mothers and one's land
so often as they are for well-publicized propaganda-mongers
who feel the need to gain more at the expense of the weak and the
    ill-informed,

I'm looking for the moment
when "moon" and "june," though thought corny,
can revitalize pure and genuine romance fevers,
thereby helping the young to stay as young and as innocent
as we have allowed them *not* to become;

I'm looking for the moment
when we can honestly say; "my country, right or wrong (*only*)
when my country is *right!*"—and not in any other instance.

I'm looking for the moment
when we shall cease believing that really we are immortal,
and realize, as dylan thomas said that we travel "from the womb to the
    tomb" in one unerring line,
nothing more, nothing less;

I'm looking for the moment
when libraries throughout our land no longer have to depend
upon hand-outs and "begging drives" to survive,
while movie houses, videos, tv's, portables, and "walkmans"
all are staging landslide business respectively—
and getting richer;

I'm looking for the moment
when family life replaces family strife
and an equanimity of trust can rule under each roof
here and throughout the broken, and breaking-down world;

and, finally,

I'm looking for the moment
when I'll no *longer* have to be:

"looking for the moment."
                september 20, 1990
                the donnell library
                manhattan, new york

For Howard Beach—A Litany Ballad of Pain
(On Dec. 20, 1986, a trio of young white fellows were among others
accused of beating three young black fellows who had entered "their"
almost-totally white neighborhood of Howard Beach, a tiny, almost insu-
lated community, a beating, so stated, which led to the auto killing of one
of the three black youths, a Michael Griffith. The subsequent furor on
both sides of the fence left the city of New York in a most distressful mood
for days and weeks.)

This following cry is for all of our city:

howard beach,
howard beach,
are you too far gone
and out of reach?

scores of your inhabitants
made clear just where they stood
(as if they could—or should!)

and with no uncertain clarity
they boasted of their insularity
as the safe, magnetic key
for a community's insured harmony,
as proof positive,
how they've lived,
and have been taught to live
(but really lives in a rusted sieve!)
beyond the space that freedom wants.

and unless, bitter ones, some greater than your own
cleanse this numbness that's invaded your bone,
a world at home and world abroad, being filled with haunts,
will turn in smouldering wonder
at "approved" hurt done by a few

134

that must foully soil each and everyone of you
for tearing decency all asunder
(and the rest of us fellow new yorkers, too.)

but silence has a power-way
of quietly saying all there is to say,
(and still more
that whatever's been pronounced before!)
without ever lifting a fist,
(though justice must and should insist)
without her naming a single name.

and yet there has to still remain
indelibly the blot of shame—
—the mark of cain—
inking within known and secret list,
whose sense of respect and fair play
is answered harshly or gently so,
pray sanity rules another day,
not pouring damning pain on pain,
watch democracy slip down the drain,
reminiscent of the nazi way
you recall fifty years ago;
and there is still such sick'ning bane!

howard beach,
howard beach,
are you too far gone
and out of reach?

and though the facts in time be known,
much of the "pride" you once possessed
has crumbled now; it all has gone.
and who it is who could have guessed
so very bitter and intense
would be your local vehemence
for perpetrators' strong defense!
is this a lack of moral sense?
(if so, o god, the recompense!)

neighbors, we hope we're not alone
because *your* woe is all *our* woe!
and can you show but callowness,

too rooted to apologize!
we here who also suffer stain—
we pray and beg so otherwise—
or dare not raise our heads again,
or face a world's sharp-probing eyes!

oh, howard beach,
oh, howard beach,
are you *far* too far gone
and so, *so* out of reach?

                                12/29/86

The Black Land
(Make-Believe Return to Normandy Beach)

The sun, the part that's left, crumples down
like a broken wheel out of sight,
leaving a dry blackness.
And a hoarse bird coughs out a failing note.
This is a world of foolish stillness
where the eyes of dead men rise up and glow
like stars with a chilly heat.
They creep over the barren land like a magnet
searching for rotted flesh and bleaching bones
the wind uses for calcium reeds, blowing the crying tunes
of a thousand silenced tongues.
This is the land that still bleeds dry blood
which the wind sifts upon unfallowed soil.

Out, out beyond the knobby hills trees stand
with their shaven heads and shiver and rasp,
still creaking the way they did when steel
cut away their greening, reaching fingers.
This is a hollow land, more dead than death itself,
more lonely than the wastes of a desert;
but this is a desert, a desert made by man,
and only frequented by the ghosts of lost youths
who re-trace their ragged steps inch by inch
in quest of the promise borne by fire,
but the fires are out. It is dark.
There will be no reaping this autumn;
this is the black year in a black land of destitution.
No hands will probe the soft bowels of the earth

to shake the potato free, to shock the corn,
for the hands have lost their strength
and the heart its faith.

This is the dead land where only the dead
are alive and living fallen.
And the voices of the youths are heard
seeping through the air, this thin, dry air.
One of the figures picks up a handful of soil and murmurs:
"Here is no seed growing. That is strange."
"Not strange," says another, "for it is past harvest time."
Then a third whispers, "There has been no harvest. There has been
    nothing."
"But I thought the land would fairly smother in grain. They promised,"
    protests a fourth one.
Then the shadowy figures with the voices shift away,
back to the ruffle-less sea.

They leave the unflourished wastes,
back into the safe arms of death;
and the wind still rises, blowing the music
through the calcium reeds over this black land,
while the hardy bird coughs his notes,
and the shaven trees rasp, their stubbled arms grasping at nothing.
                    10/49

Receiving the News of Marshall's Dying
(The Summer an English Teacher Heard the News of an Ex-Student's
Death in War) — True Account —

Now try as I might I cannot diffuse
this flypaper summer heat
with a wave of a power fan, a swig of water,
with sparkling soda and doubtful scotch,
T-shirt and Alpine-shorts,
and pull down the classroom shade of memory
for yet awhile.

And I had planned to make no plans,
(think no thoughts of pseudo or real intellectualism)
recall no verbal battles on verbs,
on the nominative predicates,
on nouns in apposition or opposition,

137

nor consider the Ancient Mariner
as ancient, modern as tomorrow morning,
think of no smudged notebooks,
reviews, spelling rules, skim-reading,
(quasi-answered quizzes)
(and multi-answered multiple choices,)
nor what Brutus' pal Julius and certain
politicians of the moment have in common,
the origin of the words we use, or should use,
and why we use them.

Oh, I had planned to make no plans,
nor turn back to canned experiences
compressed among the printer's pages,
and thus let time's zenith interlude
weave its sultry spells.

But I was wrong, young Marshall!
How very wrong I was!

Charles—you remember Charles,
Charles of "No Homework Fame,"
who sat squirming behind you through all
those tortuous days when diction and dictionary
meant not half as much as the set shot
on the schoolyard basketball court,
when Billy Shakespeare took a back seat to
the *Hotrod Journal*—
Well, Charlie I met the other night
and he told me about you,
the news of how you were spilled out in
the ash-green jungle,
how you had served your time,
had ended your tour of duty,
and how you volunteered for another round
to stare unflinching again into the yellow eye of war,
and how you died ten thousand miles from home.

Your jolting dying unwound the clock of time
and brought you back to grace that room once more,
brought you back to grace that room once more,
to grace that room once more,
from the five warm Septembers ago,

from the five crisp-blanched mid-winters now past,
from the five lettuce-fresh Aprils now historized.

I review how you did not feel the need for essay rules,
and themes and special levels of language.
You, Marshall, remember how you questioned:
"What's the use of all these special styles and rules
on how to talk and how to write?"
And I smilingly protested,
the snobbish protest of language teachers.
"To be understood and to understand
is good enough for me," you grumbled on.
And thus we reached an impasse of steel—
you stoutly gripping your point,
as if it were an iron handle to gain support,
and me seeking to shake you free
as if you were a ripening apple that refused to drop.   Throughout the
     learning season we stood our ground,
with only spring and promotion relieving you of me
and all the clattering parts of speech
that fell from the open pocket of your agile mind,
tumbling about like useless scraps of iron.

This night, Marshall, old youthful adversary,
the dead coals of yester-when
reflame a moment
and your voice re-echoes these
ten thousand miles (as the crow or B-52 flies,
whichever comes first),
returns one hundred thousand miles (as the pain of war flies),
with death shaking an angry stick,
blowing ear-splitting sounds to the be-medalled deaf,
who cannot choose but listen,
blowing ear-splitting sounds to the unimpeachable deaf,
who have called the "shots;"
(Oh, what a vicious pun,
and at your expense, my boy.
Forgive!)
"To be understood and to understand . . ."
the teen age voice trailing off again
as though a smokestack of smoke had swallowed the sounds.
But those words crackle back tonight
in sardonic prophecy.

139

How right you were!

What good could word declensions serve you
west of Da Nang,
seven kilometers south of Pleiku,
nearing Saigon, Quinhon,
the other places you could not spell nor pronounce?
What matters now that David Copperfield
was Charlie Dickens scrawled on paper;
or should it read: "if I *was* you" or "if I *were* you"?
Did you foresee this joke that I was teaching,
while you heard in some faint distance
a louder roar of a future hand grenade,
exploding along the corridors of your mind?
Did you sit there in Room 114 and sense the feeling
of real loneliness in a ghost-guarded rice paddy
when I droned that "Once upon a midnight dreary" line?

Marshall, you must have seen beyond the closed-in walls,
beyond those rigidly-lined chairs, name-marked desks,
that gray-green dust-powdered chalkboard,
for now at this pinpointed spot in time,
though fleeting and muffled,
I hear your prophetic laughter cutting this flypaper heat,
re-arranging the false calm of this July haze.

How right you were!

"Names of persons, places, or things" did not mean a single damn
the moment you lost it all among the vines in Somewhere, Vietnam.
August 12, 1968

To Look and *Not* See at the Fair
"(A slim woman in a white dress and white shoes came out of the hotel
and walked down the driveway towards a car. A man stood holding the
door for the woman. She came right past James Metcalf *and she did not
look at him.*"—Reporter Jimmy Breslin, N.Y. *Post*, 8/7/68, Miami, 1968
G.O.P. Presidential Election Campaign Convention, where James Metcalf, thirteen year-old speaker from the Poor People's Campaign, stood
with a group just outside a hotel, exhorting the Republican Party members
to consider the plight of the poor in its platform.)

—Oh, you've been so long at the fair!"....

... "And she did not look at him."
Oh, reporter with the lucid mind,
the snake-quick eye,
the elephantine memory,
she saw, Miss White Shoes, White Dress, saw!
She saw more clearly than she or any colleague
would care to remember.
She saw him long before she chose her crisp wardrobe
for this gathering at the Fountainbleau,
long before she tasted her first very dry martini,
her tossed salad, her baked blue fish, creole,
potato *au gratin, aperitif*—
much longer,
before she became enamoured of the workings of any party.
She did not look because she *saw*,
and *seeing* carries more impetus than *looking*;
for when one sees,
he perceives, absorbs the full weight of color,
measures the broad scope of sound and sight,
... and *contemplates*.

Jimmy Metcalf's pubescent voice pushed through the plush,
through the glittering glamour,
as only a child who is brimful of hope can sing,
as only a child who is bred in sorrow can sing,
as only the voices of those just beyond the "tracks,"
in the *Other* Miami of Florida can whisper,
over there, there where the tropic houses hunch together
like beaten curs in the mawkish August sun,
where the roadbeds are paved with dead palm fronds and sardine tins,
where vacant lots of the land sprout multi-colored slivers of broken glass,
where the vacant lots of the mind lay strewn with multi-colored slivers of
    broken green dreams,
and dead-end streets all lead to further dead-end streets.

Jimmy Metcalf's exhortation knifed through the mechanical
sound-tracks with the clarity of unbroken truth,
as only a child who has been bred in sorrow can sing,
as only a child who is brimful of hope can sing.
And he sang: (And his followers answered him.)
"Starvin chillun down in Marks, Mississippi!"

141

Tell it to em, brother!
"Senator Eastland throwin food into th river!"
    Stick to the case, brother, stick to the case!
"All the money for Vietnam . . ."
    stick to the case, stick to the case!"
No money for the Poor People's Campaign!"
    Oh, yes! Stick to the case, brother, stick to the case!!
"Mamas and papas got no money for their rent—
brothers and sisters got no shoes for their feet!"
Tell it to em, brother! Lord, tell it to em!
"What you goin' to do, Mister Election Man,
what you goin to do?"
Stick to the case, brother, stick to the case!
Yes, my Lord, stick, stick, stick to the case!

Above it all, this is polish-and-diamond
and so-many-hundred-bucks-a-plate-spread country,
butler-and-maid-and-governess-and-doorman-and-chauffeur
and-shoeshine-and-caddy country,
big tips-and-painted-smiles-and garnet-studs-and-stickpin
and screwdriver-and-pink-lady-and scotch-on-the-rocks-lightly
and bloody-Mary-and daquiri-and-white-lightning country.

Above it all, this is May Day in early August
and playground for the elite—
only the Convention Calendar provides the reason,
affords the legitimate excuse.

But—below it all,
under the total confrontations,
it is more than these.
And that is why the Lady of the White Shoes
did not have to look.
She knew that beneath this strip of fashions and facade,
beyond the sonorous sounds,
the orderly and ordered manners,
pinwheeled, automated gesticulations, innuendoes,
the clean jokes and the profane snickerings,
this meeting of the general mind and common accord—
this meeting is in mean and rugged terrain
of the green bereted concepts,
of the pull up by your own bootstraps mouthings,
of the sick and tired of the permissiveness attitudes

that pervade and persist;
this is forward position where the tinsel of the cinemas
has grown entangled with the tickertape of Wall Street,
and one can scarce note the difference;
this has become the domestic DMZ,
where the terms *welfare* and *crime-in-the-streets*
turn into steel fortresses in the valleys of the closed-off minds,
where compromise in war is tantamount
to submission and loss of face.
The Constitution and the Bill of Rights
are mesmerized wooden words of rotting clichés
in the deliberate mouths of the masters.

Here, at the Fair,
under a sprinkling of rapid stars
and southern evening duskiness,
where the Fountain of Youth has temporarily been found,
despite the Seminoles' misguided lurings centuries ago,
where it effervesces higher and purer than ever,
amid the computerized neon gods and goddesses,
as the real night swoops down around
the little Black Gadfly from the Delta Lands,
and around Miss White Shoes and White Dress
who did not look
because she saw too well the true image,
reaching up and out beyond this,
this beachcomber's mechanized paradise,
rising like a spectral trumpeter,
sounding a platform of warning,
while an orange moon lifts
the tenebrous tides again—
somewhere a fisherman swears softly
at his tangled nets.

                                        August, 1968

**A N.Y. Public School Teacher Ponders Recent City Corruption
Charges, and Remembers Carl Sandburg's *The People, Yes* (1936)
/ The Donald Manes Tragedy / Mar., 1986**

This cold etching winter rain,
This nail-driven sleet,
This biting snow!
Still trying to survive it all—

Though barely, though barely.

Today I am made even more cold,
More wretched,
More mentally disfigured
At revelations of such shocking dimensions—
Those strange "shenanigans"—
Some may politely name them.
I name them uncaring, despicable explosions
of the soul and heart,
Unearthed in this our Big City Rake-off Scandal,
Immense Rake-off of '86!

Headlines scream down,
Across the world,
(And within the secure and secured confines
Of my corporate being,
Of our New York City corporate being:)
Graft Runs Riot!
Bigwig Takes Life!
Corruption Runs Rampant!
And on and on they run,
Testimonies of filth and deprecation.
And here I stand (we stand)
Numbed by these shockers,
Poisons dripping of human
Of unsuspected treachery.

Poet Carl Sandburg and his long-agoed voice
From his volume, *The People, Yes*—
His voice cuts through this frozen,
This sickening atmosphere.

(And I quote):
When hush money is paid
To whom does it go,
And by whom is it paid
And where should there be a hush? . . .
And if a boy fresh from college and the classics
Offers the point: Money sometimes rots people,
He'll hear from someone:
Maybe so, but can't have too much,
Too big a surplus to take care of the future . . .

Money is power: So said another one.
Money is a cushion: So said another.
Money means freedom: So runs an old saying.
Money is bigger than talk talk.
Money buys everything except love, personality,
Freedom, immortality, silence, peace.
Money buys food, clothes, houses, land,
Guns, jewels, men, women.
Every man has his price.
Money breaks men and ruins women.
No ear is deaf to the song that gold sings.
There are some who can't be bought.
When you buy judges someone sells justice.
You can buy anything except night and day.

So wrote wise, old speculative Carl Sandburg
Some long fifty years ago,
Carl Sandburg of Galesburg, Illinois,
Who not only knew a thing or two:
He knew several things and more,
And thus his power-house words,
Vital, gripping, and prophetic,
As truth-telling as a well-oiled grandfather
Clock announcing the correct time of day,
As a Farmer's Almanac telling next year's
Days, weeks, and months on a calendar—
These words buzzsaw their monotonous way
Into the bloodstream of my (of our) total being(s)
As I look out in the gray winter-solsticed distance,
The block-topped domes of this my (our) city,
Butting their dark heads into the low-hung
and ominous clouds sweeping the world,
Domes that house
The hopeful and the hopeless,
The magnanimous and the narrow,
The raucous and the modest,
The over-glib and the under-silent:
The *haves* and the *have-nots,*
As well as the *never-will-gets.*

And these iced, iced-edge scimitars of deceit, of chicanery,
Loom more cold, more imposing, more sharp.
Trust and *faith* become words excluded from shibboleths

145

When one mentions *justice, honor,* and *fair play.*

The winter storm yet rages, grows worse,
Over-hanging and "hung-over" with polluted
Meanings, skies of acrid pain and disbelief,
Until such utterances: *Whom can you trust?*
As well as: *Why are we always to last know* syndrome,
As well as: *Why are we always so, so totally misled*
By those whom we faithfully choose?
These words themselves soon burgeon to be shibboleths
When one mentions *justice, honor,* and *fair play.*
(And here we repeat.)

The winter storm yet rages, grows worse, even worse,
As these words grow also within the realm of their own
Meanings and over-all implications.
They razor-hone themselves more keenly,
More profoundly bitter and debilitating,
With each new four-star edition of
The Daily Evening Chronicle,
The New Morning Knickerbocker Tabloid,
The Weekly Warp and Woof Gazette—
All, all ablaze with more lurid acts
And more putrid dealings!

Suddenly—suddenly I remember:
This dirt is of my (our) generation,
This shame is the shame of my (our) associates,
Compatriots, fellow-travellers, neighbors,
Of my (our) voted-for, voted-into-power grabbers
Of decency and incorruptible promises!
And who have turned the crystal waters of purity,
Of *faith,*
Into the rankest gutter sludge and impotable
Waste slime reneged upon by even the cess-pool rats!

Now what can I tell the sea of restless,
The asking faces of children, the students,
That fill the empty spaces of my *sanctuary,*
My upstairs Room Number 409,
In the middle of the building?

I peer out beyond these bolted windows now

146

And hear sleet-ice ditto
Out its crackling insistence.
I hear wild Canadian rocket gales snarl,
Then go angrily around this
Glass, stone, brick, and metal place.
And grimly I feel the pointed drill-bit of winter cold
Grinding and challenging the comfort of this place.
Yet there can be, there can bloom,
No mightier hurt
Than the pain of every day's new ugly truth
Spewing itself across the landscape,
Beyond the blotched inkspots
Of the fast printed page,
Hissed and cajoled out by newshawks
At every newsstand in this my (our) curious
And vibrant city, lashing and leaping out
Like the anti-bodies into the braincells of the mind!

Then, uneasily I pull each classroom shade,
Turn off each room incandescent
As unknown gremlins snicker and lurk
Every empty and hollowed corridor.
Carl Sandburg speaks again:

We'll see what we'll see.
This old anvil laughs at many broken hammers.
Whether the stone bumps the jug
Or the jug bumps the stone it is bad for the jug.
We all belong to the same big family and have the same smell.
Handling honey, tar, or dung, some of it sticks to the fingers.
The liar becomes to believe his own lies.
He who burns himself must sit on the blisters.
God alone understands fools.
The sea has fish for every man.
Every blade of grass has its share of dew.
The longest day must have its end.
Man's Life? A candle in the wind,
Hoar-frost on stone.
Nothing more certain than death
And nothing more uncertain than the hour.
As wave follows wave, so new men take old men's places.
The people is a tragic and comic two-face:
Hero and hoodlum: Phantom and gorilla twisting

To moan with a gargoyle mouth.
The people is a polychrome,
A spectrum and a prism.
Man is a long time coming.
Man will yet win.
Time is a great teacher.
. . . . With a great bundle of grief
The people march . . .
The people, yes . . .

And then I say to Mr. Sandburg,
"Carl, I do know it's the people, *yes*,
But I wonder when that permanent,
Nailed-down, honest-to-goodness yes . . .
When will that *yes arrive?*
But for now do I have to sing,
To paraphrase
These my failing days
With the following thing:
Do I *have* to sing:

"My country (our) country—
My (our) city,
'This of you,
Metropolis of honest hue,
To you I (we) cling.

Streets where my (our) dreams reside,
Monument to human pride,
From every landmark's side,
Can *new* hope spring?"

Hesitatingly, I close the door.
I walk out into the gale.

I bow my head.

—March 29, 1986

Long Overdue: Commentary of the Mind

it's long overdue
we stop exploring the outerspace of the cosmos
and start seriously examining the innerspace

of our hearts;

it's long overdue
we see ourselves as others see us
and respond according to the dictates
of truth and honesty,
and deep-bury the ostentatious attitudes
in which we cloak our real identities;

it's long overdue
that we face ourselves squarely in the daylight and crowds
the same way we face ourselves in the mirrors
of all our midnights and are all alone,
acknowledging we more often sin
than are sinned against;

it's long overdue
that we make our nightly prayers
more creative and less repetitive,
hammering God with patent-made words
of empty and rote supplications;

it's long overdue
that we legalize the precepts of the basic
and simple Ten Commandments,
and not use them only when we *stumble*
across a biblical quotation,
or when we are in an hour of stressful need;

it's long overdue
that we end abruptly this "battle of the sexes",
when, after all, we all know one can't honestly
survive without the other,
knowing also, and full well, the fall and denigration
of one sex signals and fall and denigration of both sexes;

it's long overdue
that before it's too late we lend help to our children
to gain or re-gain the wonders of childhood,
a thing we've taken away from them in our sense of
false *maturity* and often adulterous machinations of
complete disregard for the puerile minds and souls—
(while we curse their veneered sense of rebellion

149

and resentment)—
when deep down we know we are rebelling and resenting
our paternal failures of our own self-interest existence;

it's long overdue
that we open up our closed-off minds
the way so many of our narrow White Americans have fled
suburb-wise and closed off communication lines with
the remaining underclasses of the urban world,
offering pseudo-abhorrence at the "shocking" antics
of those *thems* left behind, when we all know the root cause
of much disenchantment rests with Majority Man's insistence
that God made America for the White Man and Big Business,
and that all "others" mere servants to the machines of industry, commerce,
and often, religious tenets which the Majority Man blueprints for his own
sense of self-esteem and false sense of superiority;

it's long overdue
that the churches, synagogues, mosques of the world would change the
spelling of *churches* to Church, meaningfully noting the capitalized
version, and not help to promote divisiveness through the strange concepts
that those present churches' "way to salvation" is the only way;

it's long overdue
that cobwebbed and "glitzy"-tongued politicians be called to task
for their continued lack of compassion for the wills and the constituents
whose hard-gained cash and votes-of-faith elevated them to such an
    honored
plane for public service,
and we should curse ourselves for being the annual, the perennial dupes
that we are that they stay or return to this plane, election after election
and vote after vote;

it's long overdue
that we de-emphasize the sphere of mammon's power that be-clouds
our impoverished minds, and we should reach for the inner peace
that "passes all understanding", leaving off the pace-setting drive
to "out-jones" the "joneses," that can only lead to soul disintegration;

it's long overdue
that we grant more personal and private attention to sex and its too-often
deviations which today's media so eagerly have thrust before us, and,

(worse), thrust before the impressionable and mixed up minds of our very,
     very young,
thus denying them the beauty and sanctity of such human relations;

it's long overdue
that we retain our private dogmas but without
going publicly *dogmatic*, or growing highly indignant in the eyes
of our (God forbid!)—detractors to such dogmatic observations;

it's long overdue
that this country become far more than the concepts of:
"only American English spoken here,"
(and with provincial interpretations!) no matter what newcomers
may say and how newcomers may feel to the contrary:

it's long overdue
that the Black Members of our Great Society stop self-denial and denigration through some foolish concept on the value of skin tones,
even within the confines of their own set aside world,
drawn up by the Caucasian-tempered ideology,
and these Black Members must emphasize the individual worth
based on the corpuscle color that courses each vein,
thereby gaining a true gauge of the nobility of self and self alone;

it's long overdue
that we accept all feelings of the Human Race,
remembering that God knew just what He was about genetically
much more than any demi-gods or social (?) scientist could project,
and see that we all travel in a straight and unerring line
from the "womb to the tomb" with no variation on this journey,
proving that the gravediggers must survive us all
until each gravedigger, in turn, must also (to paraphrase
Willie Shakespeare): "come to dust;"

it's long overdue
that we re-examine the natural vulnerability of the judge
as well as the jurors, remembering that a "jury of one's peers"
is not always a true and honest representation of "one's peers,"
remembering, as did C. Sandburg that when justice crumbles, someone
pays the judge for justice to crumble, hence making justice become one-
     eyed and soul-and-honor-slanted;

it's long overdue

151

that though we know a "leopard cannot change its spots,"
we know even more so that we are not leopards nor do we have to
depend upon circumstances of nature as provender for survival or demise;

it's long overdue
that we must realize that Life is not a lottery, nor is the
spanish phrase: *sera-sera* a clean and infallible theory
to pass on to a waiting and wondering generation
who must look to us for pure guidance,
or we'll reap (even more deadly than now) the whirlwinds
of horror of our misdeeds or the lack of our "good" deeds;

it's long overdue
that i spend more time with the mirrors in the eyes of others
and less time in the mirrors of my bathroom, when i'm sure that
no probers are about to probe, stop, look, and listen to the voice of my
    own private narcissus leanings;

it's long overdue
that we as Americans grow up and grow up quickly, if we do not wish
further embarrassments of the inequities showered upon the skies
of the inner cities, where in *real* reality is but the open manifestation
of all of America's lack of justice, fair play, honest evaluation;

it's long overdue
for the Majority Man to stop giving Black Man the sickening phrase
that reads gratingly: *my-folks-came-here-with-nothing-and-we-made-it,*
when underneath it all he forgets the damning words: *came-here* are not
    the same as *brought-here* implication,
and he knows even to this day the debt owed to Blacks (and *Native* Americans) can never be fully settled or adjusted—
for how can one measure mental pain and bodily anguish—
and the longer this concept is faithfully pursued, the longer shall
we pay in blood for such lack of reparations of the soul and spirit,
and as andy hacker, the social scientist observer, has put it: we shall
remain a nation—black and white—divided, a hell-bent idea the *"better-
    than-they"*-ism;

it is long overdue
that we must as honest human beings keep complaining
until outside there is no more raining,
no more shooting down the hailstones of unrequited justice
upon the unprotected heads and hearts of the many

who keep looking beyond the stars into the cobalted blue;

and until then, thus it will always be
long overdue!

—5/16/92
Citicorp Atrium: Manhattan

Commentaries From a Broken Mind

I'm getting fed up
with consumer reports that consume too much of my time
reporting much of which I already know;
with the war and the threat of war that rattle in the rusty throats
of decrepit and delusioned back-fence Napoleons and slick-handed
    money dealers;
with the products that swear I must grow thin or get my money back,
and when I put on 30 pounds and ask for my money back,
I find the shills have moved to another town with no forwarding address,
    setting up another row of calorie-fattened suckers;
with those under thirty who just *know* that all over thirty are dyed-in-the-
    wool "establishment,"
and all those under thirty are idealists intent on putting this Humpty-
    Dumpty Universe back together again.

I'm getting fed up
with Whites who lump all blacks in a common heap and insist they know
    the "nigger" like the "back of my hand;"
with Blacks who paint all Whites with the same paintbrush and know
    irrefutably the "Honky-cracker" like the "face on a clock;"
with clean timetables and dirty trains;
with beautiful doctors' offices and ugly doctors' bills;
with people having sexual hang-ups about birth control among the non-
    mammalians,
but don't give a damn about the welfare of Mr. and Mrs. World and
    Family.

I'm getting fed up
with Women Libbers who say they can and should "go it" alone without
    the male element of the human species,
and the male element of the human species who in many cases is willing
    to let them give it a try;
with the Middle-age Spreaders who say the new youthful religious cult is
    just a cult and nothing else;

153

with the oldsters who "live" their religion out of the corner of their mouths,
while regarding everyone else's way to Heaven as misleading or contemptible;
with the professional politicians who watch current "fad" bandwagons upon which to jump,
and then sneak off when the fervor of the novelty has worn off.

I'm getting fed up
with me admitting my shortcomings only to myself,
while extolling my virtues with a megaphone from every parapet in every town;
with those who believe that the Christian Brothers are the only real Christians in town;
with exotic-sounding perfumes used by females that destroy more than they lure;
with so many girls today who *can* cook the way "Mother used to cook;"
with folks lacking the guts to confess the truths to their rabbi, their priest, their pastor,
and their rabbi, their priest, their pastor half-listening anyway
because they have so many fears of their own.

I'm getting fed up
with children who fault their parents for all their failures,
and attribute all of their successes to their own indomitable wills;
with the drug peddler and the policeman who see things "point to point,"
"grass to grass," "powder to powder," and "cube to cube,"
and then accuse the "System" if their friendship is made known to all;
with the fanatics who push the "sec-America-first" concept, yet who
spend all of their money on overseas airline tickets and travelers' checks;
with the word "sale" in the windowshops that proclaim: *Our loss is your gain;*
with the frenzied racial outbursts by Whites who will use another guise when challenged for explanations.

I'm getting fed up
with cabbies who flash the "Off Duty" sign when they approach me black,
only to switch the sign back to "On" a scant block just past my reach;
with "ethnic" joke tellers who use "honest" presentation as an excuse for the jokes being repeated;
with the stranglehold that cheap TV fare has upon our young,
and the network's despicable tears about the wasted values of youth.

I'm getting fed up
with the puny regard with which the average Mr. America holds the
    memory
of Martin Luther King's monumental contribution to human dignity,
and the high esteem this same Mr. America retains for the football hero,
    the movie queen, and the "pop" musician;
with the way Big Business lies about: "What's good for business is good
    for the people;"
with the urgent way I whisper my prayers in moments of desperation,
and the way I grant God's ears a vacation during stress-less days,
giving credit to myself alone:

I'm getting fed up
with the rich getting richer and the "poor getting children,"
and the idolators of these favored rich whose telescopes can only spot the
    thousand-dollar banknote as a beginner,
and whose scales can only weigh bars of gold and miles of yachts,
whose peccadilloes are accepted as the mode of the seasons,
the "in" guidelines for daily living;
with those twisted Americans who indict twenty-seven million Italians for
    the sins of a few crime artists,
turning blind eyes and closed ears to Verdi, Michaelangelo, Fermi, and
    others;
with the concept that only Aryan beauty is the truest kind of beauty;
that the Bluebird of Happiness has never sounded a sour note;
with the Texan's notion that if it wasn't grown in Texas, then it can only
    be a midget at best.

I am getting fed up
with the blockbuster who destroys neighborhoods with his verbal poison
    and itching palm,
and even more with the souls who let their blocks get "busted"
because they substitute water for blood in their veins,
ice for the warmth in their hearts;
with Churches pussyfooting around political and social issues
by declaring, "That's not within the province of the pulpit,"
when the Churches know full well that Moses was an ace politician
and Jesus Christ the Number One Caseworker in and around Jerusalem.

I'm getting fed up
with those people who fail to see the Irish Cause in Broken Belfast
as the same as the Black, the Spanish Cause in Newark, the Chicano
    Cause in L.A. and El Paso;

with those who pleadingly sing, "Lead, Kindly Light," on the Sabbath,
then stumble the other six days in human darkness.

I'm getting fed up
with the ex-dreamer who swears that dreaming's out of style;
that this is really a dog-eat-dog existence
(and seeks scars to prove the bites);
with him who puts a price tag on everything,
including love;
with the many modern Jobs who revel in their self-woven sackcloths and
    their constantly-stoked ashes of despair;
with the wineglass without the wine;
with the change purse without the change;
the train fare without the train;
the map to happiness without a legend.

I'm getting fed up
with a billion false starts up Mt. Aspiration, although I know
fulfillment rests atop its highest peak!
And finally finally finally—
I'm getting fed up
with getting fed up!

                              - 9/30/72

Telegraph Wind from Cambodia: For the Children Caught in a War
    Children of Cambodia,
(Or should I say
Cambodian children)
The wind tonight works on
Hurried air wheels
For Western Telegraph,
And the message sweeps in through
The open window,
Beyond this sealed door,
Sweeping in painfully loud
And distractingly clear.

I hear the message,
And tonight when the bearer
Of such tidings, such sad tidings,
Has gone from my place,
I shall make reply,
I shall make reply.

This wind bites subtly tonight
At the tented edges of my conscience,
The place I call my body's home,
The temple of my mind.

It is not a crying wind
Like early April ones
That whine up and down
The frost-patterned wastes;
It is not a screaming wind
Like late March ones,
Antagonizing muscle and bone,
Tearing the eye.
But it is a wind of mean
Objective just the same,
For it transports to me all
The sounds of your brandnew terror,
The total terror of the forces
That invade your playground,
Upset you at the sanctuary
Of your hopscotch,
Your native version of Ring-O-Levio,
Double-Dutch jumprope steps,
Your blind man's buff,
Shutting off your personal joys again.

This is the wind that bites so,
So, so subtly tonight,
Wind fresh from the nauseating jungle morass,
Polluted streams made vile with
Past-tensed human flesh, bodies.
Bodies. Bodies. Bodies. Bodies.
Your visions of the *Sugar Plum Fairies*
Fade quickly once more
As your children's games
Grow, expand into grownup games
That play with the red-stained,
Red-steeled snarl of monstrous war,
With bloodied heads,
With slit tongues of silence.

It is a ginger wind that
Insists upon telling the truths

My television camera fails to record,
Of new hurts to your old wounds.

Now I smell the putrid heaps;
I can see active maggot worms
Drilling holes in infant skulls;
I can hear bubbling wails of
Hunger-pinched bodies.
Bodies. Bodies. Bodies. Bodies.

Oh, Cambodian babies,
Oh, latticed-ribbed Biafran babies,
What can I say that you have not
Heard, have not silently said
To an unrelenting world!
Jellied blood ripe, trembles in
Your unclosable mouths,
And flies have a field day
In the gashes of your scars.

But I do get the words the wind
Would have me know, nevertheless,
This wind that self-deciphers
All the words, all the signs.
I hear the message sweeping in
All, all too painfully loud,
And distractingly clear.

And tonight, when this bearer
Of such sickening tidings
Has gone from my place,
I shall make reply—

Nor do I know exactly what to say,
but, Children of Cambodia,
Or should I say
Cambodian Children?)
I shall make reply . . .
        I shall make reply . . .
        I *shall* make reply.

The Day a Stranger Asked about Martin Luther King, Jr.

"Say, Mister, what is this thing,
This thing about a *Martin King*
That makes so many people sing,
Calendars record, bells ring?"

Oh, Sir, where have you been,
And why haven't you heard?
Such a tremendous sin
If you've heard no word!
Not a hint of one so brave.
You must've spent years
In some sealed-up cave —
(Or in some grave).

But if you haven't heard,
I'll "put you in the know"
About a fantastic being
Who died over a score ago,
Died for *Freedom's Cause*,
To eliminate each unjust clause
That said upon this brown sod
We're all not God's children placed by God
For equality, and tried to state
That all God's children separate
Though all're chilled by the same wind,
Each and every living one,
And each one burned by the same hot sun,
Wet by the same pouring rain,
Soothed by the same love-words,
Hurt by the same human pain.

Haven't you heard of this preacher,
Man of God who faced angry mobs,
Yet swore equality's job the greatest job,
And the way to gain pride in this land
Was for every decent soul to take a stand,
Swear to the powers, sowers, the reapers:
We are our brother's keepers.
What scars Joe in Waycross, Georgia,
Wounds also Mary-Anne in Upton, Idaho,
We are responsible each to the other,
Matters not where we chance to go?

159

Though cut by stones, threatened by rifle and gun,
King and his faithful refused to run!
His great deeds, words, made us realize
We *could* reach stars that dot our skies!

When given thousands in his fight for peace,
He kept not a penny, nor did he cease
In his cry to make all Americans see
There's no such thing as *one-sided equality*!
If half of America was not free,
Then *none* of America could ever be!
It is a true fact for one and all:
If one is pulled down, then all must fall.

King even foresaw his untimely death,
Uttered words that pained his breath
When he said to a hushed, listening crowd
In icy words prophetic, not overloud,
An April Sunday when Martin paused to say:

Perhaps, folks, I may soon be forced away,
Forced to lie under worm-ruled sod,
Forced suddenly to quick-meet my God—
But I'm not worried about this dying,
So, if I go, contain your crying.
Don't make a big send-off for me;
Just say (if you need words to say still)
Say I, Marty King, just tried to do God's will.
Add this maybe, if you can:
"Martin only tried to serve his fellowman."

That was a Sunday when those words were said—
Four days later, Martin King was dead.
His prophecy rang out so true
As a Tennessee sniper's bullet
Immortalized him for *me*, and for *you*!

So, stranger, I'm right in my remembering,
And this the brief "bio" of a fantastic man . . .
And long will the world be in its remembering
About this giant of a man, Martin Luther King!
                                                    - 1/4/92

PART V

"A Gadfly's Gadabouts"
(HEART-CUTTINGS)

A Gadfly's Gadabouts

1. Gossip thrives on gossip; truth grows on truth, but truth prospers.
2. Erase lies, but underscore truths. So little of the latter seems prevalent nowadays.
3. He courts disaster? Shucks, he *married* misfortune!
4. Take me as I am—and maybe we can pick up some diverse attributes lying along the way to Self-Improvement City.
5. That you love me—that I don't doubt: It's my conceptual evaluation of myself regarding myself that has me worried.
6. The last time I thanked my *lucky stars*, a meteorite fell and punched a hole in my roof!
7. After you've come to *see* me, take a good *look*, and then go!
8. There are no disturbances of any sort on the Richter Scale, so why is our love on such *shaky ground*?
9. If I'm the "black sheep" of the family, at least my wool does not have to be dyed!
10. Maybe if I knew the meaning of *taciturn*, then maybe I wouldn't be so.
11. If your mother had known how you, Junior, would have turned out, she more than likely would have told your father to substitute a *frown* on his face for that *gleam* in his eye!
12. I've suffered so long, when I don't suffer, I suffer because I don't!
13. If you must take anything, take time to love the world, but don't necessarily expect total reciprocation in return.
14. There's no accounting how far love will go to reproduce itself—until you seek love to *extend* itself.
15. "People needing people" are the *only* people in the world, Joe!
16. Strange is the rooster that crows without an appreciative audience.
17. Remember, there are no *seconds* in a suicide!
18. No, dumb Al, internal affairs has nothing to do with upset stomachs!
19. Remember, it is better to bring *smiles* to the face than to bring *tears* to the eyes.
20. Just why *should* I doubt you?

21. When you can stop and admire yourself without a mirror, then, sister, you are in deep trouble!

22. Cry of the freed ex-housewife turned spy: "No more pots and pans; it's now—plots and plans."

23. "How're You Gonna Keep 'em Down on the Farm"—when the farm has now moved uptown?

24. At least no nudist can be a *casual* dresser—a *casualty* maybe, but certainly not *casual*!

25. The most appealing low-cut to him was the downside of a hamhock.

26. "If at first you don't succeed"—(why bother to fail again?)

27. He was so loud, even his sign language disturbed the whole neighborhood.

28. Be more hesitant to say goodbye than to say hello.

29. Be careful when she calls you the "picture of health." She may be thinking of having you framed and hung.

30. Isn't it odd how we are more concerned with fairplay mostly when we are treated unfairly?

31. Funny, how in every establishment there are always a few "left-over usables"—except in a bank!

32. Prosperous farmers love to belong to the National Garner Society having more than just *seed* money.

33. Sometimes miscellanies get all mixed up!

34. Too much of what we take for granted really shouldn't be taken at all.

35. There's no bigger fear than the fear of *not* being afraid.

36. Yes. The choice *is* mine: that's exactly why I'm so sorely distressed.

37. When you two seek to "say it with music," at least seek to *harmonize*!

38. Better sorry now and happy later than happy now and sorry later.

39. Strange, how country life generally terrifies most urban kids. Every time you say goodbye, I really expect a *good*bye!

40. Clockmakers seldom come to work on time. (And to them time is of the essence to their timeless profession.)

41. Why is it when I think of lilies, I think of funerals and funeral processions?

42. Make a meaningful *slice*—don't merely take a *stab* at life, Ed.

43. While celebrating and cerebrating upon being the finder of money, pause now and then to extend a bit of sympathy to the loser.

44. No wonder I have small wonder about you: you're not all that *wonderful*!

45.   "All Quiet on the Western Front"—but volcanic noises disrupt the other three points.

46.   Husband, of you the public thinks it knows. Of you the wife doesn't *have* to think.

47.   It's mighty tough being honest in public, isn't it, buster?

48.   Had the world let the *punishment fit the crime*, so few of us would be alive in the world today—right?

49.   I don't care if you *do* say that the *dog's bark is worse than its bite*, I possess cast iron legs, but *cotton-made ears*.

50.   Let the "dead past bury the dead," but be careful not to let the present inter tomorrow!

51.   Other than being in love, nothing else matters, really.

52.   He has a *way* with people. It's just too bad it's marked *one-way*.

53.   I haven't made up my mind about you, but when I do, I'll be the first to know.

54.   I gave up on yesterday when tomorrow kept getting in the way.

55.   Oh, I got enough of you and *still* had a lot left over!

56.   In most instances, the "best laid plans of mice and men," Robert Burns *should* go astray—and *stay*!

57.   Henry Clay opined, "I would rather be right than President." Boy, look how many candidates (and winners) have ignored his precept!

58.   'Tis said, "Heaven will protect the working girl." Boy! Think of the many females (workers) who will hastily challenge such a statement!

59.   "He that spareth the rod, hateth his son."—Proverbs XIII,24. "Oh, please, please hate me some more, Dad!" (Words from ten-year-old Ike.)

60.   You know, lover, of "Careless Love," his carelessness may just prove *deliberate*.

61.   Words from a desperate male-chaser: "Catch me if you can . . . (and I'll *crawl* away very slowly.)

62.   Sometimes, what you call *stardust* in your eyes, my deah, is in reality, merely coal dust.

63.   Spare not the horses—nor the riders!

64.   *Coming clean* may mean *washing dirty* in public.

65.   "Take me to your leader . . ." and perhaps we *both* may be rewarded.

66.   The cleanest beaches are people-free beaches. Strange, eh?

67.   Remember ascertaining is never the same as estimating—never.

68.   "Patience is a virtue . . ." (so I've heard somewhere a long time ago.)

69.   I may be *footloose*, but I sure "ain't" *fancy-free*, honey!

70. Don't "show me the way to go home." And I sure wish you could. You see, I'm homeless.

71. A wise man never admits he's wise and a fool never admits he's a fool.

72. If love chooses to remain, who must care what else should go? It hardly matters.

73. Nail-biting is not the only sign of a soul's uneasiness.

74. Only brag about your seeming longevity when tomorrow grows *securely* into yesterday.

75. Sure, there's a *doctor in the house*—(but he left his stethescope at home).

76. At least Life *precedes* Death.

77. The greater the scorn for Heaven, the greater the admiration of you for Hell.

78. Re-dredging up the dregful does not do well to re-cement old relationships.

79. How true is *true-blue*—or is there such a measurement for loyalty? (Or need there be one?)

80. If you do chop down the Flower of Wisdom, you'd better save some of its seeds.

81. Only hate should be reprehensible.

82. Learn to savor solitude. Such a commodity is so scarce today.

83. If I have to remind you to remember me, well, I'm really not worth remembering, am I?

84. If you love humanity, you have to love New York City!

85. Better a "tiger by the tail" than a lion by the nose!

86. Be careful, doting mother, that your present "little shaver" don't grow up to be a big "cut-up."

87. "I would be true . . ." but who's there to believe me?

88. Today, "Shakie," "Much O' Nothing" is long overdue.

89. I feel much closer to you "Since You Went Away."

90. The "pen *is* mightier than the sword . . ." if employed with diplomacy and delicacy.

91. Do you really know what it means to be mean? I doubt it.

92 All *great* leaders began as even *greater* followers.

93. You know, I see a whole universe of sunshine—Beyond the "Shadow of Your Smile."

94. Forgiveness is the expiation of guilt on the part of the forgiveness-seeker. A soul's peace is the recompense.

95. Young lady, shyness is not the same as ignorance.

96. Love can cover a multitude of sins, but not *that* many!

97. Sometimes, it's safer to enter through the *back*door.

98. Self-denial does not always make one a martyr.

99. The only thing you can truly be certain of is the certainty of *un*certainty.

100. He stopped before he began just in case he couldn't when he got started.

101. Pious (?) one, why use a mirror whenever you pray?

102. Odd thing about youth: The more youth seeks to be different, the more youth remains the same. Right, Mr. Frenchman—*oui?*

103. Why seek an open line with God who's 10 billion kilometers away, if you don't speak to your neighbor whose property joins yours?

104. Bravery is very becoming in a mouse when the cat's been caged.

105. So few daughters-in-law are good enough for mama's first-born males.

106. It's as easy and as painfree as sliding downhill covered with glass and you have bare knees and uncovered bottom!

107. Have you ever noticed the belligerence of some health-food addicts toward the non-health-food *nuts?*

108. Meet me ⅞th of the way, and I'll *still* complain!

109. "To dream, perchance to *sleep.*" Somnambulistic anti-Bard quotation.

110. Nothing is more cocky than a crowing rooster with very little to crow about.

111. False modesty has really given true dignity a very bad, bad name.

112. *Today,* Mr. James Otis, "taxation *with* who's representing us is *twice* as tyrannous."

114. "Each to his own taste." True, true, Mons. Rabelais, but what some folks' taste represents is bad taste, even to the most generous observer.

115. Strange how the world's *all ears*—until I open *my* mouth!

116. Shucks, he *sowed* the whirlwind!

117. Only when you can learn to regret can you even begin to approach the Highway of Contentment.

118. I took it upon myself to thank you for myself. I'm just *that* benevolent!

119. Even Robinson Crusoe didn't want to be alone—not by *Friday!*

120. When one reads of ancient cestus-fighting as a bloody sport, one can only remember the *"gory* that was Rome."

121. I loved it when poet Edna Millay wrote with passion: "O world, I cannot hold thee close enough!—(until I realized that she had penned *world* and *not girl!*)

122. Thank you. You "took the words right out of my mouth." Now Mama won't have to wash my mouth out with soap!

123. To be sure that I won't get lost, I'll carefully follow you in the *opposite* direction!
124. "Children of a Lesser God"—(all seem to grow much bigger than the other gods' offspring).
125. Chocolates and ice cream—low-fat advocates' biggest enemies.
126. Stool pigeons lose all rights to sing the blues if the messages they disclose should backfire.
127. You gave me the right to be wrong—and I like it—being wrong, that is.
128. Not: What do you think?" but in *your* case: "What? Do you *think?*"
129. Speaking of "cabbages and kings," I'll take cabbages every time.
130. "I'll See You in My Dreams"—if you insist. But please don't.
131. "O Death! the poor man's dearest friend—The kindest and the best." That may be, Bobby Burns, but try telling that to the man who has reached *that* state!
132. "The more the merrier . . ." only when *I'm* not footing the bill, Will!
133. Even *flattery* from you is distasteful.
134. Because of the new special cooling system that's been installed there, snowballs do have an excellent chance in Hell.
135. Friendship is giving more than you get, and expecting even less.
136. To me nothing is more pleasant than an "Idiot's Delight."
137. Never use another's heart as target practice.
138. Sadly, in some cases, there's very little muscle in the "strong arm of the law."
139. Leaving things up to your own devices is not always most resourceful.
140. Please change your mind—when you *get* one.
141. Show me a fool, and I'll show you a mirror.
142. Will the "love of your life" become the "death" of you yet?
143. At least let your hate be consistent and sincere.
144. "What a Difference a Day Makes" . . . especially if you thought it was *payday*—and it wasn't!
145. Racial slurs and epithets are the surest signs of individual insecurity and low self-esteem.
146. Let love be your trademark and sincerity your hallmark of compassion.
147. It's never too late to say, "I do . . ." if you haven't already.
148. "Honesty is the best policy . . ." and it needs no underwriter except the seal of sincerity.
149. When I do go, don't let it be "Death in the Afternoon." Rather, let me slip down in some quiet and softly-painted sundown.

150. Parents, straighten up before the "twig is bent."

151. True, it was "written in the stars," but he never learned sky-writing.

152. When I grown old, decrepit, and irascible, blame it on my youth. If I am nasty, one of a terrible sorts, blame it on my age.

153. "It (Was) Is a Long Way to Tipperary" . . . until the shooting war actually started.

154. *He* has madness in his *method*!

155. Before you boast that your "home is your castle," better check the security of the drawbridge and the water in the moat.

156. So often "live wires" shock themselves while getting *grounded*.

157. To somebody "Spring Will (Always) Be a Little Late (Every) Year."

158. Fear is the only thing on earth I'm *afraid* of.

159. Successful teachers listen more than they talk.

151. I think he's really chairman of the *bored*.

152. I prefer character to reputation. Don't *you*?

153. A culinary cook is only a cook overlaid with snobberism.

154. Plan your old age carefully: you'll only have one, you know.

155. Remember, the greatest use for education is sensible application—not wanton experimentation.

156. Save me from myself, please!

157. Laughter is a true purgative to a wise man; it is poison to a fool.

158. Few strippers' smiles are genuine.

159. "If you can't beat them," *cry* for mercy!

160. Give me your hand to check for *weapons*.

161. I could do small things well, but who'd have a microscope so powerful enough to detect them if I did?

162. "You had it coming to you" . . . but you had moved.

163. Love spoils no one—the lack of it has ruined and devastated millions.

164. Christ's precepts were so easy to understand, but were so, so tough for human beings to put into practice!

165. Beware of the man who strongly says: "Trust me." I tend to feel he hasn't been all that trustworthy in the past.

166. You'll probably need *elbow* room to keep your adversary at *arm's* length.

167. Sometimes, in your daringest moments, mention to an Irish fellow about the "luck of the Irish", especially if that fellow's tenured job has suddenly become *un*tenured.

168. True the "world owes me a living"—and a dying. I'm not too sure about the former, but the latter is foolproof.

169.   Sh! The Bird of *Paradise* has just sung a love aria to the Bat Out of *Hell*! My! What's the World coming to? (Oh, I guess only *Heaven* knows.)

170.   American, when you judge skin coloration or colorization, as your chief criterion, the Court of Human Behavior should hale you before the bar of Justice as soon as it convenes.

171.   The inscrutability of the general Asian make-up and the illimitable verbosity of the Western structure should strike a happy medium near the African Gold Coast.

172.   Isn't it amazing how the Black Influence via vernacular, mode of dress fashion, and musical and dance expressions have so long been a part of the larger society of America, and yet White America, whether intentionally or sublimally so, have kept itself in a state of perpetual denial? It is almost ludicrous, isn't it, Charley?

173.   Great debatable contention: Which mother makes the better mother-in-law: the son's mother or the daughter's mother? If you know the answer to this sneaky puzzler, please let me know.

174.   Your credibility is in bad shape indeed if dubiety enters my thinking even *before* you utter a single syllable!

175.   He who lies about the "facts of life" to the young and inexperienced, should have the world tell the truth here about *his* life!

176.   *Change* has a strange way of repeating itself under the guise of *change*.

177.   There really is an art even to art.

178.   Even though the plates be foodless, one still must mind his/her table manners.

179.   One pristine idea is worth a sackful of fuzzy contemplations.

179.   That public speaker there shouldn't even be allowed to speak in *private*!

180.   Most children are not goaded or teased or lead into show enough concern where reading is concerned, parents.

181.   She left her calling card, but I was too deaf to answer.

181.   Before you choose to "go with the flow," it's best to know the *destination* and *objective(s)* of the flow, Susie!

182.   Too often the apology only exacerbates the offense.

183.   Keep pointing out my faults and ignoring my attributes, and pretty soon the former will at least triple the former.

184.   "Wait till it happens to you" . . . and maybe it never will.

185.   Please "Save the Last Dance for Me" . . . until late *next* year.

186.   Keep looking back at yesterday, and you won't recognize tomorrow until tomorrow becomes your yesterday.

187   History is what most of us wish never had occurred.

188.   We live by example, good or bad, if we live at all.

189.   Ancillary rights are better than no rights at all.

190.   Knowing what to say is not half as effective a knowing what to *do*!

191.   Townsfolks came out to give their "all-conquering hero"—*hell*.

192.   I've tried my best to doubt you, but your spotless innocence kept getting in the way of my nefarious motive.

193.   Happily he makes room for yesterday.

194.   The shadow hurt me more than the substance.

195.   After years and years *and* years of waiting. . . . I'm *still* waiting!

196.   Each time they declare "love is just around the corner," someone keeps straightening out each bend in my road to romance!

197.   It's lucky for the world that I am successful!

198.   Our first anniversary, dear, is nothing like the last one was, is it?

199.   "Clothes (do) make the man," O Didactic Poet, but not at a nudist colony, buster!

200.   Bigoted White Man, how can you honestly say your nightly prayers when God knows you've hated me, the Black One, long, long before the sun went down?

201.   "In the beginning was . . ." *this writer*, and all things subsequent are of miniscule consequence!

202.   What motivates me can often put you to sleep. *Often?* Heck, it generally does!

203.   The lives we eventually live are rarely the lives we set out to live.

204.   Isn't it strange (and yet so abysmally human) how we lay at the doorsteps of fate most or all of our manifested shortcomings?

205.   Merchant, don't let your sales pitch loom more bizarre than your bazaar here.

206.   What you do with your life *is* a concern of mine, neighbor, since we're all a "part of all that we met."

207.   Doubt me, so I can experience such a rarity among the wisdom-seekers of this world.

208.   Misquote me; folks'll believe what I say anyway. (Or is it because you *mis*quote me that their own lucid opinions are formed?)

209.   I have the right to be right, but, shucks, who cares?

210.   When you swear that you admire me, why do you always say it while you're looking intently into a mirror?

211.   True, even I can be wrong sometimes, but don't remind me. It might occur just because of such careless "remarkings."

212.   Even fools are believed, and wise men doubted.

213.   "Fools rush in where wise men . . ." fortunately escaped *from*!

214.   If it doesn't toll for *me*, what care I for *whom* the bell tolls?

215. There's an *enormous* price tag on your head simply because the "best things in life are *free!*"
216. Why wait till it's done before you believe it can be?
217. Falling in love puts the *faller* into a great unfair bind, if he/she can never pick him/herself up.
218. What is true lasts; however, what is last is not always true.
219. Discretion can often lead to a clear-cut victory to the patient.
220. "I'm a stranger here myself." . . . (That's why so many folks claim to know me.)
221. "Distance makes the heart grow . . ." but not always *fonder.* Never trust completely your new surroundings. Sit awhile and survey.
222. Eve to Adam after the Apple Fiasco: "Share the fame? Share the blame."
223. Even roosters know when it's time to shut up.
224. *New Testament:* "Physician, heal thyself." Jim Morris: "Physician, heal thyself . . ." or see your *nurse* or your *wife.*
225. The Devil can play politics. Shucks, the Devil *is* politics!
226. Most epigrams are best when *mis*quoted.
227. Yeah, "familiarity breeds contempt—and children," declares Mrs. Markus Twain, *I* declare, "Nowadays, just leave off 'familiarity.' "
228. Of course, I bring out the "best" in you! What else can there be in you, sweetest love-pip?
229. "Fame is the spur . . ." even when trying to ride a *dead horse!*
230. I would fervently seek to be famous, but just suppose one day all full-sized mirrors were broken!
231. Forsake me, but don't forewarn me.
232. *Old Testament:* "How the mighty are fallen!" Old Jim Morris: "That is O.K. with me: I have my own phoenix just waiting to rise, kid!"
233. "Herb" Spencer opined, (in so many words) "Civilization is a progress from an indefinite . . . homogeneity toward a definite heterogeneity." Don't you think, according to today's narrowing societal outlook and regard, that good old "Herb" S. is lucky to have lived over 100 years past?)
234. Weeping willows, rose gardenias, mockingbirds in song—what more does a lover of nature could ever long for? Or *need,* Francie?
235. There is something most infectious even listening to the genuine laughter of a fool.
236. Waiting is time unfulfilled.
237. Rabelais, you're right, pal, "Everything comes to those who can wait." And the rent, gas, and light bills come even if you cannot wait!

238. Funny, how we ascribe our sinning to a matter of being taught and/or fed misinformation—no thing of *our* own mis-doing.

239. Since "I've grown accustomed to your touch . . ." keep your hands off me!

240. In fact, more than every now and then, the scales of justice must be re-checked and re-adjusted for fear of a possible imbalance.

241. Only when you fail to recognize that you are a failure can anyone call you one.

242. When Death takes *me*, Edna St. Vincent Millay, why *shouldn't* he "be proud?"

243. Real, wondering young lovers, make your living one long poetic expression, but more metaphorical than "*simile-tic*".

244. I bet most of my ancestors are very sorry that they are.

245. Remember, alliances mean trust in the *first* place.

246. In the River of Life, be more concerned with what waters are emptying into, rather than where they spring from.

247. When do even octogenarians and nonagenarians all say, "Age before beauty?"

248. To many, "accidents" just "happen" to be accidents.

249. Too many of our ambassadors of *goodwill* become ambassadors of *pure evil*!

250. Let's build a bridge *now*, so we won't have to build one when we *get* there.

251. Nine times out of ten, if you wish to create utter contempt, if not total bewilderment, just mention the phrase "the good old days" to a Black Man!

252. In my case, I bet Sir Adversity pays a bigger tithe to Fate than does Lady Good Fortune.

253. Why, that accident took place on *purpose*! I'd swear to that.

254. Come to think of it, Clarence, when's the last time you saw an *angry* angel?

255. Despite those Rights Laws enacted by Congress in the mid-turbulent sixties, countless white architects of hate are still drawing up blueprints of perpetuation of discrimination. And thirty years later!

256. When all the "facts are in," Love and the Laws of True Love will win. (Now don't press me on a specific dateline, for there are far too many "facts still pending," Jose.)

257. As long as you need me . . ." see my brother Basil anytime.

258. I wonder, cowpokes of civilization, just who'd be around *after* the *Last Roundup*?

259. Often you can tell a man by the breath he wears.

260. Birdwatchers, check modernity and surveillance progress today. Now birds carry telescopes!

261. He got completely lost and discombobulated all because he let his *conscience be his guide*.

262. Sir, it seems that I made more progress after I *dispensed* with *blessing*.

263. A brothel is a social prison without the bars and jailhouse keys.

264. Your boldness has made me shy.

265. "Christ in Concrete" . . . or Christ in Cornfield—it really does not matter to the true believer.

266. Being *citified* is not the same as being *cosmopolitan*, Nan.

267. Out of chaos can come calm, but the deliverer of the chaos and recipient of it both must work or wish it so—and no one else.

268. Men love to show how much they've *spent*; women, how much they've *saved*.

269. Misery comes in all forms—so does a healthy outlook. The choice belongs to the receiver.

270. It takes courage to display courage.

271. Brutality should only be left to the brutes; after all, they invented the act.

272. Remember, wisdom does not come by the cupfuls, but by the eye-dropper holderfuls.

273. Recall more of life's beautiful occurrences, and less of the misfortunate ones, and, presto! before you know it, even the ugly take on a more amber and softer glow upon the segments of your memory.

274. Remember, not all our guesses are *educated* nor all estimations *conservative*.

275. Often, pessimists, open umbrellas give clouds ideas that hadn't even crossed the thresholds of their minds.

276. Shall we cry after the cheering has stopped?

277. Isn't it inane to say, "I *thought* to *myself*?"

278. Chauvinism has nothing, buster, at all to do with patriotism, war-lovers notwithstanding.

279. If you must cheat, make your chiselling neat, at least!

280. Always feel that the "wages of sin" are still too small.

281. Good and great melodies are never, never out of tune—singer and performer may be, but never such melodies.

282. You caused me to love! (And I was doing so very well *hating* the world.)

283. So often nowadays, I see, married couples get married life mixed up with wildlife, or have the two terms always been so easily interchangeable?

284. Young at heart   old in body (and *mind!*)
285. The whole point of the needle is to *have* one.
286. Had I known you in the old days, you wouldn't have the inestimable honor of knowing me *today!*
287. One of the language's major heights of redundancy is the many-times used phrase: "It was a *free gift.*"
288. Don't dare label yourself a legitimate farmer until you have had your first *genuine* harvest.
289. Did he leave the "Scene of the crime?" (Naw, he never *left* the place!)
290. As *long* as you're *leaving*, why take so *long*?
291. Hey, what's so *filthy* about being *rich*?
292. "Let us break bread together . . ." even if we're both not so hungry. (Or was the prophet referring to *another* kind of feast?)
293. Many a parsimonious employer will give no quarters to servants.
234. What's so unnatural about "loving thy neighbor," huh? (Or maybe I should address *myself* first on this issue?)
235. Remember you can never put out water with fire.
236. When you set out to be a hero, usually the heroic moment and circumstance never materialize.
237. Sugar or foul, flies don't discriminate.
238. At least by running around in circles, you can't get lost in unexplored territory.
239. Always save a little bit of the dream, even though it has mostly come to fruition.
240. In the face of battle: "To the rear—*run!*"
241. Even if the delivery is off, the material is awful, and presentation horrendous, please be indulgent to the up-and-coming-who-should-be-out-and-going-swiftly inept comedian.
242. I know "fame is fleeting," but I'm a very fast runner, kid!
243. "Shooting pains" often result from pains from shooting, Ed.
244. Remember, targets are for more than practice.
245. Why are the "idle" rich so *lazy*?
246. Greenness does not always refer to a state of ineptness.
247. The word discrimination is tough to spell, but even worse to practice.
248. It's not *what* you give that counts so much as to *how* you donate your object.
249. I'd much rather be a graduate of Ft. Knox than be a graduate of the School of Hard Knocks.
250. An absolute awareness of God automatically insures and assures you an awareness of Humankind.
251. It's so wonderful to be right . . . whenever you *can!*

252. Hate hits right where it hurts: in the *heart*!
253. The only thing that pessimists *smile* about is their constant ability to *frown*.
254. I wasn't headed this way, but the sign to disaster got turned around.
255. At least *he* aimed for something.
256. If you have faith in yourself, don't you be the *only* one.
257. Consider your faults, even if you cannot clearly see any avenue for rectification at the moment.
258. When you become the center of your universe, it's past time for you to search for newer worlds to explore.
259. My road that I walk may be straight, but, honey, it sure "ain't" *narrow*!
260. Did you know that many recluses lose their house keys deliberately?
261. That couple is so loving, a cross word to them would indeed be a puzzle.
262. If you don't worry about having to worry, chances are great that you won't *have* to.
263. Wisdom is simply mind muscles developed through hours and hours of rigid and tough thought processes at work diligently.
264. The gossip transmitters, when they've "heard it all," they still listen and hope for *more*.
265. The speaker developed great delivery technique, but there were none to receive his thoughtful and deliberative "goods."
266. When the heart of the matter does not matter, re-examine the matter of the heart.
267. When's the last time, Mother, you heard some sibling proclaim, "I meant to do *your* work today"?
268. She gave me a *complement*, and I smiled, thinking she was handing out a *compliment*. (Oh, the curses of improper *pro* and *e* nunciation!)
269. Please praise me, if you will, but please praise me with tongue in cheek. (It'll still sound, I'm afraid, just as sincere.)
270. Nightly, after hay-and-oats-chomping, the equine members of the world say prayers for the inventor(s) of the now indispensable horse*less* carriage.
271. For ideas to become more than ideas, substantives must be added with special and definitive deliberation, Son.
272. Even mosquitoes can teach the human specimen a thing or two about selectivity and perspicacity with a *bite* to it.
273. Fast lover speedster, don't laugh too heartily over your track record. You'd better check the skid marks on the byways and highways of your heart.

274. Why should you *have* to ask someone to: "Give me your *honest* opinion?

275. Mother and Father are inevitably caught between Yesterday and Tomorrow when Grandparents' Grand-dear comes upon the scene. Yes, truly, Mother and Father are problem-targets, no matter what.

276. Some of the worst-wearing apparel can be found in a *boutique*, Kathy.

277. Do it the hard way and real hard things will later become easy.

278. Call me parsimonious, stingy, close, whatever, but not *covetous*.

279. Old-fashioned lemonade *still* tastes like old-fashioned lemonade, no matter how update and "chic" *she* may appear to be, Charlie.

280. I charge you the going rate, so, Buster, get *going*!

281. You, chiefly, learn to *earn*.

282. Blind shopper must purchase "sight unseen."

283. Computer-poetry creations take the personal touch out of the poem.

284. Trust me and even *I'll* be sorry.

285. It's always good to know the source of your embarrassment, lest you re-submerge your senses into the same murky waters of the Sea of Shame.

286. Be careful when you raise your voice that you don't lower your self-respect.

287. Often many times, to say, "I'm sorry," is not nearly enough to assuage the tender feelings.

288. Sure, save yourself, but be sure to know for *whom* the saving is made.

289. I most assure you, depressed one, a large dose of pure laughter will cure you.

290. No matter how you slice it, the cake is *still* inedible, Maude.

291. Sue, don't hesitate about asking one's forgiveness, irrespective as to the gravity of the offense.

292. If you do not save you for me, please save yourself for an impeccable rival, at least!

293. Imitation is the spice of most lives.

294. For too many ersatz athletes, it's not the game, but the "name of the game" that impresses.

295. Most mirrors should only be glanced at at best, or simply quickly passed by.

296. Don't you find the terms "dusk" and "twilight" more romantically endearing than the phrase "early evening"? I certainly do.

297. Don't forget you can't lease love.

177

298. You shouldn't feel as though you'd be an imposition. Heaven has enough room for everybody.

299. I suggest we who love people should stage a collection and purchase a one-way ticket to East Nowhere for Mr. and Mrs. Segregator.

300. Even the Grand Prize came as no surprise.

301. The sound of *money* has such a *rich* sound—even paper money.

302. In the desert environs a single raindrop is worth ten times as much as any pearl drop.

303. Since man's moon-walking expeditions, do young lovers see the moon as a loving ally in romance-seeking? I doubt it.

304. Maggots make the biggest of us human beings infinitesimal, in the final analysis, you know. (Or had you forgotten so quickly?)

305. "Bargain seekers" to bargain seekers are *not* bargain seekers. They are merely "astute shoppers."

306. Sipping cider through a straw or simply gulping it down with a wide mouth—either way, tipsiness will overcome the consistent consumer in a matter of time.

307. All the world *is* my province—until tax-paying time each annum.

308. Nothing upsets youth as much as advice from old age.

309. Most of the things I am today are nothing I had planned and/or surmised yesterday.

310. Tell me, is science an art or is art a science . . . (or does it really matter?)

311. Even so, Love survives—and thrives.

312. In the first place, racial, ethnic, and/or discrimination is so, so inelegant, isn't it?

313. Maybe, Ian, your wherewithal is not all that much here or anywhere!

314. Doesn't even the thought of summer make you feel good all over—that is, unless you're some starving furrier, huh?

315. If lies make you smile and truths fill you with chagrin, brother, how little of the good life that you're cognizant of!

316. The *Bible* declares that the "poor is always with us," so we might as well not move, huh, Jane?

317. She's even too proud to look down to see if her shoes are untied: too tired, or too lazy.

318. If you cannot *do* me well, as things are between us, at least *wish* me well.

319. I wonder what American, black, white, or in between really grasps the total and wide-ranging artistry of a man they name "Satchmo" Armstrong! (And that's only the genius with a fourth-grade exposure!)

320. Old man, don't confuse your hearing aid with your bifocals. It has been done before, you know.

321. Personally, I think mirrors should not be on sale for everyone, including *yours truly.*

322. Too many long (and short) telephone calls are too *phony*—and no pun intended here at all.

323. I bet (and I don't wager generally) if Christ were alive today on earth among us, what with morality's decadence so heavy, he'd cry, and cry uncontrollably.

324. Rising waters always mean lowering hopes of some worried souls.

325. To seal the famous crack in that equally famous Liberty Bell would be sacriligeous to history.

326. Remember, some painkillers kill more than pain.

327. Fears don't have to be cultivated to ripen and fall into harvest.

328. Deny me your presence when I desperately need it, and I'll likely rejoice in your absence when you'll desperately need it to maintain your balance.

329. I'm beginning to acutely wonder if all judges should be addressed as "your *honor.*"

330. Youth never goes out softly, nor does old age sweep in with a bang.

331. Isn't it a causeless statement, the one about "It's just a matter of time"? Hex, you and I know, as well as every other soul hereabouts, know that with *everything*, it's just a "matter of time!"

332. "*Mourning* (may) Become Electra," but her brother laughs nastily all through the *wake.*

333. A good mouth can take in more than gossip to sustain the whole body's general make-up and healthy outlook on life.

334. Without a doubt I see that you doubt.

335. Not only is *conscience* almost hard to spell, it's impossible to evade for all that long.

336. Sure, Phineas Fletcher, "Faint heart never wins the fair lady," but an over-zealous Lochinvar has lost thousands, fair and otherwise!

337. "The groves were God's first temples," but why are so many trees being cut down lately?

338. "X" marked the spot, but someone has come along and erased the spot.

339. He or she who must wait to pray at prayer meetings only, can seldom pray *anywhere* at anytime in earnest.

340. Her lips were made more for gossiping than for kissing.

341. In *your* case, "laugh, and the world laughs (*at*) you." "Weep, and the world laughs at *you still!*"

342. Some princes, worthy or unworthy, never become kings.

343. In our case, Love, it was a chance meeting on purpose.

344. Smile not upon manual labor. Recall the greatest of philosophers was a Carpenter's Son who also learned the trade.

345. Return to me at a winter's midnight when powderpuff snowflakes are drifting down to cover my footsteps so any still-not-abed neighbor may not realize your return.

346. Appeasement does not mean the lowering of one's self-esteem.

347. Self-denigration is almost as bad as self-adoration—but not quite.

348. Justice is not *blind*, as it is supposed to be, but Lord in Heaven, it certainly *should* be!

349. He swears by love but not by romance. He also swears there's a vast difference.

350. Remember, after the substance there's but shadow behind shadow behind shadow.

351. "Whom the Lord loveth, He chasteneth"—*Hebrews* XII, 6. (Boy, my grandmother who reared me after my mother's passing, must have loved me almost to pieces!)

352. Privacy be doomed, if secrecy harbors a narrowed outlook on mankind at large.

353. Life at best should make one live joyously even if cautiously . . . if such a combination is possible, Clarice.)

354. Speculation becomes fact if the speculator "happens" to be right.

355. Why does marriage take all the fun out of romance, Mary-Anne?

356. Wrinkles come from smiling, too, but not as many as from frowning. (But in your case, Evie, who cares, or can note the difference?)

357. It's too bad "all our *yesterdays*" have so much adverse bearing upon most of our *tomorrows*.

358. Always hang on to your heart; that's really the only thing of value worth caring for, the mind notwithstanding.

359. Be sure the "ways of the world" are the ways that don't lead you *out* of this world.

360. Does the "love of your life" exemplify a love *for* life? You'd better take a second and closer look at her, Franklin.

361. Before the luckless ones end their sojourn here, may they all have more than a *rockinghorse winner in the fifth race* somewhere in this world.

362. Jail wardens can be the loneliest of people.

363. S'funny, but some pet lovers let their pets pass judgment on the owners' social prospects.

364. I made no heed, but the evening warned me of the next morning.

365. First date kissing can often lead to second date missing.

366. The middle child in the family's siblings fight harder to achieve because it knows there're one or more ahead that it can't surpass, and there're one or more behind it dare not let it/them overtake him or her! It's really frightening, isn't it, Middle "Sib"?

367. If you wish to test a host's friendship strength, bring the whole family—and bring it unannounced on a rainy day in winter!

368. Sometimes it takes the grave to explain the life one has lived.

369. You *live*, but you don't necessarily have to *learn*! *You* are proof!

370. Ever notice how so many *late* love consummations end in *early* divorces?

371. Remember, freedom really isn't *free*.

372. God, grant me the power to see me as I truly am, and grant me even greater power to make all the necessary adjustments for immediate improvement.

373. Misery comes in all forms—as does happiness.

374. When marriage becomes a competitive experience, happiness and peace of mind become the luckless losers.

375. Make ground rules for love, and soon you'll be lost somewhere ever wandering in space friendless and forlorn.

376. Keep your eyes on the road . . . even if you're *not* the driver.

377. Words thrust harshly enough to cut can wound far more than any rapier ever could.

378. No woman feels she is as pretty yet as observers say she is.

379 Though they live rent-free, mice run the house.

380. Burn your hand *once*, will wear heavy glove *twice*!

381. When love becomes a chore, love seeks to linger no more.

382. Ice slows down the swiftest stream.

383 Time is the chief hangman of us all.

384. Wave hello more than you wave goodbye and loneliness will not be your nemesis—ever.

385. Don't let too many "better things in life" sour you on the sweet things of life.

386. Why seek to raise the "windows of the world" while you keep the heavy drapes so tightly drawn?

387. Keeping your enemy at "arm's length" might demand more than "elbow room", Garth.

388. *Shame* sounds so much uglier than *embarrassment*, but it's so much easier to spell and pronounce.

389. He pronounced them "husband and wife!" but the groom didn't hear him—or pretended *not* to.

390. When Love forgets, Hate leans in the wings, all set for downfront and center stage!

391. Lord, if I could turn "water to wine," I'm afraid my motives wouldn't be the same as *yours* were!

392. The Lord above knows we may need more heroes and heroines, but no more *martyrs*!

393. Perhaps if we spelled the first name *Martyr* instead of *Martin*, the morality-losing world today would adhere more and more to the philosophies of Dr. *Martin* Luther King, Jr.

394. One must work extremely hard to be funny without being offensive or obnoxious, for good clean humor is hard to come by, you *would-be-smut comics*.

395. I know a Mr. Ray said it clearly and directly when he said, "He who fights and runs away, may live to fight another day." Well, let *me* put it *my* way: "He who fights and runs away, may live to *run* another way." Shucks, *my* way makes more sense, Mr. Ray.

396. If your "world of tomorrow" should suddenly pop before you, could you really handle it, right, *right* now?"

397. Don't mention "love" to me if you don't include life, for love and life are inseparable, Francine.

398. I'm really sorry, Bob Frost, but "good fences make good neighbors?" Nah, Kid, I swear, "Good *neighbors* make good *fences!*"

399. When someone says he lives a "stone's throw away," be doubly sure his aim is erratic, or you don't live in a *glass* house!

400. Don't let love of self out-distance the love for others.

401. Don't let too much self-denial create the evil suspicions of sincerity in others. You know *people*, Ernest.

402. Philosopher Thales is said to have opined, "Know thy self." Now, *I* opine, "Do I have to? I may learn an ugly side of me."

403. Even a moron's laughter can create a feeling of well-being in the body of a sage.

404. Honesty lives in a glass house; honesty can well afford it.

405. Does the hangman really enjoy a good night's snooze?

406. Good gravy does not always mean good meat.

407. As long as you love me, I don't have to love myself all that much.

408. The world is my garden, but I keep forgetting to pull the weeds.

409. Save me from myself, please!

410. When you're in love, the season is always summer at high noon.

411. You say, Robert Burns, "To see her is to love her." Well, if we're talking about the same lassie, that's why my eyes are always so tightly closed!

412. Speaking of taxes, but why should I?

413. Never kiss with your mouth full, Edwardo.

414. "When you come to the end of a perfect day," don't expect another one soon, if ever again.

415. He put his "best foot forward . . ." and nearly broke his neck!

416. Don't let them say when you are through that your biggest offense was living a month after the day you were born.

417. When you let friends choose your mate, you deserve whatever your fate.

418. Friendship is the fruit of a well-tended tree.

419. "Forgive us our trespasses as we forgive those that trespass against us." . . . (even though the trespasses may be numerous.)

420. Anyway, who measures the territorial range of a fool?

421. Valorous be your name, coward, to those who were not near in battle with you.

422. Dear, if "love is the name of the game," let's "op" for *tennis*!

423. Save your *best* for *last*; I'm going home *early*.

424. One of the White Man's most demeaning old remarks about a successful Black was, "He is a credit to his *race*."

425. When "all the world becomes a stage," Shakie, as you were wont to contend, I'm getting me a comfortable orchestra seat, and truly enjoy the *comedy of errors*!

426. Until your concern becomes my concern, all prayerful gesticulations will be of little or no concern.

427. A house is not necessarily a home, but a home is always a house.

428. The tricky part of life is just learning how to know *how* to live!

429. Often many "cramped" styles should be cramped even *more* so, Mary-Ellen.

430. Have you ever been too ashamed to be even embarrassed? Well, *I* have.

431. The voices of Belafonte and Johnny Mathis are two of the most endearing, haunting, and most enduring voices ever.

432. Remember: Even second-hand hearts can be refurbished like new—and some will be far better than before.

433. The more we segregate our bodies, the more we isolate our souls!

434. City White Escapers, crime doesn't stop at the City Line. Sometimes it *starts* there—and often in those mansions.

435. Since we are a "part of all that we've met," I guess there are really no strangers among us. No?

436. I suppose one tires of being good all the time, but then again, in *my* case I wouldn't know.

437. Not all followers make ideal followers, or do they? You see, *I* wouldn't, never having *had* to be one.

438. I dove into the Sea of Futility—and almost made it to the other side!

439. The trick is to be an *aimful* wanderer.

440. "Breaking up *is* hard to do!" (But I'll manage somehow—*happily*.)

441. Oh, yes, the deal was *cut*, but it sure wasn't *dried*, buster!

442. Changing establishments' cognomens from *foodstops* to *gourmet emporiums* will not change the taste of the local viands, although some fanatical semanticists or philologists may feel otherwise, not to mention the foodstops' owners *themselves*.

443. Lyricist, I know "many a tear has to fall," but should not be "all in the game." Good grief!

444. He "stuck his neck out," but withdrew his head, which really then did not matter, did it, hangman?

445. "The Lord loves a cheerful giver." (And so do *I*, as a willing, able, and cheerful *recipient*, of course.)

446. Why don't you aspire to a judgeship? His answer, "I am a devout *Bible* follower, and God said pointedly, "Judge *not!*"

447. By offering me a "piece of your mind," you run the risk of *total* imbecility, pal.

448. As practitioners of love of the world, we sure do need far more clients, don't we?

449. "The evil that men live *by*" should be made to change living quarters.

450. If love is a heartsore, let's defy all health rules and aggravate the awful painful conditions that plague the heart.

451. I can draw the line between right and wrong, but all of my pens and pencils are lost, stolen, or broken.

452. When your "word is law," you don't need a huge thesaurus-loaded mouth.

453. I'd trust others only after I trust myself—or should it be the *other* way around?

454. Nowadays, many cities give jungles a bad name.

455. When there is a "call to *arms*," be careful not to lose your *head*.

456. Sure, the world will bless me long, long after I am gone—*good!* But I sure hope that blessing time does not approach anytime too *soon!*

457. You cannot make a fool out of a wise man nor can you make a wise man out of a fool.

458. Having the "time of your life" certainly does not mean serving a jail term, Jocko!

459. It's not the bold type that does us in; it's the fine print that so often incarcerates.

460. Who determines *aristocracy*—and *why?*

461. Funny, how war-loving generals in armchairs can't spell beyond the word *armaments*.

462. A man is known by the *wife* who keeps him!

463. Ever since Adam's index finger pointed at Eve for *both* of their monumental indiscretion, man has been pointing to the female of the species.

464. Browning said, "Grow old along with me!" But *I* offer this selfish additive: "And maybe then folks won't notice *my* crumbling condition as much.

465. To re-quote the prophet Joel, "Old men shall think wanly of yesterday, and young men shall picture enthusiastically on tomorrow."

466. Why don't you ever *mis*quote me, so people will believe implicitly in my sagacity.

467. Love long enough, I hope, so you can truly appreciate your younger, vitalized seasons.

468. Make all your alliances as proud to know you as you are proud to know *them*.

469. No transported American can ever be a true American until he acknowledges and respects the First American—the American Indian.

470. Why "look homeward, angel?" Your folks moved last year and they left no forwarding address.

471. "Beauty is as beauty does:" so get busy, laboring diligently day and night, day and night, my dear.

472. Don't get me wrong: I'd "beard the lion in his den," but I'm no wildlife tonsoralist. Besides, my shears are dull, not to mention my razor (or my wimpy courage.)

473. "Hail Caesar; those who are about to die, salute thee!"—Suetonius. (But *this* observer adds: "But only if, 'Caes,' you go first!")

474. Capitalism is the bane of the broke man and boon to the affluent.

475. Revenge, in a way, augments the original offense.

476. Mr. "Willie" Wordsworth, a brief word, my man; (If "the child is father of the man," say, why doesn't he bring a weekly or bi-weekly paycheck home? Good grief, "Billy!"

477. Let's pass a law having Christmas 366 days out of every year. What a great world this would be, eh, St. Nick?

478. What really are "creature comforts?"

479. Benedicts' (or Benedectine Monks' Motto." "To labor is to pray." (May I, Brother Monks, drop in a bit of awry-inducing nastiness by adding, or saying, "In most cases, to pray is labor.")

480.   She was slow to smile or laugh, but when it, or better, when she
        did either one, the whole community stayed bright for many
        months to come, Sally!

481.   Thanks for thanking me: (I get the *hint*, Judy.)

482.   Perhaps the most heinous, or at least, the saddest phrase so
        familiar to Derpression-Era Children is "make-do."

483.   "I've Got a Pocketful of Dreams" . . . (but there's a huge hole in
        my pocket.)

484.   "Saturday Night Is the Loneliest Night of the Week . . ."
        whenever *you* choose to call.

485.   "When the Lights Go On Again All Over the World . . . (Boy,
        won't Con Ed be happy!)

486.   "Just the Way You Look Tonight . . ." (you ought to leave your
        cosmetologist in your will, Nell!)

487.   "I Don't Want to Walk Without You . . ." (In fact, I don't want
        to *walk*!)

488.   "Somebody Else Is Taking My Place" . . . (and please remind me
        to thank that person profusely, dear.)

489.   "I Get Along Without You Very Well . . ." (so don't bother to
        come back—or *call*!)

490.   Caruso, you pointedly sang: "La Donna E Mobile . . ." (but,
        shucks, kid, ain't we *all*?)

491.   (I may fall, . . . but ("I'll Never Fall in Love Again!")

492.   Forgiveness would be my middle name (*if* I had a middle name.)

493.   There's nothing funny about melancholia—*strange*, but certainly
        nothing funny.

494.   Everything decays but *Time.*

495.   When Love flexes its muscles, look out, you *strong* boy!

496.   "When I Fall in Love," call the nearest precinct, night or day.
        I'll not care.

497.   "St. Louis Woman," I'm gonna pack *your* bag and make *your*
        getaway!

498.   Thank you so much for so little.

499.   I wish someone would create a Heimlich Method for the foul-
        mouthed.

500.   Isn't it funny how everything, including me, plans to become less
        sinful "Come Sunday"?

501.   Gossips's Request: Tell me the whole story, and don't *spare me
        the details.*

502.   A good dosage of chauvinism greatly reduces a man's stature in
        the eyes of the world, other males included.

503.   Be careful: Don't let your Tomorrow pass you unobtrusively
        late Yesterday.

504. "They asked me how I knew my true-love was true . . ." (I couldn't for the life of me tell them, so I just lied.)

505. Which seems nicer: *hobo* or *vagabond*? Is one an opprobrious nomenclature of the other? Or is *vagabond* merely a *hobo* with a clean face?

506. Wordsworth, she *was* a Phantom of delight . . ." (until reality set in!)

507. Nothing pains a general more in having to re-tell pointedly of a *glorious* battle that he *lost*!

508. Blindness creates an inner light far more radiant than any visible one to the sighted ones.

509. Masters rule their dogs; cats rule their masters.

510. If you sign your name with a pseudonym, I'll pay your wage in counterfeit bills, so things even themselves out.

511. *Character* is what you make of yourself from whole stuff.

512. No wonder relief rolls are treated so nicely and are so overloaded, and have been for over 125 years. Remember Lincoln's proclamation which our country has yet to realize fully for all people?

513. He got abysmally lost letting his "conscience be his guide."

514. Anything grows lushly in the *Field of Dreams*.

515. My worst adversary treats me better than my professed-to-be warmest friend.

516. Belligerency has no spot at the Feast Table of Love.

517. The word *potpourri* always leaves me all *mixed* up.

518. Beware of the sewed-on smile and the glued-on grin: thread rots, glue dries up.

519. The two warring lovers-to-be moved *upstairs* to make a fuss *over* her.

520. Even some "bonafide" evidence becomes suspect in the hands of an unscrupulous judge.

521. When greed outgrows the need, disgust enters and rules indeed!

522. "Fun" at another's *expense* is a sure way to *bankrupt* your own soul!

523. Over-the-counter romances are far too cheap to be of any lasting value, Pearline.

524. You always appear to exercise *my* rights. What? You have none of your own left?

525. He showed us no pity, but we wouldn't have looked at any of it anyway.

526. He was such a *brave* coward!

527. Aw, come on—*Eternity* can't last *forever*!

528. Say, dear, what are Love's curfew hours?

529. Egoism is the art of self-comparisons, and not being able to determine which image is finer, or finest.

530. Being epigrammatic is not always dramatic or even dogmatic. It can prove to be merely being verbally erratic.

531. Is it true: *Hangmen* do work at *breakneck* speed?

532. Oh, would I had the ambition to be less ambitious!

533. The White Man is the burden around the Black Man's neck, though few Whites have ever considered acknowledging such a painful observation.

534. "You take the high road, and I'll take the low road, and I'll be Scotland before ye . . ." (Shucks, you *should*! The high road is at least 40 miles *shorter*!)

535. Immorality and dishonesty have a way of saying to our friends only what our friends *wish* to hear.

536. If giving to charity evokes a sense of magnanimity and not of genuine empathy toward or for the designated recipient, far, far better you should offer your goods to pigs in a muddy and foul sty!

536. Once I get myself straightened out, I'll stop running around in circles, trying to discover new angles for living.

537. So, live so far above reproach that when reproach-givers label you (and some there are who certainly will), like waterdrops on a duck's back, such reproach will really roll off to a vast sea of anonymity and insignificance.

538. Peace-time soldiering can be more stressful than battlefield encounters at times.

539. You get up out of my chair, Joel! You know the *Old Testament* psalm that runs: ". . . Nor sitteth in the seat of the scornful."

540. "I'll Remember April and You . . ."—and income tax abberations!

541. "Little Things Mean a Lot . . ." Yeah, kid, if you call *pearls* and *diamonds diminutive*.

542. Oh, yes, "Per" Como, "Catch a Falling Star . . ." and get knocked silly into late tomorrow night, too!

543. "I'll Never Smile Again . . ." (Why bother to stop now? You've already embarrassed half of the world!)

544. (Every time I visit the psychiatric ward) . . . "These Foolish Things Remind Me of You."

545. "Make Someone Happy" . . . as a matter of fact, Lucie, *move* and make everybody delirious!

546. Don't lose our lease (leash?) on love.

547. "A friend in need is . . ." (no friend of *mine*!)

548. Keep giving me all that I want, and soon I'll not want anything that I need.

549. I suppose I'm such a monster that when they say, "All's fair in love and war," I'll shoot Cupid and declare instant giant armament ban on ALL elements and indications of romance!

550. Don't reach for Tomorrow until you have fully let go of Yesterday.

551. "The early bird (got) the worm . . ." and the falconer got them both. (The falconer was also an avid fisherman, see.)

552. "Keep your eye on the prize . . ." even if you do have to use a special *giant* microscope.

553. Ah! At my funeral I can hear the sounds of the moans, the tears, and hear the sounds of sighs as they all must cry," Oh, Lord, what ever took him so long!"

554. One kiss from you should last a lifetime—if I *live* that long!

555. Since I can only do the rhumba, please save the "last waltz for me."

556. Although it may be preferred by the loquacious over the simpler term *pity*, I still like the word over its synonym: *compassion*. You do, too, don't you?

557. I'd like to be my "brother's keeper," but our baby sister won't move!

558. Far better to be the "flower-of-the-month" than be the "stinkweed-of-the-year."

559. A nasty mind seeks to manipulate its conscience.

560. Don't let your achieved degree of contentment be so loud as to drown your neighbor's cries of anguish, please!

561. Doesn't *cosmopolitan* infer or imply a gentler emotion than *urbanized* for the big city dwellers! I think so.

562. Never let your host/hostess be *required* to tell you goodbye.

563. Just a crazy thought, romancers: Don't all love involvements border on the ridiculous?

564. You can never be truly a giver from the heart when you feel the need to place a price tag on the commodity that you have to offer.

565. When your creditor can give you a warm smile after a five-year old debt, then you are the most admired (or) pitied son-of-a-gun alive.

566. With instant cooking and ovenware employment, there's no worry about "too many cooks spoiling the broth."

549. "The public be damned . . ." if your conscience is clear. (But, please, please examine with utmost diligence that conscience of yours.)

550. Dear, your face and figure must become an eternal laugh-producing frieze—according to the poet who said, "A thing of beauty is a joy forever."

189

551. Better begin going around in semi-circles if the same old circles are getting you nowhere.

552. For years, it seems, the Wright Brothers couldn't get their idea off the ground—until they took a good *flying*-start.

553 Courage is not the absent of fear, my child; it is the convenient containment thereof.

554. Why does "chiseler" carry a more distasteful connotation than the term *cheater*?

555. Speaking of Christian and Christianity: The real Christian does *practice* Christianity—he or she *lives* it.

556. Now that I've overcome myself, I can overcome the world.

557. Why is it, geologists, nature students, etc. that rivers are more celebrated than the springs of their sources. It really doesn't seem right or "kosher."

558. And here all that time I thought the *Ladies' Home Companion* was a loving and dutiful spouse! Humph! Just shows again just how *little* I do know, eh?

559. Just suppose my hometown address was Chattahoochie, Tennessee! Boy! you'd soon grow arm and finger weary just writing *that* much. (And I haven't put down the street address yet!)

560. I do hope "Charity starts (over at) *your* home . . ." and quickly spreads over to my house.

561. Not every crisis has its own solution, no matter who *starts* it.

562. Don't worry, little lady; what's in fashion *now*, will indubitably be in fashion *then*. Just sit back and gulp in God's fresh air.

563. I'm really afraid to be afraid. Scared? Yes, but not *afraid*.

564. Better "fool that I *was*" than "fool that I *am*."

565. If smiles were dollars, he would have been quite a *pauper* years and years ago!

566. She was so clever she put my foot in my mouth.

567. "Fame is fleeting." (But I don't mind running at breakneck speed.)

586. Why talk about your "pie in the sky" when either your airship's out of fuel or your own wings are broken and featherless?

587. Trees that bend in the wind, or bend with the wind, are smarter than trees that resist the gale.

588. The deadliest condescending statement made by (sometimes) the most "liberal" of whites about black-white relations is this remark: "Why, some of best friends are black!" To this *I* say, "Yes, and some of *my* best friends are humans. So!")

588. Sparrows, though the lowliest of aviary members, are by far the strongest, mighty eagles notwithstanding.

589. Innocent young lady pulls the night shade down carefully *after* she has undressed for bed. (*Innocent* . . . or really *daring? You* make the choice.)

590. 'Tis a pity horses can't at least once in awhile select their own riders.

591. He has a superior key and lock but the door has no hinges.

592. Save me for your dad's approval. After all, he will have to foot the ceremonies of the wedding, you know, Annettie.

593. I went to investigate for myself. They *still* were right!

594. He was head over heels, but the poor slob didn't know the difference. He was in *love!*

595. You know, dear, I look upon you as a *friend*—not as my *wife!*

596. No wonder you're so wonderful: you love *me!!*

597. Don't rub your belly when your back aches.

598. Can't *see* for *looking;* can't *listen* for *hearing.*

599. Put yourself in my shoes for ten minutes, and you'll probably go barefoot the rest of your life.

600. That guard was paid double not to guard, and that's how the company saved and made so much money.

601. Believe him when children fall in love with dentists and homework!

602. Gee! I had my chance to love. And, thank God, I "flubbed" it so successfully!

603. It's not easy to be easy.

604. Give me the right to be wrong, and, buster, believe me, I never shall!

605. I got totally lost "On the Road to Mandalay."

606. She loved putting on "see-throughs", but folks never cared to ever see through!

607. Small minds come at more than a dime a gross.

608. Some eggs do seek re-entry into the safe confines of their shells.

609. I don't even like the word *cahoots!*

610. A busybody often results from an idle mind.

611. She has nothing to do, and, Lordy, she does that *so* well!

612. Covetous rose leaves hide the most treacherous thorns while the fresh rosebuds blush so innocent-appearing.

613. "Sweethearts or Strangers," dear, you make the choice.

614. Forget your preachments, dad—youth and tomorrow simply are synonymous.

615. It could be said that "He was his own worst enemy," but too many countless ones lifted their voices in sharpest protest.

616. I've always wondered where echoes go when they cease "echoing" jobs. I suppose they graciously slip back into the sweet confines of silence.

617. I guess the world is *round* simply because it's been *around* for so *long*.

618. He's not used for target practice. He's the *real object* they're aiming at.

619. Humor, placed inappropriately, can result in the deadliest of confrontations—no laughing matter, Robbie.

620. Talking can be injurious to your well-being at times. Just you picture this: We *struck* up a lively conversation, and *hit* it off right away, especially after I had *kicked* in a few *bon mots*.

621. She kept her eyes wide open on her blind date.

622. The *Bible* says, that "faith can move mountains." I wonder if Mohammad didn't seek to operate on that same concept.

623. Right or wrong, somehow I always feel that I'm right. Or that I don't feel that I'm wrong.

624. Ah, "shure," he "got my *goat*," but not before I "cooked his *goose!*"

625. It's better to have been loved than not having to love.

626. Great-grandma Harriet, part Indian, refused to forsake Black slave husband to go to Oklahoma and/or Texas territories. I guess the grand old lady said, "Why not stay in this tight Alabama segregation colony and not migrate to a larger, and unbelievable larger arena of human misery and human denial, eh?"

627. You said we go together like "hand and glove." But I noticed you didn't say: "hand *in* glove!"

628. The "pot called the kettle black" but kettle didn't mind for kettle had found itself a "home on the range."

629. A thing of duty is a bore forever!

630. "I want the girls just like the girls that married dear *owed* dad."

631. May the world long remember, never forget that there once was a real word called *chastity*.

632. You appeal only to those unappealing to the world at large.

633. I can't get enough of you because you don't give *enough* of you.

634. Change is but repetition adopting a new and camouflaged form.

635. He was my rabid admirer until I failed to re-pay him a five-spot.

636. I've never been able to figure this one out: "But, honey, I thought lipstick was used to hold loose lips together."

637. Sometimes, thievery *can* get you some*wear!*

638. You say that you want a little peace and quiet? Why, aren't they synonymous, Sarah-Marie?

639. At least, old geezer, most birds know when to migrate. (And you call them "bird-brained"!)

640. There's even an art to ambulance-chasing.

641. Laugh at yourself before others do, (and you'll be labelled a first-rate fool for the rest of your life.)

642. I am my worst enemy, and all my friends planned it that way.

643. Better to be late than always on time.

644. Looking out for Number One always upsets Numbers Two, Three, Etc.

645. I've arranged it for you to commit suicide, Kermit.

646. Sometimes I think Texas is even bigger than Texas thinks it is.

647. *Everywhere* or *anywhere* is a long ways to go if you must *walk* to get there!

648. Some people I know say more through ten hours of silence than you reveal in ten years of talking.

649. "Nobody knows you when you're down and out . . ." (except those who are down and out.)

650. Nothing gets under the skin more than a gadfly who announces that he's gotten under your skin.

651. I go out frequently with my ex-wife because she is my *ex*-wife!

652. She sought to tie him down with no strings attached, but soon found out that she faced a knotty problem.

653. The more I see you, the more I wish for new bifocals in sunshades.

654. "Stand by Your Man . . ." even if he doesn't offer you his seat.

655. She was fit to be tied, but the groom was just stringing her along.

656. "I'd Climb Every Mountain . . ." if you'd stay in every *valley*, dear.

657. Nowhere does barbed wit ever fit.

658. Even losing has its fine points of refinement.

659. I've searched for you all my life but the search wasn't that thorough, nor have I lived so long.

660. Make my house, please, your point of no return.

661. Love is not the way to go when you're in a hurry.

662. "To each his own . . ." and I want part of *yours*, too, at least.

663. Love demands great sacrifices, so start pawning your adulterated heart.

664. Friederick Nietzsche must have been born in a lemon grove.

665. But you must remember, foot soldier, *valorousness* has no connection with *discretion*.

666. No army soldier can ever forget his terror life in a foxhole, whether it was for one hour or for six months!

667. Most generals hate the Black spiritual: "Down by the Riverside."

668. I took it upon myself to love you. (Now I see what happens to the strong-willed and firm of purpose "old cuss.")

669. Most cocktail parties are simply elegant ways of getting intoxicated in a pseudo-sophisticated manner, nothing more, nothing less.

670. No, philosopher, we only "pass this way but once." (And, believe me, brother, I wouldn't have passed this way now had I been *barefoot!*)

671. God is alive and well—but no thanks to these human practitioners He created in His own image—which, I feel, was God's first error!

672. Everything matters, Arthur Balfour; it's just a matter of degree in each thing's substantive value.

673. Just because "The Price Is Right" does not mean that my billfold *is.*

674. Why do most of us "critics" treat criticism as a one-way street?

675. Angry gossips' complaint: "Why 'privatize' a public affair?"

676. Hey! Ow! My last and best dream was stored in that red balloon that you just burst!

677. Prejudice is the hallmark and curse of a very disillusioned family. Thank heavens I'm not related!

678. I'm sorry, accuser, sometimes the only *end* to go off *is* the deepend.

679. I wonder how real today is most of our "real McCoys"?

680. That would-be comedian gives excellent humorous material a very bad, bad name!

681. You recall, dear, the "heart is a lonely hunter;" so why'd you bring up such a crowd in quest of mine?

682. Far better a "clinging vine" than an over-exposed single sap!

683. Never tell a woman that she *looks good for her age*—even though you may be more than right.

684. With all of humanity's unspeakable, disrespectful carryings-on in the valley, once sympathetic gods have locked themselves like eagles in their impregnable eyries. Can't much blame 'em either.

685. It's only right that you should be wrong now and then, but, Lord, not time and time and time and time again!

686. Pray. Never mind about wasting God's time. Remember, He made the world.

687. Never veto *all* your dreams.

688. The mimosa tree is truly God's flower tree whose delicate aromatic petals are worn in the angel's hair without a doubt.

689. "People Will Say We're in Love . . ." (Huh? Who puts any faith in *people!*)

690. "They Asked Me How I Knew My Truelove Was True." (I lied: I said that you swore you did on a stack of *Life Magazines*.)

691. Omit the words. Just hum the tune. You know, words have a way of *prevaricating*, to phrase it nicely.

692. After you've said goodbye, why hang around for a brandnew hello?

693. Prejudice, blatantly flaunted in Dixie or subtly displayed in the North or West or East, is still a most sickening and reprehensible act, America.

694. Sometimes, I feel the Melting Pot was taken off the Flame of Equality far, far too soon.

695. Nothing can take the place of a warm friend meeting a warm friend—not even on television. (And I might add, particularly on television.)

696. "You and the Night and the Music . . ." (Of the three, one of you make me sick!)

697. Which is better, and what really is the difference: to go down in a "blaze of glory," or to go down in a "hail of bullets"? In either way, buster, you go down, and you'll not be around to reap any benefits, if such there be.

698. Perish the thought: Just suppose we arise one morning in spring especially, to find all the birds have a severe case of laryngitis!

699. Upset motorist, stalled for hours and hours on the famed L.A. *throughway*, exasperates: "Now whoever named this highway a *throughway* must've had a very warped sense of humor. I haven't gotten *through* this *way* in over six hours here!"

700. Tell me: Just what is the *body politic—deadheads in Congress?*

701. Be careful lest the "Peg O My Heart" becomes the *peg in* your *heart!*

702. Anybody can be President, but not everybody has a *mind* to.

703. *That* Sleeping Beauty should have remained just so.

704. I know it's *tough*, but "Love Me *Tender*."

705. "There Goes My Everything." (I knew I shouldn't have stayed so long out of the apartment!)

706. "You Are My Sunshine" . . . (At "Three O'Clock in the Morning . . .")

707. Don't the ever-continued acts of hate vented toward Blacks, Jews, and all the other minorities in this country today make the senseless vituperative spewings of Blacks against Jews and Jews against Blacks seem so, so utterly reprehensible, Asians, Latinos, Etc.? Or is this generation so unaware of the efforts of these groups in the Civil Rights Movement of the sixties and earlier (and later) or is this generation too lazy to "check out" history today?

708. "Ain't it funny today how so many "matches made in heaven" wind up as mis-mates in hell"?

709. When sleeping becomes your full pastime, it's past time you wake up.

710. Do paid mourners ever change by the number of tears they shed for the dearly departed, or by the voltage of their outcries?

711. You would think that the special emphasis that is placed on forgiveness in our Common Prayer, you'd think we would just know the efficacy and need for our practicing forgiveness. Right?

712. Perhaps because we're science-fiction and fairytale oriented as a nation, is the reason why we do so poorly in historical facts about our real past and present.

713. I may be far off the mark (and I usually am so), but shouldn't *alimony* be properly spelled: a-l-i-*m-o-n-e-y*?

714. Leaving this *universe* would make a *world* of difference.

715. "To know you is to love you . . ." so let's remain very distant strangers, huh?

716. Clearly I remember "The First Time Ever I Saw Your Face . . ." (and that *was* your face, eh?)

717. Decimate my love, but please don't desecrate my love. I've worked too hard and long to have it spoiled now.

718. Thank God Life's Clock shows it's always too late to hate!

719. Thank Jehovah the term *social acceptability* is always so relative, (and minor, too!)

720. A man with a cane does not always use it for walking aid.

721. "Tomorrow and tomorrow . . ." (creeps) . . . (I beg your pardon, Brother Macbeth. After 40, "tomorrow and tomorrow *races* by to give one pause to reflect.")

722. Jealousy does not need to advertise.

723. I'm still amazed at the wisdom and clarity found in King Solomon's ancient teachings! (Aren't you, too?)

724. I've never met a man I liked (if he owed me money, plus interest.)

725. Socially, economically, and emotionally, things won't be easy for you in the U.S. if you're Black and Latino *and* wearing the Star of David around your neck, buster!

726. Why is it bad news makes the front page, while *rejoiceful* news hardly makes the "back page" in very fine print?

727. "Feelin' tomorrow just like I feel today, I'm gonna pack my suitcase and . . . and" (make myself gladly stay!)

728. Believe it or not, but on July 12, on a mid-town bus, in New York City, I saw an old lady chewing tobacco from a pouch—(and this was in the year of 1993!)

729. No, my brother's no marathon walker—but a marathon talker, and he has yet to come in first!
730. Smiling should be banned except for dark and dreary Februaries from now on.
731. My righteous censor censors his own mail.
732. I finally found myself right in the middle of Nowhere. (And here I thought all the time that I was *lost!*)
733. All music is serious—and especially badly written music, for upon hearing it, one must exclaim, "Aw, that composer couldn't be serious!"
734. Remember, fools aren't measured by the inch or pound, but are measured by the sheer weight of their stupidity.
735. All across America "The bells are ringing for thee and my *pal.*"
736. Before he turned psychotic, you were the *last* thing, dear, he had in mind.
737. Prove that I'm ever wrong once, and I'll not speak to you again on your own terms!
738. Tell me, is there a sequel to love? (Should there be one?)
739. Mary's little *Lamb* went a *fur* piece.
740. It matters not how pristine the objective to wage *war to end war,* it is a sin before the Maker.
741. Shucks! His manners were hardly worth minding.
742. The last time that I was lucky was *tomorrow.*
743. I had forgotten to remember: so that's why I forget.
744. The only beautiful thing about slavery in America is that it ended; the ugliest thing about slavery in America is that it started.
745. I've lost the address "On the Street Where You Live." (Goody!)
746. The funeral ceremonies all complete, you should see the Merry Widow *Waltz!*
747. No wonder you're so poverty-stricken: You've been getting only "*Pennies* from Heaven."
748. Why don't you *finish Symphony* #8, Schubert?
749. "When Your Lover Has Gone," (here's my telephone number, honey.)
750. You'd be shocked if you could see yourself "Just the Way You Look Tonight"!
751. Isn't it downright sad that after at least four wars to settle differences as we speed along toward Century Twenty-One, the awful truth is that too many *yet* wish to practice and activate the conscience-rot of prejudice? Now isn't it sad?
752. Oh, yes, Neighbor, I could exist without you, but I could not *live!*
753. I'd like to change my mind, dear. May I for once?
754. At least let the suit of Hate that you wear to be a borrowed suit.

755. Violin background chords should enhance the worst vocalist's presentation . . . honest!

756. Never be so stupid as to ask for a jury of your *peers*.

757. If you must ask someone: "Am I boring you?" don't bother to wait for an answer. Chances are you already have.

758. The square root of life is love multiplied countless times over and over—and then some more!

759. Sometimes, a kiss can be far more hurtful and insulting that a slap in the mouth.

760. Be careful not to trip when you and the "special one" "trip the light fantastic."

761. Ah, yes, he's "light on his feet," but so gosh-awful *heavy* on *mine*!

762. Dear fashion model, when modelling a banana fruit dress, be sure it's not a banana split!

763. Hey now, *tell it to the judge* may not prove all that efficacious at all times!

774. Do you realize, O generalizer of concepts, that some cats and dogs live peacefully together?

775. If my "fate is in your hands," at least wash your hands before picking up my fate—*please*!

776. Sorry Fireside Philos, but I've seen some mighty *dirty whistles* in my time.

777. Say what you will (oh, but you will anyway!)

778. I have faith. (At least *someone* has it.)

779. "A burned child dreads the fire." . . . Not today's headstrong group!

780. "*When You and I Were Young, Maggie*" . . . (you *still* were 20 years my senior . . . and today, you're 20 years my junior!)

781. "Be My Love . . ." only when I can be reached by you through a forgetful, senile carrier pigeon at night.

782. "There's Nothing Like a Dame . . ." except perhaps another woman.

783. "It Seems Like *Old* Times . . ." the way you keep tinting and dyeing your locks.

784. "Give credit where credit is due!" (Heck, not until you pay back what you already owe me, Charley!)

785. She gave him a *glancing* blow, but knocked him out with her *eyes*.

786. America, America, it's never too late to integrate!

787. I starved to death by letting "well enough alone."

788. "After You've Gone and Left Me Crying . . ." there'll be the biggest freedom rally celebration in the history of Hooked Romantics the world has ever seen!)

789. Me dubious about *tomorrow?* Shucks and greasepit, I'm still raising questions about *yesterday!*

790. I think there's nothing and no one more sickening than a White or Black supra-patriot on Memorial Day or on the Fourth of July!

791. "Oh, My Heart Belongs to Daddy . . ." (and to his stocks and bonds especially, honey! Believe me!)

792. "I'm Just Wild About Harry" (who in turn, is wild about Annie, who, in turn, is frantic about Joel, who, etc. (You get the picture.)

793. I'm such a universal advocator, I even advocate advocating!

794. Generally, you drown when you're in "over your head," Francine!

795. Just in case you choose to leave, depart in any season except Spring. No, no, never in Spring!

796. You poor dear, didn't you know that girls' wrists are for bracelets and/or other bright baubles—not for *razors* or *razor blades!*

797. Love long enough and you'll forget about having to leave because your "mother is calling."

798. The river does need crossing, but first we need a *bridge!*

799. Death sets its own timetable plan, so don't try to alter it.

800. Sometimes, noise can be good to be able to appreciate silence.

801. Why twist my arm to straighten me out?

802. Since you are my biographer, make my life an open book, please.

803. But the drowning man said the water felt so good!

804. Can you really "get away from it all . . ." (or) "get away *with* it all?"

805. Forgiveness-supplicator-seekers, how can you nightly pray, "Our *Father* who art in heaven" when you can't whisper "my *brother*" to the neighbor across the back fence?

806. How can you "raise the roof" when there's no ceiling to begin with?

807. The food looked *better* and was *tastier before* you cooked it, Mamie.

808. When you begin talking, it's always forever*more*—never the *less!*

809. Youth, a foul mouth is not as disrespectful for your parents as much as it is for the future offspring you will eventually mother and father in tomorrow's world. Disrespect grows and hardens with time. It does *not* lessen or soften with the passage of time.

810. Love does form a strong circle, but it can be gladly broken if an honest and gentle request is made for a new entry.

811. Years ago, a generous baywindow was considered (in men) evidence of *opulence*. However, nowadays, it's deemed *corpulence*, men.

812. By the way so many Dallasians (?) brag the only thing bigger than Texas is taxes . . . (and even that's hard pressed to prove.)

813. "All the world's a stage." And thank Providence I'm the director of such pathetic drama!

814. He "showed me the way to go home. . ." (But my wife had moved earlier in the day with no new address noted.)

815. Wanna watch the "world go by?" Well, stand at high noon on Fifth Avenue and Forty-second Street, Midtown Manhattan, and you'll surely see the world go by—and some souls are even *out* of this world!

816. Spring sneaks in when Winter's back is turned, poking cold fun at dead Autumn, who had just snickered at the late Summer's dying throes!

817. By clearing up the matter, you are beclouding my mind.

818. The average suburban, white inner city escapist artist wouldn't mind black me moving in if his neighbors didn't move *out*!

819. "With a Song in My Heart . . ." (O.K., but leave it there; it's so nice and quiet here in the outer world.)

820. Some of my *best* friends used to be my *best* friends.

821. At *least* Lot's wife made biblical history. Not many other ancient girls can attest to that—that is, not a *(L)ot*.

822. Far better a mere figurine of little note than one of blubberization and all bloat!

823. I've given you the "benefit of the doubt" so often till I'm beginning to doubt its benefit.

824. To remove much of the contentiousness from race-mixing, try this simple solution: Integrate only between 9:00 P.M. and 2:00 A.M. far away from all incandescence or lunar assistance, so by "dawn's early (revelatory) bright" it'll be old hat all during the rest of the day. See?

825. Ah! The *old* me is dead, folks, dead! (Voice: Thank God, and let us pray for no rigid elements of any old phoenix and ashes!)

826. If you wish the "lion's share," check with his wife, Mrs. Lionness, first and the baby lionettes and lion juniors! You'd *better*!

827. Honesty was in the cards, but he gave me a fast shuffle.

828. Dancing bears may be pretty to watch, but certainly not to do a wild fandango with!

829. Please, none of your superlatives over my worth and my great qualities, lest when I really grow famous your accolades become tiresome, limited, and far, far too *inadequate*!

830. Public bathroom wall scribblings tell far more about society's moral and mental sickness than any talk show could ever produce.

831. Say, "noble and pure" Christian bigots, wasn't Christ a Jew, and wasn't one of the Three Wisemen ebony-toned? (Maybe we don't, or haven't explored faithfully the same *Bible*. Huh?)

832. When it's pure cacophony, don't you just despise the "Sound of Music?"

833. Just as I *thought*—then the lights went out.

834. He was a "picture of health," but a little touch up job was vitally needed in several paint-worn spots.

835. Many bald men feel a great need to grow an enormous moustache and beard. I, a bald one, wonder why?

836. How long have you been broke, Bill? (Bill: Ever since this country fled the gold standard.)

837. Don't ask a man of his character. Ask his maid or butler, if you really want to know the truth . . . especially if she or he is no longer employed by said "character."

838. I'll fight *any*body, *any*time, *any*where who's willing, ready, and able to *lose*!

839. Love sets up the stage; Hate pulls down the curtains. (Ah! Ah! what masterful drama, kid!)

840. Three women together: two will "size up" the third.

841. Having the "gift of gab" is really no gift at all.

842. Blame me stoutheartedly (when no mirrors are available for yourself.)

843. "Still waters run deep." (O.K., but they *still* run.)

844. "Still waters run deep." (That's O.K.; I'm great drinker and a deepsea diver.)

845. "Gather ye rosebuds while ye may . . ." (because the insidious thorns are waiting for your first dumb slip-up!)

846. "O, call back yesterday . . ."—Salisbury—*Richard II*. Morris cry to Time: "O Time, no you don't! I still owe some back alimoney to all four of them! My gracious!"

847. "Truth has a quiet breast . . ."—Mowbray—*Richard II*. (Of course. Lies have to yell and repeat themselves often enough to be heard, believed, and respected!)

848. "Let me play the fool . . ."—Gratiano—*Merchant of Venice*. (Well, *you* can, "Gratti," but my cousin Al's not *playing*!)

849. No, I did *not* say that you were "wise beyond your years!" I said you were wise beyond your *peers*! But upon second thought, being that *sagacious within your generation* of *today*, is not saying all that much for wisdom.

850. If "Life is just a bowl of jello," don't you think it's time to sort of "shake" things up?"

851. "The Devil can cite Scriptures for his own purpose . . ."—Antonio—*The Merchant of Venice*. (Yeah, but he can only *cite*, not *write*!)

852. Love *is* blind," even wearing double bifocals! (With twin telescopic lenses yet!)

853. "O, that this too, too solid flesh would melt!"—Hamlet—*Hamlet*. (Don't worry, "Ham," another hot N.Y.C. July, like that old hot July of '93, there'll be no need to beggar that request, old buddy!)

854. "What a piece of work is man!"—Hamlet—*Hamlet*. (He *did* He did say "piece" and *not* "pieces," eh? And he did further say "man" and *not* "woman?")

855. And as Gertrude exclaimed in *Hamlet*: "Sweets to the sweet." But *I* add, "Sweets to the sweet, *lemon*-face!"

856. "I Heard You Crying in the Chapel . . ." (and it was *music to my ears!*)

857. Even tombstones don't mind lying, and plainly so, for all the living to pause and read.

858. Oh, I could handle it, if it *had* one!

859. You needn't laugh—unless you really want to.

860. Now, dear, it's *my* turn to turn . . . *away!*

861. Does watching the new day *break* give you the same sensation as seeing the old night *fall?*

862. "A hundred Years from Today . . ." will be as vituperative?" You say I "ain't" seen nothin' yet? (Ooh, gee, I can hardly wait!)

863. When the "body runs down," why not "accelerate the heart?"

864. May all your days blossom into a wild field field of flowers to be picked with complete abandonment from your countless waiting tomorrows.

865. Does it really matter if the coffin eventually leaks?

866. May one, single bright tomorrow erase cleanly your innumerable yesterdays of private and public shame.

867. Joe, he was training to be a thief, but he was left back because of a large streak of Honesty-Class 102-S.S. in his freshman year.

868. I cannot quite make up your mind to make me a loan.

869. Some troubles follow even with the brakes on going downhill!

870. And with a knife, never confuse the *blade* with the *handle*.

871. There's nothing *right* in *wrong*doing—ever!

872. Even should the sky rumble, crack, and fall, there are some souls who will still not believe (From the Prophet-Sage Chicken Licken.)

873. Because evil Jack Frost lurks ever near, it takes more than one blade of grass and one clover bloom to establish the *Rites of Spring*.

874. I *am* my "brother's keeper," and your crime is my crime, whether I ever wish to accept this fact or not.

875. Nothing is inevitable except the quick changes (and warning-less) in the weather of New York City.

876. I forgot the giant bouquet of roses you gave, but I do vividly recall the *single* thorn that you forgot to remove, Susi-Lee.

877. Now it seems, our lesser gods all have lesser gods. (So what's a fearful and fearing body to do?)

878. He was inappropriately undressed for the sunbathers' academy.

879. Never try to plug the holes in your bleeding heart that caused the holes to be there in the first place.

880. Love does not have to be gift-wrapped—that's how *real* love comes anyway, Dummy!

881. Water cannot purify itself—especially in today's questionable environment.

882. The drowning man reached for what he thought to be a straw, but which in reality was a *log*.

883. Speak to me only with thine eyes, and I'll understand; but, dear, not on a starless midnight! Shucks! There *are* limits, you know!

884. Didn't you know that a beloved Black boxer in the 1920's in France was the cause of the wearing of black as a "fashion statement" instead of only for mourning? (Aw, of course *you* knew!)

885. "Oh, When the Saints Go Marching In," (Lord, just let me be a lowly drum major. I wouldn't mind a bit, Sir!)

886. "The Song Is Ended . . ." (but you keep mumbling those gosh-awful words!)

887. "You and the Night and the Music . . ." (make it pretty crowded in here, my deah.)

888. Today, the way talk shows, bonafide and pseudo-sociologists, and the like, have all tended to "clinical-ize" the whole business has stripped away all romanticism from mankind's most intimate relationships. (And, dear Jesus, that's the pity of it all!)

889. I'm afraid we attribute far more Solomon-esque-like intuitiveness to today's judges than they are able to display and/or accept.

890. There is no way so many of the "rap" music lyricists can justify smut and derrogative words used in any presentation, and under the thinly-veiled guise of the bastardized catch-phrase: "telling it like it is."

891. Punctuality isn't always the finest of attributes. Imagine heading for your hanging, for example.

892. "Everybody Loves My Baby . . ." (so why should *I* bother? She certainly doesn't my tiny romantic input, now does she?)

893. Aw, who repaired the church bell's clapper? (Sonny, it must've been your *conscience*. As for me, I don't hear a thing!)

894. He has a tongue of *silver* but a purse of *lead*.

895. Doctors can "con" everyone except private nurses and private secretaries. Right?

896. Don't soar so high that you forget what the *terra firma* once felt like.

897. I spent a whole lifetime *not* in search of you, and now you've turned up!

898. The battle ended in a draw, and both sides cheered lustily at the victory results.

899. Yes, Al Tennyson, "Age has yet its toil . . ." (It *has* to nowadays because youth refuse to even *look* at labor!)

900. Better the slowest ride on a camel's back than a breakneck pace on the back of a jaguar!

901. It's amazing how many pints can get into two quarts of milk when you're *buying*, and how few pints make up two quarts when you're *selling*!

902. "Spittle" sounds more polite and sanitary in public than "spit;" don't you agree?

903. Touch me even with the *sheerest* gloves, and you really haven't touched me at all.

904. Not everything that pours is water, you must remember.

905. I swear I'll be just as kind to history as history will be to *me*—no more, no less.

906. Strong drink imbibers all seem to love getting into the "spirits" of things. (And this has nothing to do with ghosts at all!)

907. Maybe it's the *color* of the cabs of New York City that makes drivers *afraid* to often pick up *black* me. (Oh, just a little rumination.)

908. Most Important Commandment is the Eleventh Commandment, which admonishes: *Keep the first ten!*

909. "When I Grow Too Old the Dream . . ." I'll *still* pretend that I'm able to.

910. Really, what's so great about a hand-me-down love, even if the hand-me-down love has truly been superbly re-polished up?

911. "And it came to *pass* . . ." but he was no *quarterback*, therefore, he "*played the field*" of the love-*game* . . . (And got quite a *boot* out of it.)

912. He was a real fashion plate, but only at a nudist colony.

913. Which makes the most sense?
(1) "The summer of my last resort . . ." or
(2) "The resort of my last summer . . ." or

(3) "Neither one."

914. Every force is my task force because my force is a task within itself!

915. Let *nothing* come between us but . . . *goodbye*, please!

915. He "played the field . . . (and got buried by the plowblades of over-confidence . . . and to make it worse, there were no *ashes* from which any *phoenix* could *ever* rise, Malvine!

916. I *do* believe in reincarnation, so I'll come back later as a *watchdog* with a severe case of *rabies*! (Of course, I'll put the *bite* on you!)

917. "I Want a Sunday Kind of Love . . ." not like the other six days' laboring presentations!

918. When you die, try to make someone as sad as you'll make the undertaker *happy to hear*, hear?

919. Unlike synthetics, Love does not have to mix, or be mixed, with anything else to be potent.

920. You can't pay luck to play favorites.

921. A well-lived life, like a well-toned, and turned autumn leaf, has no regrets for impending winter of deep content.

922. Remember, you must always take advantage of the dream.

923. White Bigot, to me as your considered rival or nemesis, your blatant and overt acts of prejudice, like a slyly-moving away from me on the street, with an underglance of suspicion whenever we pass, a throat-clearing signal to a white "brother" of my presence, and so on—these are the gestures and *acts* that I am talking about. (But you clearly know this already. What evidently pains you is my chary and often keen observance of these, your *acts* of pure *innocence*!)

924. The trouble that I find with realism in life: It leaves nothing to the *imagination*!

925. Remember, when you change your mind, you might as well change your socks, too. They both are pretty dirty, you know.

926. Don't let your Life be the dust of inaction upon the back shelf of the world.

927. Those Black Southerners who lived in the ante-bellum Civil Rights Days, or Years, wasn't it weird and stupid how Mr. Southern White Man who swore no possible genetic contamination with "Negra plasma", so stupidly made the connection more ludicrous when he'd address our mothers as *auntie*, and our fathers as *uncle*? (My God, *what price Corey*!)

928. (From Morris' Extremely Sick Pun Dept.:) Q.: Now that you have been able to conceive, Alice, where will you go? Alice: Oh, *From Here to Maternity*, I suppose.)

929. Don't ever let *Hate* fill the void where *Self-pity* used to dwell!

930. The bean was too big for the pot.
931. The guests of *mine* knew better, but they all came along hungry anyway.
932. It matters little how old you think old-ness is, if you never attain that circumstance or condition anyway, Sam.
933. He burned the house down just to have ashes to save.
934. My dear, yes, "Thanks for the Memory . . ." but let's not try to *refresh it*, please!
935. Ask exactly *why* I love you, and I'll probably discontinue this very personal act.
936. Remember, one board left does not make for a safe bridge.
937. True sincerity, like a loaded wagon, makes no hollow or noisy sound.
938. Even if you're not, say you're sorry; perhaps I'll never detect the true difference. (And if I do find out, *I'll* pretend I never knew the truth of your sentiments.)
939. Always leave one another just a little bit hungry for more love.
940. "Necessity *is* the mother of invention . . ." but thank God so many truths are *still-born*!
941. Sure, I had enough rope to hang myself, but *your* neck didn't seem all that uninviting, and, besides, you were only a *scant* swing away.
942. You really flatter me with all your flattery. (Or have you stopped, and this is the "real McCoy" that emanates?)
943. One doesn't always have to be an executioner to be "dressed to kill."
944. "Count Your Blessings Instead of Sheep . . ." (and you'll be the starvingest shepherd in the whole valley!)
945. "The Night Is Young . . . and You're So Beautiful . . ." (Notice I didn't say, You're So *Young*!")
946. (It may not matter now,) but . . . "I'll Never Smile Again.")
947. Since petrol prices have skyrocketed, and shoe leather has grown rather prohibitive, "I Don't Get Around Much Anymore."
948. "When I Fall in Love," . . . I'll never skin both knees again, I promise.
949. "The *Anniversary* Waltz" is probably danced *yearly*, or at best every *twelve months*, don't you think, Katie?
90. "When You Were Sweet Sixteen," (I was a bitter forty-six, kid.)
951. Nowadays, it seems everyone toasts to everything, and with everything—but sliced *bread*!
952. Henry, you're a *natural*. Graveyard worms really relish your type. And when you go, I bet you won't *worm* your way out of that!

953. "You Light Up My Life . . ." (and, boy, is the electric power company upset!)

954. "Every Time You Say Goodbye . . ." ("You Keep Coming Back Like a Song!")

955. Ma said there would be days like these. (I'm only sorry that Ma was so right!)

956. Please ask that stand-up comic to quickly sit down.

957. It's not fantasy, but reality that shocks youth today.

958. Most hasty persons get severely bitten from making snap judgments.

959. She was so distraught she'd commit suicide every other fourth Tuesday night.

960. Don't be upset: Longevity is just a matter of time.

961. Only iron eggs should be used as battle weapons if best results are desired. Ask Sir Humpty-Dumpty.

962. Soul and heart? Soul is the mind; heart is of the body.

963. Dear, friendship is never a by-product of love. Friendship is the outgrowth of love, and it grows as love grows, if nurtured.

964. Don't forget: Wherever you go, you must go alone, no matter what or where or why.

965. So self-centered and self-assured is he that he answers all of the questions months and months before they are asked.

966. Moonlight cannot cook your eggs, but it can present them in such a lovely light.

967. Bill collectors have a nasty way of pouring swamp water over the honeymoon bouquets.

968. Her face mask was badly torn, but no one knew the difference — nor did anyone care!

969. I'm sorry, many members of the Jewish persuasion, the Irish Catholic persuasion, and other persuasions, who join forces with the Majority Wasp American by ostracizing the Black, Latino, and Native American, also, can't you realize how you're being used to your own personal detriment at this late date? Didn't many of you flee to this country to escape exactly the same concept that you are advertently or inadvertently promoting against the Black, Latino, and Native American individual? Well, this American of the Black-Indian persuasion seems to feel so. (Please inform this writer if he's right or wrong, you hear?)

970. The other night I mailed a postcard prayer to Heaven. The card came back marked: "Postage Due." Were the postal angels trying to tell me something, Gladys?

971. I said I'd call you. You said it could be the start of something big! It was: You said goodbye!

207

972. So eager to see comic symbols relating to marriage, she swore the rings around Saturn were Heavenly wedding rings waiting for nuptial ceremonies that would be out of this world!

973. I cannot refer to you my lawyer because my lawyer himself is seeking legal aid from an unmindful judge who needs legalistic advice also!

974. Often when people are at *logger*heads, it seems, or it simply means someone was *bark*ing up the wrong *tree*, and it's past time to *branch* out and *leaf* things alone.

975. It is so dreadfully sad how all of America for the most part treats school teachers with such low regard when we *all* know that teachers are the promulgators of all our children's oncoming tomorrows! Other cultures, I'm afraid to say, do not display such disregard for the academicians.

976. Don't you get tired of just being *tired*?

977. I know where "you're coming from," but I don't even worry about "where you're going—" so long as you *go*!

978. In the Country-of-know-It-All, signpost arguing has long been popularized.

979. Mountain peaks seem to daily grow taller above the Valley of the Damned.

980. "Nothing succeeds like success!" Yeah, and nothing "fails like failure!"

981. I'd rather it be brandnew than for it to be a new brand.

982. Be sure to count *me* among your blessings!

983. If love comes a dime a dozen, check your change for the nine cents that's due you.

984. I could quickly, dancing lover, get you off my mind if I could get you off my *feet* first!

985. It takes a dark, ominous sky for one to appreciate a spotless full moon.

986. Counting on you is like putting faith in a broken down adding machine.

987. Let love be the cornerstone for justice.

988. Remember: *Love* that becomes competitive is only recognizable in a *tennis* match, my dear.

989. The bright child sympathizes with a dull mother.

990. Eat all you want, but, please, want all you eat.

991. To prove that summer is preferred to winter, notice how many love songs involving summer, as compared to love lyrics scribbled in deference to winter (or the other two seasons, for that matter.)

992. He poked his eyes out, thinking that would sharpen his hearing facilities. (It worked, but not enough to compensate for the loss of sight.)

993. It takes a brave "vet" to pull a lion's teeth without the use of anesthesia (on *both* lion's *and* "vet's" part!)

994. Doesn't "temple" and "cathedral" sound more majestic than "church"? Yet, come to think of it, *groves* were God's first places of worship.

995. Nations are born out of manifested hope, and are laid to rest out disillusionment shrouded in despair.

996. The marriage ceremony put the groom to sleep, and only *after* the honeymoon did he wake up!

997. "Love Makes the World go 'Round . . ." and Hate applies the brakes, bud!

998. In *bush* country, *twigs* are more in demand than *logs* or *branches*.

999. Although infinitesimal to human beings, fleas are big things in a dog's life. (Perhaps that's why human beings don't like to lead a dog's life. You think so, huh?)

1000. Food or the lack of food, first and last, determines the operation of the world. Let no one tell you otherwise.

1001. You owe it to your children to make them owe you *and* themselves genuine respect and self-respect, Mom and Dad.

1002. The beast was tamed, but the lion tamer went wild.

1003. Heaven is just around the corner, but don't turn the curve too sharply, or you, in unmerited haste, may overleap its station and/or location.

1004. When drinking becomes more than a pastime, it's past time you stop drinking.

1005. Most marital fights begin over little nothings—and end up on even less. (But, wisely, in most cases, they end amicably so.)

1006. Politics to most politicians is like coffee to most coffee addicts: its taste and flavor are not as important as the fact that it is vote-gaining (taste-sustaining) in the final analysis.

1007. That "devout" parishioner goes to church twice daily, hoping the church doors are securely bolted from the *inside*!

1008. It's generally best to have the territory before demanding territorial rights, Clancy!

1009. I bet Mr. Noah didn't even hire life-guards!

1010. Too close for comfort, and yet not far enough away for fear.

1011. Yes, Oh, how the mighty have fallen!" . . . (all upon *me*!)

1012. Give me a chance to explain yourself.

1013. "Somebody Loves Me . . ." (But does it have to be *you*?)

1014. Twice he was at death's door, but no one would answer the knock.

1015. Finally, when I walked out, ("Love Walked In . . .")

1016. "Love Me or Leave Me"? (No! "Love me *and* Leave Me!" . . .)

1017. Make my life more meaningful: Pay me the ten-spot you owed me half of my life.

1018. "Twice bitten—(at least twenty times) shy," buster!

1019. There she sat playing the "Beer Barrel Polka" when the atmosphere demanded champagne!

1020. Remember, whatever you select, the choice is *mine*.

1021. He said, "You certainly know how to treat a guy: you never overdo it." Doggone it!

1022. The *repentant* thief was ashamed (of his *ineptitude!*)

1023. Love is really inexcusable.

1024. Anxiety knows no limits.

1025. Filled his pail, then proceeded to pollute the well.

1026. Beautiful saucepan, but no soup.

1027. Count your blessings—not *mine!*

1028. "You'd Be So Nice to Come Home To . . ." (*if* the rent's paid at least six years in *advance*, Lucy.)

1029. Hey, you walked out on me! (What took you so long!)

11030. Why, you're so much beneath me, and I'm so spiritual, even my worst derogative remarks about you will induce all kinds of pristine haloes to revolve around your head forever!

1031. Sir, I doubt you most definitely when you add: "believe-me's" to every declaration that you must utter or make.

1032. A library is to the mind what a church must be to the soul.

1033. Leniency should be on every offended one's conscience.

1034. The evil man at least shows you the one to avoid.

1035. Love is blind. Marriage affords the strong bifocals.

1036. If only I had spoken when spoken to, as the wise (?) adage goes, I would have been a deaf mute over fifty annums ago, and then some!

1037. Water seeks its own level, but you shouldn't have any trouble seeing where to drown.

1038. "Handsome is as handsome does." (No wonder you're so *lazy!*)

1039. Dry your tears, but not on *my* shoulder! Please!

1040. Sometimes I stand on Fifty-seventh Street at Fifth Avenue and watch the world go by, by, by, by, by, by, by, etc.!

1041. Let nothing come between you and me . . . (except another more alluring, richer, and prettier gal, honey.) Don't relax; that shouldn't take long.

1042. The most cutting words in the language that I know is, "Ya see, I *told* you so!"

1043. "Free at last! Free at last!" (And here I've been *paying* $4.95 for them for the past five years!)

1044. *Surreptitious* even *sounds* sneaky.

1045. I *worry* when people go out of their way to make me *happy*.

1046. He was a seasoned recruit.

1047. To aid in the war effort, he volunteered to stay out.

1048. I worry about you when you don't worry about me.

1049. "To the victor belongs the spoils . . ." (To each his own, but I can't stand spoiled and/or rancid food!)

1050. "The best is yet to be," but I can't stick around for 150 years!

1051. What is this: Are *all* disasters *natural*?

1052. In my divorce proceedings, one word led to another, and the judge had me led to jail.

1053. I suppose Plato was much loved by a lot of people, for so much love is even to this day *Platonic*.

1054. Love comes in two sizes: Full Size to Fit All or Not At All.

1055. I'm deeply in love with a *married* woman! (And *lucky* for me she happens to be my *wife*!)

1056. Of course, people who marry a lot are long distance runners. They enter *marrythons*, stupid!

1057. Cynics are merely salty critics.

1058. Old age beats young death any day, buster!

1059. It takes a great loser to boast about his loss—either he's a great loser or an even greater *fool*!

1060. I really wanted to call you, but I didn't exactly know just *what* to call you.

1061. Doing *your* level best can't be that much at best.

1062. Don't forget to learn how to live. Age will appreciate you for it a long ways down the road.

1063. "The voice of the turtle is *heard* in the land . . ." but no one is *listening*.

1064. The broken heart anguishes more when love drops off in many, many infinite *unpickable* pieces.

1065. *Nowadays*, "the child is *(god)* father to the *man*."

1066. So sorry, plastic cosmetician-physician, some (or many) of your incisions badly need revisions.

1067. Boy, he was "taken to the cleaners!" . . . but came back ever dirtier!

1068. Love should be a *seasonal* thing, renewed *four* times a year.

1069. The pessimist is he who sits in a "house by the side of the road" while the "*best* of the world goes by."

1070. She was "up for grabs," but all of the fellows kept their hands in their pockets, leaving her "all up in the air."

1071. He made quite a "dashing figure," and all ladies, after one good look, were seen making a "dash" the *other* way!

1072. After years of research and genetic-transplants, it is possible for you, buster, to have *your* type deemed human. (Boy, but what a job and what a time!)

1073. A real metaphor for laughter is this: It is a rash of tears overflowing with glasses of rainbowed champagne and bright music.

1074. We clipped the wings of the Bird of Paradise—but it flew even higher and faster (*away*) from us!

1075. You can easily tell if a man is dying or dead if he refuses to do anything for love or money—especially the *shekels* end of the proposition.

1076. Love showed me the way out—out the *back* door at *that*.

1077. If I fail to thank you, don't get upset; Oh, please understand that's *exactly* how it was planned!

1078. Remember, the root comes *before* the branch.

1079. I would have roundly and soundly denounced you, but my severe case of laryngitis would not allow such *accolades*.

1080. Yes, Lucille was *real*, but Christine was *pristine*!

1081. He promised her the world and all that was in it or on it, but the globe he finally brought was a tiny job he picked up at Woolworth's. (And what a *world* of difference!)

1081. Dad *quadrupled* his allowance and junior *still* had nothing!

1082. (From the World's Nastiest Crack): "Please wash your hands after eating, Junior." (Junior): Why, Ma, is the food *that* dirty?"

1083. He's the only daredevil who wouldn't dare the devil.

1084. Even her smiles had me worried.

1085. When the poor and *un*famous steal, it's pure "thievery;" when the rich and influential do so, it's merely "embezzlement." This is a strange environment that we live it, "ain't" it, Maurice?

1086. *His* proverbs taught you what *not* to do and say.

1087. Mirrors, remember, never make faces.

1088. Sure God's a pretty busy real estate and life-operator, but He's not *that* involved to take time to lend an ear to your and to my *worthwhile* prayers, Marjorie.

1089. Wake me up only if you *have* to, but not to whisper that you love me. That'll probably put me back into much *deeper* realms of sweet slumber.

1090. Sure, God'll grant you water to drink, but you'll have to open your mouth.

1091. Your skin's pretty enough to wear on the outside.

1092. At least a debt will keep us in touch.

1093. *Two pairs* of shoes with only *one pair* of feet. My! My! What extravagance will you think of next, Wifie-Dear?

1094. There must be *something lacking* about you, newcomer: No one's a *complete* stranger.

1095. I would charge it to Cousin Al, but he's already in debt.

1096. Your words, in the long run, will prove much bigger than your two fists put together.

1097. If *you* do the best you can, I can only suggest that you should quit before you start!

1098. Once I get rich, can I truly appreciate the state of poverty (which, incidentally), is quite a large state!

1099. Waiting for you can put such a stress on you.

1100. A handshake can say more about your personality than a thousand words poured out in very fine print can.

1101. Women don't always get together and talk about men, but generally they do.

1102. Feed the singer only after he's sung the melody through at least ten times! (Must be crooner Tommy Tucker, eh?)

1103. The Near East is not as near as you would suppose, Judson.

1104. I devour your words most ravenously; your *silence* I ponder over with meticulous care for days and days.

1105. As I *live and breathe*! I must constantly repeat that act.

1106. The power of forgiveness can rival the atom bomb explosion, if it's that genuinely sincere.

1107. He called my bluff, but only he could hear it answer so weakly.

1108. The rabbit still resents the bad news publicity put out by the tortoise elements of the prejudiced news world.

1109. He's brought the ashes to prove that his house has really burned down.

1110. I really resent your not resenting me more than once a day.

1111. No wonder God didn't put lips on mirrors!

1112. He tried to straighten out a crooked shadow . . . (and nearly succeeded.)

1113. (The real story involving Priscilla and John Alden): Priscilla: Why don't you speak for yourself, John Alden?"—Johnny Boy: "O.K., I will: Don't you have a prettier sis, Pris?"

1114. *Cat's got your tongue?* (Now who'd ever want *that* cat around!)

1115. Yes, it's a *pity*, but not a *shame*.

1116. Tobacco can only fight back when you chew, dip, or smoke it. (And tobacco is so patient, Charlie!)

1117. Rags fit him far better than a Lord and Taylor elegant tux does!

1118. Wow! And just suppose butterflies could sing also!

1119. How you arrive here I don't need to know, how you leave, I already know: via one big throw from me. (Sure, we're on the twenty-third floor—the air will do us both some good: my staying, your going by the open window direct route, believe me!)

1120. Honey is so good. Why do bees have to sting? (Maybe that's *why* they sting, Mavis!)

1121. He loudly raised the question: incredibly, I lowered the answer.

1122. We *wreck*onciled our differences.

1123. Because he was *puny*, he took *puny*-tive measures easily.

1124. The rice tasted better before she cooked it. She seemed to have gone against the *grain*.

1125. Not all big trees cast large shade, nor do all small ones cast small ones.

1126. The braggart has *two* boats, and they *both* leak!

1127. Often *tongue and teeth fall out*, and no one's more happy than a broke dentist (and his starving family!)

1128. Nowadays, the blind lead the sighted ones, and do a far better job than the old other way around.

1129. He worked awfully hard to get "Up a Lazy River . . ."

1130. He always wanted to rollerskate on a bamboo floor.

1131. Some greedy gossipmongers rush to valleys just to hear echoes give them more to gossip about.

1132. He tied his dreams in a huge bundle but the Dept. of Trashportation refused to pick them up without gloves and noseguards on.

1133. Remember, no one's too young to live—or die.

1134. Why's the air in here so suddenly foul? Answer: Because those two characters over there decided to air their differences in here.

1135. "To the winner belongs the spoils!" Why? Give it to the loser: he's a rotten loser anyway!

1136. You must take me as you find me, Paul! (Paul: Naw, I'd rather lose you *since* I've found you!)

1137. Winds of change are not always for the better, you know.

1138. One does not have to brag about the good deeds he's rendered. If they were *that* good, they will speak for themselves.

1139. Upwind or downwind, the skunk's smell still radiates the same odor of obnoxiety.

1140. Sometimes *pairs* don't always mean *couples*, lonesome lover-boy!

1141. You don't have to be an Iowan farmer to be *corny*, you know.

1142. She remembers only each day that follows yesterday.

1143. You don't need hollow eggs to play the shell game.

1144. Tears evaporate—residue remains often to bring on a fresh supply of tears.

1145. To believe him is not to love him, believe me!

1146. Some fruits: sweet in the beginning, sour in the end. Other fruits: sour at the start, sweet in the end. Yours is the choice.

1147. I'd gladly rejoice if only I knew the occasion. On second thought, in today's rough world, who *needs* the occasion?

1148. Most overworn clichés of our day:
(1) "This is the bottom line."
(2) "It's a whole new ball game."
(3) "Check out the scenario."
Now don't they just grate on your semantic-philologic nerves!

1149. A dimpled chin greatly enhances *any* chin—even a double one.

1150. Yes, Didactic poet: "A little learning *is* a dangerous thing;" but, kid versifier, *total* ignorance is more deadly than forty-five megatrons ready to blast off in seconds!

1151. Shy girls, dispense with your shyness now and then. Kick love in the pants to wake Cupid up once in awhile.

1152. Such a sad commentary, but it seems the term *chastity* is a laughable term. Well, if such be true, we are living on the sharp edge of fatal darkness.

1153 You have to let someone describe your back with accuracy, or you won't know what you look like walking away.

1154. If there are, as spoken in *Julius Caesar*, "words before blows," sometimes the *latter* is not necessary.

1155. Maybe most Latinos and Blacks here in America suspect each move the white man makes because the white man initiates the cause. *But*, even so, retaliation should *not* be a prime motive for abstinence from inter-social relation attempts.

1156. Love came by and left her calling card, but it was the wrong number!

1157. Charm is the worst of all female vices.

1158. As far as I'm concerned, after God made the rose, the giant marigold, and the 'mum, He could've just stopped his floral creations. That is, as far as *I'm* concerned.

1159. Shucks, if I watch what I'm doing, I can't ever see a thing that goes on!

1160. Man with forked tongue often makes cutting remarks.

1161. When, and *if* Love drops in, pull up a chair, offer Love some lemonade or coffee. Love just might feel so welcome, he just may sit a long spell, like, say, a whole lifetime, at least.

1162. He *drives a hard bargain*—until he runs out of gas.

1163. Why have clean table talk with dirty napkins and filthy tablecloth?

1164. I quickly set out when rigor mortis set in!

1165. *Margaritas* are much more appealing as girls than as *drinks, Tom Collins.*

1166. No! I said wait *on* me—not *for* me! Good gracious!

1167. Sometimes, it seems I get more assistance from my tutelary gods than from my regular overseers. How about that!

1168. Who *can* you trust nowadays! (Well, don't look at *me*!)

1169. Hadn't planned it that way, but Love made me a staunch recividist. (All, all against my iron (?) will, too!)

1170. And speaking of Flaming Youth, most become Cold Ashes long before Middle Age.

1171. His mock trial delivered a sentence much more strong than any *real* one would have produced.

1172. That "wayward bus" was not as "wayward" as the winking bus driver would have the riders suppose.

1173. The truth of the matter is that there is no truth in the matter.

1174. Many so-called backlashes are merely excuses for exercising *justifiable* (?) heinous acts of ungoverned violence.

1175. Wisdom is the grossest of drawbacks in the community of fools.

1176. I simply just want the right to *be*!

1177. Some things only exist *within* the shadow of a doubt.

1178. Sometimes, there's not always a beaten path to follow, junior.

1179. Shoot, *all* truths *should* and *must* be self-evident. Only the hearer here may tend to becloud their clarity.

1180. It may not seem so, but heaven's always just a prayer-stop away.

1181. A pig doesn't have to worry if its socks don't match . . . so . . . in *your* case. . . .

1182. "There's Music in the Air" . . . so stop singing and listen to a real melody, Frances!

1183. Cursing doesn't *expiate*—it *excruciates*. (Deep down for the curser.)

1184. You are also known by the friends who *avoid* you.

1185. Lightning strikes its own chord; thunder has the drum roll.

1186. Just how far and how much is *over and beyond*, orator?

1187. He was tarred and feathered for trying to whitewash a *lie* . . . (and that's the *truth*!)

1188. Enough is *more* than enough when you're already full (by most folks' standards.)

1189. Sorry, Hank Longfellow, "lives of great men (only) remind me" how hard work really is, especially if wife and mama are the only *pushy* types!

1190. Some straight lines (deep down) wish to be crooked.

1191. Studied world and government foundations for one day. Now he seeks to teach world geography and history at an advanced college level!

1192. Let me emulate *you*, not you copy *me*, for then all my failures can be placed at *your* future doorstep.

1193. Live in one place long enough, and you'd be a fool to move elsewhere.

1194. Remember, success and admiration seeker, *cream rises to the top*, but *sugar* clings to the *bottom*.

1195. Graveyard greedy worms promptly sent the too-mean-to-live rascal back to the undertaker.

1196. When's the last time you've sat in a *genuine* rose garden?

1197. What he knows best, he won't talk about—*himself*. (Can't blame the *conscience-ridden* fellow.)

1198. Just because you're *home*, does not mean that you are *free*.

1199. Is it that you and she are only "comrades in arms"?

1200. Deny me when we're alone, but, please, not in the Public Square!

1201. The plethora of the output and the wearing what is so conveniently called "baggies," and often beltless, can only cause this old observer from Time's Frontsteps to label this the "Bag Age".

1202. With sex, sex on talk shows endlessly, in newsprint, without stopping, and its professed interpreters "explaining" this sad and open forum dissertative hammering, one must conclude that America is such an infantile territory, and sex was discovered or revealed to this country some scant twenty-four short hours ago!

1203. When you grow angry at the whole world, it becomes *sore*-ciety, doesn't it, Kermit?

1204. Generally, men carry handkerchiefs for *blowing*, ladies, for *showing*.

1205. It's a very rare steer that does not deeply resent beefburger emporiums.

1206. The trouble with *you* . . . is *you*!

1207. Remember, *calculating* is never the same as *speculating*.

1208. *Baywindows* on the male human frame generally give the owners great *panes*, eh?

1209. The physical beauty of the populace of N.Y.C. lies not in its singular beauty, but in the multi-pigmented faces that dance, loiter, or pass along her avenues and byways.

1210. Ugly words soon produce even uglier faces and figures.

1211. You move me to tears—not shake me to laughter.

1212. Juniors, *washcloths* are still to be used with more determination for dirt removal than *towels*! My goodness!

1213. "The more things change . . . the more . . ." (*you* do, too, dear.)

1214. Yes, I did say "take *time*," but I did not mean my *antique grandfather's clock*!

217

1215. Horse racing and dog racing *still*, to this inconsequential observer, are horror games forced upon these captured and harnessed animals, queens, kings, and other "dignitaries," to the contrary.

1216. Love *only* in Spring—and the other three remaining seasons always.

1217. If Hate takes you away, there is nothing harmful or embarrassing if you let *Love* bring you right back.

1218. Save the *best* part for the *first*. Who knows that we listeners can last until the *end*?

1219. Whites, you who keep turning a blind eye and drumless ear to the pseudo-supra and neo-narrow-minded bigots, are going to harvest a bucket of blood and an acre of indelible shame, unless you rise as honest and devout believers of human dignities as the birthright of all, and not keep "escaping" to pseudo-enclaves of *one-ness*, for soon the evil will include your doorsteps and your doors will wind up in a pitiful heap of immemorial ashes!

1220. Cameras don't lie, but darkrooms *do*!

1221. Parents of the Skinheads, my God, what are you *rearing*—no, I mean what are you *raising* today? (And I hope you do get the full significance of my distinction here.)

1222. Constructive anger is the only kind of anger there should be, if there should be. (Remember Jesus upbraiding the money-lenders in God's House?)

1223. The sad love song stated, "I'd rather have a buddy, and not a sweetheart, for buddies never make you cry." But the lonely little old maid said, "Ah, I know, but I'm willing to take my chances!"

1224. Speaking of "rank and file," the disgusted "topkick" muttered, regarding his raw 'cruits,' "I've got the *file*, and they sure are *rank!*"

1225. She seemed so quiet until she *closed* her mouth.

1226. He quickly found his old ways in his new country.

1227. I don't trust *men*, so I won't send it by *male*.

1228. Women, and especially style-conscious young ladies, the more you show or expose of yourself body-wise, that is, upon the public streets, the less he'll wish to see in the privacy of the shade-draw boudoir. Believe this old gaffer, ladies, please!

1229. If a dream needs propping up, most likely it's better to cut it down and plant a new one in its place. (And nurture it, of course.)

1230. I gave up drinking until my throat got dry.

1231. Isn't tomorrow's dawn an extended nightmare when you're with someone not too pleasing to be with? (Oh, I know: *she* told *me* so several times, doggonit!)

218

1232. Over-use of *swear words* eventually makes them *nowhere* words, if ever they had a viable place in mixed company in the first place!

1233. Dear John, the last time you kissed me was the *last* time you'll kiss me!

1234. In the Furnace of Love, Love never overheats, but adjusts its thermostat to afford a pleasing air of comfort, adjusting to the temperatures of each dream.

1235. I didn't quite get the *compliment* when she said, "Oh, you look so much better without your face!"

1236. Greedy One's Proclamation: "Give me more—never the less!"

1237. Sir, when she says *tentatively*, she means *always*—or *never*.

1238. Please obey your mother—*after* you have failed *decisively*, Ron.

1239. Never promise *more* than you will *receive!*

1240. Say you love me, and I'll slowly deny it; say hate you, and I'll quickly try it!

1241. To tell me honestly that you don't love me does not make the announcement more bearable. Here in this instance the truth is *not* beautiful.

1242. "Our Love Is Here to Stay" . . . (That's why I'm *leaving*, Babs!)

1243. "The best things are free." (Heck, they *should* be! The *worst* things cost too darned much!)

1244. Yes, I'm Black, and do you know: some of my worst friends are Black, too!

1245. You'd scarce believe it, but some of my best friends are—*friends!*

1246. Say, dear, let's re-*new* "Love's *Old* Sweet Song . . ." even if we're both off-key now.

1247. "I Don't Wanna Set the World on Fire . . .") but arson seems to run in my family with such a burning desire!)

1248. "I'm Gonna Sit Right Down and Write Myself a Letter . . ." (but probably forget enough postage!)

1249. "Three Little Words . . ." (*Please go home!*)

1250. "Nobody Knows You When You're Down and Out . . ." (Shucks, in *your* case, you're so obnoxious, Nobody, "Nobody Knows *You* When You're Up and *In!*")

1251. I'll always love you, dearest, when ("Autumn Leaves") turn bright green again!)

1252. You left me a "Room Full of Roses . . ." (and a backyard blooming in *crab*grass!)

1253. Beware of the world outside when bluebirds forget to sing.

1254. Love needs no mirror to convince itself.

1255. Flamingoes and egrets are ready-made artist canvas subjects.

1256. *All* girls know they are pretty; only some know they are *prettier* than *others!*

1257. I'm very daring, so don't be *afraid* to let me *follow* in *your* footsteps!

1258. Alas, the "Three Blind Mice" couldn't see the approaching ravenous cat.

1259. I may be a bit too presumptuous, but your soul seems to bear the earmarks of a broken dream or two.

1260. If you can realize the success of *one complete* dream in a lifetime, consider yourself most fortunate. Some of us aren't even *half* that lucky.

1261. Needing "elbow" room often is a lazy man's excuse for not *shouldering* responsibilities.

1262. You're some newly-canonized "saint" if you can't tell the difference between the *blessed* and the *damned*.

1263. To put the old saw another way—and more personally in a gender way—: *You never miss your hair till your head runs bald.*

1264. Nowadays, too much is blamed on Mother Nature and not enough on Father Time!

1265. Gosh-O-Willikens! I had *your* chance, and flubbed it!

1266. *Too much of a good thing* is just about right for *me*!

1267. "Everytime I Feel the Spirit Moving in *Your* Heart, I Will Pray!"

1268. Shea always wished me *well*—until I got *sick*.

1269. Hands covered with crumbs, and he still cries for cake.

1270. You should be ashamed of myself!

1271. Do eagles ever get too proud to soar with hawks?

1272. Maggots asked prison wardens to consider sending down a better grade of specimen.

1273. The poor may help to make up the laws, but the rich insert each clause.

1274. He's damned if he does—and damned *after* he does it.

1275. Oh, I'm having the *time of my life*! (In case I forgot to tell you, I'm in *jail*, of course.)

1276. Hey, I just saw Yesterday rush by and overtake Tomorrow. Now I'd rather hang around with Today, but there's no Future in it.

1277. Isn't it amazing and alarming how the White Man has still ignored and denigrated the First Settlers of this country, the Indians! Notice, too, how such a discourse generally creates silence on the part of the White Man almost every time? Is this due to embarrassment or callousness on his part?

1278. As long as you're the target, I'll just keep on *practicing*.

1279. "Of Thee I('d) Sing . . ." (if I knew the words and melody.)

280. Surmising can so often be surprising.

1281. "Till I Waltz Again With You . . ." (keep on sitting out all the other steps.)

1282. "Long Ago and Far Away . . ." (You meant so much to me, but, remember, that was *very, very* long ago and *very, very* far away!)

1283. O.K., Americans, when you develop lung cancer or throat cancer from the inherent dangers of tobacco, don't blame those Iroquis folks; just remember the horrendous Manhattan Island Real Estate Deal for something like twenty-four smackers. Isn't there something called a reciprocal trade-off deal that is *still* extant?

1284. Don't gloat over achievements. Last year's successes may prove to be this year's failures.

1285. It always gives me a sad jolt to see a tender spring-green leaf escape a tree in such an early part of the season.

1286. Every time I whisper *goodbye*, why do you always yell out *hello*?

1287. Isn't it amazing how communicative and caring we become to our fellow-beings during giant crises, and how hostile and uncaring we grow in times of relative ease and calm? Does it take fear of survival alone to make us see each other as brother (and sister) beyond the skin?

1288. The element of surprise always *only* if that element of surprise is pleasing, of course. Do you hear?

1289. Life in the *Old Days* weren't *better* — they were just *older*.

1290. Old Age has arrived when you, after looking down, forget to tie your shoes, and when you *do* remember, you *still* can't do it.

1291. Age doesn't have to don boxing gloves to fight the ravages of Time.

1292. Philosophers insist on identifying some as members of the "common man" gender, while no man considers himself as being *common!*

1293. They say island dwellers make the best soldiers, while others declare the best soldiers make the island dwellers. *You* choose.

1294. Prejudice is nurtured on the "milk of (un)human kindness," Mr. Billy Shakespeare, to quote you out of context.

1295. The taproot of love needs deep watering and nourishment if the tree is to grow and flourish, couples there.

1296. Super-conceited is he who only works with a chisel to handle crossword puzzles to carve in stone. He's super-conceited — or — is lost beyond all common sense redemption.

1297. You're not anemic, but in *your* case, you certainly *should* be!

1298. You ask me why do I love you. I can only answer, "Be darned if I know, and if I knew, more than likely, I wouldn't!"

1299. King Lear had "girl trouble . . ." his own murder-inspiring daughters. At least it was kept in the family.

1300. Shakespeare is so easy to quote nowadays because: (1) Who reads the Bard today anyway anymore, and (2) Most folks don't understand "Shakie" now, nor ever did!

1301.   Henry Ford learned to "drive a hard bargain"—until it eventually ran out of petrol.

1302.   Even "Siggy" Freud didn't understand "Siggy" Freud most of the time.

1303.   The most overworn and insipid adjective at the top of the female's descriptive list is *cute*—with the male, it's phrase: the *greatest*. Are our verbal developmental stages halted through *indifference*—or *ignorance*?

1304.   Nothing picks up a love's sagging heart like a pink rose when it's fifteen below outside. That's why florists are the most envied of men, I suppose.

1305.   When love has to offer a warranty (as a constancy stipulation), far better one should *love* a lawyer in the *stipulatory* business.

1306.   That counter clerk there is a *jerk* even without a *soda-making* machine in sight!

1307.   If one cannot remain happy and pleasant at least one hundred times longer than one experiences anger and displeasure, then such a life would fare better playing the role of Crusoe-before-Friday-days forever!

1308.   I may not seem as *sweet* as *sugar*, but I've had my *lumps*!

1309.   Corn and wheat growers get upset when Nature goes *against the grain*.

1310.   Don't let Summer bring out the Winter of your life.

1311.   Lord, why is it that I can utter *I'm sorry* only once, and (grudgingly) to my shouting "*It's all your fault* twenty times or more?

1312.   Boy, if Old Age came before Youth, only one-tenth of one percent of us would be willing to wait for it!

1313.   Redundancy and circumlocution—take these verbal guides away from the average public speaker, and such a peace and calm that *passeth all understanding* would so heavenly prevail we wouldn't even ask for the whereabouts of Miss Solitude!

1314.   You never say, "I dare you to love me" because you know I'd never take up such a commanding and demanding impossibility.

1315.   Sure, one must suffer for love, but, my dear, why make me your personal *martyr*?

1316.   Words can be weapons, so be careful and not *shoot* your mouth off!

1317.   Small minds can never generate great ideas.

1318.   He *landed* a big one, but couldn't eat it.

1319.   Remember: Just because he's your *color*, he does *not* have to be your *kind*.

1320.   It was done *simultaneously*, and also it was done at the *same time*.

1321. Deny me, but don't defy me!

1322. Conceitedness has made some entertainment "stars" really feel they do rival right now the biggest heavenly bodies—thanks entirely to a materialistic-worshipping and blind public.

1323. Nothing can age you more quickly and permanently than being *elderly*.

1324 You'd better contact a good caterer if you can't "Guess Who's Coming to Dinner?"

1325. Isn't it amazingly tragic how minorities, for a "place" in the "sun" controlled by Majority Man, fight minorities, and how it is Majority Man who profits by such blind pettinesses?

1326. "Love Makes the World Go 'Round . . ." (Hate brings it to a grinding halt!)

1327. Playing "musical chairs" with love can often mean there's SRO, you would-be-specialty-"picky" lover!

1328. Many a time he or she who plays "second fiddle," simply should have the *strings* tightened.

1329. He's always looking beyond to yesterday.

1330. I'd grant you the right to be wrong, but you seem to always do all things in giant *excess*.

1331. Wait for me here, dear; I'll be conveniently *gone!*

1332. Love: applying truth to promise, and maintaining and/or augmenting the assignment. That's all that love really is.

1333. I only wish I could wish you happiness, but, darling, you know how I detest flatterers.

1334. You have such an insecure way of assuring me of your security. Is it because you love to live *dangerously?* (If you call that living?)

1335. Indignation can also be displayed passively—and with as much conviction.

1336. Perhaps, after all, promiscuity is the greatest adversary to "safe sex."

1337. Let nothing come between us—except our nightly private prayers.

1338. Catch me if you can while I'm standing still.

1339. Tears of joy, tears of pain: Their proximity is so great neither one can boast of supremacy.

1340. Public Speaker, be careful; perhaps the public doesn't care for the introduction, the middle part, or the ending of your speech. The Public may be much smarter than you realize, buster!

1341. Lies are knives that leave such deep scars upon unsuspecting hearts.

1342. A toothless tiger as a housepet is a wise choice, but keep it away from an unscrupulous "vet"-dentist!

1343. We met as friends—we part as strangers.

1344. Those eight other fingers are jealous of the rule of thumb, and they've voted without pointing accusing finger, hands down.

1345. It's not the rhythm but the drum sounds that send her into paroxysms of uncontrollable joy.

1346. Biting off the nose to spite one's face can have advantages. Expensive mirrors, for example, would be totally unnecessary.

1347. With today's heavy influx of counterfeit currency, it's *Seller, beware!*

1348. Most kings were funnier by far than their jesters any day were—only the kings didn't know it.

1349. Say, tell me when do our "tender years" really begin—or end, for that matter?

1350. Take a special pride in being proud (but only for the *right* reason.)

1351. What do you mean: "Pride comes before a fall?" Heck, in *his* case there, he's never been up!

1352. "And a little child shall lead them." What! Without a compass or map? Aw, come now!

1353. He believed my twenty-five lies but doubted my single truth.

1354. What's this, gravediggers and cemetery caretakers, you're starting a new tombstone territory before you fill up the first? You must be anticipating a lot new trade, eh?

1355. Having brunch is simply another way of serving "franks" on French roll with special mustard on the side next to the inelegant "dills," listening to recordings by "Far and-Awaythoven."

1356. I was to be "taken for a ride" by hoods, but the vehicle broke down, so we all had to push.

1357. Judge to recividist: "These are the crimes that 'fry' men's souls!"

1358. Singer: "I'll Get By." (Nasty Voice in the Crowd: "Yeah, but *why?*")

1359. What kind of opposing views are these: One voice intones, "The grass is greener in the other yard," and then bluesfully sings of the "Green, Green Grass of Home"? (Please, somebody, make up his mind!)

1360. "I Wonder Who's Kissing Her Now?" (—now that her wrinkle-grease is running down her chin. . . .)

1361. "I've Got a Gal in Kalamazoo . . ." (Big deal! I've got four in the Bronx Zoo!)

1362. "I Can't Stop Loving You . . ." (unless you stop *paying* me.)

1363. "You Are Always in My Heart . . ." (That's why I've undergone sixteen by-passes and ten valve replacements, too.)

1364. "Tonight We Love . . ." (Tomorrow we "split"!)

1365. "If You Knew Susie Like I Know Susie . . ." you'd triple her *paying* price!)

1366. "You're the Object of My Affection . . ." (And I object to *any* romantic overtures from you regarding the affection . . . or infection!)

1367. "I Don't Want to Set the World on Fire . . ." (I just want to get the fire started in my *furnace.*)

1368. "I Don't Want to Walk Without You . . ." (so I brought along ample cab fare, kid.)

1369. I said, "Let's be seen "Dancing Cheek to Cheek . . ." (I did *not* say "Check to Check"—unless you're covering *both.*)

1370. Sometimes things are too hazardous to "play it safe."

1371. You are free to love any married woman—as long as that "any married woman" is *your* wife!

1372. You can never replace a dissatisfied god; try to appease the old.

1373. The older you get, the more beautiful a sparrow's chirp becomes.

1374. Don't worry over Summer—Autumn always return. Just worry about *your* return.

1375. Measure the tree's root system before you dig the hole.

1376. At least *pretend* you're brave in front of your kids, dad!

1377. I always salvage what I do not want.

1378. The finest silk frock still impresses no silkworms.

1379. Worst Pun Div.: The inveterate pianist was drawn to scale.

1380. Not all open mouths are conducive to housefly visitation explorations.

1381. When the lantern goes out, why not go out with it?

1382. I substituted for my brother's incarceration period, so I was having the "time of *his* life."

1383. Hello, Mr. *Alone,* I see you are known by the *friends* you keep.

1384. And another thing, "All work and no *pay* makes Jack a dull debtor."

1385. In *your* case, you'd better make new friends beyond the grave for you're in bad shape on *this* side.

1386. You cut the tree down, and *then* you ask me to climb it.

1387. He burned his house down to warm his hands.

1388. Thief, generally, no pre-planned avenue of escape means post-concocted one sets you up as easy capture target.

1389. You wonder just what cranes have to *whoop* about—their *coughing?*

1390. Always contemplate about yesterday when tomorrow has arrived.

1391. Somehow, I've always felt sorry for my wife's husband.

1392. Never let me forget to forget about you.

1393. Why spoil such a beautiful day, John, by *your* waking up?

1394. It's a good thing some mountain peaks can't reverse themselves.

1395. The *sight* of you makes me hard of *hearing*.

1396. In the cremation, why say, "Ashes to ashes and dust to dust"? The urn speaks for itself—and graphically so.

1397. He guffaws loudly at my *tiniest* miscue; he half-smiles at his biggest *faux pas*.

1398. Make no mistake: *I* make no mistakes!

1399. Darling, please tango . . . "Till I Waltz Again With You."

1400. Not because my maternal grandmother was part Indian, but I feel one of the most devilishly innocuous, yet demeaning phrases that we've employed for scores of years is *honest Injun*. And don't forget the equally demeaning term, or statement: *"Don't be an Indian giver."*

1401. Yes, *Bible*, the "poor are always with us," but the rich are always *over* us.

1402. Noise can only produce more noise and little noises.

1403. God is never, never a God of condescension.

1404. What is *one's distance* when one is asked to *stay*—and how is it *measured*—centimeters or miles?

1405. Possess, but never be *By Love Possessed*.

1406. Johnny, *outer space* is not the same as being *spaced out*!

1407. By all means, if the coffin does not fit, don't force. At least last rites should be last *rights*.

1408. When you say, "I can handle it," be sure the pail has one.

1409. When you're finally *ripe* for living, old age has to come in and spoil it all.

1410. No one has to be taught to love—just taught to *unlove*. And, Lord, that's the pity of it all, and shame upon the consciences of the responsible tutors and mentors!

1411. A blind man will heap adulation even upon the one-eyed compatriot.

1412. Show me *how* to fall in love, and then maybe the tumble won't be all that painful.

1413. Pure music requires no special instrument, just an understanding and proficient instrumentalist.

1414. Why not reach for the moon—you couldn't catch and hold on to the sun, Fred!

1415. I never worry about "star wars." These here on *earth* are more than damning and damnable enough!

1416. Keep on going around and around, and eventually you'll meet yourself coming back!

1417. Well-prepared food deserves to be ritualistically honored, as well as the cook.

1418. When you drill or sink a well, sink it deeper with your neighbor in mind, please.

1419. I tried to not touch you, but the *tactisty* of love was most too potent for my weakened nature. I didn't lose that *touch*.

1420. No, Mary-Jane, he didn't say you were "sloe-eyed" like a deer. He said you were "slow-eyed" like a bat! Gosh, you don't listen closely, do you?

1421. Thank God, this Headed-for-Death Ship has sprung a leak!

1422. Do hangmen ever hold annual confabs to compare job analyses and totals?

1423. Crows attacked bluebirds because crows thought bluebirds were *poor voice instructors* in matin madrigals! (Can you imagine!)

1424. "I Can't Stop Loving You . . ." (And God knows I've tried!)

1425. A true friend will visit even if he knows the cupboard is totally and abysmally bare of all viands!

1426. Hell stops just short of this block. That's why it doesn't pay for me to move.

1427. I said "wake me up . . ." not "shake me up!" Heavens!

1428. Don't live so far from Earth that Heaven will have little use for you as well.

1429. I took the back way home because my wife had the front way blocked and the door bolted. (See, I'm not all *that* stupid!)

1430. There is no sin like a sin repeated.

1431. I'll never forget and forgive you the pain you *almost* caused me!

1432. Even his vaunted dynamism is over-loaded with a special lethargy.

1433. The maligned minority victim who witnesses a foul verbal attack on another minority group and glorifies in such a vile repesentation is almost as guilty as the originator of the heinous act. He may be even more reprehensible because he affords silent tacit approval.

1434. Love may be careless at times, but never contentious at *any* time.

1435. Gray hair doesn't necessarily bespeak of wisdom, but gray hair at least has had *time* on its side.

1436. Money changing hands does not lower the money's value—only if it's counterfeit.

1437. I would give you my *all*, but, lady, I have *already*!

1438. A Hell on Earth can be no more disagreeable and unbearable than the hell that is really in Hell.

1439. A desperate man will resort to any extreme—even to *Love*!

1440. The sweet Life takes the bitter taste out of an imposing Death.

1441. Child, only if you *ask* me will I say *no*!

1442. "Thanks for the Memory . . ." (that I have already *forgotten*!")

1443. Don't curse the curative powers now that you're well again.

1444. Isn't it sad how fewer young brains are heeding each September's academic bells for higher learning!

1445. Many times it's really pointless to be so blunt.

1446. Termites are eating into the statue made of steel the town erected in my honor last week.

1447. My insufficiency is *more* than enough for you.

1448. Farmer, you said, "The devil take the hindmost." But that's where the milk is! Boy, you must be really disgusted with it all!

1449. A south wind is most welcome in a northern January calendar time.

1450. Like faulty pancake batter, you didn't stir me at all, sister!

1451. He's so stingy he's too tight to open his fist for fear of losing what he even doesn't have!

1452. Beware of the cocky rooster that crows at high noon on a bright June day! Cook him or sue the rascal for lying!

1453. Better take me as I am, for there "ain't" *that* much left now!

1454. Again from the Bad Pun Office: Honey, *bee* yourself "Until I *Wasp* Again With You" (in my sharp and stinging *yellowjacket*.)

1455. Sir, you being ninety-six proves the adage: "The *good die young*!"

1456. In Life's devious machinations, the trick is *not* to get tricked.

1457. Too often, conformist, one gets drowned, and quickly so, by "going with the flow."

1458. There's something pretty macabre about a stand-up comedian act in a cemetery. (Maybe he's there (or she's) there, to avoid those "more-than-likely boos" so likely to emanate. And comedian will be caught there *dead* to right!

1459. We can never know how many would've been soldiers' parents with *means* helped their sons to live safe-states-side unbarracked lives. Can we?

1460. Say, being a foxhole G.I. in W.W.II, and the son of a Black doughboy in W.W.I, I can honestly ask: How many times has a flag won a battle? Not that I don't love Old Glory as much as the next patriot; it's that it's often those who wave the hardest have done or will do the least when it really comes to that *combat* stuff.

1461. If lies are "music to your ears," you'd better check on the score and on your eardrums. Both are in question.

1462. The "truth never hurts . . ." (unless it's *discovered*!)

1463. The smartest worms I know work from without to within. They don't trust the other way around.

1464. Enough irritable discord can even get a bald-headed man's "dandruff up!"

1465. Not all doves and pigeons are kind and docile, the jealous hawk notwithstanding, folks.

1466. Not all personnel carry the *Wall Street Journal* for reading and perusing purposes.

1467. My Grandma Nora would say, "Treat him/her with a long-handled spoon." I've found using a twenty-foot ladle is even *better*!

1468. When I say, dear, "Let's face it," I mean the problem—not at *me*! Oh, you say that I *am* the problem? Forget I even inquired.)

1469. Pity the poor housewife and mother. (Few do.)

1470. Remember, you can't slice your meat morsel and chew it at the same time.

1471. We played the game of "*Follow*-the-Leader . . ." (only we played it *backwards*—and had more fun!)

1472. Whites fear Blacks far more than Blacks fear Whites. Yet the former wields the most potency against fear—*monetary solvency*.

1473. William, remember: One can be loud without displaying any degree of garrulity.

1474. Be sure your adamancy for a cause is well worth such a stand.

1475. The worse statement you must never say to a desert dweller: "Sorry, but the case won't hold water."

1476. We must rise as one, or go down in bunches, Humanity.

1477. Who listens to stop anymore? (Or who stops to listen?)

1478. Most parishioners nowadays seem to feel churches, mosques, and temples are bolted from the *inside*!

1479. You say the sea is our mother? Well, why not right now go and let "Mother" bathe you!

1480. Reaching for Tomorrow and he hasn't even found *Yesterday*!

1481. With apologies to Bill Cullen Bryant's great poem, "Thanatopsis, a look at life and death, that says in part, "So live that when thy summons come . . . etc." . . . I say, *So live when thy summons come, you'll go quietly and pay the speeding violation ticket*, Bub!

1482. You insist, "Take me as I am," but *I* say there must be something of value to take in the first place, m'deah!

1483. He was such a vain soloist, he tried to outsing the "Anvil Chorus!"

1484. I'm in a kind of dilemma about the cemetery problem: When I depart this "terrain of tears," will the present occupants be glad to receive me, and will the *upright populace* be glad to "dump" me? I really do *not* wish an answer. It's purely rhetorical, you know.

1485. Perhaps the Worst Sight-and-Sound Pun Ever in the King's Court: "Frank Lee, speak, King!"

1486. The journey's awfully tough when there are more leaders than followers.

1487. Isn't it a sin how too much of America's social *and* moral life is based on skin coloring?

1488. If nothing else, all of the citizens respect the town's water tank.

1489. If Love strikes, why not play the old bomerang game, and with greater accuracy.

1490. Don't you hate the word *retaliate?* Well, *I*—certainly do!

1491. "I Found a Million Dollar Baby at a Five and Ten Cent Store . . ." (but that store's long been bankrupt, love-seeker!)

1492. Is *goodness* passé today? (Oh, my *goodness!*)

1493. Sure, I want "Someone to Watch Over Me . . ."—but you have such poor eyesight! Besides, you're too much in love with *mirrors* (which is a bad *reflection* on your part, too.)

1494. Don't bother to knock. . . . (In fact, don't *bother!*)

1495. Spare me the *gory details;* for you see, I, too, plan to *marry!*

1496. It's a long, long ways back home, if you were chased out in the first place.

1497. He argued over the check even before he ordered the meal.

1498. "Man appoints," while God *dis*appoints. (Or is it the *other* way around, folks?)

1499. "My house is your home . . ." (as soon as I *move* out, or am *thrown* so.)

1500. She sees more with her *ears* than most folks see with their *eyes!*

PART VI

Measured Verse
"Sing a Song of Sonnets"

Had I Not

Had I not lost time hating you,
And all concocted visions held
That made me think of voodoo's brew,
All evil prophecies unfulfilled
Or taken time when skies were blue
To quietly call you to my side,
Pointing some special cloud to you
That fierce sunrays had sought to hide,
Or had I heeded inner tone
That spoke the need of simple trust,
Perhaps I would not lean alone
While bone-dry years flake off as rust.

Your loving ways would've made me glad—
And what a time we *could* have had!

-11/93

Stubbornness Pays a Price

They say you loved me 'way back then,
When bud and flower burst in bloom,
That you knew when just to say when
And beg us watch some rose in bloom.
They also swear, reiterate,
That you showed patience of old Job,
And pleaded long for us to wait,
Dress ourselves in restraintful robes;
That loves does not jump times ahead,
Run headlong into tomorrow.
Too many hasty hearts had bled,
And brought such hearts unto sorrow.

But who was I to heed advice?
I was proud soul. I wouldn't think *twice!*

-11/93

From a Protected Child to His Dead Mother

To spare me pain was your intent,
And shield me from hurts of the street,
To curtail certain embarrassment

233

You knew that I would surely meet.
You knew our fine, our cultured ways
Had to steer clear of ghetto tone
That would darken my moods and days.
Though such might mean moving alone,
And so my hands stayed spotless-clean,
While other worlds escaped our door,
Safe we in our time machine—
Abstention would reign evermore!

Now you've gone. Mother, you're dead—
Where can I turn *bewildered* head?

On the Thirtieth Anniversary of Great
Freedom March—Aug. 28, 1963)

We marched on Washington, felt good,
Held burning hands and knew that we
Had no more need to *knock on wood*—
Ours more than promised victory.
We heard a slight man with a *dream*
Roar out at last that we had come
To ache no more from Hate's extremes,
Nor just equality for some.
We'd hide no more Truth's looking glass;
Together strong, we'd hew a stone
To tell the world: "New days will pass—
Black and White shall rise as *one*!

Today we re-search Langston's word:
What happen(ed) *to* (our) *dream deferred?*
-11/93

Trying to Write a Sonnet on Trying to Write the Sonnet

How I've tried to coin the sonnet!
Have tried and cried—to no avail—
Hours of pain wasted upon it,
Yet every effort doomed to fail.
Oh, I could get the meter right,
Words carved with diligence, and more,
Words of pure beauty, swept in flight—
Only to lose the metaphor!

Or after putting this in place,
I would forget transition's line.
So there I'd sit, "egg on my face,"
Wishing to heaven *thing* not mine!

I'll live the hour only to rue it:
Stand by me—someday I'll *do* it!
                    -8/1/87

But No Comparison Here

Funny how love plays with the brain,
Denying brain the art to think,
And yet, inuring cells to pain
Like one who's had too much to drink,
Or like buoyed swimmer facing wave,
Though long ago all strength was spent,
And should have meekly welcomed grave,
Nor watchers know the path he went;
Or like a willow snatched by storm,
Roots left to blacken sharp with frost,
Widely exposed to every harm
Summarily, and left for lost.

I would compare our love as such,
But we two care so *overmuch*!
                    -8/1/87

Love and Luck: Gambler's Choice

I've had no luck at all,
And yet I've held great need, and more
To serve a warmth and comfort shawl,
To serve as lock upon a door.
Perhaps it is the curse of gods
Who'd dare compete with mortals here,
But yet must know such bitter rods
Must flagellate with curse severe.
There is perhaps another cause,
Just why I have so been denied,
Just why they've been preventive laws"
Said I'm unworthy. (They have lied!)

235

Just *you* could change such circumstance,
If you would say, "I'll risk romance!"
                                        -8/1/87

You, the Query-Raiser

I used to count myself as wise,
Among the wisest of this age,
Granted perception to surmise
Thoughts from the most respected sage,
Even before I'd read or heard
And met philosopher discreet
Who'd seek to clarify the word,
To make each reasoning complete.
So thus I moved from hour to hour,
Basked in wisdom I possessed,
So proudly strutting with this power—
Nothing wondered, nothing guessed—
Until you posed this question tough:
Why is it hard for man to love?
                                        8/1/87

A Lesson Learned Here

After living so many lives,
Each one far grander than the last,
And each on blind ego thrives,
Being both character *and* cast,
So proud and self-contained, a sphinx,
Demanding homage to my feet,
And knew mine were the *missing links*
That made knowledge final, complete.
I knew that I was Tomorrow,
The Present Tense, also the Then.
Who'd believe I'd embrace sorrow,
Not only once, but yet again?

It filled me to the brim with rage.
Oh, but *once* I did hold *front stage*!
                                        -8/1/87

236

Black American Query
(Modern Tense)

I try to cover bruise with smile,
Pretend my mouth's not crammed with dirt,
That pain does not escort each mile;
There is no subtle nor binding hurt.
I try to say each hill's less steep,
And each day filled with one less stone,
That no ill—ease invades my sleep,
Or rips the throat with mocking moan.
God knows I fight to catechize,
To weigh each face by its own weight,
Fight to repel angers that rise,
Envy that would contaminate.

This I ask, Christ: (I must be weak!)
"How can I still turn the 'other cheek' "?
8/1/87

American Indian Youth Speak-out

I'm no *poor, wayfaring stranger,*
A-trudging on some barren land."
I have long been linked to danger,
This native soil on which I stand.
Chief Sitting Bull or Pontiac—
They were redmen, steeped full of pride;
Today, cabined, we want it back,
And, though unseen, their spirits ride:
"Good Cherokee, you wait no more!
This land is yours as much as theirs!
Where is that pride that was before
From Crow tribes down to Delawares?"

So, watch, White Man, we've things to prove:
You'd best respond. *We rise to move!*
-8/1/87

Upon a Special Spouse's Passing

"Ashes to ashes . . ." I have heard,
Rendering final, no reprieve,

237

Brutal as any spoken word
For any soul to up and leave.
Heart-crushed, indeed, and sore enough
To de-marrow, turning to stone
The gentlest of most human stuff,
Then fragmentize the sternest bone,
And bring to life beyond the dreams
A terror borne of loneliness,
Which makes the dead more than it seems,
And denigrates beyond regress.

Such is the passing of her I've made,
Cursing dank shadows deep in shade.
4/11/87

Of Course, if It's for *Love!*

I'd love you till Hades should freeze
And sprout icicles from its vaults,
Swearing love's no dream all made to tease
And say my faults were normal faults;
I'd hold you close till Euphrates
Becomes dustbed for new Stone Age
And even longer, gods to please,
And keep our love down-center-stage;
I'd swear the rose worst bloom with stem,
That crabgrass puts to shame each rose,
That beauty wears false diadem
And no thing's right as we'd suppose.

Such fabrications gladly make
If for the *truth* and *true* love's sake!
4/11/87

Losing and Houses

At last the open house was shut.
At last the rafters would not shake.
No more would window ask: "What's what?",
Nor door beams creak as if to break,
Come tumbling down in frenzied heap
As if angry ghosts controlled the scene;
Red flames dare do little more than peep

238

Not as they roared skywardly keen,
Bringing a calm I had not known
Before Life dealt me vicious blow
And search for moan-below-a-moan
Since so abrupt you had to go.

Yet, I'd endure great holocaust
Could I re-gain what I have lost.

4/11/87

A Note to the World

"O world, I cannot hold thee close enough. . . !"
Who scribed those words before I crossed the scene?
Is such impassioned cry more showboat stuff
So sharp observer will not probe between,
Or shallow listener's assent only pose,
Eager to please but in duplicity?
And who will substitute each flaming rose
For lesser bloom and immorality?
Or was it neither one listed above,
But soul more timid, yet with brighter fire
To tell the world it is a case of love,
Of unadulterated heart's desire?

The way you, world, has made me toe the line,
You know no such confession dare be *mine*.

4/12/87

Honest, I've Been True!

I've been so true in this affair,
Though normally I'm otherwise:
With flightful heart, with roving eyes
That tend to wander everywhere
If flirting skirt is passing there
To catch a codger by surprise,
Especially one who can't surmise
A reason for *promised* affair.

I tell you this and nothing more
Because I'm not my *old* self now,
Nor vagabond I used to be.

239

Perhaps you dread things as before,
But, really, I have changed somehow:
Love makes me drink sobriety.

                    -4/12/87

For Us the Living-Dead
(Sonnet Sequence)

O foolish world, arm-locked with fear,
With broken teeth that clatter in your head,
(Or are those bones up-rising from the dead,
That fall like splitting rock upon the ear?)
While from afar, beyond time's hemisphere,
A knife-edge wail, a single word is said.
Is this the weeping Christ whose blood streamed red
And drenched a hill in some imprudent year?
I do not know. A gray-white dove flies high,
Afraid to perch upon a window-sill;
For it, like Truth, will surely have to die,
Crushed, caught between Man's stubborn fist of will.

Unclasp yourself, blind man, and reconcile—
There still is time, though but a fleeting while.

Yet no hand moves about this rancid air
To chain the dove of peace that circles on;
No eye looks up into a paling dawn
To search a hope, nor lift a mouth in prayer.
(For only fools, they say, take time to care,
Fall moaning to sky when day has gone!)
And who is he that dares to rise alone
While futile might of earth spreads everywhere?
So all the bones lie still, re-couch in dust,
And winds stir softly through a bed of leaves,
Charging the air with every passing gust,
But only Love tramps in the night and grieves.

Christ the Penitent speaks no further word:
Only the ring of hammer blows is heard.
                    8/50

240

In Memoriam: Pvt. Logan Johnson
(Died of Wounds in France in
My Outfit)

And you who always had the ready smile,
The freshest laughter in the August sun
That blistered man and earth mile after mile,
And gnawed into the mouth of every gun,
Clearly I see the smile you wore that lone
Bare day. When Death crashed down in GI style,
Struck you across the face, and then was gone,
I forgot all strength, and fright hugged me a while.

Yet you who never courted fear or dread,
Crumpled beside me like an emptied bag,
Clothed in that blank surprise worn by the dead—
Still *smiled*, your curving mouth refused to sag.
And now that guns, that wars, are laid aside,
I must remember France and how you died.
                        8/45

Was Love Sincere?

I chased Love from the great outdoors,
And followed Love before hearth-held fire,
Feeling Love would resist no more
My wild attempt to quell desire.
"Love," said I, "these cozy walls
Are just ideal for satisfaction."
"Ah, no," said Love, "ah, not at all—
Too little chance for sharp distraction."
"You're right, Love." I agreed with him.
"Such indoor setting *is* not the thing.
Your maddening flame should now grow dim:
And we need wait for brandnew spring!"

(Spring came (and went) with labelled blue—
The way Love passed on quietly, too!
                        9/9/86

241

Sonnet for One Poised on a Bridge to Die

Oh, you, divested of Life's wonder now,
Mind cleanly swept of pathway to a star,
Lost sailor undesirous of your prow,
Or whether Heaven's point be near or far!
Oh, you, who turned away the looking glass
For fear of hurt you would discover there,
Knowing full well remorse just would not pass,
Mixing with other cries to say, "Not fair
For Life to hand me 'flip-side' of dreams,
To offer me no respite in the end.
Why is it even bleaker than it seems,
And was not every highway built to bend?"

Pretend that all these years you've been asleep,
And, in so thinking, you negate this leap.
-4/12/79

Turnabout for Love

Turn down the book and read no more.
The light's grown dimmer in your eyes.
You now have learned less than before,
And yet you seem so very wise!
Turn from Picasso on this wall;
The colors move too grossly grim.
He scarce would recognize at all
Such "masters" poured from brush by him.
Listen no more to organ's tune;
Recorded notes have turned to lie,
And you can't quit it all too soon,
And both of us know reason why:

Come, take my hand, let us join hearts.
They follow *us* — not *we* the Arts!
4/12/79

242

Coffin Attire

When I have closed these my eyes at last to sight
To breathe no more my favorite New York air,
Nor picture seagulls wheeling deep in light,
Feeling that they were God's lone objects there;
When street boys argue over score of game

As honking drivers scream invectives shrill,
Although they know it will remain the same:
Boys will be boys and they forever will;
Do not adorn me in a velvet suit,
Nor in some fancied, tailored shirt and tie.
Just robe me in pajamas, then refute
A friend or stranger who would raise an eye.

Oh, yes, *pajamas*. Here is why I say:
I shall have turned to slumber anyway!
                                        4/13/79

In Defense of "Glancing"

Again you've called me horrid name
For winking at another curl.
But it has never been the same:
Always indeed another girl.
In your confusion you have cried,
Asked no forgiveness from you then.
Yet have I sworn—I've really tried—
Never to smile their way again!
And often just a glance slips out
When such a pretty face wisps by.
Nor is it cause for you to pout
Or let a new invective fly!

Now this is solely my intent:
Comparison's a compliment!
                                -4/16/79

Not at All Ungrateful

Grand Lord of Love, you must now know
Although I'm here entombed alone,
Where only fetid air must blow
And add to aching of each bone,
Where other cries of fallen men
Sound out against these tempered bars,
And where these ears re-echo pain,
While my red eyes still dream of stars,
Ungracious host, you swear to me
Entombment's for my own welfare:
Wild dangers roam extensively
Both in the woods and in the air.

Protector, thank you for concern,
But free me now and let me learn.
                              4/16/79

I Must Be Winter, Love, to You

I must be winter time to you,
Nor do I have a link to spring,
Just as the thorn cannot be yew,
Or any other living thing.
Times gone by, I might've been autumn,
Rich with the swirls of flying leaf,
As red winds so swiftly caught them.
I can't be summer filled with grief
For having been so left alone
While beauty's cup swelled to the brim,
But still unoffered for my own
As coppered summer wept to dim.

Now after other seasons go,
You slip to me, arms piled with *snow*!
                              4/17/79

Father to Son or Daughter

If reasonless, or so it seems,
I do berate you without cease,
And thus upset your private dreams,

244

Nor give you one moment of peace,
But "grind and hammer" till your ears
Seem near the bursting point with hate,
And all your fears grow bigger fears,
While you wish me beyond the "Gate,"
So things you've planned go on as planned—
Not stirred at all by old *gadfly*.
A matter I can understand,
But you'd refuse the reason *why*.

Because I pray that you do well,
I point you pitfalls where I fell.

4/18/79

The Elderly Couple Takes a Tour
After Countless Moons

We board this bus with hungry eyes
To drink in sights we've never seen,
As we await each new surprise
And all such wonders in between
As compensation overdue
When lean years held us homebound fast,
Provincial-minded, just us two,
Slipped into mold we did not cast.
But now this is another day
And both our fancies can take flight,
For we can *up, up, and away*,
And turn our dreams into delight.

Yet something sad envelopes you:
Were dreams too long in coming true?

4/19/79

Imperturbability, Death Notwithstanding
(Sonnet in Trimeter Form)

I'll have nothing for you,
Not anything at all,
Though you may plead me to
Through honey-coated call
Or silver-vision, Death.
Where luring is an art

245

And heavy measured breath
Would upset normal heart,
And pain a glowing trail,
I will have none of it.
My honor will prevail—
I'll not succumb one bit!

Is that a waltz you play?
Dark Dancer, lead the way!

4/20/79

For Forsythia Blooming in Early Spring

O gray-tan branch alive with stars,
Stars of a ripened cadmiun hue,
Blazed forth to cover winter's scars
And cheer springtime along with you,
While skies remain a doubtful gray
And late snows scud the nearby hill,
Reminding us frost still holds sway,
(And seems that it forever will),
I'll long savor this early gold
When summer comes and floods the scene,
In colors riotous to behold,
And you have toned to duller green.

Some may forget your early fling,
But I'll remember you brought spring!

4/20/79

To a Seventeen-Year-Old Girl on a Stoop

Intertwining your long slender fingers,
Sitting there in the shadows all alone,
Desire straining flesh from reluctant bone,
Like wet clothes from rough iron wringers,
Girl of seventeen, caught between an age
That has no place for an inquiring mind,
Ahead lies a void—dull memory behind
Which chains you to a past, locked in a cage.

What doubts rise on this eve of womanhood

Despair that you can never understand—
Is this world to you wholly gay and good,
With dreams of romance floating across your land?
Perhaps you sit absorbing the world's woe,
Or maybe there is no desire to know.
11/47

A Black Brother's Prayer
(Blank Verse Sonnet with Couplet)

Lord, press wide the eyelids of my own eyes
That I may shun the vile iniquities
Of hate that clasps too close and often binds
So many of my whiter brothers' minds.
It is so hard to be hated and not hate,
To turn the other cheek, to shift the weight
And smile as if neither feel nor care
Though my face burn, a million fires flare!
The cloud looms large before the waiting dawn;
The ominous bird of doom flies fiercely on,
Swooping here, there, belching its poisonous slime,
Flung across the noble breast of time.

Lord, open my own mind and heart as well,
For I, too, sometimes worship in Hate's citadel.
2/48

PART VII

Dedication Verse
(POETRY)
"Songs for the 'Dream' King"

Songs for the "Dream" King

1. Modus Operandi

(For Dr. King, John F. Kennedy, Jimmy Jackson, Andrew Goodman, James Chaney, Michael Schwerner, Medgar Evers, James Reeb, Viola Liuzzo . . .) Poem below appeared in newspaper, *Het Schakel Blad Newspaper*, Holland, May, 1968

"*Door een kogel zwijgt de stem*
Van verzet en droom; voor hem
Een eeuwigdurend Requiem."

"He who does not exactly suit our whim,
A sniper's bullet we save for him,
Lasting, lasting, everlasting,
Granitized requiem!"

6/68

2. Death Appreciation

Thank you, O Blind Assassin,
At whose hands Martin King has died:
You gave us a Charcoal Jesus
And updated our Eastertide!

4/68

3. No Taller Need

"I have a dream!" that voice of magic roared
From deepened valley straight to highest hill.
Nor can any of us afford
Not to have such smouldering dream here still.
Each rugged mountain must be made more low
And every dark valley made dry to rise.

251

And each child's dream must have that chance to grow
Beyond the fog-mists in those searching eyes.
Else all are but lies in those Structured Laws—
Else all is dead for Democracy's Cause.

5/68

4. Gladly, America, I Answer!

America, you've raised the query
Just why Black me remains contrary.
Well, every time that sun goes down
I must recall old White John Brown
Hanged for the *Cause* at Harper's Ferry.
And it has been a long-time sign,
And "home's" *still* not yet fully mine!

-12/29/87

5. Martin Luther King—Dead in Spring

Somehow this spring
Is not the spring I used to know—
Not like last year's—
Or three springs ago.
Oh, I know
Grass again bends green
And fresh winds blow.
Even so . . .
Boys and girls,
Quick shadows in glad sun,
Seem to have lost much fun.
Each one . . .
Somehow bird-songs that rise
Above dew-fields
Are madrigals of lies,
And sincerity cries.
Yet, beyond this season's dismal,
Black-draped tone,
There rises a drone,
A monotone.
Beyond this chlorined tear,
This year,
I hear hope tramping to a distant drum.
One *Voice* rings evenly clear!
We shall still. We shall overcome!

4/6/68

6. Martin Luther King, Born in Winter

On this day one step in time,
In one particular year,
Martin King came here . . .
A cold-fisted East-North-East wind
Rattles without the frozen door
While snickering frost paints
Flower-fingers on each thickened windowpane.
(And with blue cold so heightened,
It seems to blunt each worthwhile thought insane.)
In a nail-tough winter moment of our bitter fear.
But on this day one step in time,
In one particular year,
Martin King came here.
Yet, how can we really raise up
An honored banner, a flag,
With these fingers grown ice-sticks
From this relentless cold?
How can we really pay tribute, really brag
That in *our* time *we* knew one man so bold
As to challenge the damning forces
Of mankind's valley of *hate*
With a sky-tall *love* transcending
all land-bound spheres,
He who sought to bring lasting peace
Within every sealed-up mental gate?
Still, we must recall, relate
On this day one step in time
In one particular year,
Martin King came here.

                    10/77

7. Martin Luther King Blues

It could be these blues I sing
Ain't nothing new, Martin L. King.
But one's tired of the same refrain,
Tired of standing in unrelenting rain,
And still see freedom a *mean old thing*.
Could be these blues that I profess
Only mirage in *bag-man* dress,
That there's sweeter music after all

253

Played by God over this high wall,
Softly singing in some hope-lit hall.
But I been fooled so many times,
Looked for dollars, but just got dimes,
I now don't trust a doggone thing.
But that's the way some things are still,
And some folks swear they always will,
Good Brother Martin Luther King.
Therefore, man, I can't help but choose
These mean old *Martin Luther Blues.*
(And, man, you know I've *paid my dues*!)
                                    12/87

8. Not Quite Sure About Hating You

Were I dead sure I hated you,
I'd say, *Hey, you I really hate!*
But since I'm not too sure that is true,
I'll stick with *love*. Old *hate* can wait.
My good friend, wouldn't *you*?
                                    2/88

9. About Dr. King

The special thing
About Dr. King
That has spun in my head
Is: He *lived* everything
That he preached or said!
                                    1/8/88

10. Reason for Seasons to Change

In winter's coldest frame,
Martin Luther, he came.
With newest-blooming spring:
Out he went—our Martin King.
                                    1/8/88

11. Some Things and Time

Ah! Some things they just linger so!
Creating yet our stranger fears.
Can you imagine, really know,
Since so abrupt, King had to go,
It now has been full twenty years!
And yet how some things linger so!
                              1/8/88

12. Me? Too Bad I Wasn't Around

The one thing that makes me,
The one thing that shakes me,
And brims me up with dark regret,
Is fact that I was nowhere near
To laugh aloud or burn a tear
When Dr. King preached so of love,
And marched his way right on through here!
                              1/8/88

13. God, the Great Sculptor

No, friend, M. King has long been gone.
His image? Not another one!
See, when God sculpted from purest gold,
Our Sculptor God just broke the mold!
                              1/8/88

14. Sorry, Not *I*! Not *I*!

If one would spit right in my face,
Then should I pause and give *embrace*,
And simply call attacker *dumb*,
Then shout that *I shall overcome*,
Get down on my knees and pray
Attacker flee his evil way?
And should you ask me how could I?
Gosh! I don't think I'd even try!
(I'd be *mad* enough to *die*!
And, being human, you know why.)
                              1/8/88

15. Long Live Dr. King

Eighty seasons gone
Is such a long-time gone,
O my! a long time gone,
A mighty long time gone!
Seventy-three hundred nights and days!
Memory creates such layered dust;
Even metal gives way to rust.
This may be true of other things,
Like statuettes and copper rings—
Not the power-imaged Martin King!

For though it's been a full round score,
Seems that he's just passed out Life's Door.
And should you pause to question me,
Now I say such will *always* be!
And you can take it here from me!
So, let us rise and proudly sing:
Long live King! Long live the King!
(And here we do mean *Martin* King!)
1/8/88

16. Despite the Loss of Noble Blood

Despite spilled blood
Of Martin King,
Freedom's still a good,
Good far-off thing.
In fact, so far
I have to wonder:
Is that freedom's star
A-hanging 'way out yonder?
Or last year's leaves
All dried and brown
Under early sunset
Going down?
8/22/86

17. An Old Back-of-the-Bus Rider Remembers

Lord Jesus! Poor me!
Rode so long
In the back of the bus
When I ride up front,
I think the bus's
Going in *reverse*!

And to prove here
The thing I say:
I asked bus driver
Only the other day:
"Son, you gonna *back* home,
All the way?"

(Lord Jesus! Poor me!)

8/88

18. A Prayer for All on Martin King's Birthday

O great and puissant God,
God of Almighty Wind and Wave,
Awake in us upon this sod
Your awesome, yet gentle will to save!
We who here so confusedly stand,
And have so thus stood for many years
As shadowed robots of blind command,
To play fool hosts to streams of fears,
Grant that we might—that now we must—
Must swift-unwind this tightened reel
That's spun most dreams almost to dust.
Grant us the love to *truly* feel
Another's tarnished, or battered, trust,
Another's faltering loss of faith,
As did mount-gazing Martin King,
Whose beaconed life, though stilled by death,
Left Hope with us a Song to sing!

11/77

19. "To Keep Alive the Name of Martin"

Let not the leaves of calendars,
Nor fingers pointing to Time's clock,
Shut out the *Dream* he held with stars,
While posed upon this earth-bound rock.

How often, and again, too soon,
Do deed of worth escape the tongue,
While acts of hate serve but as boon
To resurrect each human wrong.

But let us not, forging ahead,
Fail to remember this at all:
Hate, made our ruler, fountainhead,
In time, will make whole body fall.

So, let's re-live a moment's shame,
Cast by a single shot one night,
And see that glory's enlarged his name,
A face that casts a wonder-light
And flowers still more red the flame!
                                    9/76

20. No Taller Need

I have a dream! that voice of magic roared
From deepened valley straight to highest hill,
Nor can any one of us afford
Not to have such potent dream here still.

Each rugged mountain must be made more low
And every dark valley made to rise,
And children's dreams must have that chance to grow
Beyond the fog-mists in their searching eyes.
Else all are but lies in those Structured Laws—
Else all is dead for Democracy's Cause.
                                    7/77

258

21. From Winter to Spring
(For Martin King's Birthday)

The skies were dark that January day,
And so many such days most surely are.
But all future smiled on that very day
When *love* lowered to earth its *destined star*.

Winds might have screamed sharp in a biting gale,
And not one bluebird poised nearby to sing.
But neither wind nor rain nor slash of hail
Could stop the advent of this giant *King*!

And true: From '29 to '68,
It is such a shortened, narrowed span.
Yet within those years stretched a mind so great,
For *freedom*, proud, had made an *all-year* man!

Perhaps it was right to arrive in snow,
In such a frost-time for Martin L. King,
When man's *wintered* hopes feel only woe,
Then leave a world full in the arms of *spring*.

11/71

22. Celebrating King's Day

This is Martin King's holiday!
Why not step out to celebrate
In such a most resounding way
So worlds will hear us dedicate,
Recalling him with shouts and cheers,
With flags high-flying down each street,
Recalling all those bitter years
King led with voice, with burning feet!

No. No wild shouts or blaring bands:
Let's quietly sit and join our hands.
Martin King would smile: He'd understand . . .

6/69

23.Remembering Martin King
(A Villanelle)

The dream he dreamed has never died,
But has grown taller with the years,
For hope's never quite crucified.
And yet how often have we tried
To introduce a rash of fears!
The dream he dreamed has never died.
Though pessimists seek to deride,
Deep thoughts will be made clear;
For hope's never quite crucified.
We feel he moves right here beside
When doubts increase a flow of tears,
For hope's never quite crucified.
We can't deny our fratricide,
Nor raise a round of lusty cheers—
The dream he dreamed has never died.
We must press on, each, side by side,
Destroy despair both far and wide.
The dream he dreamed has never died,
For *Hope's* never quite crucified.

10/3/79

24. A Sad Birthday Poem for Dr. M. L. King

Why is the snow powdering down
On this some quiet winter town,
From cloud-filled spaces 'way up there,
Like lady bowed beneath white shawl,
Bending so softly deep in prayer?

Don't you remember it at all?
This is our Dr. King's birthday,
The atmosphere seems to recall
And settles quietly through a pall,
Mourning again this passing day
As though that year hadn't slipped away,
As though that total aching pain
Will, like November freezing rain,
Return and still return
For caring hearts to burn
Sadly again, and yet again,
To say mankind will never learn!

1/1/91

25. Dr. King's Legacy
(A Song-Poem for Children)

We have this thing
About Martin King:
He believed in us children
Far more than anything!
You recall that *Washington Speech*
In a certain August of '63,
And how he would pray
For some special day
When all children could play,
Could learn, could *love*,
In harmony?
And although today
The dream still seems far away,
We have faith increasingly
That such a day will be—
Eventually!
Now you grown-up folks,
You may disagree,
But you just wait and see,
For we, the World's Children,
Are Dr. King's great—
His cherished *legacy*!

1/1/91

26. We the Children Remember Dr. King

Let us the children now all sing
Once more, again, of Martin King,
Who turns long winters into Spring,
Through acts of love!
He said the word *discriminate*
Was blood-brother to vicious *hate*—
A curse he never could tolerate
By all above!
Despair's a word we cannot know
That signifies visions of woe,
And such for us is never so—
Nor winds may chill!
Now he's gone, and how years have sped,
Yet some fears still becloud the head,

Yet still we walk the way *he* led—
And always will!
We toss flowers to Yesterday,
Pretend each day the First of May,
Still hearing what he had to say
That long ago!
We do know Truth can never die,
But stretch and bloom beneath God's sky,
To dwarf, then kill hate's biggest lie,
So Hope may grow!
So, let us strike the Freedom Bell,
And let each stroke resounding, swell
That we may say, *Martin, sleep well*
Beneath smooth stone.
We've caught the beauty of that spark
That clarifies each doubter's dark.
We see Ambition's glowing ark
Lead on and on!
   Envoi
And, Dr. Martin King,
We shall go *on* remembering!

                              1/1/87

27. Passing Stranger

Right here in hate-scarred room,
Walls ruined from segregation's aim,
Sluicing away mistrust and gloom
With cleansing power, in *he* came.
Then left a song.
Who was this figure, and his name,
From what far country, and for just how long—
This master cleanser of hate and shame?
Now who was *he*, he'd never say,
And silently he slipped away,
Slipped the same
As how *he* came.
(But I shall not forget the day!)

                              12/29/87

28. 1963 *Dream-March* Remembered

We were there, quarter million plus,
Each one a visionary soul,
Who'd come to gain strength renewed
And keep the *dream* well in control.
Now five and twenty years later,
With mere memory-glance of *him*,
There still remains much hate and hater.
How slow the mills that justice grinds,
How stubborn tradition fights and fights,
How still sealed in the closed-off mind!
It refuses to see the *light*,
Hoping that *dream* die a labored death,
While we, like Ruth, in *alien corn*,
Bend our backs and gasp for breath,
Refusing to curse when *dream* was born.

Will we forgt the fights we fought?
O, Martin King, perish the thought,
Perish the thought! Perish the thought!
We know how honest dreams are wrought!
8/88

29. Freedom Marcher to Grandson Joe Today

Say, Joe, sometimes you start me off
To some lowdown old wondering,
As if you've never heard a word
That was intoned by Marty King—
Seems it does not mean a *thing*!
8/88

30. Grandma Reflects on Marty's March on Washington

You say, son, it's twenty-five years
Since Marty King's most famous *dream*?
It's more like only yesterday,
Or that's the way it sure does seem.
But I suppose this sad old way
Shows how my status seems to stay.
So, it might as well've *been* yesterday.
And, son, it's enough to bring on tears.
8/88

31. The Time Since Aug. 28, 1963

Say, I wonder if that dawn
That Langston and Marty spoke of
Has up, daybroke, and—gone?
But I sure hope it just "ain't" so.
But nowadays, you never know;
You never know.

8/88

32. Bitter Weed, Parasite Vine

Better a bitter weed
Or parasitic vine
Than share here indeed
Such bitter wine
Poured freely into this life of mine!
I thought Viet Nam would *turn the trick*.
But discrimination still makes me sick,
Feeling more alone than in Pluto's mine!

8/88

33. On King's 20th Anniversary

Look here, Mister, the fife?
Why do you loudly bang that drum?
I'd've bet you anybody's life
That we at last had *overcome*!

(Better you should use my "crying towel"
Twenty years later, hate's *still* the prowl!)

8/88

34. At Martin's Gravesite (1988)

Oh, Martin L., as we lean here
Under early red April moon,
We bleed yet a redder tear.

You left us, Martin, much too soon,
For angry fires still dance your bier,
And fear still croons a bitter tune.

8/88
12/29/87

264

35. Owed by America

Long ago, American, you made me,
And still make me what I am.
But, like rich asset, you mislaid me,
And it seems you don't give a damn!
I'm angry, too, because it is I
Who yet must demand fair *cut of pie*,
While you expect me mere silent clam,
But all *those* days have rotted by!

12/29/87

36. No More Jan. 15, but Apr. 4

Martin, never again upon God's great,
Green earth
Will I note January fifteenth,
Date set aside to praise your birth.
I'm not seditious, mean —
Rather, I'll stand silent in April rain
For Spring's re-newal again
To grant a sweetness to my breath.
I'll mourn *April fourth*, sundown of your *death*!

12/29/87

37. Beyond the Grave With Black Martyrs

Sorry, but I must up and go,
Go now before I might forget
Where *Fred, Sojourner,* and *Harriet*
Have somewhere below a sundown met
To see if the *dream's* unrealized yet.
How many more martyred ghosts must thrust
Questions death-side of Jordan's stream
Shedding ghost-tears of rank regret
For unfulfillment of our *dream,*
That still unpaid and growing debt?

America, why must you yet forget?
(Dead voices still in anguish scream.)

12/29/87

38. Psst! Our Late Dr. King Must Never Know!

Martin King,
Delete your fears.
No blues we sing
To pierce your ears.
Equality's denied
All tears again.
What you thought we cried
Was mere late,
Cold springtime rain.
Martin King,
Erase your fears.
No blues we sing
To rock the spheres . . .
(And have not here
In twenty years. . . !)

                              12/30/87

39. A Brief Note to Dr. King

Dr. King, again I say to you,
(Again and again it should be so stated):
Since that time when you came through,
Although my *dream* may not be new,
The *dream* has certainly been renovated!

                              12/31/87

40. If I Never, Dr. Martin King

If I never read another line,
Never again raise voice to sing,
I'll not forget the *peace design*
That you created, Dr. King!

                              12/31/87

41. Despair for M. L. K.—or Any Truth Seeker Slain for the Cause"

Let them search for you, "scrounge" for you,
In the deep waywardness of empty music,
In the vapidity of strandless songs,
Doggerel and line-less cliché,
Among broken eyries of lost eagles.

266

They have foolishly unravelled from
The hidden skeins of history,
Stolen from the artistic looms of creativity.
But do not come back to this point,
This point of your well-promised beginning,
Where you laid down with your life a dream-gilded heritage,
And they need you now, need you more than ever,
But let them reach through broken windowpanes
And sever their hopes, their *dreams*.
Let their fears rise and mourn sonorous and pitiable—
Only now they seek your *truth*,
Only now they wish to commune with
The saints of understanding,
Only now they wish to erect monuments of
The soul in your newly-uncovered memory.

Make it too late! Make it too late! Too, too late!
They will only pock-mark history,
Enshroud again your beauty in emptiness,
The essence of your pristine yearning.

Stay, stay, modern prophet!
Let no desire encourage your returning!
2/20/83

PART VIII

"A Foray Into Oriental Verse"
(POETRY)
A. "Taking a Haiku to the Orient"
B. "Tinkering With the Tanka"
(BLUES IN TANKA TIME)

Taking a Haiku to the Orient (Oriental Efforts) Part I.

1. Willow Lover, Indeed!

When willow trees bloom
I do not care if summer
Ever comes to town!

4/26/80

2. Love-Hate Comparison

The measure of love
Is, Oh! doubly sweeter than
Measurement of hate.

4/26/80

3. A Moon Wish

I can only wish
The moon had not become real
Before I knew *you*.

4/26/80

4. Dream Assurance

Lean on every dream
The way you strive for rainbows
After every storm.

4/26/80

5. The Painful Page

Page you wrote upon
Even burns with anger now.
Laughter long has fled.

4/26/80

271

6. Not As They Seem

Bluebirds on a limb
Sing not to welcome late spring,
But to mourn for *snow*.

4/26/80

7. Moon Power

A sharp-quartered moon
Will still afford glow enough
For a heart of hope.

4/26/80

8. Indication of Sorrow

The white lines of frost
Tell me dramatically
That once you were *here*.

4/26/80

9. Consolation

In twilight's velvet
I wrap my familiar fears
Of a brutal day!

4/26/80

10. Regarding Flower Petals

No one spoke to me
Of such beauty on each bloom—
Blooms speak for *themselves*!

4/26/80

11. Cautionary Measures

I must forsake you
Before I should remember
Not to leave at all!

4/26/80

12. Sheep Grazing

Sheep in luscious fields
Don't recall a stubbled earth —
Just grass before them.

4/26/80

13. Daylight Sadness

Daylight finds me sad,
Wishing for last night's stars
To guide me safely.

4/26/80

14. Music-Maker You

You are the sound of
Your own beautiful music
As well as my own.

4/26/80

15. Broken Reed Music

A dry, broken reed
Makes the sweetest of music
When one is lonely.

4/26/80

16. The Worshiped One

Admiration knows
No bounds, dear, with *you* alone
As divining rod!

4/26/80

17. On a Certain Street

On this street at night
No one follows painted stars
Who longs for daylight.

4/26/80

18. Such a Magician

Stiffened winter stream
Races to a waiting sea
When *you* kiss its face!

4/26/80

19. For Any Suburban Complex

Suburban complex
Rests uneasily tonight,
As it's always done.

4/26/80

20. The Snow Owl

The snow owl hooting
Does not call for flakes of snow—
But for *summer's glow*!

4/26/80

21. When Sparrows Are Kings

Sparrows are kings
When grand, winter-fleeing birds
Head for safer things.

4/26/80

22. Wave-Tips Comparison

Like green-white wave-tips
Posing at their utmost height,
Your dark eyes find mine!

4/26/80

23. Leaves That *Un*cling in Winter

Like opiates' dreams,
Falling winter leaves just now
Can't remember spring.

4/26/80

24. Fearful Discovery

I thought I was brave.
You've slipped away in shadows—
So has bravery.

4/26/80

25. Limited Appreciation

In my spring gardens
Magnificent flowers grow—
Loved only by bees.

4/26/80

26. Disturbance

The winds laugh loudly
As I whisper: *Happiness*
In a driving rain.

4/26/80

27. Egotism, Nevertheless

To make you just sing
So loudly in praise of me
Is so infantile!

4/26/80

28. Not Privy

Apparently, Love,
All birds knew your gentleness
Far better than I.

4/26/80

29. Question Is Raised

For the best *or* worst—
But why is it Evil's side
Has to rise up *first!*

4/26/80

30. Concerning Your Whisper

Your velvet whisper,
Calling me to prayer's the same
As 10,000 bells.

4/26/90

31. Sleep Panthers

There lie sleep-panthers
Waiting now beneath my bed,
To rip me to shreds!

4/26/80

32. Regarding Your Loneliness

Angry thunderstorms
Roar across the dry deserts
Of your loneliness.

4/26/80

33. Constellation Advice

Never turn to stars—
Unless you seek honesty
Resting deep within.

4/26/80

34. Night Cloudburst

Maddened horses leap
An angrier sky tonight!
Where sleeps God or Zeus?

4/26/80

35. For You So Coy!

Why are you so shy?
Butterflies are here seeking
Beauty tips from you.

4/26/80

For a Certain Realist

Milk's made to be spilt!
(Yes, but so are dreams, my friend,
Made to be *re*built!)

4/26/80

This Black Man Will Wonder No More

On a pitch-black night
I don't have to wonder
Just what white is like.

1/29/93

Wishful Thinking?

Hope time approaches
When inquiring child will ask:
What's segregation?

1/29/93

Klan Destined?

Why, in broad daylight
I saw the K. K. K. clan
Pretend it was *night*!

1/29/93

Black Homeless Man

Poor, black homeless man,
Giant eyesore to the world—
Bigger to *himself*!

12/29/93

Tinkering with the Tanka

1. blues in tanka time *blues*

blues, why did you have to
go and break this heart of mine?
what am i to do
while i'm still fresh on the vine?
(now who's lied that love's divine?)

4/4/91

277

2. broke in tanka time *blues*

for every dollar
that years past i used to own,
decades of squalor
have wickedly pared to bone
wealthy days i should have known.
4/4/91

3. the case for the happy *blues*?

you say there are blues
which end on a happy note?
i'd love to diffuse,
grab that liar by his throat,
make him crawl without his shoes!
4/4/91

4. indebted *blues*

world owes me a dream
that i paid for long ago.
world owes me a dream
and i've searched both high and low.
but world swears that it "ain't" so!
4/4/91

5. bad luck personified *blues*

talking about pain,
man, you ought to take a look.
lose more than i gain:
evil times were such a crook
came and burned my pocketbook!
4/4/91

6. all but one *blues*

if i had the chance
to repeat goodbye again,
i'd yell out: "drop dead, romance;
you have only brought me pain!"
(unless *she's* ella mc vance!)
4/4/91

7. missing "paree" blues

o blues, ooh, la-la!
wrongest blues i ever saw,
when not in "paree."
mean old blues grabs hold of me,
stays with me until "paree"!

4/4/91

8. gun for my love blues

plan to buy my love
a big, shiny forty-four
that i'll buy my love,
and then knock upon her door—
but i'll have to knock no more!

4/4/91

9. tears and laughter blues

'twixt laughter and tears?
there's no in between:
either it's all cheers
or blood-loss upon the scene.
(i hope you get what i mean.)

4/4/91

10. love-and-blind blues

love can change your mind—
desire it or no—
open a lifetime blind.
please ask me, for this i know,
(though i went blind years ago!)

4/4/91

11. black girl dancing blues

see that black girl whirl!
erase shadows from the floor!
whirl, you proud black girl,
as lecher wolves howl for more!
(let none see tears held in store.)

4/4/91

279

12. found me a nickel *blues*

done found a nickel
after years of waking broke.
at long last lost that yoke,
and i sure don't mind a bit
(but, say, is this *counterfeit?*)

4/4/91

13. bad, but could be worse *blues*

life's an empty shell.
this must be my living curse,
far as i can tell.
couldn't be worse, far's i can see . . .
(unless *you* return to me!)

4/4/91

14. can't get over you *blues*

i can't get over
this my getting over you.
couldn't be a rover.
ah! that much i'd've sworn was true.
(some surprise in day or two!)

4/4/91

15. anti-mavelle *blues*

i just cannot tell
what tomorrow will bring me:
disaster bell,
or bell-tone of victory?
(long as it "ain't" you, mavelle!)

4/4/91

16. planting blues-seeds *blues*

used to plant "blues-seeds,
just to see if seeds would grow,
if they'd grow or no.
today i can't understand:
giant redwoods spread my land!

4/4/91

17. on a diet *blues*

got on a diet
to shed me two hundred pounds.
today a riot:
my shadow can't dent the ground,
and i cannot run around!

4/4/91

PART IX

"Glancing at Drama"
(DRAMA)
Skit: "Dillon Vs. Dillon"

"Dillon Vs. Dillon"
(The Reader Must Determine the Outcome)

Scene and Problem: Late 1960's or early 1970's. Henry Dillon, a respected black professor of chemistry at Whitby College in a particular Southern town. The college is virtually an all-white institution. He lives with his wife, Edie, just off campus. Dillon is faced with a serious problem: He has promised to march in protest over some conditions there on campus with black student leader, a John Vickers. Edie is fearful and cautious about her husband's involvement. She fears for his safety—in part—but she fears more over his almost sure expulsion from the school. Yet she knows her husband will make a decision one way or the other.

Drama Structure: Dillon has just walked in from a late evening class. He does not know that Vickers is waiting in the livingroom for an answer from him to march with the pupils, the few blacks and a larger smattering of whites. These students bear the now familiar title of *radical*. Edie is seen talking in guarded tones to her husband about the request and the presence of the student in the next room.

Scene: The kitchen. Edie is standing near the table where Henry is about to sit. She stops his movement.

Edie: Henry, you know that boy is here—in the living room.

Dillon: What boy? Oh, yeah, John Vickers. I told his roommate to tell him he could come over one night after a late Tuesday class and I would give him my decision about the protest march.

Edie: Now listen, honey, let's not go over all that again. I know that you are not going to get involved. I just know it!

Dillon: Look, Edie, let's face it; I'm *already* involved! By virtue of the fact that I'm here teaching on this formerly totally milk-and-cream white campus. I have no choice.

285

Edie: You know what I mean, Henry. You fought like a dog to go through, to get through Columbia to get your degrees—tears, dejection, rejection, insults. And I'm not going to sit idly by like some Anne on a silver throne and see you destroy your chance to be a real asset. What do these kids know about protest anyway?

Dillon: They know a heckuva lot of things that we used to take for granted. They are on to the lies and subterfuges that have been handed down to them. It's not just the war in Vietnam and racism, and . . .

Edie: Hold it, St. Stephen, you who are about to be stoned! You know exactly what I'm trying to say. The answer, the very answer, very best answer, to fight such things is in the *classroom*—not *outside*! Our weapon, if we have ever had a weapon, has been through education—*learning, not burning*!

Dillon: (Sharply)—Edie, that philosophy went out the window when Malcolm and Martin King got it. And, furthermore the day of the ostrich is over. Remember, he who puts his head in the sand is a double fool: First, he can see and hear nothing around him, and, second, he leaves his rear end exposed to the very thing he seeks to avoid!

Edie: You can speak in patrician tones all you wish, Henry, but this I know: Such an attitude and such involvement certainly won't keep Carolann up there in Vassar! And you know it, too!

Dillon: There you go, preaching, preaching, preaching, and worrying about Carolann! And money!

Edie: And if I don't, who else will? *You* certainly won't, Henry. Let them get someone else—import some of those professional ones—what do you call them—the professional "rads"? Besides, you're a science man—not a *social* science one—a physical-chemistry science one. And a darned good one, too.

Dillon: That's beside the point. In our struggle to set this country, set the whites, and especially the southern whites, straight, there is no line of demarcation. An engineer has to speak out against an injustice as readily as a minister. Else he is not discharging his duty as a human being.

Edie: (Flushed)—Your *first* duty, your *very* first duty, is to your family—that is the mark of a concerned person. And, another thing, what specifics are these kids demanding? Is everything spelled out?

Dillon: No, everything is *not* spelled out. Perhaps nothing is clear to them in ways of attacking the problem. That's expected of them because they are young. They are asking for moral adult commitment, leadership. That is why they're seeking me out.

Edie: All the more reason for you to keep away from these hotheads!

Dillon: All the *more* reason why I should *not*, Edie!

Edie: Do you really feel involved, Henry, or is this an act of fear of a lowering of your image in the sight of some students if you refuse to participate?

Dillon: (Angry, voice rising)—You know that was a rotten thing to say . . . a rotten thing to say, and you know it! Do I have to *buy* my respect from these students? *Do* I?

Edie: (Sarcastic): —Are you asking me? Or should some things be left better unsaid? Huh?

Dillon: Very funny! Very funny! That was just about as funny as a barbed wire lynching scene—just about as funny. I don't have to act the part of a martyr to achieve recognition here, or at any *other* school!

Edie: Lower your voice, else Vickers will hear of your dilemma through these walls. But the way you seem bent upon marching with these students will help to make you a fantastic martyr, my Sir Gally, quicker than you can say, "Nine naughty gnats nipped Nellie Knox's narrow nose!" Believe me!

Dillon (Turning toward the door leading to the rest of the house): I've got a responsibility that really transcends test tubes, graduated cylinders, textbooks. A black man has got to be more of what he is. Edie, Whitey knows that. And I owe it to kids like that boy out there waiting for my answer. God, we as black men have sat on our bottoms long enough! And when concerned black youth *and* concerned white youth, also, come to us for guidance, we ease back into a welter of mumbo-jumbo words.

Edie: The mere fact that you are spending so much time right now with these mumbo-jumbo word battles that you are having, shows the doubt about the whole situation. Now go, tell him how easy it is for you to say: "Yes, yes, young man, I'll lead the march through the streets of the campus of Whitby and through the streets of Marketville!"

Dillon: Aw, Edie, shut up, will you! Doggonnit, shut the heck up!

Edie: O.K., ungrateful one, but just remember when you were up there in that Columbia University world, I was working in the five-and-dime on Delancey Street ten hours a day, six days a week, and I waited tables many a Sunday besides. This was done to help you *overcome*, so to speak—or have you forgotten so soon, little man?

Dillon: That's just like you—you use a mechanism against which I have no defense. I know you worked like blazes for us—for me. I know it. I can't knock it. But this, this decision is still a struggle for personal dignity, you know, Edie. And, Edie, I just *have* to take a stand!

Edie: Is that your answer, Henry, is it—that you have to take a *stand*? Well, go and tell him, Mr. Vickers, how pride, and pride alone, will pay for all the remaining payments on this house note. Tell young Mr. Vickers that dignity, that real dignity, will substitute very nicely, thank you, for that loan for Carolann's remaining two years at Vassar. Tell him at the same time that the old 1966 Chevy will be maintained the same way, the very same way! Please go tell him, will you?

Dillon: Oh, Edie, you can never understand!

Edie: Oh, but I can, and *do*! That's the problem. I undestand only too well. Too well, Henry, too well!

Dillon (Turning, walking toward the door. He pauses, frowning): Well, I'll go and straighten this out once and for all. (He does not move, but looks back at his wife, who is wiping her eyes.)

Edie: Well, Henry, Henry Ralph Dillon, go on. What are you waiting for?

Dillon (Still not moving): Edie, Edie, Edie, I don't know, I don't know. Truly, I just don't know! Why the heck did I have to be born a *black* man in America? Why? Why? Why?

CURTAIN—)

Your Problem, Reader:

You tell us in your own words what decision this troubled man made. Tell us *why* you made such a choice. Thank you for getting "involved".

—1972